SHATTERED SPIRITS

A DRAGON SPIRIT NOVEL: BOOK 2

C.I. BLACK

Gryphon's Gate Publishing

Gryphon's Gate Publishing

550 King St. N.

PO Box 42088 Conestoga

Waterloo, ON

N2L 6K5

ebook ISBN978-0-9919229-9-4

Print ISBN978-0-9937651-0-0

PROLOGUE

The boy pounded on the glass of the top floor window, mouth open in a scream that couldn't be heard. Smoke billowed from the four-story tenement. It cast a ghostly haze over the moon and enveloped the streetlights at the entrance.

Flames licked out of the windows on all floors, bright streamers straining toward the neighboring buildings only a narrow alley away. Sirens wailed in the distance. People gathered to watch the chaos.

Ryan shoved through the crowd and raced across the street to the tired, sagging steps.

A thunderous boom shook the ground.

Flames shot from the roof, showering him with stinging ash and debris. He stumbled under the faded yellow and white striped awning and yanked open the door. Black smoke engulfed him, burning his lungs with every quick inhalation.

Coughing, he pulled the front of his T-shirt over his mouth and nose and barreled up the stairs. One flight. Two flights. Three.

The smoke was thicker here, black and hot. He squinted, looking for signs of movement. The window had been on the front corner and the child had been screaming. He rushed to the left, straining to hear anything, but the fire roared around him, crackling and snapping, consuming sounds as well as the building.

He'd just have to pray he'd get there in time.

He *had* to get there in time. This was his chance to do what he'd been unable to do all those years ago.

The smoke gusted up to the ceiling, revealing the door at the end. He rushed toward it.

His eyes watered, but he kept focused on his goal. Smoke billowed around him again, but the path to the door remained clear. His chest burned, each breath heavy.

Just a few more feet.

The hallway flickered, darkness sweeping along the edge of his vision. He reached for the doorknob, but it was a foot farther than anticipated. Smoke ebbed around his feet. He leapt closer. The door moved back and the hall flickered again, like ripples on dark water.

His breath caught in his throat.

It was a future flash. Only a vision of what was to come. It wasn't actually happening right now.

He squeezed his eyes shut, concentrating on slowing his racing heart. The fire continued to roar. His breath burned and his chest ached.

It wasn't real. Not yet. If he could break free, he could save the kid.

He pressed his hands over his ears, but the blaze roared inside his head. There had to be a way to control his visions. He needed to concentrate. Block everything out. Focus on his body.

But his body thought he was in the middle of an inferno. His heart continued to race, his skin burned, and his muscles trembled. His curse controlled him, and no matter how hard he tried, it wouldn't release him until it was ready.

Heat blasted him in the face, and his eyes flew open.

He sat in his car, parked under a flickering streetlight on a quiet street. Across from him sat a brown tenement, looking worn down even in the dark. Its stairs sagged under a faded yellow and white awning. Just like the stairs in his vision.

There was still time to save the boy. He leapt out of his car, and the building exploded into flames.

C apri kicked the snow from her boots and entered the Newgate Medical Examiner's office through the heavy back door. It was never a good sign when her friend Hiro called her to her office. In fact, it had been years since the last time. It usually meant the kind of off-the-books work that could have a dragon reborn for treason.

Of course, Hiro knew that, and Capri doubted the chief medical examiner would have left the cryptic message on her phone if it hadn't been important. The timing was terrible given that the dragon prince was on a rampage, looking for traitors after the failed coup two weeks ago.

She unwrapped her scarf and headed to the main examination room. Movement down a side hall caught her attention, and she paused to get a better look.

Eric stood at the far end, talking with someone.

Her heart skipped a beat, and she jerked her gaze away.

It wasn't Eric. God above, it was not Eric. He was dead. He'd died years ago, and she'd been forced to leave him years before that. Dragon law was specific about how long a relationship with a human could last, and she'd done what her prince had commanded.

And regretted it every day of her immortal life.

She'd thought she'd put Eric's ghost to rest. When he'd died of old age, and she was still in the ageless human body her dragon spirit had been put into during the late twelfth century, she'd thought she'd accepted that leaving him had been right. But she never stopped aching for him. And since meeting Detective Ryan Miller—the man who could have been Eric's twin—she now saw him everywhere... Eric, not Miller. She saw him in glances down halls, walking on the other side of the street, in her dreams, even in the Dragon Court.

With every passing day, her yearning for him became worse. She'd even caught herself yesterday daydreaming that Miller was really Eric and they'd renewed their intimacy.

But Miller wasn't Eric. She didn't know the detective, and if she wanted to be a good drake and follow the rules, she'd never know him. Besides, he wasn't in Newgate, and the odds of seeing him again were slim.

Which was good.

Really.

She ground her teeth and shoved open the swinging doors to the main exam room. Best to focus on work, or in this case, under-the-table work.

Hiro glanced up from the naked body on the stainless steel table. The victim's chest lay open and the top of his ribcage sat on a trolley, along with the man's head.

"I'd ask if you know the cause of death, but it's a little obvious. Same as Kardas?" Two decapitated drakes were the perfect distraction. If, of course, this one was a dragon. Capri didn't recognize him, but that didn't mean he hadn't been one.

"The murders look identical."

"That's two bodies in a week and a half." Not good. Most dragons had accelerated healing, making them difficult to kill. The only sure way to kill one was to remove his head, and there were only two possible situations for what had happened to the guy on the table—if he was, in fact, a drake. Neither of them was good news for dragonkind.

"His driver's license says his name is Andy Reynolds. Now, he's not in the registry—" Hiro pulled off her gloves and grabbed a file from her desk. "But with Kardas last week, I thought I'd give you a heads-up... no pun intended."

"Thanks." Not being in the drake registry didn't mean he wasn't a dragon. It could just mean he'd managed to slip under Prince Regis's radar—something many drakes aspired toward. But with his soul gone, there was no way to tell if he'd had a dragon's aura or not. Not until someone did some poking around into his private life.

"And even if this one was human, it's still suspicious." Hiro made a note in her file.

"Two beheadings so close together—suspicious is an understatement." It wasn't impossible to think a psychopath who decapitated his victims was on the loose. It had happened before. But the odds that he'd chosen a drake, possibly two, and killed them while unaware that they were dragons was slim. Killing a drake took planning and an understanding of dragon capabilities—like knowing you had one swing to do the job or needed to incapacitate the drake first, and it took enough sedative to knock out a rhinoceros for that.

"There are really only two options. A human knows about us or—"

"Or Regis is auditioning new assassins." Capri resisted the urge to bare her teeth. It was inappropriate to show her pleasure over the situation, given how serious it was. But this was the perfect distraction. A few deaths, a little intrigue. Just enough to keep her occupied, albeit on her toes.

"If Regis is in the process of hiring, this assassin is doing a terrible job. This is a mess," Hiro said.

"And one I haven't been asked to clean up." Which didn't necessarily prove or disprove the theory that these were sanctioned assassinations. Although, if it had been a human murderer, Capri and the rest of the North American Clean Team would have been rushed in to eliminate any evidence of dragonkind. But if Regis was behind the killings and wanted to send a message to all drakes living outside of Court—and essentially outside of his immediate protection—leaving the mess might that message.

Hiro pursed her lips. "Regis has done this before."

"Yes, but technology has changed since the 1500s. If it is him, it's sloppy to let two bodies stack up in so short a time." Capri bit back a growl. "That drake only follows his laws when it suits his needs, and then I get to clean up the mess when the humans start noticing." But that was the way it was. Regis could do as he pleased because he was the prince, and she'd had to give up the only man she'd ever loved.

Keep dragonkind a secret, Capri. Clean up the mess, Capri.

Follow the rules and you won't be reborn with all your memories erased.

Hiro cleared her throat, and Capri jerked her gaze up. She hadn't realized she'd been staring at the corpse.

"I didn't ask you here for a pity-party," Hiro said.

"No. If you had, you would've made margaritas." Capri needed to focus on the job. Even if this wasn't an official job, it could turn into one at any moment, and the more information she had, the easier it would be. And she liked this, liked the rush. She just had to stop thinking about Eric and everything would go back to the way it had been.

Hiro cocked her head, pulling Capri back to the conversation again. "Ptolemy has Cooper on the investigation, so we're covered there. But just in case politics are involved, I thought you should know."

Capri offered a smile. It felt forced, but it was the best she could manage at the moment. "Of course."

All the bases were covered. The two drakes situated in the Newgate Police Department, Ptolemy, chief of police, and Ilan Cooper, detective, had the traditional angle, and when the shit hit the fan, Capri could swoop in, flash her FBI badge, and keep dragonkind safe.

Hiro made a note in her file and snapped it shut. "So, you still on for girls' night tonight?"

"It all depends on what's going on with work."

Hiro raised a delicate eyebrow. "You haven't missed girls' night for a hundred years. Until the last two weeks, that is. If you miss again, I'll think something is up."

"You already think something is up."

"There is that."

Capri pursed her lips and focused all her attention on the corpse. Very few drakes knew about her indiscretion with a human, and Hiro wasn't one of them. And even though she and Hiro were from different coteries, Capri had been friends with the other blue drake since the early 1800s. She didn't think Hiro would see her confession about having a human lover as an opportunity to take advantage of her, but some instincts were hard to ignore, and she, like most drakes, had been protecting her emotional vulnerabilities for centuries.

The door to the examination room whooshed open.

"How's my favorite medical examiner?" an oh-so familiar voice asked. Shivers raced over Capri, and her heart plummeted into her stomach.

Eric.

No, Eric was dead.

Which meant she hadn't been imagining him in the hall. It had to be—

2

Capri turned, afraid to, yet knowing who she'd face in the exam room's door. "Detective Miller."

Miller stopped mid-step, his eyes locked on Capri. "Special Agent Jones." His gaze dipped to the corpse on the table, then back to Capri.

Just a look from him made her heart flutter and ache. God, she was pathetic. One coffee with him two weeks ago while on the job, and all she could think of was Eric. One look now, and all she wanted was for him to *be* Eric.

Mother of All! She wasn't some silly youngling freshly hatched. Just because he looked like her lover didn't mean he was.

"What brings you to Newgate, Detective?" The last time she'd seen him had been in Elmsville. He hadn't seemed happy as a detective for such a small town. Perhaps he'd transferred. That would be just her luck. A constant reminder of what she couldn't have, walking around town. Her imaginings had been bad enough.

"Saying hello to Dr. Yoshida. I'm in town for a few days, thought I'd stop by, see if she's available for lunch."

Everything within Capri froze. He couldn't ask Hiro out for lunch. How the hell did she know Eric... no, Detective Miller?

Shit. Get a grip. Miller wasn't Eric, and Hiro could be friends with anyone she liked.

"And you make it a habit to just walk in? Ever heard of a phone?" Oh yeah, that was mature. The urge to call her earth magic and manipulate his thoughts into wanting to have lunch with *her* was overwhelming. Except she still felt guilty over the last time she'd enspelled him.

"If I'd known I needed to stand in line for the good doctor's time, maybe I would've called." Miller's gaze dipped again to the corpse, and Capri wondered if he'd seen such a graphic death before. A small-town detective probably hadn't witnessed much action. Although if he knew Hiro enough to ask her out to lunch, perhaps he wasn't as small-town as Capri thought.

None of which mattered. Miller was bad news for her, trouble just to look at him. And no, she would not use her magic on him. Even just to make him go away. "No, sorry. Dr. Yoshida and I have just finished."

She shot Hiro a glance. The blue drake's eyebrows were practically in her hairline. Girls' night was going to be an onslaught of questions—if Hiro didn't call and start asking the moment Miller left the exam room.

"So, lunch?" Miller asked. He didn't seem nearly so cocky anymore.

Capri couldn't decide if that made her happy or not.

"I've got a full house." Hiro gestured at the exam room.

Thank the Mother of All.

"But I will need to take a dinner break."

Capri's traitorous heart did another flip in her chest. This was not happening. Her best friend was not going on a date with a man who could have been her dead lover's identical twin.

Miller pulled a business card from the back pocket of his jeans. "Call when you're ready." He set it on a trolley by the door and left.

"What was that?" Hiro asked.

"Nothing." Capri slid Miller's card from the stainless steel surface, and Hiro plucked it from her fingers.

"Didn't look like nothing to me."

Capri fought the urge to grab the card back.

"You should get your vision checked, then."

"Whatever you say, Special Agent Jones," Hiro said, her tone saying she knew something was up, and if Capri didn't fill in the blanks, she'd make her own assumptions. Which were probably going to be right.

"I met Miller cleaning up that mess two weeks ago."

"Uh huh."

"I did." Jeez. Now she was on the defensive. How pathetic was that?

Hiro slid the file into a rack on the wall. "Maybe *you* should take the dinner date."

"I don't want your date." Well, Capri did, but that was the worst idea ever. Miller probably still had questions from their last encounter. The more time she spent with him, the harder it would be to hide the truth.

And the harder it would be to keep her feelings straight. She was messed up already and they'd spent less than twenty minutes together.

"You sure?" If the twinkle in Hiro's eyes got any brighter, they'd glow.

A growl bubbled at the back of Capri's throat, but her phone rang, saving her from having to think up a nasty retort. "What?"

Swipe, her second in command, harrumphed into the phone. "I see we're having the same kind of day."

She doubted it, but she wasn't going to argue with him. That would just open her up to questions she didn't want to answer. "What have you got?"

"Work time. Diablo found another of the mage's abandoned hideouts."

Which meant he needed her to watch his and Gig's back while they used their earth magic to clean up any evidence left behind. It had been like that for almost two weeks. Always one step behind those human mages created to fight Zenobia's coup. Not that her Clean Team was assigned to apprehend any of them—that was Diablo's job as a member of the Asar Nergal. Her team just cleaned up afterward.

"I'm on my way," she said. Swipe gave her the address then hung up. She pocketed her phone and turned to Hiro. "Duty calls."

"Have fun."

"You know I do."

Hiro jerked her thumb at the corpse on the table. "Ptolemy and I can keep this quiet for forty-eight hours, but then we'll have to tell Tobias."

"You should probably tell Tobias right away." But if Regis really was behind the beheadings, Tobias, the prince's chamberlain and Capri's boss, likely knew about it already, and then it was really just a political land mine.

"Well, he could be human, and that would make Kardas's death merely a coincidence."

Capri rolled her eyes. "Politics."

If she stuck her nose in the prince's business and he took offense, she'd be tortured for years because he felt like it. If she didn't check this out, she could be caught off guard and be tortured for years because Regis felt like it. Because of the coup, Regis would be on edge for at least a century.

Right now, it was dangerous to be a dragon in the prince's employ. Of course, it was even more dangerous for a dragon to try to leave the prince's employ. Resignation equaled treason. Which left her in the middle of a tightrope with two corpses and her regular job to do.

Here was hoping it was enough to help her forget Eric and his doppelgänger, Detective Miller.

3

R yan sat on the edge of the concrete divider separating the narrow parking lot from the four-lane road running behind the Newgate Medical Examiner's office, trying to figure out the mess of churning emotions within him. Special Agent Jones had been there, and she was more alluring than ever. Except he'd never expected that she, of all people, would be at the Newgate M.E. office, and he didn't know if that complicated anything.

He had hoped he could slip in and sweet-talk Hiro into revealing details about the corpse. That was all. Because while the name the media had released last night wasn't Pete Matthews, the picture certainly had been his.

The body on the table had sure looked like Pete as well... or rather his head on that trolley. It wasn't surprising that the news hadn't mentioned anything about the victim being decapitated. This was now the second decapitation in less than two weeks. One would make the public nervous. Two would make the public scared, and he suspected the police didn't want a panic until they had a better idea of what was going on.

But that was the only thing about this situation that made sense. Top of his list of confusion: how could someone who'd died fifteen years ago now lie in the M.E.'s office, having been beheaded yesterday?

It had to be a coincidence. The victim was Pete's double. They—

whoever *they* were—said everyone had a double somewhere in the world. What were the odds that Pete's double would live in the same city and also be killed in a public way? Not that Ryan was a betting man, but even if he was, he wouldn't take the bet. Besides, if Pete hadn't died in that fire, he would have contacted Ryan. They'd been best friends. They'd shared everything.

Except if Pete had faked his death—for reasons Ryan couldn't fathom—childhood friendship wouldn't have meant anything. No matter how much Ryan wanted it to. They might not have really shared anything... if that body was in fact Pete.

Ryan rubbed his face, trying to focus. There were so many bad memories with Newgate, and his friend's fiery death had been the first. He was such a fool to return. Even more of a fool to step into the Newgate Medical Examiner's office and hope no one would notice or ask questions. Those were odds he shouldn't have bet on.

Of course, Special Agent Jones knew nothing about him, save that they'd crossed paths again so soon, but she didn't strike him as the kind to let coincidences go. He didn't want her to start asking questions and certainly not figure out why he'd ended up as a detective in small-town Elmsville.

Of all the people he could have run into, why did it have to be her? There was something enticing and mysterious about her. When she found out the truth about him, he didn't want to see her look at him with the same disappointment everyone else did.

No, he wanted that ferocious something he sensed coiled within her five-foot-nothing frame staring at him with desire and nothing else. Perhaps it was the strawberry blond hair that made him think she was ferocious, vivacious. Everyone thought redheads were fire-crackers, right? Except there was something else that made her alluring. He just couldn't figure out what.

And if he wanted to prove he hadn't lost his mind and seen the decapitated body of a fifteen-year-old ghost, he needed to stay as far away from Special Agent Jones as possible.

With luck, Hiro would call, they'd make that dinner date, and he'd learn the truth about the body in her exam room.

But he hadn't gotten into his car and driven away. Against all common sense, he waited, pretending not to stare at the back door. Not that Special Agent Jones couldn't leave by the front, which would make him even more the fool, but the urge to catch just a glimpse of her again was undeniable.

The door swung open, and Melissa Slater, perky reporter and backstabbing bitch, stepped into the lot, stopping when she saw him.

Just great.

Her cameraman jerked back before tripping over her, but she didn't notice. A hint of a smile pulled at her perfectly lip-glossed lips, and she sauntered toward Ryan, her hips moving in an exaggerated sway.

The day just got better and better. It was insult to injury that his ex would show up while he irrationally waited for Special Agent Jones. If he was smart, he'd get in his car and leave.

"Ryan." Melissa slid his name out, her sultry alto an unwanted reminder of their past relationship.

"Ms. Slater," he said, doing nothing to hide the chill in his voice.

She pursed her lips, and Ryan bit back a nasty barb to add to his acknowledgment of her. He was beyond that. Not that the bitch didn't deserve it. She'd not only abandoned him when Internal Affairs had begun its investigation of him, she'd turned him into a stepping-stone for her TV career.

"What brings you to town?" she asked.

Not you. "I'm visiting my sister."

Melissa nodded. He could practically see the wheels turning in her head as she tried to figure out what angle she wanted to take.

"I heard you transferred to Elmsville."

The street wavered, like air over sweltering asphalt, even though it was mid-January. A dark hallway, fluctuating and translucent, transposed itself over the parking lot.

Ryan clenched his jaw and tried to act normal. Now was not the time for a future flash. Not that it really mattered if Melissa thought he was crazy, but he didn't want to give her more career-advancing material.

"I heard you moved to KDKA."

She said something, but her words were muffled. The vision was too strong. Plain, pale cinder block walls—probably beige—surged into focus.

He gripped the barrier beneath him, struggling to root himself back into the M.E.'s parking lot. Through the wavering hall, Melissa frowned. She said something else. She expected an answer.

"Hunh."

Her frown deepened. Guess that was the wrong answer.

Something crashed, making him jump. He dug his nails into the concrete barrier, struggling not to glance in the direction of the imaginary noise.

From over Melissa's shoulder, Special Agent Jones rushed into the hall through a metal security door, sidearm held ready. Her pale eyes pierced him as if this vision of her could see him. Blood was smeared across her cheek and stained her shirt at her side. With a growl, she turned and ran into the darkness. A bang sent his heart racing. Then another and a scream. Gunfire. In the direction Jones had gone.

He jerked to his feet.

The security door flew open again, and Special Agent Jones stepped back into the hall.

But the hall darkened and rippled.

"Detective," the imaginary Jones said.

Something within him popped, and the hall disappeared, but Jones remained. The real Special Agent, not the vision. He had no idea if she'd been the one in the vision who'd gotten shot, and he had no idea when the future flash would happen. But she had been injured, and his visions had never not happened.

"Jeez, Ryan. You can't even pretend to be happy for me," Melissa said.

"What?"

"I got a promotion last year."

"Great." He couldn't stop looking at Jones.

Jones raised an eyebrow and stepped into the light from the shadows of the M.E.'s office.

He had to warn her about what he'd seen. "Special Agent Jones."

"Special Agent?" Melissa swung around and held out her hand. "Melissa Slater."

Jones looked at Melissa's hand, but made no move to shake it.

"I'm with KDKA, Newgate's News Specialists. Are you a Special Agent with the FBI?" She glanced at her cameraman, and he lifted his camera to his shoulder.

Capri rolled her eyes. "Excuse me." She turned and headed to a black SUV parked a few feet away.

"Wait. I want to know about the murder victim. That's two in less than two weeks. Are they connected? Is the FBI on the case?"

Ryan shoved past Melissa and raced after Jones. For all he knew, she was headed into the situation he'd just seen. "Jones, wait."

She didn't look back, just got into the SUV.

Shit.

"FBI?" Melissa turned to Ryan, her tone sugary sweet.

If Jones wouldn't listen here, he had to follow her. Maybe she'd go someplace safe and outdoors. Like a park. He rushed to his car.

"What's the FBI doing here?"

Jones backed out of her spot.

"I don't know." Ryan yanked open his car door.

"Come on, Ryan."

Jones pulled out of the lot. He had to hurry up. "Bye, Melissa."

"Ryan—"

He shut the door on her and squealed out of the lot. It felt good to give the bitch her due. Perhaps things were changing for him. Maybe this time he could save someone.

4

C apri pulled into a lot of churned, muddy snow and parked beside Swipe's black van. Twenty feet away sat a nineteenth century three-story factory, with crumbling brown bricks and broken and boarded windows.

The building looked deserted. Except the mess in the parking lot indicated someone—likely many someones—had stopped here recently. It was probably the local teen hangout. On the outskirts of town, settled between two hills without another building in sight, it made a great spot for an illicit party.

Swipe and Gig stood by a battered open door with Diablo, their team's contact with the Asar Nergal—the organization assigned to eliminate human mages. Mages hadn't been so much of a problem that her Clean Team had needed to be brought in to work with the Asar Nergal since early in the 1600s. Usually the Asar Nergal were the sole hunters of those humans who'd shared a body with a dragon and had their connection to the earth's magic activated. She imagined, given that most drakes valued their lives, the Asar Nergal had been bored for over four hundred years.

Diablo glanced at her. Yep, must have been bored. He'd grown his hair out. Again. Braided back, the black strands brushed his waist, making his body's Native American heritage clear. Not that the black drake knew anything about the Navajo people. It was just luck of the draw his body had come from this continent the last time he'd been reborn into an empty vessel.

She got out, her low-heeled boots crunching in the gravel and snow.

Gig, the youngest member of her team, waved vigorously, the motion making his shaggy locks bounce around his head. Swipe ignored him, while Diablo glared.

"Well, hello to you, too," Capri said.

Diablo's glare deepened. She hadn't thought it was possible to look so sour.

"The site's all yours." With a whoosh, he used his earth magic to form a gate—a black vortex appearing under his feet—and disappeared.

Ah, ever the man of many words. Obviously, he hadn't found the human mages and needed to regroup in private. He didn't take failure well, and from what she'd heard, the last of these mages were proving more challenging to apprehend than anticipated.

She turned to Swipe and raised an eyebrow, trying not to laugh. "Someone's in a good mood."

"He was still swearing when we showed up," Gig said.

Capri bit back a chuckle. As much as it was bad that the mages were still out there, it was kind of amusing to see Diablo struggle. Mr. Perfect wasn't quite so perfect. As well, it meant more of a distraction. Maybe if she was too busy working, she wouldn't be thinking about Eric or Detective Miller.

She shook away her thoughts and stepped into the warehouse. "Let's see what we've got here, shall we?"

The first ten feet of the inside were clear, just debris and garbage piled on the floor. Beyond lay a maze of machinery and shelves and a lot more garbage. Dust danced in the sunbeams cutting through the slats over the windows, and the reek of a sewer permeated the area, overlaid with the more expected smell of age and mold. She could just imagine what the second and third stories looked and smelled like.

This was going to take some time. The bigger the location, the longer the spell's duration and the more energy it would take for Swipe to use his magic to remove all traces that dragons—and in this case, human mages as well—existed.

Turning back to the parking lot, she let the weak winter sun warm her face. With no one around, and therefore no one to use her magic on, this was going to be one big hurry up and wait kind of assignment. Normally she wouldn't mind. It gave her time to think, but thinking was the last thing she wanted to do right now.

She resisted the urge to sigh—it wouldn't do for her teammates to think something was wrong—and looked at Gig. "Anything for you here?"

The silver drake's gaze grew unfocused. His earth magic ability to communicate with technology never ceased to amaze her. She couldn't begin to imagine how it worked. He didn't even have to be touching the device. Although perhaps it worked a little like how she reached into a human's mind and changed his or her memories.

Gig sucked in a slow breath, held it, and dug his toe into the ground. With a burst, he let the breath out and flashed her a wild grin. "There's a cell phone in there. Want to see what's on it and see if it gives us a lead on the mages? See if Diablo missed something?"

"Absolutely." There was no guarantee it had anything to do with the human mages, but the thought of one-upping Diablo with new information was the best thing that had happened all day.

She turned to Swipe, always handsome in his black tailored winter coat, short-cropped blond hair, and square jaw. "How much time are you going to need?"

"A while." The Texan accent he'd been working on last week was gone. Guess he'd gotten sick of struggling with it. "The mages were here for over a day, and that leaves a lot of stuff." Stuff being DNA evidence, fingerprints, hair, footprints, anything that might be traced. Anything that wasn't technology. Swipe could remove the DNA and fingerprints from the phone, but not the contents within it.

"Well, have fun. Gig and I are going to look for a cell phone."

"In that mess? I think I should be telling you to have fun. At least I don't have to touch anything." Swipe flashed her a hint of teeth and trudged through the snow along the side of the building, already working on setting up a magical perimeter for his spell. With so much evidence in such a large space, setting the perimeter would help focus his magic and hopefully shorten the duration required to remove all traces.

Capri turned to Gig. "All right, lead the way."

He clicked his tongue, and his gaze grew unfocused again. He couldn't have looked any more different from Swipe in his baggy, worn-down clothes and hair in desperate need of a cut. He'd unzipped his jacket and underneath was a comic T-shirt reading, "Do not meddle in the affairs of dragons, for you are crunchy and taste good with ketchup." He tilted his head left then right, then back to left. "It's this way...and up."

She nodded. She'd learned a while ago that if she said anything, he wouldn't respond, not without her raising her voice and giving him a good shake, and that would break his connection, and he'd have to refocus.

He shuffled along the wall through the open area to a narrow hall created between towering shelves and looming machinery. More weak bands of sunlight shot through holes in the grimy windows, making it too bright for her night vision to kick in and yet dark enough to soften the details of the garbage piled on the floor.

At the back of the factory, they found a set of rickety wooden stairs and followed them up to the second floor into a dark hall lined with doorways, some with doors, some without. Her night vision wavered in and out, showing glimpses of broken doors and furniture crowding the walls and moldy fast-food packaging.

"It's really close. In here." Gig stepped through a doorway a few feet down.

Inside, shelves had been cleared to the right wall, and a rat-eaten couch sat in the middle of the room, facing two large windows with most of the panes broken or missing. Ice and coarse snow slicked the floor.

To the left stood an open doorway, the door lying on its side against the wall. Empty beer cans and liquor bottles and more rotting take-out bags and pizza boxes were strewn about. Wonderful. This was going to take forever. Somewhere in this mess was a phone.

RYAN ENTERED THE ABANDONED FACTORY AND WAITED FOR HIS EYES TO adjust to the dim light. When he'd driven past, Jones had been standing in the doorway with two men. He hadn't gotten a good look at them, and by the time he'd pulled a U-turn out of sight down the road, they were gone. Jones's SUV and a van, however, remained, and Ryan could only assume everyone was inside. From the look of the place, he didn't think this was where his future flash would happen, but he couldn't be sure. Besides, even if it wasn't, he still needed to tell her.

But tell her what? That he'd seen the future, and she was going to get shot... maybe? She was going to think he was crazy. Hell, there were days when he wondered if he was crazy.

Yet he couldn't stop if he'd wanted to. If there was a chance, any chance, that he could save her, he had to take it. And it had nothing to do with his attraction to her. Really. Honestly. Besides, trying to warn her would probably ruin all hope of anything happening between them.

He knelt and examined the footprints on the muddy floor. There were a jumble of them, all different shapes and sizes, confirming his suspicion that this was a local hangout for the neighborhood youth. It didn't, however, explain why the FBI was here. If he was lucky, it would have something to do with the decapitated body in the M.E.'s examination room. And if he was really lucky, he'd be able to get some details from Special Agent Jones.

Yeah, right. If looks could kill, she would have killed him back at Hiro's office. She hadn't looked happy to see him, and he doubted she'd be even more impressed to learn he'd followed her here.

Two sets of fresh tracks, still damp from the snow, led along the left wall to the back of the building: one small enough to be a petite woman's, and the other most likely a man's. It looked like the second man had stayed outside.

A bang exploded above and to his left. Then another.

Ryan's heart leapt into a quick tattoo. Gunfire. Maybe this *was* where the future flash happened.

He drew his sidearm and raced after the tracks. They led to rickety stairs. He took them two at a time.

Bang. Bang.

Someone yelled. It sounded like a man, but he couldn't be sure.

Another bang.

He paused at the top of the stairs. Beyond lay a dark hall with doorways and partially opened doors allowing weak light to reveal mounds of debris. A large shadowy figure at the end of the hall, with a gun held at the ready, slipped from one room to the next.

The urge to race to the end of the hall and confront whomever it was swept through Ryan, but he needed to clear the closer rooms first. Besides, he had no idea if that man was friend or foe.

Another volley of gunfire. Close. But which room?

Ryan eased to the first doorway and glanced in. Empty. Debris littered the room, and a partially blocked doorway indicated the rooms were interconnected.

A man yelled, "Give it up."

Someone screamed.

Ryan rushed to the next doorway. Silent, efficient, like he'd been trained.

Another quick glance, and there was Jones, crouched behind an overturned desk, weapon in one hand and reaching into a pile of garbage on a shelf with the other.

What the hell was she doing?

Two more shots exploded in the room. Chips from the desk flew into the air. She didn't even flinch.

Movement to her right caught his attention. A heavyset man jumped out a doorway faster than Ryan would have thought possible, gun pointed at Jones' head.

She glanced up, hand still in the garbage, gun trained on the man in the other doorway.

Instinct kicked in. Ryan squeezed off a shot and dove for Jones. The man's shot exploded. Ryan tackled her, and they skidded across the floor through a pile of something foul. Chips of floorboard, shattered from the bullets, flew past his head.

Another gunshot sounded. Ryan kicked the shelf, knocking it over for more cover, and garbage and debris tumbled behind them. Jones wrenched in his grip, rolling on top of him, her Glock pointed at his head.

Her eyes widened.

Time froze, suspended between one breath and the next. All sound vanished. The reek of rot and decay, even the threat of danger, disappeared. There was only Special Agent Jones... straddling him. The heat of her thighs, pressed tight against his, seeped through his jeans. Her hair had fallen free of its knot and framed her delicate face in a strawberry blond halo. Bright blue eyes held him prisoner. Her surprise was clear. She was the most beautiful woman he'd ever seen. She captivated him, and he couldn't explain why, as if something deep inside him, something he hadn't even known existed, flickered awake when she was near.

Then her expression hardened.

The world rushed back in, the smell, the gloom, and the roar of gunfire.

She leaned close, nose to nose, the length of her body hot against his. "What the hell are you doing here?" she growled.

Anticipation shivered through him. God, what did he say? That he'd seen her in trouble and thought she needed help. She was an FBI agent, for goodness sake. With a team. He didn't doubt she was more than competent, and, now that he thought about it, his instinct had made him look ridiculous.

Bang. Bang.

Someone yelled, and footsteps pounded away.

Jones inched up and glanced over the fallen shelf, but didn't move her gun from his temple, and didn't stop straddling him.

A man swore, and more footsteps pounded away.

"Shit," Jones hissed. She shoved Ryan in the chest, using more force than necessary to get to her feet, and leaving him cold where her body had been.

"Why are you following me, Miller?" Her gun stayed trained on him.

"Saw the guys sneak in behind you. Thought I'd give you a heads-up." See, he could come up with something intelligent, even with her gun pointed at him.

"Oh, really?"

He became aware of the silence in the room beyond.

A man whose clean-cut look screamed federal agent—well-tailored coat, close-cropped blond hair, and hard profile—stepped into the doorway. Something dark glimmered against his shoulder like water or blood, but with the weak light and his black coat, Ryan couldn't quite tell what. The man's gaze slid from Jones to Ryan, then back to Jones.

"We shot one," the man said, "but he won't be talking."

Capri rolled her eyes. "That'll make Diablo happy."

"And I got the phone," a young tenor said. A man in his very early twenties—he might have even been a teenager—shoved past Mr. Clean-cut, holding a mangled phone. It looked like it had gotten shot. The young man stumbled to a stop, staring at Ryan. "Who's this?"

"Special Agent Patterson, Special Agent Valverdis," Jones said, "meet Detective Miller."

This was not the way he'd wanted to meet her coworkers: prone, covered in something disgusting, and held at Capri's gunpoint.

5

S wipe met Capri's gaze. Blood seeped through the shoulder of his
black coat, clear in the dim light because her night sight had
kicked in. He'd been shot. Just great. Not that it would kill him, but
he'd be grumpy for days.

His frown deepened. Definitely not happy thoughts. Well, she
wasn't particularly happy, either. Miller was going to need to do a lot
of explaining for following her and then getting involved in the
gunfight.

As if he could hear her thoughts, he stood and holstered his gun.

"Make it fast." Swipe grabbed Gig by his collar and yanked him
away.

Right. She'd just rip into Miller's mind so Swipe could get home
sooner. She resisted the urge to bare her teeth. Neither a sign of
aggression or sexual attraction was appropriate with the human
watching. He wouldn't understand either meaning of the action.

She turned to him. "Detective Miller."

He squared his shoulders, not bothering to brush the dirt and goo
from his clothes. His winter coat strained against his broad chest, as
if he'd put on more muscle since he'd bought it. Nothing for a detective to do in Elmsville but work out? Mother of All, she'd love to see
what lay beneath the heavy material.

The memory of running her hands over tight muscles flashed

through her mind. But it wasn't *his* chest she remembered, it was Eric's.

And that just tossed cold water on the fantasy.

"Special Agent Jones." He stepped toward her, moving his face into a narrow beam of sunlight cutting through a crack in the boarded window. It struck his cheek and glanced across his eyes, making them glow as if he possessed magic that radiated from his green irises.

"You're interfering with a federal investigation." Maybe she could just get him to go without messing with his mind.

"I thought I was saving your life."

"I can take care of myself." For a heartbeat she didn't want to. It was foolish. She'd seemed to have lost all common sense the other week when she'd been in the coffee shop with him, too. But a gunshot wouldn't kill her, even if it struck her heart. It would hurt like a bitch, but it wouldn't kill her. She really didn't need his protection.

He reached for her cheek, but didn't make contact. The heat from his fingers simmered along her jaw. If she leaned, ever so slightly, she'd complete the connection and touch flesh to flesh. Her chest ached with the need. But he was human, and there were rules.

God dammit, there were rules!

She shoved him back with her free hand and rammed her Glock into her hip holster. "Do I get an answer, or do I arrest you?"

A hint of a smile pulled at his lips. "If you arrest me, do you pull out your cuffs?"

Wouldn't he like that. "Special Agent Patterson does."

His smile wavered. "I saw your car, heard the gunshots, and thought you were in trouble."

That was the stupidest thing she'd ever heard. "Your story isn't getting any better. We've already established that I'm more than capable of taking care of myself."

Swipe growled in the next room. He was getting impatient. They still had a cleanup to do that now involved getting rid of a body. As much as she wanted to know why the detective had been following her, she didn't have the time to find out.

"I don't doubt that."

She raised an eyebrow. "Doubt what?"

"That you can take care of yourself."

"And that's why you came running in?"

Miller pursed his lips. Obviously, he didn't want to tell her the truth. It was much more difficult to use her magic to get someone to do something they didn't want to do—like tell whatever truth they were hiding. It was easier to suggest something they were going to do in the first place—like go home. It was also easier to make him forget something, just have it slip his mind—in this case whatever ridiculous reason had motivated him to follow her in the first place.

Fine. It'd be a slap-dash job, but it would do. A little suggestion, a small mental wall, and she'd be set. She wouldn't get any answers, but Miller would be gone, and Swipe would be happy—more or less.

She subvocalized her power word. Her earth magic flared, and she slid a thread of energy into Miller's thoughts.

Or rather, she tried.

The thread slipped around him, brushing against his consciousness but not entering.

She pushed a little harder, willing her magic to enter his mind. He was tired and needed to go home. Whatever he was looking for, it wasn't worth getting on the bad side of the FBI. "Consider this your warning."

He pursed his lips. "Really, Special Agent, are we going to play that game?"

The thread slipped past him again.

Jeez, what was wrong with her? She really was losing her focus. It would be so much easier if she knew why the hell he was here. Yeah, and if she kept telling herself that—

Swipe barked something at Gig. Miller glanced in the direction of their room, and Capri grabbed his chin, forcing him to look at her. His pale gaze met hers, and desire swept through her. Mother of All, he was so much like Eric.

"This isn't a game." She shoved her magic harder, spearing it into his mind, locking it into place. Pain flared across her temples, and she ground her teeth against it and against what she wanted from him.

"It's not—" he said.

She wove her magic into a blanket, forced it into his mind, and twisted the blanket over the last twenty-four hours of his memory.

He gasped.

She wrapped it tighter. It was a sloppy job, but in a couple of days, the sense that he was forgetting something would pass, and he'd continue on.

Miller's eyes flickered shut, his neck went slack, and his chin pressed against her hand. His breath caressed her thumb and forefinger. She yearned to capture that breath with hers, return the caress with lips and hands and—

She released his chin and slapped his shoulder. He jerked to attention.

"It was good to see you again. Thanks for your assistance." She forced a smile. Her gut churned at tearing into his mind and at how much she wanted him to be Eric—at how much she was willing to pretend he *was* Eric.

But it was better for him to forget her and for her to keep her distance. The more encounters they had, particularly since he was on the threshold of dragon activities, the more evasive the changes to his memories would have to be. And that was dangerous. Too much, too soon, and the damage to his mind could be permanent.

Miller blinked. A line formed between his brows, and he glanced left and right. "Excuse me?"

She gave him a gentle pull and led him toward the staircase. "The FBI can't thank you enough for your help."

The wooden stairs creaked beneath them.

"Ah..."

They shuffled down the narrow aisle toward the open area and the outside door. He looked like he was moving on autopilot. He'd probably be out of it for another couple of minutes, and slightly confused for at least a few hours, but instincts would still work. He'd still be able to drive a car and defend himself if he needed to.

"Thanks again." She held out her hand, not wanting to offer it, yet burning with the need for him to take it.

"Sure." His gaze dipped to her hand, but he didn't capture it with his own, just stared at it as if he couldn't remember what it meant. "Not a problem."

She crossed her arms, hiding her hands at her sides. Her chest ached at the thought that he wouldn't even remember this parting, and that she'd never see him again. But this was for the best. She couldn't abandon Eric a second time, and she certainly couldn't go to his funeral again, no matter how long he lived.

Miller crossed the lot to the road, his boots crunching in the slush and ice, and got into a navy Camaro. The engine started, and he drove away.

Capri's uneasy stomach continued to churn. Messing with his mind like that was a new low and indelicately done. What she really wanted was to tell him everything, a way of making amends for having abandoned Eric. But that wouldn't solve anything, and it wouldn't heal the ache within her. It would probably make everything worse. The human mind could only handle so much. The truth usually drove them insane.

She kicked a chunk of ice into a puddle a few feet away. Her day just kept getting better and better. Two mysterious beheadings which could be her prince flexing his less-than-diplomatic muscles, and now she'd violated Miller's mind, the twin of the man she'd never stopped loving. To top it off, she still had to go to the Dragon Court with all its political pitfalls and report.

6

Four hours later, Capri pulled up behind Swipe's van in the underground garage of their headquarters. The van's door flew open and Swipe stepped out. His rage simmered around him, ferocious and deadly. Obviously he'd been holding it all in while he cast his earth magic to clean the scene. Which meant it was well and truly boiled.

"You took care of the human?"

He'd been too focused on his spell to notice when Miller had left, and she hadn't been stupid enough to bother him then. "Do you really have to ask?"

"The human?" Swipe growled.

She got out of her vehicle and resisted the urge to check her sidearm. "Detective Miller is not a problem."

"Doesn't look like it to me."

"He's my problem, and it's been taken care of." Badly and without any kind of honor, but it had been taken care of.

"I got shot. That makes it my problem as well."

She bit the inside of her cheek. Even on a good day, Swipe wasn't a drake she wanted to piss off. He was bigger than her, his soul magic was just as fast at healing as hers, and he could gate as well as she between anchored gates. They were evenly matched until it came to size. At over six feet, he towered above her, and if she didn't fight dirty, he could easily kick her ass. To top it off, she'd have to work extra hard to hide his corpse, while all he had to do to hide evidence of hers was cast his earth magic. And yet, if she wanted to remain in control of her team, she needed to prove she was still the dominant drake. "I said I'd take care of it, and I did."

"I know he's that cop from Elmsville. I don't know what's going on—"

She grabbed the front of his coat and yanked him close, nose to nose. "Nothing is going on. If anything was, I'd tell you. You're the team's Second, *my* Second. That's the way Tobias assigned it. Besides, you healed within a minute of being shot."

"I still have a hole in my coat."

She shoved him, ramming his back against his van. "I'll buy you a new one."

"You've got crappy taste." Swipe bared his perfect teeth and growled—not a sexual invitation. "I'll send you my bill."

He grabbed the dead mage in the body bag from the back of the van, slung it over his shoulder, and stormed to the stairwell. Guess he didn't have the patience to wait for the elevator.

Gig slunk around from the other side of the van and shrugged, as if Capri and Swipe had this kind of argument every day. Okay, maybe as if they had it every sixty or so years, which was closer to the truth. Of course, Gig was so young, he might not have been able to remember her and Swipe's last fight. That had been in the early 1940s, when Hunter had gone on an unsanctioned killing spree, just after Gig had been reborn. Before then, Gig had been Payne: team leader, older than her, and witness to dozens of spats with Swipe.

Gig hit the button to call the elevator, crossed his arms, and rocked back and forth on his heels.

He was waiting for her.

She didn't know why the Handmaiden had rebirthed him. It hadn't been demanded by his coterie's doyen or Regis—the only two ways for a dragon to be forced to have his soul reborn. He'd also been put back into the same body, something else that wasn't done. Every time she looked at him, she saw her friend and mentor under all that teenaged clothing and haircut. Now Swipe was on her case, she couldn't confide in Payne because he was now Gig, and she couldn't stop thinking about Miller... no, Eric... no—

Shit.

She punched the car door, splitting open her first two knuckles.

"Tobias isn't going to like it if you break another car," Gig said.

Thin runnels of blood wound around her fingers, then the wounds scabbed over and healed. "I don't care what Tobias thinks."

"Yeah, right."

The elevator door slid open.

Capri got in, and Gig wisely remained silent for the ride down. Since Newgate was the preferred place of residence for most of the drakes living in the human dimension, the North American Clean Team had established a permanent base of operations here. Surrounded by hills and not much else, the one-story office building had been built on the side of a steep hill. Across the street sat a large truck mechanic shop and a deserted Victorian house that had seen better days. A mile up the road, and therefore down and then up another hill, was a struggling strip mall.

Regardless of why the building had been constructed at least five miles from anywhere, it had been the perfect location for the team when Tobias had finally agreed they needed a base in the area, its isolation being the primary factor for suitability.

The office on top had remained the same, with the addition of extra thick blinds covering the windows, and an underground complex had been constructed, complete with suites, guest rooms, debriefing room, cells, records room, a kitchen and living room area for team members, gym, pool, and gateroom.

The elevator opened into a hall running left and right. Left to the living areas, right to the business areas. Far to her left, Swipe jerked open the fridge in the kitchen and stared in. He'd cool off soon enough. At least she hoped he would. It would be a shame if she had to beat or shoot some sense into him. He already had one hole in that suit and coat, and she knew how expensive it was. Bet he'd buy something twice as expensive just to see if she'd pay the bill. Not that she, or even he, didn't have the money to replace it, but he was particular about his clothes and would do it just to spite her.

All of which she'd deal with later. She needed to report to Tobias and dig around for some information about the corpse in Hiro's exam room.

The image of Miller reaching to touch her cheek flashed through her mind's eye. It morphed into Eric doing the same action while he lay naked in her bed so many years ago.

Her heart fluttered.

Shit. She was turning into one of those insipid heroines, the kind in those black and white movies her friend Grey loved, always sighing and fainting and weeping and periodically breaking into song.

She ground her teeth. Focus on work. Surely, Tobias and the body were enough to distract her.

She headed to the gateroom, Gig still at her heels. Tobias wouldn't be pleased to hear the mages had returned and that Diablo had screwed up by claiming they weren't around. He should have stayed for the clean up. But then, he never had before and there hadn't been anything about this situation to imply it was different from any other. Which meant there might actually be something on that cell phone connected to the mages.

Regardless, Diablo—Mr. I-am-death-to-all-human-mages—was going to get an earful. That almost made her smile. Too bad she didn't get to do it. She really needed to yell at someone.

Gig squeaked beside her, and she realized she was growling.

She was also in the gateroom and hadn't noticed the walk down the hall.

She swallowed back another growl. "See what you can get off the phone."

Gig nodded, his swarthy complexion pale under the harsh institutional-style lighting.

Jeez. She couldn't even focus for two minutes.

"And Gig—" If Regis was behind the two decapitations, she'd need to do damage control in the future and find a human scapegoat. Particularly if the media sensationalized the deaths, and with the reporter being at the M.E.'s office, that could be any time now.

The biggest question, however, was if Regis was sending a message, why kill one known drake and one unknown drake, possibly a human? If the second victim, Andy Reynolds, was human, he had to have known something to have been considered a threat to dragonkind. "I also need you to look into someone."

"Sure thing, boss."

"But it needs to be kept under the radar."

"I'm good with keeping things quiet."

No, he wasn't. But she wasn't going to say that. He was young. Naiveté practically evaporated from his sweat. A hundred years ago, he'd been so sophisticated, so old. Older than her. He'd been the boss. And the Handmaiden had taken that from her.

Which wasn't fair, either.

"I need you to find out what you can about an Andrew Charles Reynolds. His local address is 27 Mapleton Ave."

"Okay."

While he wasn't good at keeping things secret, he was great for doing things without question. "I'm working on a hunch, but I don't want Tobias to worry about it until I know anything for certain."

"You mean you don't want Regis getting wind of it. I'll get right on it." He sauntered away, trying too hard to look cool and therefore failing—a very Payne thing to do to lighten the mood.

She raised an eyebrow. Maybe there was a hint of Payne in there after all. And maybe she just saw what she wanted to. For the second time that day she was forced to ask what the hell was wrong with her? Wanting Eric and Payne back? People would think she'd become soft. She needed to get a grip because a soft drake was a dead one.

7

Capri gated into the Dragon Court's gateroom and headed to Tobias's office, passing more than a dozen royal guards stationed along the passageways as well as three two-man patrols walking 'beats' like policemen. Security had never been so high in Court before. There certainly had never been patrols. She wished— not for the first time—that she had stronger gating abilities and could gate from anywhere to anywhere like Grey could. But she couldn't and no matter how hard she concentrated, she couldn't open a gate without a magical anchor and couldn't move through dimensions without an anchor on the other end.

Save for the guards and patrolmen, the halls at Court, hidden in an interdimensional sphere discovered by the Handmaiden centuries ago, were unnervingly empty even for mid-afternoon. But it had only been two weeks since Zenobia's failed coup and the disaster it had wrought. Prince Regis was still on a rampage looking for more traitors, and doyens were keeping their coterie members close, either to protect them or control them—although the odds of that preventing Regis from losing his temper and rebirthing any of them was slim.

Except now rebirth was impossible. Regis's preferred punishment was off the table. The Handmaiden, the dragons' only true sorcerer and the only one capable of casting the rebirth spell, had left and no one knew where she'd gone or when she'd return.

Her leaving was a disaster, especially when everything was in turmoil. Dragonkind was an endangered species to begin with. Stuck in a parasitic spirit state, inhabiting and reanimating human corpses using the magic in their dragon souls put them in a precarious situation. They couldn't reproduce. Their numbers were finite. While able to rapidly heal, accidents—and sometimes things not even close to accidents—still happened. Their only salvation was the medallion, which could absorb a dragon's soul and keep it safe until the Handmaiden could cast the rebirth spell. Except the medallion could only keep the soul cohesive for a short period of time. If the Handmaiden didn't return soon, too many souls in their already diminished numbers could be lost.

Only something of great importance could have taken her away, but Capri couldn't fathom what. She'd never known the mind of the Handmaiden. No one did. The only drake who'd ever gotten close to her was Grey, and Capri got the impression he still didn't know a fraction of the Handmaiden's secrets.

Capri stepped onto the Greater Promenade, heading to the end where the chamberlain's offices lay. Grey emerged from the opened double doors, brow creased.

"Hey, Grey."

He squinted, as if looking at her from a great distance even though he only stood a few feet away.

"Grey?" She could only imagine the challenges he'd faced since the coup. Being in the Handmaiden's services had alienated him from his coterie, putting him in even more of an allegiance limbo than her. When the Handmaiden had disappeared and Grey's friend Hunter had left his position in the Royal Coterie as the prince's assassin, Grey had aligned himself with Hunter instead of joining the Royal Coterie. And while others also flocked to Hunter's banner, Hunter had yet to solidify his coterie. Hell, he hadn't even proclaimed he was starting a new one, drakes just gathered around him in hope that he, the only drake who could now take dragon form, would take the throne and lead them with the compassion that had been missing for centuries.

Which made Regis, as heir apparent, the last of two gold drakes— and the only one sane enough to rule—even more psychologically unbalanced.

Grey stumbled to a halt and sucked in a ragged breath. His gaze settled on her, and he tilted his head to the side. "Capri?"

"So I'm not invisible."

He furrowed his brow.

Was that sweat at his temples?

"Rough day." He rubbed his face.

She could relate. "And it isn't even dinner yet."

"You won't want to mention that." He jerked his chin in the direction of the Chamberlain's Office. "Barna insists on going ahead with his annual charity dinner for the humans, and Regis is on the verge of proclaiming him a traitor."

Capri rolled her eyes. This was ridiculous. She didn't know how, but it looked like the prince was becoming soul sick, and if that happened, Court would fall into more chaos. It was barely holding together as it was.

"Well, we can't hide from the humans' realm every time we're upset." Although she suspected Regis would love just that. And not only when he was upset. The drake was becoming more paranoid by the day, just like his father.

A strange expression swept across Grey's face, then vanished. "Yeah."

He flashed her a hint of teeth, then snapped his lips closed and strode away.

It had looked like he was actually going to flirt with her. Had he finally given up on desiring something between them? He only flirted with women he wasn't serious about. But the moment of flirtation hadn't lasted. It hadn't even really manifested. Nothing about Grey seemed right, but she couldn't put her finger on the how or why.

Of course, maybe it wasn't Grey. Maybe the mess of her emotions was making her see things. Which didn't help her avoid the need to report.

She strode through the maze of desks, partitions, and office equipment to Tobias's small office at the back. A quick check through his open door assured her he wasn't on a rampage. Not that the former pirate rampaged. He was too slick for that. He'd more likely knife you in the back or while you slept.

He leaned over documents spread out on his desk, his wild black pirate hair, similar to Gig's and yet more sophisticated on his muscular frame, veiling his face. She crossed the threshold and before she could make a sound to announce her presence, he glanced up.

"Report."

"What, no small talk?" Even for him this was terse.

"It's been a busy day, about to become a busy evening."

He had a point.

"The hideout wasn't as deserted as Diablo thought. We ran into a bit of trouble. One mage is dead, another is in the wind, along with who-knows-how-many more."

Tobias pursed his lips. He didn't look happy. Of course, he hadn't looked happy when she'd entered, so perhaps it wasn't *her* news pissing him off.

"We did find a cell phone that they seemed to have come back for. Gig's got it, and he's working his magic, although it did sustain some damage."

"Damage?"

"It got shot."

Tobias raised an eyebrow. "How does something so small take gunfire?"

In a complete disaster of a gunfight, that's how. If Miller hadn't distracted her, she would have gotten the phone and everything would have been fine.

"You don't want to know." She rubbed her temples. "Hopefully, he'll have something soon, and we can track the others down. Perhaps get a handle on how many remain."

"Wouldn't that be nice." Tobias flashed a hint of teeth, revealing his displeasure.

Yeah, well, she was displeased as well, but she wasn't going to draw attention to it. The chamberlain's troubles were better left alone. Particularly right now.

"Are there any other leads?"

"No." And finding leads wasn't her job. It was Diablo's. Something else she wasn't going to point out to Tobias.

"I'll talk to the Dugga of the Asar Nergal and have him assign Diablo to your team for the duration. Maybe that will get something done."

Capri's heart skipped a beat. "You'll what?"

She couldn't have the leader of the Asar Nergal commanding Diablo to hang around while she investigated the decapitations in secret. Well, she supposed she could, since it wouldn't mean much to Diablo. But the idea of him poking his nose in her business—business she didn't even want Tobias to know about until she was ready—didn't sit well.

"Is there a problem?"

Shit, she'd waited too long to answer. She rubbed her face with her hands, playing up her exhaustion. "No, I just doubt Diablo will agree. He's very much a lone drake."

"That's his problem."

"Actually, it will become my problem if you force him onto my team."

"You can't handle him?"

"Oh, I can handle him fine. I just hate wasting the bullets."

Tobias sighed and closed the folder on his desk. "Try not to shoot him." He opened another folder. "At least not too many times. There's more than enough politics to go around right now. I don't want any of it from you."

"Aye aye, Captain."

Tobias flashed his teeth, this time in pleasure, and she left. She needed to get back to Gig. Hopefully he'd found something about this Andy Reynolds, and she could figure out if his murder was connected to Court before it became a public problem—and before Diablo could show up, making things even more complicated.

She headed back down the Greater Promenade to the gateroom and rounded the corner. More than a dozen drakes glanced at her and she froze. Most were Regis's sycophants, but she counted at least three guards with them. The sycophants were a collection of drakes who'd sworn allegiance to the Royal Coterie but didn't hold any position of importance other than to follow Regis around and make him feel good. As if on cue—and, knowing Regis, it could have been orchestrated—the drakes parted, revealing the prince, who stood waiting at the gate.

A young drake, dressed in creams to match Regis's over-dramatic, Henry the 8th attire, cleared his throat. "Your Highness."

"What?" Regis barked. He turned and his gaze landed on Capri. A bright, evil pleasure curled his lips and lit his eyes. "Capri. So good of you to join me. Shouldn't you be at work, chasing down mages?"

Capri plastered on a fake smile, showing just enough teeth to be polite and not be mistaken as the aggression she wanted to show. "Just reporting to the chamberlain, Your Highness. I really should gate back to Newgate and carry on."

"But my summons," Regis said.

"Your—?" Right. There'd been a text message on her phone, summoning all drakes to Court at 4 p.m. exactly. Royal decree and all that. Normally she would have just sucked it up and gone, but given Regis's mood lately and the current mess with the mages, she figured it would be safer to be too busy for whatever Regis had in mind. "I really should get back to work."

"And disobey a decree?" Regis asked, his voice syrupy.

"Of course not. I shall attend at Your Highness's pleasure."

"And not perform your duties." Regis's tone darkened, and he flashed his teeth.

"Your Highness." The trap was obvious and there was no way to avoid it. "I am at Your Highness's disposal."

"With the Handmaiden gone, unfortunately you're not." Implying he'd *dispose* of her by rebirthing her—probably just for the thrill of it. He'd do it, even though her new body wouldn't have the earth magic ability to manipulate humans' minds and that she'd lose all of her memories. Her soul would be reset back to her most primal state, that she was a blue drake and a baby drake at that, and then she'd be useless as leader of the Clean Team.

A black void erupted against the far wall in the hall as the gate was activated, and Barna, the doyen of the Major Brown Coterie, and his Second lurched through.

"About time," Regis growled. "Come along. You, too, Capri." He strode from the hall with a wake of drakes dressed to match his cream doublet, breeches, and cape trailing behind him.

Barna, a drake in the body of a middle-aged man of Greek descent, turned his lined, swarthy face to Capri, his dark eyebrows raised.

"I don't know what's going on," she said, and followed after Regis and his entourage.

Behind her, Barna's Second, a drake in a young, mid-twenties body, snorted. Yeah, that's how she felt, too. With luck, whatever this was wouldn't last long.

Regis sauntered down the hall to the main stairs—a wide, curling staircase that connected the arteries of Court. They took the stairs up one flight, then down a secondary promenade to a wide, ornamented hall.

Capri's heart sank. Only the halls with royal significance were ornamented, as if to point out to the rest of dragonkind that the Royal Coterie was so much more important than they were. This hall led to the royal booth in the arena.

It shouldn't have surprised her. Regis had summoned everyone. He had a point to make, and the best way to make it was in the arena. But it couldn't be a duel. Surely, she would have heard if someone had called a *wasu tahazu*. Even if someone had, Regis couldn't allow it. Yes, the medallion at the heart of the arena absorbed the soul of any drake killed during a fight. But without the Handmaiden to cast the rebirth spell, the soul—without a body to maintain its cohesion—would disintegrate.

Regis passed through a massive, ornamented arch and sat on the cushioned throne in the center of the box. His entourage crowded behind him on cushioned benches, leaving the uncushioned bench in front of him free for his *guests*.

"Have a seat, Barna. I think you'll find this entertaining." Regis leaned back. "You, too, Capri."

Fantastic. There was no getting out of this, and certainly no hanging out at the back of the box and sneaking away once whatever Regis had planned began.

She followed Barna and his Second and sat.

Regis leaned forward. "Now, watch carefully. This is important."

A nervous energy filled the arena. It was too quiet with so many drakes in attendance. More drakes were here than had been at the *pahar* two weeks ago—but then the *pahar* was really for the doyens, their Seconds and Thirds, to play Regis's political games, and not much more.

This, however, was for every drake. Regis had summoned them all, and any who hadn't shown had been noticed and not in a way anyone wanted. Regis was pissed and no one knew if it was safer to avoid him or play his games. Even Grey was here. He sat on a bench a quarter of the way around the arena from her, near the back. In the bright light filling the stadium, Grey still didn't look well. He was even more gray in complexion than before.

Movement in the main arch, across from her on the arena floor, caught her attention. Regis giggled and Barna stiffened. The doyen of the Major Brown Coterie knew whatever was going to happen was a not-so-veiled threat. Would it be effective?

Half a dozen guards, dressed in all black with a gold rampant dragon embroidered over their hearts, stepped out of the shadows. Behind them, collared and on a chain leash like a dog, followed Zenobia. She stood straight and proud, a testament to the Syrian queen she'd once been, but her posture was also tight with agony. Her black hair hung wild about her head, accentuating the silver half-mask covering the left side of her face, the reason for her pain. Regis had dressed her in a low-cut green gown. Runnels of blood seeped down her neck, parting at her shoulder to ooze down her back and over her chest between her breasts.

The guard holding her leash jerked it, and Zenobia stumbled but didn't fall.

"Kneel," Regis roared, his voice booming through the arena.

The muscle in Barna's jaw twitched.

Zenobia eased to her knees, her head held up defiantly. The guard grabbed her mask and pulled it off.

A gasp raced through the crowd. The skin on Zenobia's face scabbed over a raw wound but then burst apart before fully healing. Blood seeped down her jaw and over her neck. The wound scabbed and burst again and again in a constant state of healing and disintegration.

She should have been dead. Disintegrating touch was one of the few things that could kill a drake. But her soul magic healing was so strong and so fast she had somehow survived—if in an agonizing state of constant disintegration was actually surviving.

Someone else moved just inside the arch. More whispers hissed through the arena. Then a hint of something pale shifted and caught light, forming a silver halo.

Capri's mind stuttered.

It couldn't be.

She blinked, but only one drake had a halo like that. Odyne.

The silver drake eased from the shadows and stepped into the arena. She was a study in opposites to Zenobia, with skin so white she looked bloodless. Her silver hair hung to her waist, a match to her silver eyes. She wore all black: boots, pants, long-sleeved shirt, and calf-length, high-collared coat. She clasped black-gloved hands before her and turned an impassive expression toward Regis as if she were above all this.

Maybe she was. She'd been a recluse, hiding in an obscure wing of the Dragon Court for centuries, longer than Capri could remember. Rumor had it she'd been Constantine's Torturer, using her earth magic gift of searing touch to cause excruciating pain to anyone Constantine condemned. Rumor had it she couldn't control her gift, it was always active, and any touch, any slight brushing of skin on skin, caused a pain so agonizing you wished you were dead.

The Handmaiden's ban on using Odyne's gift for torture certainly gave credence to the rumor. Regardless of what was true, the Handmaiden had made her proclamation centuries ago and Odyne had withdrawn from dragon society. But now with the Handmaiden gone…

"I wonder," Regis said. "What do you think hurts more? Zenobia's state of constant disintegration or Odyne's touch?"

Silence filled the arena. No one wanted to find out if the power of Odyne's magic was exaggerated.

"I asked you a question, Barna," Regis growled.

The muscle in Barna's jaw twitched again, then stilled. "And it's a good question," he said, no sign of fear in his voice. "Your Torturer's touch only lasts for so long. Zenobia's current state is forever."

"Are you suggesting we don't punish Zenobia for her treason? She murdered drakes. She made mages. She broke the laws we hold most sacred."

"I'm not saying we don't punish her—"

"Sure sounds like it to me." Regis stood and jerked his chin.

Odyne slid off a glove. The guards around Zenobia tensed. No one wanted to find out if the rumors about Odyne were true.

"Put dragonkind in danger," Regis said. He was looking at Zenobia, but it was clear he addressed the entire arena. He dropped his gaze to Barna, smirked, then turned back to Zenobia. "Willingly or not, and you'll wish I'd killed you."

Odyne brushed a finger across Zenobia's good cheek then put her glove back on. Zenobia's eyes flashed wide, she swallowed a scream, and blew out a ragged breath.

That was it? Guess the rumors about Odyne's touch were just that, rumors. It didn't look as if it had been anywhere near as painful as Zenobia's already melting face.

But then Zenobia's eyes widened again. She gasped, then gasped again, quick, desperate pants. Her body clenched, the muscles in her neck straining, and the good side of her face turned red with effort.

Regis chuckled with dark satisfaction. "That's it. Fight it, bitch."

Zenobia's body trembled. She opened her mouth, gasped again, and then started screaming. She screamed and screamed, doubling over and still screamed, wrenching, agonizing, horrific wails.

Mother of All. One touch. Just a caress of Odyne's finger was all it had taken. The myths were real, and with the Handmaiden gone, there was no one to stop him from using Odyne's touch on anyone he wanted. Capri had no idea what Regis had on Odyne. She was old enough to remember the time before the Great Scourge when dragons still had their corporeal forms and all drakes had sworn their loyalty to the gold drakes of the Royal Coterie. Some of the old drakes refused to be oath-breakers no matter what Regis did. Maybe Odyne was one of them.

Regardless, no drake was safe. Anyone could raise Regis's ire, even a drake sworn to his employ like Capri. With Odyne back in his service, the punishment was terrifying.

8

G rey gated into Hunter's front hall, his pulse racing and sweat slicking his brow. Zenobia's screams still rang in his ears. Screams he'd never be able to forget. There'd been reasons the Handmaiden had banned King Constantine from using Odyne's magic for torture. No one deserved to endure that. And Odyne shouldn't be forced to inflict it.

But with the Handmaiden gone, there was nothing holding Regis back. And using Odyne wasn't just the first step. Regis had already started *detaining* drakes without cause. He claimed they'd been involved in the coup, but there was no evidence to the fact. Regis had to be stopped, and the only drake who might be powerful enough to do that was Hunter.

Grey headed down the hall to the living room. A fire burned in the hearth but the room was empty.

"Hunter?" The drake needed to know what was going on no matter how much Grey didn't want to interrupt the lovebirds.

That thought stung. Grey was even more alone now than he had been before. He hadn't thought that possible. Sure, Hunter had been a mostly absent friend for the last couple hundred years, but they *had* been friends. They still were. Just now there was someone else in Hunter's life. His inamorata.

The hall darkened and water dripped behind Grey.

He sucked in a quick breath and focused on the fire crackling in the fieldstone hearth.

Not. Now.

It had only been two weeks since the Handmaiden had soothed his clamoring memories into a foggy haze. It was too soon for them to come crowding in. But a lot had happened in those two weeks.

Like almost getting killed in the humans' realm. Again. And because he never forgot, not even the slightest detail, the memories now swarmed through his head, weakening his hold that kept the rest of them at bay.

Drip. Drip.

Mother of All, why did he have to keep reliving that horrible night? It had been years ago.

Drip—

Keep focused.

"Hey, Hunter." Grey crossed the open concept kitchen-family room to the back of the house. Focus. Hunter needed to know what was going on. Surely if he saw that Regis stood on the edge of insanity, he'd step up and take the throne. He had the Royal Coterie's medallion and likely the, albeit reluctant, support of most of the Counseling Coteries.

The kitchen was sleek and new. All stainless steel, white granite, and dark wood. It blended into a plush sitting area with a matching hardwood floor and furniture in various shades of gray. If it wasn't for the vase of red roses and the red and pink throw cushions, Grey would have assumed the place was a bachelor pad, all slick and dark. But the more Grey looked, the more he saw little feminine touches: a bowl of fruit on the counter, a decorative stained-glass pane in the window over the sink, and huddles of candles on shelves and in corners.

A massive painting of a sky at sunset hung over the fireplace, but that was Hunter's. More paintings and photos of skies were scattered throughout the room, but not as obviously as the art over the mantel. Grey had been sneaking Hunter's hoard of sky-art from his suite at Court to him over the last couple of days. After taking the risk with the one big piece, Hunter had told Grey to only take the small stuff and then not too often. He didn't want to risk Grey upsetting Regis any more than he already was.

Grey crossed to the large bank of floor-to-ceiling windows and the back door. A trail of man-sized footsteps led away in the snow off the deck, and into the woodlot behind the house. It was hard to tell if they were new tracks or not. For a fire drake who hated winter, Hunter was certainly spending a lot of time outside on the hundred acres of farmland he'd purchased in Canada—although farmland seemed a misnomer. Even if it wasn't currently knee-high—and higher in some places—in snow, the landscape was too rugged, with jagged jutting rock and gnarled pines, for any kind of sensible farming. It was cold, and rocky, and Hunter was pretty sure given how everyone knew his dislike for the cold that no one would suspect him of willingly moving to Northern Ontario. And since he'd been able to take dragon form, outside, in the cold that he hated so much, was the most likely place to find him.

A blast of frigid wind hit Grey in the face, heavy with the scent of pine and cedar. The snow crunched under his boots and clung to his pant legs. He crossed into the shadow of the forest and the chill seeped through his slacks and coat.

The trail led around a massive oak, revealing a gentle slope into a clearing filled with an enormous red drake. The drake faced away from Grey, offering a spectacular view of his tail and haunches. The dying day's light shimmered in his scales of varying shades of red with hints of gold and black. The ridges of his spine stood up sharply like another ridge of pines.

No wonder humans had found them so terrifying. They'd been enormous.

"I'm sure the question you're itching to ask is, does this dragon form make your ass look big?" Grey said.

The dragon, Hunter, stretched his wings and shifted. His massive head swiveled toward Grey and one large slitted eye examined him. Smoke drifted from Hunter's nostrils and for a moment, Grey feared his friend wouldn't recognize him in his frail human vessel.

Anaea assures me it's just the right size. Hunter's mental voice boomed in Grey's head.

"That's what all inamoratas say."

True. Love is blind. Hunter's form trembled. His neck shortened and his snout squashed back. With a groan, he shrank and morphed back into his human shape. Goose bumps leapt across his naked body. He hugged himself and rushed for a pile of clothes a few feet from Grey.

"You pick the best places to run around naked." It made Grey shiver just looking at him.

Hunter glared at Grey and dragged on a pair of jeans, a sweater, and the medallion—which hung on a thick masculine chain. "You have news?"

"Yeah, but let's do this inside." Grey grabbed Hunter's shoulder and formed a gate beneath them. The vortex transported them back into the house, tossing them out of a gate that lay against the bank of windows. The jerk, from falling through to lurching forward, shook through Grey's legs, but he—along with Hunter—managed to keep his balance.

Heat wrapped around Grey, sudden and stifling in contrast to the stinging cold outside. The fire in the fireplace crackled beside them, reminding Grey of—

Things he wasn't going to remember right now. Focus.

"So." Hunter rubbed his hands and leaned closer to the fire. "How bad is it?"

"On a scale of one to ten... worse than the Inquisition."

"That good, huh?"

The Inquisition had been bad times for the dragon community. Somehow, some humans had discovered the dragons' existence and in typical human nature tried to destroy what they feared. Dragons became good at playing dead and, as a result, half of Regis's laws controlling the dragon population had been made.

Light trembled at the edge of Grey's vision. Water on sunlight. Impossible in the dimly lit living room.

More light flickered. It wasn't real. It was just a memory. But Mother of All—

A voice screamed, "Witch," and a roar of approval followed. Grey fought the urge to look and acknowledge the vision.

As if just thinking about not looking gave it strength, the sunlight flashed again, this time in his face, blinding him. He blinked. Hunter's living room vanished and a muddy village square shimmered around him. Sunlight sparkled from a bucket filled with water sitting beside the well. The vision was serene. There wasn't a soul in sight. A warm spring breeze caressed his skin. Reflected sunlight danced across his face.

A woman's scream filled the air, and a crowd roared. Between one heartbeat and the next people materialized, filling the square and pressing close. The reek of unwashed bodies choked Grey. Smoke billowed from the smithy's furnace on the other side of the square. The woman wrenched against the grasp of two burly men as they dragged her closer to the doorway. She cried and begged, tears pouring down her cheeks, but the overweight middle-aged priest in the smithy's doorway, clutching his Bible in one hand and a smoldering metal brand in the other, only grimaced.

The woman hadn't been a dragon or a witch. Just some woman who'd given Grey a kind word.

"—Grey?"

The priest's face morphed, turning long and lean with a shock of black hair cut close to his scalp. He reached out, and Grey jerked back.

"Grey?"

Hunter. It was Hunter bleeding into his memory.

It felt so real—it *had been* real. Grey had watched the woman tortured into a confession and then tied to a stake and burned to death, unable to save her. So many deaths at his hands because of what he was.

Darkness rippled over the square, turning it into a wet alley at midnight. "How fast can you heal, dragon?" a voice hissed.

Grey shoved at the memory. Get a grip. It wasn't real. Hunter and his fireplace were real. That was real. Focus.

"Earth to Grey?"

"Sorry." He clenched his jaw, struggling to see past the memories to Hunter. "Just don't want to be Regis's next target. With the Handmaiden missing, it seems Regis now has permission to be... medieval in his punishments."

"He always was medieval," Hunter growled.

"He brought Odyne back into service."

"But the Handmaiden forbade it."

"She's not around, now, is she? You have to proclaim your coterie and take the throne." It was the only way to stabilize dragon politics.

"I'm not of royal blood, and I don't have the Handmaiden's

backing."

"No one has the Handmaiden's backing. The other doyens will support you. Hell, I'm sure even Zenobia will support you."

Hunter sagged into a leather armchair by the hearth and rubbed his face. "I'm not a king."

"Then at least offer shelter to those drakes without a coterie."

"And I'm not a doyen."

"You can take dragon form. You're the only one who can." Couldn't he see how important that was to the other drakes?

"And I'm certainly not the savior of dragonkind."

"I'm not saying that you are, just—"

"Yes, you are. Everyone is. But I'm just the prince's assassin." He snorted. "I'm not even that anymore."

"Even if you ignore Regis, he won't ignore you. Your inamorata is a human sorcerer. You know he's planning to come after you."

Hunter growled and flashed teeth. "Don't think I don't know that."

"Then do something before he does." It was never good to be put on the defensive. They'd had enough experiences during the Crusades to know that—not to mention all the other wars they'd been a part of. "It's a dangerous time to be a drake. And the humans have nothing to do with it this time." If Hunter would just step up. More than half of the doyens were sure to support him. Drakes would leave their coteries to flock to his banner. Handmaiden's support or not, Hunter had to take the throne before Regis destroyed them.

Hunter jerked toward Grey. He braced himself, ready for the attack, but Hunter stormed past him to the dark window overlooking the path to the clearing and pressed his hands to the glass instead.

"It's always a dangerous time to be a drake. Regis won't just step down. Drakes will die if I make a move."

"Drakes will die if you don't. His first step is Odyne, the next is to start eliminating those he thinks are a threat. And he won't wait for the Handmaiden to return to rebirth them. He'll kill them for good."

"I need to protect Anaea."

"With Regis in charge, she'll never be safe. None of us will."

"Not without the Handmaiden."

It always came back to that. Without the Handmaiden, drag-onkind was helpless. If their human vessels were so damaged that they died, they died for real. And their species took one more step closer to becoming extinct. They needed her magic to rebirth them. There were so few of them to begin with and even fewer now, but that wouldn't stop Regis.

Mother of All, why hadn't she just told him where she was going? Why had she even left in the first place?

Light shimmered on water again at the edge of his vision. His pulse jumped and sweat slicked his palms.

And why had she left him? Every day his memories grew stronger, more consuming. If she didn't return and use her magic to help him regain control, he'd fall into them and never be able to find his way out.

She had to come back. She always did. "The Handmaiden will return. She has to."

"But will it be soon enough?" Hunter asked.

Grey pushed the memories back. Trembles shook his hands, and he shoved them into his pockets. "You can't wait. You have to take the throne."

"I'm not willing to risk that without her support." Hunter blew out a long sigh. His gaze, through the reflection in the window, caught Grey's. "I need you to watch Anaea. I need you to keep her safe."

"Isn't that your job?" But ice seeped into Grey's gut. There were very few reasons for an inamorated drake to ask someone to watch over his beloved, and none of them were good.

"I have to find the Handmaiden. Someone has to. But Anaea needs to learn to control her magic. She can't come with me."

"And I'm sure you two have discussed this."

"No, and if I talk to her I won't have the strength to leave." Hunter's expression hardened. "I've spent a lot of time thinking about this. It's the only way."

"So you're what? Going to leave her a text message? Oh, that's slick. Even I know that's bad form."

"You need to let her know I'll be in touch when I can. She'll understand how important this is."

"Gee, thanks. She's a sorcerer. The only thing that has more fury than a woman scorned is a sorcerer scorned. And you're asking me to play messenger."

"And bodyguard." Hunter pulled the medallion's chain over his head and set it on the coffee table beside him. "She's at Nero's. Keep her safe."

With a whoosh, Hunter gated from the house.

The fire snapped, its image flickering in the dark window where Hunter had stood.

This was just great. Regis was on a dragon hunt. Hunter, the only drake in a position to take over, was gone, and Grey had just been put in charge of keeping Anaea safe.

Sunlight danced at the edge of his vision. He could barely keep himself in the here and now, let alone keep Hunter's inamorata safe. If anything happened to her, not even the Handmaiden would be able to save Grey from Hunter's wrath.

The sound of a gate forming whooshed in the front hall.

"I'm home and I brought wine from Nero's collection," Anaea called.

Hunter had terrible timing.

"What are we celebrating?" Grey asked.

Anaea strode into the kitchen. "Hey, Grey. Is Hunter still outside flexing his wings? Give a drake shiny new scales and he becomes vain." She set the bottle of wine and a bag of groceries on the counter and unzipped her coat.

"Actually, he…" Jeez. Where did he begin? She was Hunter's inamorata. This kind of leaving didn't happen. It would feel too much like heart-wrenching abandonment this early in their relationship. "Maybe we should open that wine and sit."

Anaea's eyes widened. "What's happened? Has Regis done something?" She closed her eyes and frowned. "Hunter isn't answering me. He's blocking my mind call."

The stemware in the glassed-in cupboard behind her started to rattle.

"If he responds, he'll come back and he can't do that. Not yet."

"But he promised he wouldn't return to Court without discussing it with me. If Regis has done something to him—" The cupboard door flew open. A glass leapt out and shattered on the counter, making her jump. "Shit."

Another glass tumbled out and smashed.

"No no no." She squeezed her eyes shut and drew in a slow breath, then another.

The glasses stopped rattling.

"Long day?" Grey asked, trying for nonchalance. It wasn't every day he watched stemware commit suicide, but it wasn't outside the realm of possibility in his world. Last time he'd seen Anaea, her telekinesis had just started to develop. Looked like it had gotten stronger.

"Long two weeks." She pursed her lips and stared at the broken glass. "It's getting so hard to control it. All of it. Yesterday, I almost set Nero's library on fire, and I'd just been reading a book."

And losing her inamorato—even just for a temporary absence—was going to make it even more difficult to control her magic. Unstable emotions equaled unstable earth magic. But Grey still had to tell her about Hunter.

"Take off your coat. I'll clean up the glass."

"And you'll tell me what my stubborn drake has done?" The glasses rattled again, and she sucked in another breath.

"Hunter has gone to find the Handmaiden." Grey pointed to the medallion on the coffee table.

"Thank God. It's about time." She strode to the medallion and hung it around her neck. "Although that means you'll have to come with me to face my soon-to-be ex-husband's lawyers tomorrow."

"Jeez, Hunter couldn't have waited a day?" Sure, Grey was managing not to have a panic attack every second he was in the human realm, but most of that time he was in safe, confined spaces. An office, with strange humans, was not safe.

"I hadn't told him. He's been so worried, I didn't want to bother him."

"You're too kind," Grey said, letting playful sarcasm color his tone. "But couldn't you postpone it? I'm sure finding the Handmaiden won't take long."

Anaea's expression turned serious. "I hope it doesn't. Dragonkind needs her and so do I. I'm terrified I'm going to kill someone."

"You're not going to kill anyone."

The glasses in the cupboard rattled again. "You so sure?"

9

R yan kicked his shoes off in the front hall of his childhood home. A fog had settled around him, and he couldn't seem to shake it. He couldn't remember why or how he'd become so exhausted. Or even why he'd returned home to Newgate. There was something he needed to do. Something he had to...

Jess, his ten-year-old niece, squealed from the kitchen and appeared at the end of the hall. She rushed to him, her ponytail swishing behind her in a curly brown cloud.

"Not so fast, young lady." Trisha had taken her place in the archway to the kitchen. "You can hug him after he cleans up."

He glanced at his clothes. How—? What—? He was covered in dirt and a sticky something that was hardening into a clump along his arm. He couldn't remember getting filthy, or even being in a situation that could have covered him in dirt... or was that dust?

He picked at the goop with a nail, but only managed to smear it. He'd been doing something... What the hell had he been doing?

Jess stuck out her bottom lip. Her mother raised an eyebrow at that, and the pout disappeared.

"So how does rolling around in the dirt get you your job back?"

"I—" How did getting filthy get him his job back? No, he had a job. He'd transferred to Elmsville after Internal Affairs had started asking about that apartment fire and how he'd gotten to the scene so fast. It was as if he'd known before anyone else, and he knew where that would go—accusations of setting the fire and charges for the death of that kid he couldn't save.

But he couldn't tell them the truth, that he *had* known before everyone else. They wouldn't have believed him, and the possibility of being declared criminally insane could be added to the list of terrible options.

Something boomed. He jerked back. Special Agent Jones crashed into the wall beside him, her head slamming against it. Blood stained her side and smeared across her face. Another gunshot hit the beige concrete blocks beside her temple, and shrapnel sliced her cheek and forehead.

His heart pounded. The next shot could kill her. He had to do something. Had to stop it.

He reached for his gun at his hip.

The hall wavered.

No. Not the hall. Jones wavered. Ripples on a still lake.

His breath burned, and he couldn't draw enough air to fill his lungs.

The image wavered again, and Jones's features blurred, melting into a broad forehead and cheeks, her hair darkening and lying still around her face.

"You look beat." Trisha's frown deepened.

The vision snapped, lancing through him and stealing the rest of his breath.

He gasped, drawing in warm air tinged with the aroma of popcorn. He was back in the hall of the house he'd grown up in, now owned by his sister. She hadn't changed anything. He didn't know if she didn't want to, or if she just hadn't had the time. Probably didn't have the time. She'd moved in within a month of her husband's passing four years ago and had struggled to keep everything as close to normal as she could for Jess's sake.

He blinked and drew in another unsteady breath.

He was alone in the hall. Trisha was back in the kitchen and water whooshed from the tap, presumably to fill the kettle. When she didn't know what to do, she made tea.

"Orange pekoe or green tea?" she called.

He shuffled into the kitchen and sat at the worn, linoleum-topped, table. Shoeboxes, old photos, and photo albums covered it. Jess cleared a corner for Ryan.

"I think there's another box of albums in the attic. Why don't you go up and see if you can find them for Uncle Ryan?" Trisha said.

"Sure." Jess jumped from the table and raced out of the kitchen.

Trisha pulled two mugs from the cupboard beside the sink and tea from a white ceramic jar on the scarred counter. Everything was where it was supposed to be. Him. Trisha. The house.

Except... it wasn't. He was forgetting something. It was on the tip of his tongue, something about not belonging, or wanting to belong, or being somewhere...

The thought that he needed to go home kept going through his mind, over and over again. Except he was home... no, home was his apartment on Railroad Street. But that wasn't right, either. He lived in Elmsville now, not Newgate.

He slid his gaze over the photos. The closest one was of him and Trisha at Christmas when they were kids. The photo had yellowed, or maybe it had always been slightly yellow. Beside it was a family photo on vacation at Disney. Mom and Dad, him and Trisha. All grinning from ear to ear, wearing those ridiculous Mickey Mouse hats. This was his life... no, it *had* been his life. Dad had died on duty, trying to stop a convenience store robbery three months after the Disney vacation. When Trisha's husband passed, Mom had sold her the family house and moved into a modern semi-detached bungalow on the other side of town.

A black and white picture poked out from underneath another Disney snapshot. Ryan pushed the other photos aside. He hadn't realized they still had anything this old. Two couples in the stuffy clothes of the early 1900s stood on the front porch of the house. Mom had said the house had been in the family for generations. He'd just never known there was proof.

A cup of tea slid into the clear place on the table before him.

"Great-great-great-aunt Sarah and her brother, Eric."

Ryan smoothed his thumb over the photo's corner. None of them were smiling, but they all looked happy. Especially the woman standing beside his great-great-great-uncle. She almost looked like Jones.

"You look a lot like Eric," Trisha said.

He dragged his gaze up to his sister. For a moment, her hair was strawberry blond, her face heart-shaped. God, he was seeing Special Agent Jones everywhere. In his sister, in that woman in the photo.

Fear snapped through him. Jones was in trouble. He just didn't know when and where. That was why he was back in Newgate.

No, that wasn't right, either. Well, not entirely right. Jones *was* in trouble. He'd seen it, and his flashes of the future always came true. The question now was whether her trouble was related to Pete's death... or rather second death, if in fact the body in the M.E.'s exam room was Pete.

He jerked to his feet. That was it. He was back because Pete's picture had shown up on the news.

How could he have forgotten that? How could he have forgotten that the friend who'd died in high school had somehow been murdered yesterday?

Trisha raised an eyebrow, and he eased back into his seat. She sat in the other chair at the table and hugged her mug of tea. From her pursed lips and slightly veiled eyes, he knew she was dying to ask what was going on. But even if he did know, he couldn't tell her. He hadn't told her the complete truth in years.

"Well, it's certainly been—" He glanced at the kitchen window. It was dark. Twilight was setting in. He hadn't just lost the minutes where he'd managed to get covered in filth. He'd lost almost the entire day. What the hell had happened? What had he done?

The fog in his head billowed. He'd followed up on a few leads but nothing had come of it, save that he'd gotten filthy. He hadn't answered any questions, but he hadn't gained new ones. Which meant he hadn't done anything important. That was all. Nothing important. Just exhausting. Yes. "It's certainly been a day."

"I can see that."

He blew steam from his mug. She wanted him to say more, explain why he'd called this morning and said he was visiting. Or rather, more of an explanation than his original lie of it would get him transferred back to town.

Maybe investigating Pete's murder *would* get him back in Newgate. A guy could hope. He hated Elmsville. Nothing happened, save local kids smoking pot, painting graffiti, and stealing street signs for entertainment. At least, nothing had happened until last

week, when Special Agent Jones had walked into the police department and took away the only interesting case he'd seen in over a
year.

Trisha tapped her nails against her mug. "So…"

"So—" He was going to need to think up something, explain why
he was covered in crap, but he couldn't get his mind to work. He
couldn't remember how it had happened in the first place.

His cell phone chirped, saving him from coming up with an
explanation, or at least one right away. "Miller."

"It's Hiro. I'm going on break in about half an hour. Care to buy
me dinner?"

"Absolutely." The fog slid away. "Name the place and I'll be there."

"Bistro 57."

He stood and pocketed his phone. "I've got to go. Tell Jess I'll look
at the album when I come back."

Trisha raised an eyebrow. He could see the questions in her eyes.
Rushing off to dinner? Was it a woman? Please let it be a woman.

And it was, just not the one he wanted. It wasn't Special Agent
Jones.

Wow, where had that thought come from?

He shoved it aside, offered Trisha a half smile—she'd make of it
what she wanted, she always did—and headed back to his coat. Jones
was a distraction he couldn't afford to have, and yet he couldn't
avoid her. He'd seen her in danger. He had to figure out a way to save
her, or even just warn her.

But first things first. Dinner with Hiro and answers about a
corpse that shouldn't be fresh.

10

The restaurant Hiro had picked was a few blocks from the Medical Examiner's office. With simple stylish decor in tan and chrome, it seemed out of place in the tired neighborhood—and so did his filthy coat and jeans. He should have changed at Trisha's, but it hadn't occurred to him until halfway to the restaurant and then he couldn't turn back. Not without being inundated with all those questions his sister was dying to ask.

Inside, there were only two dozen tables lining the sides of the narrow space, but more than half had customers. The hostess gave Ryan a quick glance and, with a hard expression that said in no uncertain terms she disapproved of his attire, led him along the right side to a table halfway into the room. He sat with his back to the wall so he could catch Hiro when she entered.

It had been a long time since he'd had a meal with Newgate's Chief Medical Examiner. Well, it had been as long as he'd been stuck in Elmsville. They used to have lunch or dinner every couple of months. It wasn't because there was anything between them, although she was certainly pretty. He'd just felt comfortable with her, like he could be himself, and that included the part of himself that had flashes of the future. Not that he'd ever told her. The only person he'd ever confessed that to had been Pete.

And now he was dead, again... maybe.

The door opened and Hiro entered. For a moment, he was disappointed. Not because it was Hiro, but because it wasn't Jones.

There was that irrational desire again. One that was guaranteed to get him into trouble. She wanted nothing to do with him, and she couldn't have made it more obvious when…? When they'd been lying in the dirt at the…? Where was that…?

Hiro waved, and he shoved the questions aside. If he wanted answers about Pete, he couldn't let questions about the day distract him. He hadn't done anything important that day. That was all.

He stood as Hiro approached.

"Glad to see you dressed up," she said, her tone wry.

He brushed a hand over the dirt on his pants but didn't dislodge anything. "Sorry, I didn't have time to change."

"So." She hung her coat on the back of her chair and sat. "What do you need?"

Ryan sat again and leaned forward. She'd always been direct, but never this direct before. Maybe three years without much communication was too much for their friendship. "Wow, straight to business."

"Kind of like someone I know." A smile pulled at her lips, but he wasn't sure who she was thinking of. She rubbed the back of her neck. "I don't have a lot of time. Nick called in sick so we're short-handed. And you wouldn't have shown up three years after your transfer without a reason."

"I can't just ask a friend out to dinner?"

"You can. But before you noticed Capri, you looked like you had a question."

"Capri?"

Hiro flipped open the menu, but didn't look away from him. "Special Agent Jones."

"Capri." He rolled her name over his tongue, spinning it through his thoughts. An unusual name, just like her.

The waitress took their drink order. Hiro continued to watch him from over the top of her menu.

"So, your question?" she asked, her tone softening.

"I'm curious about the body in your exam room."

"It's a little out of your town."

"By about a three-hour drive. I know. This isn't official."

"I wouldn't imagine so." Hiro eased her menu shut. "Cooper's on the case, so whatever you want to dig around in, it's covered."

"That's not—"

She raised an eyebrow.

"All right, maybe I do need to nose around."

The waitress arrived with their drinks, and Ryan sat back. If Detective Cooper was on the case, Ryan was going to have to be careful poking into anything. Cooper had been the first cop in line to help Internal Affairs find him guilty of arson and murder, and Ryan doubted the man had lost a night's sleep over it.

But that only meant Ryan would have to tread lightly. It certainly didn't mean he was going to give up trying to find the truth. The waitress put Hiro's coffee and Ryan's beer on the table, took their dinner orders, and left.

Ryan leaned forward again. "I just have… questions."

"What kind of questions?"

Ah, shit. Now he had no idea how much to ask Hiro. He didn't know how good her relationship with Detective Cooper was, but if they were friends, it could be trouble for him. And it didn't explain why Special Agent Jones had been in the exam room when he'd walked in. "If the case is Cooper's, why was the FBI there?"

"Covering my bases." Hiro picked up her coffee and took a long sip.

"You don't just cover your bases without letting the lead detective know."

Hiro raised a delicate eyebrow.

"And we both know Detective Cooper would be less than impressed to find out you'd invited the FBI into his investigation." Ryan lifted the beer to his lips, but kept his gaze on Hiro to judge her reaction.

"Maybe I have his say-so."

"Then why say you were covering your bases?"

"Touché," Hiro said, a smile pulling at her lips. "Capri is a friend, and she likes unusual cases."

"And what makes this murder unusual? And don't tell me it's the decapitation, because while that's uncommon, I'm not sure if it's unusual."

Hiro's smile deepened. "I'm not at liberty to say. What about it has your interest?"

"The victim was…" He wasn't sure what to say. He didn't know the victim, didn't even know his name, so he couldn't claim an association. If he did and the man was involved in less-than-legal activities, it might get him in hot water, particularly with Cooper on the case. And if he didn't say something soon, Hiro was bound to notice the hesitation—if she hadn't noticed already. "He was a person of interest in a case I had a while back. One that wasn't satisfactorily resolved."

Of course, at the time, he'd thought it had been resolved. They'd found Pete's charred corpse in the ruins of his house and buried him. But then, maybe this victim wasn't Pete Matthews.

"So you want to what? Dig around to try and resolve your old case?"

"Something like that."

The waitress brought their food, and Ryan waited for Hiro to respond. She would either help him or she wouldn't—and so far she hadn't even dropped the victim's name. He contemplated his options if she didn't help him. Digging around for the man's address might prove challenging given the size of Newgate, and when he'd agreed to the transfer he'd all but admitted his guilt, leaving him with no friends in the department.

Hiro set her coffee down and picked up her fork, holding it poised above her salad. "I don't have to warn you about getting in Cooper's way."

"No."

She pushed a candied pecan into the dressing and scooped it up. "But I probably should warn you about Capri."

"I just want to answer a few simple questions. That's all."

Hiro laughed, and for a moment, Ryan yearned for it to be Jones sitting across from him, laughing. Which was ridiculous. Why would he even care?

"In this business, few questions are simple."

"Just give me the address to our victim's residence, and I'll be out of your way."

"It's not my way you need to be careful of."

And he doubted it was Cooper's. "You mean Jones."

"When she's got her teeth into something, you don't want to be standing between it and her."

That, he could believe. She'd been determined to take his case from him in Elmsville, and she'd been less than happy to see him this morning. Yet he still wanted to find himself in her way.

He suppressed a shiver of attraction. "All I need is an address, and I'll be done by tonight."

"I doubt that." Hiro popped the nut in her mouth. "But let's finish dinner. When I get back to the office, I'll text you the info. Now tell me all about the thrilling metropolis of Elmsville."

"Oh, thrilling is right." But it wasn't the small town that had him thinking of thrills. He was going to find out if this victim was really Pete Matthews and there was a chance—albeit a small chance, but a chance nonetheless—that he'd run into Special Agent Capri Jones.

He fought the anticipation racing through him. He shouldn't want to run into Jones again, and yet, he had to see her.

11

Capri parked her SUV on the street a dozen houses down from Andy Reynolds's bungalow, not because she couldn't explain to a curious neighbor why she was searching a murder victim's house, but because she didn't want to. Not until she was ready. While her FBI credentials usually gave her a free pass at just about anything, if a neighbor called the police before learning she was FBI, Tobias was sure to find out, and then he'd know she was working off the books. At the moment, it was better to avoid any more attention than necessary.

Besides, she wasn't sure what she was looking for. She might not find anything and she'd hate to have this whole situation blow up on her if her search came up empty. There had to be some kind of evidence that this man was a dragon or that he had a connection to dragons. Except she wasn't sure what that would be.

Whatever it was, it was going to be difficult to find. If given enough time, and what looked like painful concentration, Swipe would be able to find the detail, no matter how minuscule. But she wasn't going to get him involved in this until Tobias made it official... if Tobias made it official.

If looking into this incurred Regis's wrath—and given that she didn't have a royal decree, any action she took could be interpreted as treason—she was going to take the fall and keep the rest of her team safe. It didn't matter that she could argue what she did was for the good of dragonkind. Regis would see her actions-without-permission as disrespect, and he wouldn't be able to let it go. He'd have to punish her to keep in control of his coterie and Court.

Which left her searching for some small, likely impossible to find detail, on her own.

Right. Well, when the team didn't have much to go on, they went with the basics: gain a sense of who the victim was.

Gig's initial search for Andy Reynolds hadn't turned up much. He had little debt—save for the mortgage on this house—no family in the area, and he received regular deposits every second Friday from his job as a youth counselor. All of that made her think he was more likely a human than a dragon. Admittedly it was just an initial search, but usually drakes lived a more upscale kind of life with whatever wealth they'd accumulated over the centuries.

She walked up Andy's shoveled driveway. His house was a small structure with pale siding. In daylight, the siding would have been an unwashed-white, but under the glare of the streetlight it looked more gray or pale brown.

It sat on the middle of a slope surrounded by similar houses on a street twisting down a hill. Tall trees, a mix of maple and pine, dotted the front lawns covered with an inch of snow. Behind loomed a woodlot, with more towering shadows of maples and pines, barely illuminated by the light of the quarter moon.

She avoided the front steps, which were partially covered in snow. Given that it hadn't snowed since before Reynolds was murdered, the uncleared snow at the front of the house suggested he used the back door as his primary entrance. True to the assumption, the walk along the side of the house was clear, and she followed it to the back.

Darkness enveloped her. She blinked a couple of times, pausing for a heartbeat to let her eyes adjust. With her job, she counted herself lucky to be a drake not only with a strong earth magic, but with a few enhanced abilities—better night sight being one of them.

She was also stronger than the average human, which meant she could force the back door open. But that would leave unnecessary evidence, and she'd spent a lot of time learning how to avoid leaving evidence, particularly stuff that would make Swipe complain—even if it was fun to listen to him grumble.

Three snow-free cement steps led up to a new set of doors. She opened the screen, held it with her shoulder, and knelt to get a better look at the deadbolt. Standard lock. Good.

She pulled out her tension wrench and rake pick and slid them into the lock. Early in her career, and sick and tired of listening to Swipe bitch about how difficult it was to fix a broken door, she'd turned to the prince's assassin, Hunter, for a few breaking and entering lessons—which then had to be done all over again when tumbler locks came into common use around the 1800s.

With a wiggle and twist, she unlocked the door. Not her best pick. Not her worst, either. No matter how much Hunter had growled at her, she really wasn't that skilled at lock picking. It had taken her close to a hundred years to get that fast. Thank the Mother of All her human cover was in law enforcement and not crime.

She eased the door open. The knob squeaked and the hinges groaned. She glanced around, but there was no movement at either neighboring house to indicate anyone was outside and had heard anything. Thank goodness for freezing temperatures. Everyone huddled inside, and no one had a window open. Of course, with the snow, she had to be careful about leaving footprints. There were advantages and disadvantages to everything.

A cloud scuttled across the moon. She stepped into a small kitchen onto a dark mat, the color indistinguishable in the gloom. To her immediate left stood a small closet with half a dozen coats and a pile of boots and shoes in front of it, making it impossible to close.

The cloud moved away, and the white floor and cupboards gleamed in the returning moonlight. They were a stark contrast to the black granite countertop running the length of the kitchen to her right. Before her stood the arch to the living room, and to her left was a small table covered with papers. There were two plastic bowls underneath, one filled with water, one empty. It looked like Andy Reynolds used to have a pet. Since nothing came to check her out, someone must have already taken it.

She shifted through the piles of papers—mostly bills and flyers. Nothing useful, so she moved into the living room, a small space crowded with a large TV and a matching black leather couch and recliner. It looked recently decorated. And actually, the kitchen looked recently renovated as well. His counselor job didn't pay *that* much. He would have had to be particularly frugal to afford the recent changes.

Maybe there was more to this Reynolds than met the eye. Modest house on the outside, swank bachelor's pad on the inside. Wonder what kind of car he drove? She'd been so distracted by seeing Miller at the M.E.'s office, she'd forgotten to ask Hiro for a copy of the file. But she suspected the victim drove something that screamed male and single. The rest of his house did.

The knob on the back door squeaked.

Shit.

She leapt to the arch leading from the kitchen to the living room and pressed her back against the wall beside it. She needed a moment to think. If it was a neighbor, how did she explain her wandering through Reynolds's house in the dark?

She couldn't. Not really.

The door opened with a groan, then clicked shut.

Subvocalizing her power word, she activated her earth magic.

This was going to take some skill and a whole lot of power, since there was no easy way to explain what she was doing. She'd probably need a complete memory wipe of the last ten or so minutes and a replacement memory, which was the second most difficult thing she could cast—a *complete* memory wipe and *total* replacement being the most difficult. It had been a long time since she'd had to cast such an invasive spell, and there was always the risk it wouldn't hold or worse, she'd permanently scar the human's mind.

The kitchen light didn't turn on.

Huh. Perhaps this wasn't a friend.

A beam of light shot through the living room and dropped to the floor. Flashlight. Definitely not a friend. Friends didn't use flashlights. People who didn't want to be noticed by the neighbors did.

New plan.

Whoever this was could be the connection to dragonkind she was looking for. Or better yet, evidence there was no connection and Reynolds's murder was a coincidence. But two decapitations within a week and a half wasn't a likely coincidence, as much as she wished it was.

She eased back the curl of magic she'd released, letting the spell dissipate, and shifted her weight to the balls of her feet.

Two soft thuds on the linoleum floor and then the sigh of paper being shifted around. Whoever had entered was doing what she'd done. Except he, or she, had gotten to the table in two steps, making him a foot taller than her. Likely a man, given the length and weight of the stride.

The papers stopped rustling, and the beam of light slid through the arch along the living room floor. Guess he hadn't found anything, either.

She lengthened her stance and waited.

While having the help of surprise on her side, she'd still need to move fast if she wanted to subdue him. She might be stronger than the average human woman, but she was still only five feet tall and a hundred pounds. If he got a good grip on her, she'd be forced to use her magic in an attack guaranteed to do mental damage.

The footsteps drew closer.

Just a little farther. All she needed was his wrist.

The head of the flashlight inched into the living room.

One more step.

His hand crossed the threshold. She lunged and grabbed his wrist. With a twist, she yanked him around and slammed him face-first into the wall, drawing a surprised grunt. The flashlight bounced on the carpet, the light dancing over the walls.

He jerked against her grip. She yanked his wrist up his back and leaned her weight against him, securing her hold. The rich, masculine scent of shaving cream and soap slid over her. He smelled so good... and so familiar.

He bucked against her. She skidded back, proving she wasn't going to be able to hold him like that. She wrenched him around, yanked his elbow and shoulder joints into a painful lock, and forced him to his knees.

"Who are you, and what are you doing here?" She leaned in, putting more pressure on his arm.

He grunted again and glanced at her.

Her heart skipped a beat.

It was Miller.

"I'd like to ask you the same question, Special Agent Jones."

"I'm working."

"In the dark?" His tone implied there were other things they could be doing in the dark… or was that just her imagination?

Heat seeped up her neck to her cheeks, and she was grateful for the cover of night. "You didn't answer my question."

He pulled against her grip. For a moment, she considered keeping him in the painful joint lock, but that kept her holding him. And as much as she wanted to keep holding him, just his wrist wasn't exactly where she wanted her hands.

She shoved him away, turned, and paced into the center of the room. She had to get ahold of herself. He wasn't Eric. He didn't love her, and she didn't love him—she wouldn't let herself love a human again. That would only mean repeating the agony of the past, obeying dragon law, and leaving far too soon.

"I'm still waiting for an answer," she growled. "What are you doing here?"

"And I'm still waiting for mine." His gaze locked on hers.

More heat welled within her, pooling low. Light flashed from his eyes, and for a moment, no longer than a heartbeat, she could have sworn he was a drake. An intensity burned there, a determination, and a desire. The shadows accentuated the strong lines of his face. His breath expanded his chest, raising his back and shoulders, making him momentarily bigger, more dangerous.

Mother of All, it turned her on. The sense of power radiating from him was a match to her drake hiding within. He promised ferocious passion. More than what Eric had ever been able to give her. It crackled against her senses as if it were his earth magic. Which was impossible. He wasn't a drake. He was human. God damn it. He. Was. Human. She wasn't supposed to desire him.

She jerked away from him to the window. But turning her back on him did little to still the liquid desire scorching her veins. There was something very, very wrong with her. She was soul sick. That was it.

But soul sickness didn't manifest as lust. And really, it couldn't be lust for Miller. It was heartbreak for Eric. It was just coming out hot and needy and all wrong.

Outside, a shadow moved at the bottom of the driveway. She inched aside the sheers and peered through the crack. Diablo strode up the steps to the front door.

Just great. What the hell was Diablo doing here? And if she didn't want him knowing she was investigating something she hadn't been assigned, she needed to leave. Now. Could this night get any more complicated?

She grabbed Miller's arm, resisting the urge to use her full strength to get him to move. "We have to leave."

Diablo's picks rattled in the front door. No, they didn't sound right. It wasn't a pick, but a key. The man had a key. She tucked that information away for when she had time to consider all the implications having a key might mean.

Miller's gaze shot over her shoulder to the door, then he turned, and together they rushed through the kitchen and out the back door.

Capri scrambled off the stairs and ducked into the space under the kitchen window. Miller shoved in beside her, squeezing them between the concrete steps and a prickly shrub. He gave her a questioning look, probably wondering why they weren't making a mad dash across the backyard into the woodlot. He was probably wondering a lot of things.

But Diablo's night sight was just as good as hers, and if he glanced out the window, he'd see them.

The kitchen light turned on, sending a swath of illumination across the undisturbed snow blanketing the yard. She hadn't thought Diablo was so cocky... okay, who was she kidding, everything about Diablo screamed cocky. He probably didn't care if the neighbors saw him poking around. He'd just offer them that sexy smile of his, and man or woman, they'd forget what their problem was.

She resisted the urge to peek inside to see what he was doing. If she got desperate, which she doubted she would, she'd work Reynolds's murder into casual conversation and see what Diablo's reaction was. She didn't think she'd get much, which was why she'd save it for when she was desperate.

Which was highly unlikely, because Detective Miller here was going to give her answers... about Reynolds, not the desire she was sure she'd imagined radiating from him.

She subvocalized her power word and leveled her gaze on him. "We have an unfinished conversation."

Ryan's pulse jumped at Jones's look. It sizzled through him, filling him with so much want, he ached. This woman was going to drive him crazy. What was he thinking? She already *was* driving him crazy, and he barely knew her.

Oh, man. Now was not the time or place. It wasn't the time or place for a conversation, either, but whatever was between them certainly wasn't finished. He had questions, like if she was here on duty, why was she searching in the dark without a flashlight, and why flee when someone else showed up?

"Meeting three times in one day is not a coincidence," she hissed.

"The second time wasn't a coin—" The words blurted out before he could stop them. He snapped his mouth shut. Where had that come from? Aside from the fact that the abandoned factory had been off the beaten path, he was pretty sure he hadn't told her outright that he'd followed her. Except he was still having trouble remembering all the details about today.

Cold seeped through his coat where his back pressed against the siding. It slid up his neck, and over his skull, and tingled in his sinuses behind his eyes. Jeez, he hadn't thought it was that cold. Perhaps the lack of activity made him feel it more.

"The second time? At the old factory?" Jones rolled her eyes, the whites catching a hint of the light coming from the window. "Yes, that much was obvious. Care to tell me why?"

He opened his mouth to speak then snapped it shut. What the heck was he doing? The words were on the tip of his tongue, ready to spill out, but there wasn't anything he could say that wouldn't look bad. He certainly couldn't tell her the truth, that she was going to be hurt, maybe even die sometime in the future, and he had to stop it. As it was, she could charge him with interfering with a federal investigation. Although if she was on a case, it didn't explain why they were currently hiding. "Want to explain why we're sitting here in the cold?"

"No." She pursed her lips. She was so close. If he was less of a gentleman, he'd swoop down and capture her mouth with his. Maybe he should. And now he really wanted to.

He imagined her moment of shock, then the glorious feel of her melting into his embrace, pressing her body against his. Even though she wore a heavy winter coat, and probably layers of clothing underneath to keep warm just like he did, he would savor the feel of her curves against him.

Yeah, and then he'd be feeling the hard muzzle of her sidearm because fantasy did not equal invitation.

This was not good. They were hiding in the snow, she was probably on the verge of arresting him, and all he could think about was kissing her... and more.

He shook his head.

He should just tell her what he was really up to. The urge to say everything was overwhelming. The cold in his head muddled his thoughts, and he struggled to concentrate. All he needed to do was explain himself, explain about his curse, that he could see the future, and how Pete, or rather Andy Reynolds—at least that was the name on the information Hiro had sent him—was already dead, and...

And then she'd lock him up in the psych ward. No, he couldn't reveal that he saw the future. But he needed to tell her something. If his vision of her in danger was true, he needed a reason to stay close to her.

The cold now burned in his sinuses. He struggled to focus. "I knew Pete— Andy Reynolds. I can help your investigation. Andy and I—" He bit the inside of his cheek. He'd been about to say they had been friends when they were kids, but if she didn't think his knowledge of Reynolds was recent, she might not want his help. "We're old friends."

"So that explains why you were illegally searching his house?" Her tone said she didn't believe him.

"Listen, I just want to find out what happened." He needed to think up an explanation, something she'd believe. "We lost touch when I trans—" God damn it, was he going to tell her everything? He almost mentioned the forced transfer to Elmsville as the reason he'd lost touch with Pete... no, Andy. Shit. What was wrong with him?

They were sitting in the dark. There was nothing about this situation that would compel him to open up to this stranger. But perhaps that was it. She was a beautiful, mysterious FBI agent, all fire and fight coiled in a seductively tiny package, and he wanted to know her better.

Her eyes narrowed. "When you what?"

"Excuse me?"

"You didn't finish your sentence."

No. He hadn't. And he didn't want to continue. "We lost touch."

"There was more to that sentence before."

Yes, there had been, and from the look in her eyes, he didn't think he'd get away without saying more. "We lost touch when I transferred to Elmsville." Please don't let her ask about that right now. If she did, he knew the words would come spilling out, and, well, an Internal Affairs investigation and transfer to small-town-nowhere Pennsylvania didn't make a man look good. It made him look guilty.

The wind picked up, and the trees on the yard's other side creaked. The cold in his face eased away. Guess he was getting used to it, but his hips and knees were going numb from staying crouched for so long. Now he was even more aware of the heat of Capri's body beside him and the rectangle of light falling through the kitchen window making the snow sparkle.

He clenched and unclenched his hands, trying to keep them warm as well as to keep from reaching for her.

"I want to find out what happened, too. Perhaps we should join forces." Her whisper sent shivers racing over him, and the chill in his face returned. "I have a few ground rules, though."

Of course she did. But why the change of heart? Why did she

suddenly want to work with him? "Why don't we negotiate this when we're someplace warm?"

She raised an eyebrow. "This is not up for negotiation."

The light in the kitchen flicked off and heavy footsteps moved away into the living room. Jones inched up, peeking in the window. The front door thudded shut, and she stood but didn't relax.

Ryan strained to hear the crunch of feet coming closer, but instead, a vehicle started. He glanced around the side of the house, and a dark-colored Jeep pulled away from the curb and drove off.

"So." Jones stood and brushed snow from the rear of her coat. "Find anything during your search?"

"I didn't have a lot of time, but I wasn't sure I'd find anything. We'd probably have more luck looking into his phone records and financial statements." He hadn't really thought he'd find anything at the house. All he really wanted was evidence that the victim was or wasn't also Pete Matthews. He hadn't expected to find a birth certificate lying around, but a part of him had hoped it would be something as simple.

"I agree. I've got a man looking into that. I suggest, since Reynolds was found in an alley near his work, we start there."

"Okay, good."

She crossed her arms. "Good."

He didn't know what else to say. Attraction hung between them, full and heavy, caught in an eternity of silence and heat and uncertainty.

Moonlight broke from the clouds above and reflected in the crystalline snow. The light danced through the gentle swells of drifts behind her, like a swarm of illuminated creatures, flashing in and out of life, darting this way and that. Darkness followed, another cloud passing over the moon, enveloping Capri and the yard in gray, but a light still emanated from her eyes.

Ryan blinked. Her eyes really weren't glowing. It was the contrast between her pupils and pale irises. But the illusion didn't disappear. In fact, for a heartbeat, he swore it grew, radiating across her cheeks and forehead until a hint of light haloed her. An angel fallen from heaven. An angel with a dusting of freckles across her nose. She opened her mouth, ever so slightly, and a breath, frozen in the chill, curled out, caressing her cheeks.

God, to be that breath, to touch her face and warm her skin.

As if reading his thoughts, she reached for him. Her fingers trembled, drawing closer and closer to his jaw. Her gaze held him captive: breath, body, and soul. There was nothing else in the world but her and the promise of her touch. He ached for her to close the distance, even with just her fingers.

Her index finger brushed his jaw. Lightning zinged through him, crackling along his senses and swirling around his heart.

Her other fingers joined the first, sliding from his jaw into his hairline to cup his cheek. With lips parted even more, she leaned closer. Her breath entwined with his, easing warm and moist across his face.

He was crazy to want to kiss her. She didn't like him, never wanted to see him again. Or at least, that's what he'd thought from their last encounter. From this one as well. Yet everything about him was on fire, and she was close, so very close.

The chill billowed across his face, tingling his skin. His mind whirled, filled only with the desire to know how she'd feel and taste. He dipped forward, brushing his lips against hers.

She froze.

He froze in response. What the hell was he doing? He should stop, back off—

With a growl, she grabbed the front of his jacket and kissed him back, hungry, commanding, as if she needed his breath to survive. Warmth, chill, everything vanished, save for the feel of her against him and the passion promised with her lips. He'd never experienced such fire, such need.

And it burned both ways. Kissing him had to be proof of that. But a kiss wasn't going to be enough for them. One night wouldn't be enough. Even if he lived a hundred lifetimes, it still wouldn't be enough to satisfy the ferocious desire filling him, or the ferocious woman who'd just kissed him. But damn, he loved a challenge.

She growled again and jerked away.

He stumbled at the sudden loss of contact, and cold rushed across his skin where her breath had warmed it. "That was—" What could he say? Unbelievable? Incredible? Stupid?

Her chest heaved with quick breaths, and the air about her

billowed with mist. Her blue eyes glowed with that eerie light, and the desire with which she'd all but consumed him simmered there.

"That was inappropriate," she said, her voice low.

In so many ways, and yet he couldn't think of any of those ways at the moment. God, he had never had a kiss like that before.

"If we're going to work together, we need to concentrate on that. Work." But her gaze still said she wanted him naked right now, and she didn't care that they were outside in the snow.

She growled again, punched the siding beside her, and drew in a harsh breath. With a blink, the desire in her eyes disappeared, but the glow remained. Ice bled into his sinuses again. They needed to work together. Kissing her had been a mistake. He didn't really desire her.

Of course he did—

No, he didn't. Focus on finding the truth about Andy Reynolds. That's what they needed to do.

But that kiss had been wonderful, amazing—

Not real?

He couldn't get his thoughts straight. He and Capri… no, Special Agent Jones, needed to work together. Focus on the job. But—

"I'll meet you at the Newgate Youth Center, 10 a.m.," she said.

There was something he wanted to do, but he couldn't remember what. It had something to do with Jones and her lips and…

"10 a.m.," she said again, jerking her chin toward the path leading to the front of the house and his car.

"10 a.m." Tomorrow he'd get answers about the body in the morgue and be able to keep an eye on Jones. He was sure he was forgetting something, but he'd worry about that when it came up.

13

C apri forced herself not to punch the house again.

Shit.

Shit shit shit.

She'd lost her mind. She had to have. Kissing Miller. What the hell had she been thinking?

She hadn't been. That was the problem. He looked so much like Eric, and she missed him so much, and she just had to kiss him one more time.

Except that wasn't true. She'd known Miller wasn't Eric. They might be twins, but there were differences in their personalities. Whereas Eric had been a gentle professor, Miller had that cop's edge, the one that said he'd seen trouble before and knew how to handle it. Eric had treated her like a princess, worshiped her with soft gauzy love that had made her feel like she was floating all the time. Miller would challenge her, bring out her drake, make her growl.

Mother of All, he *had* made her growl. It had taken everything she'd had within her not to bare her teeth in invitation.

Miller's footsteps crunched down the driveway and up the street.

Capri's lips curled back of their own volition, and she hissed out a cloudy breath. She shouldn't have used her magic to distract him and make him forget what she'd done, but she hadn't been able to think of anything else to do.

Oh, Mother. He looked like Eric. That was all.

Eric. Dead Eric. Eric who she'd had to rip her heart into pieces to leave. If she gave in to her desires for Miller, she'd be faced with the same agony. She would stay young, he would grow old, and dragon law demanded she'd have to leave.

She couldn't do that again. Never again.

She marched to her car and drove home. She didn't even know anything about Detective Miller. Even if she wasn't going to continue kissing him—but Mother of All, she really wanted to—she was still going to work with him. At the very least, she needed to know who she had at her back.

And if Tobias or anyone else found out, she was in deep, deep shit. Working with a human on an unsanctioned case that involved drakes was a surefire way to get reborn.

But the man kept showing up everywhere. He had a vested interest in the case. She doubted it actually was that he and Reynolds had been friends. Regardless, he was going to keep getting underfoot unless she started working with him.

She stepped into her front foyer, locked the heavy oak door behind her, and tossed her keys into the dish on the sleek round table in the center of the wide space. In the dim light, it was hard to tell the entrance was decorated in gleaming cherry and gold. Eric had loved how it had shimmered under the light of the then-candle chandelier hanging above.

Stop thinking about Eric, damn it.

Focus on Miller. Her best way to deal with him was to use him and whatever insight he brought to the case then erase his memory.

The thought made her sick.

But it was the only way. If she kept him away from her fellow drakes, creating new memories would be easier, but it would still be intrusive... and painful.

Her lips burned at the memory of kissing him.

She had no choice. It was the only way to deal with him. No matter how much she wanted to deal with him in other, more satisfying ways. Her stomach flip-flopped again, and her lips burned hotter.

No choice. No choice. God damned dragon laws.

She grabbed her laptop from the hall table and stormed through her kitchen to her greenhouse. She flicked on the light, illuminating a mass of greenery, vines, shrubs, miniature trees, and orchids. Hundreds of beautiful, mesmerizing orchids.

The sweet aroma of her *cymbidium tracyanum* slid across her senses. Everything would be all right. She'd figure it out. And she'd resist the need to kindle a romance with the twin of her dead lover. A man she still knew nothing about.

She eased onto a plush-cushioned couch in the heart of her hoard and booted up her laptop. The glass wall of the greenhouse reflected a stunned woman. Her eyes were too big, her face too pale, and half of her strawberry blond locks had fallen from her chignon.

This was ridiculous. She was a dragon. Sure, she was a water drake, not as fierce as a fire drake, but she was still a predator. A man, a human man at that, didn't break her. And yet, that's what being with Eric had done to her. Leaving him had shattered her, making her carry on while missing pieces. And now with Miller—

Her phone beeped. She jerked. Her laptop teetered on her lap, and she grabbed it before it fell to the ceramic tiled floor.

"Jones," she said.

"I think you've forgotten something," Hiro said.

"Forgotten?" Ah, shit, what time was it? After eleven. Girls' night.

"Or has someone distracted you?" Hiro asked, sliding out the word *someone*.

Yeah, they both knew who that *someone* was. Detective Ryan Miller. "Really? You think I'd mess around with a human?"

"You could do worse."

Right. From the way Miller had entered Hiro's exam room and invited her to dinner, they had to know each other. How convenient she and the good doctor were about to share margaritas. If she was going to work with him, she had to know more about him. Really. That was the only reason she wanted to know more about the man.

RYAN PULLED INTO HIS SISTER'S DRIVEWAY, CUT THE ENGINE, AND squeezed the steering wheel. He couldn't remember leaving Pete's—

No, Andy Reynolds's house. He also couldn't remember getting into his car or the drive to this side of Newgate. But he could remember the kiss. Oh, God, could he remember the kiss.

His body burned at the memory. It hadn't stopped burning. Even when Jones had pulled away and the cold had shot through his face, he'd still burned. The ferocious fire in her eyes had fueled his internal inferno. He wanted to kiss her again. Wanted to do more with her.

Thank goodness, he'd somehow regained his senses and left. Except he wasn't sure that's what had really happened.

The fog in his head billowed, a chilly swell that seeped into his sinuses just like it had at the house, but then receded. Kissing her again would only create problems. Yep, that was it. She was FBI and he was a cop who shouldn't even be in town. He couldn't kiss her and lie about Pete or Andy or whoever the hell he was. Relationships were built on trust and—

Relationships! When had he jumped from kissing her to a relationship?

Oh jeez, he had to get his head back into the game. One kiss didn't mean anything, even if it was clear the attraction went both ways. Both sizzling ways. He'd known Special Agent Jones was a force to be reckoned with the moment he'd met her in Elmsville, but he'd never imagined he'd be the focus of all that ferocity.

And he wanted more.

This was bad. So very very bad. He had to get a grip. The only person who'd be worse for him than Capri—

No, keep it impersonal, use her last name. Jones. The only person worse for him than Jones was his ex.

Someone rapped on the car window. "Ryan?"

He jerked toward the voice. Soft, feminine. For a moment, he thought it was Capri—Jones—and desire shot through him.

Get. A. Grip.

He focused on the face behind the glass. Brown hair, perfectly coiffed. Crap. Definitely not Jones.

"Come on, Ryan. Roll down your window," Melissa said.

This had to be his punishment for kissing Jones. But fate didn't work that way. It was just his punishment for returning to Newgate. A man could run away from his old life, but it seemed that life never forgot him. It would be easy if Melissa thought he wasn't worth her time anymore. But nothing with that woman was ever easy. He'd been at the M.E.'s office and had talked to the FBI. According to that, he had to know something, and if their engagement hadn't meant anything to her in the face of career advancement, then respecting his privacy meant even less. Clearly, that was true, since she was standing in his sister's driveway in the middle of the night.

He opened the door, forcing Melissa to step back. "What? No camera guy?"

"I'm not here on business."

Yeah, right. "Then why are you here?"

"I thought—" She dropped her gaze and dug her toe into the snow.

Nice try. Acting meek and contrite wasn't going to work. "What do you want?"

She sighed, her breath billowing around her face. "I don't like how we left things."

Something they had in common.

"I've been wanting to call you." She slid her dark gaze up to his.

He'd loved those eyes, loved how she'd looked at him. He'd loved her. But now the looks she'd used to give him didn't seem so sincere. A reporter with a cop. That kind of relationship was doomed from the start. Probably just as doomed as a small town detective with a cloud hanging over his career and an FBI agent.

"I've been wondering how you've been doing." She offered a hint of a smile. Her genuine one, not the one she gave the camera.

Maybe she really did regret what had happened. There *had* been something between them before the I.A. investigation. They'd been together for over a year. He'd been thinking of proposing that Valentine's Day.

"How have you been doing?" she asked, and he realized he hadn't answered any of her questions.

"Fine—" He cleared the frog in his throat. "I've been fine."

"We should do coffee."

"Yeah. Sure."

Her gaze jumped to his car then back to him. "I'm not doing anything now. You?"

"Now?"

"Why not?" She inched closer. "We can talk about the good old days and what brings you back to town."

Everything within him froze. "What brings me back to town?"

"Yeah."

"I'm visiting my sister." Could Melissa be any more obvious? She didn't want to catch up or make amends. She wanted a scoop.

"And your trip to the morgue? That was what?"

"Me visiting a friend."

"Special Agent Jones?" Melissa asked. "Is she this friend?"

"Yes."

"Really."

"How much of a friend?" Melissa's tone turned dark, the implication that friend equaled lover.

"That's none of your business."

"What was Jones doing at the M.E.'s office?"

"That's even less of your business." This was ridiculous. He shouldn't even be talking to this woman. She'd twist his words, and he'd be back where he started, neck deep in an I.A. investigation—and there really wasn't a town smaller than Elmsville where they could send him. The next step would be to fire him.

"Come on, Ryan. Surely she told you something. What's going on with the decapitation case?"

"Nothing is going on with the decapitation case." He shoved past her, heading to the porch.

"I won't spoil your girlfriend's case."

"She's not my girlfriend." And Melissa sure as hell would spoil everything.

"Didn't look like that to me."

"Then you need to get your eyes checked." He took the porch steps in two giant leaps and shoved his key into the lock. "Go chase an ambulance or something."

"If you don't tell me what's going on, I'll have to report my own conclusions."

He jerked around. "Are you threatening me?"

She sneered at him. "People deserve to know what's going on."

"Even if it's a lie?"

"Oh, I never lie. I gather evidence and report on it. FBI agent in a relationship with a disgraced detective."

"We are not in a relationship."

"I've cut some video of you two talking that would prove otherwise."

Son of a—

The bitch was going to destroy Capri, just like she'd destroyed him. His breath clouded the air around him with each rushed exhalation. His muscles burned with the effort to stay on the porch. Grabbing Melissa wouldn't help. There wasn't anything physically he could do. "What do you want?"

"Give me an exclusive, and I'll make sure your new girlfriend gets positive press."

"We don't have anything yet." He needed to stall, give himself time to figure out how to deal with this.

"You've been to the morgue. I'm sure you have something."

"Not enough for a story."

"I'll be the one to determine that."

God dammit. Just take the stall. "You want it to be good, don't you? Jones and I will have more tomorrow evening."

Melissa narrowed her eyes. Her breath curled around her face like demon smoke. She was calculating her best move, the best way to destroy or manipulate him. How had he ever loved this woman?

"Fine," she said. "Tomorrow. Midnight at the—" She chuckled. "At the boat house."

"You really are a cold-hearted bitch." The boat house was where they used to have midnight trysts when they were first dating.

"Now, now. Name calling isn't nice. Tomorrow at the boat house or I run my story on you and the FBI agent." She flipped her perfect hair and strode down the driveway to her car, her boots crunching in the snow.

What was he going to tell her? He couldn't compromise Jones's investigation. He probably already had compromised it. Melissa would twist whatever he told her to suit her agenda, and that agenda would ruin Jones's career. He couldn't even step away from the investigation. Melissa would never accept that. And, irrationally, he didn't want to stop seeing Capri.

14

Hiro lived in an old converted warehouse on the top of a hill near the Medical Examiner's office. The spacious loft took up half of the third floor with the living room on the end, giving it three walls of floor-to-ceiling windows that overlooked the city. The view was spectacular, all shimmering streetlights and illuminated windows in office towers, but Capri couldn't focus on it. She could barely focus on Hiro, sitting across from her on the couch, shaking a bottle of nail polish and preparing to paint her toenails. Capri's thoughts kept going back, over and over again, to Miller and their kiss.

"Jeez, Capri. Are you going to drink that or just wait for the ice to melt?" Hiro pointed her polish bottle at the margarita in Capri's hand.

Capri dragged her attention to the glass. The drink was more liquid than slushy, and water beaded on the outside of the glass and was about to drip into her lap. "Sorry, I was thinking."

"About anyone in particular?"

"No. The case."

"You sure you're not really thinking about a hot detective who happened to walk into my morgue this morning?"

"No." Heat raced over Capri's cheeks, and she took a gulp of her margarita to hide her reaction. The ice hit her sinuses with an agonizing bite. "Shit."

Hiro chuckled. "Well, that was slick. I was sure you had more game than that."

"I have lots of game and none of it involves Detective Miller." Not anymore, at least. There would be no more kisses. None. Even if they could have a relationship, it wouldn't be fair to him because he wasn't Eric. And who she really wanted was Eric. Honestly. "Did your autopsy offer any insights into our latest victim?"

"You don't get to change the subject that easily."

"Sure I do."

Hiro flashed a wicked grin. "Pick a color for your toes. You'll want them to be pretty for the detective."

"You did not just say that." Capri wasn't that kind of girl. And yet a part of her really did want to paint her toenails for him. Mother of All, she really shouldn't have kissed him.

"Pick a color, paint your toes, and I'll talk about the case."

"We need to discuss the case regardless." Blood red? Or a sassy blue to go with her name?

"We should probably also discuss Ryan." All playfulness disappeared from Hiro's tone.

Capri's heart skipped a beat. "If it's that bad, why are you encouraging me to paint my nails for him?"

"Because it's been, what? A century? You need a fling. And for a fling, Ryan's an excellent choice. Longer term... well, that might get challenging. He has a history."

"You realize you're doing a terrible job of convincing me that anything with Miller is a good idea." And yet, she didn't care—

No. She cared. No more relationships with humans. She couldn't leave Eric all over again even if she just had a one-night stand. Hundreds of years of getting to know herself proved she just didn't work that way. She wasn't a promiscuous drake.

"What kind of history are we talking about?" she asked. Because his history might affect her investigation. That's all she cared about. Really.

"Internal Affairs kind of history and Ryan leaving Newgate for Elmsville."

"What was he charged with?"

"He wasn't officially charged. But there was talk about arson and murder."

"Do you think it was true?" She couldn't believe Miller would purposefully start fires, but she didn't really know the man.

"I don't. But a local reporter jumped all over the charges and used it to further her career. It didn't matter what anyone thought, she'd already charged him in the court of public opinion. He had to leave town."

"And this is the human you're trying to set me up with?"

"Well, you're obviously not interested in a drake." Hiro nudged the bottle of blue polish toward Capri. "Grey has been in love with you for centuries, and you don't even give him a second glance."

"Great. Does everyone know about Grey?" His courtship had actually been an anti-courtship. He flirted like mad with every other woman, but never with her. That's how she knew he was serious.

"I'm more observant than your average drake," Hiro said. "Makes me good at my job."

"Among other things." Like snooping and noticing that moment between Capri and Ryan in the exam room.

Hiro leaned forward, her gaze locking on Capri's. "I've never seen you look at anyone like that."

Heat seeped up Capri's neck. Just the thought of that look made her heart thrum. And she'd done more than just look at him tonight.

"Now I know you're thinking of him. Man, when you blush it goes right to your roots."

Capri jerked to her feet, sloshing her margarita over the lip of her glass onto her hand. "Damn it." She shoved her hand over the coffee table before she dripped on the carpet.

Hiro chuckled. "He's really gotten under your skin. With just one look, too."

"It wasn't just one look." Mother of All, Capri couldn't focus. She wanted to roar and rage, vent her frustration somehow. For the love of—

He was just one man. One human, at that.

"Oh, my God. Have you—? But you just met." Hiro grabbed some tissue and handed it to Capri. "Do share."

Capri wiped her hand, her glass, and the table. "It's not— We haven't—" Oh, jeez. "You're not going to give up until you have all the details?"

"All the juicy details. Details are my thing."

If Capri hadn't known Hiro hoarded dragon figurines, she'd have guessed the drake collected details. Big details, small details, anything she could observe, gather, or correlate.

Capri sank back onto the couch. "Fine, but you have to swear this stays between us." The request was useless. If Hiro was going to use it against Capri, there was nothing she could do about it, but surely their friendship meant something. "No political maneuverings, no telling your doyen, or lover, or best friend."

"You are my best friend." She said it as if Capri not knowing that was ridiculous.

Something eased in Capri's chest, a tension she hadn't known was there. "I met Detective Miller two weeks ago, cleaning up Hunter's mess in Elmsville, and—"

"And you had a night of wild passion?" Hiro asked.

"No."

"Well, that's disappointing."

"Would you just listen! I can't have a relationship with Miller because he's a dead ringer for someone else I had to give up."

Hiro gasped. "Your mystery man?"

"Yeah." She and Hiro had been friends for hundreds of years until Capri had met Eric. Then she'd withdrawn from everything dragon to keep him safe. All Hiro had known was there'd been a man, and then there wasn't.

"You're saying Miller looks like mystery man?"

"They could be twins."

"You disappeared for years," Hiro said. She was putting it all together.

"I really loved him, Hiro." Capri's insides twisted. "I wasn't inamorated, but I loved him."

"And he was human."

"I had to obey the law. He wouldn't have understood how I stayed young while he aged."

"Oh, honey." Hiro held out a hand.

Capri took it, her throat tightening. She'd left Eric almost a century ago, and it still hurt. How could something so old still be so raw? "Looking at Miller brings up all those emotions. All that pain." All that yearning.

"I'll get rid of him," Hiro said.

"No." Please no, and yet, please yes. Yes would make it easy. He'd be gone. Except it wouldn't be easy. It was never easy. She'd know he was out there. "I think he knows something about our second victim."

"Andy Reynolds?"

"Yes. I need to figure out what, exactly." It was the best way to deal with a bad situation.

Hiro sighed. "At least it won't be for long. I have to report everything to Tobias tomorrow night."

Which only gave Capri twenty-four hours to figure out what was going on.

DIABLO GATED FROM HIS KITCHEN TO HIS LIVING ROOM AND BACK again, fury burning through him. His whole body shook with it. The need to move, to take action, consumed him.

He shoved his hands into his pockets, gated back into his living room to the bank of windows overlooking the river, and ground his teeth against summoning his magic and gating anywhere else.

He needed to hit something, kill someone, *do* something. Andy was dead, and there wasn't a damn thing he could do about it. He couldn't even ask any of the drakes in the Newgate P.D. because he wasn't supposed to care about humans. But someone needed to pay.

A roar bubbled deep within him. He fought it, every muscle burning with the effort. He would not lose his temper. He. Would. Not.

Except Andy was dead.

The roar burst through, and he slammed his fists into the cinder block wall beside the windows.

He wrenched around to face the room. His drake needed to break, tear, claw something, *anything*, to pieces. Whatever it took to satisfy the beast. But nothing could satisfy it. Not even ripping out the throat of whoever had killed his best friend.

Diablo's gaze jumped to the pale blue vase on the spindly-legged table, close to the front door of his apartment. They were the only things in his place that were new and delicate. Everything else was old and solid and had been repaired numerous times—it was too embarrassing to always buy new furniture after his beast raged.

He snorted. Other drakes joked about this drake or that going on a rampage, but they didn't know what that really meant. They were all beasts trapped in their fragile human bodies, but his beast was so much more. It was as if there were two of him, one sane and normal —or at least normal for a dragon—and the other a monster that turned the world red and destroyed everything in its path. It always burned within him, ready to roar to life at a moment's notice. A monster he couldn't control.

Not until Andy, at least.

Andy had given him the vase and table, determined to prove to Diablo that he could control his beast and have nice things.

Diablo gated to the vase and shoved his hands back into his pockets. He wouldn't touch it, wouldn't risk letting the beast crush it.

But the beast was so strong. Stronger now than it had been when he'd found a confused kid with an out-of-control empathic ability. Andy—Pete at the time—had barely been able to figure out which emotion was his. His parents had been on the verge of locking him in a mental institution. Schizophrenia, the doctors had proclaimed. They wouldn't have known schizophrenia if it had roared at them in the face.

His hand swiped at the vase and he jerked up his magic, gating away before destroying the one thing that represented everything Andy had done for him.

Who would have thought a sixteen-year-old human mage would have helped a four-hundred-year-old drake? But he had. They had helped each other.

And Andy was supposed to have lived a long human life. Diablo should have gotten at least fifty more years with him.

He growled again, but a tentative meow stopped him.

Two green-gold eyes peered at him from the shadows of the hall leading to his bedroom and office. Andy's kitten—Darkness—had come out of hiding.

Diablo's beast stilled. He needed to be in control until he could hand Darkness off to someone more appropriate. It had been evening when he'd remembered to retrieve the kitten, and then even later that evening when he'd remembered to go back to get *all* of the cat's stuff—like its food and litter box. After that, he hadn't wanted to wake or disturb anyone.

The sleek black kitten eased from the shadows, sniffed at his pant leg, then rubbed against him.

He squatted and held out his hand for her to smell, and she butted her head against his fingers.

"I'll find whoever killed him." He didn't know how, but he would find a way. He owed so much more to his friend, but finding justice would have to suffice. It was the only thing left he could do for Andy and the only thought that calmed his beast.

The kitten butted his hand again.

The beast growled. "I promise."

GREY GATED INTO HIS SUITE AT COURT. HE HADN'T WANTED TO LEAVE Anaea but the compulsion to return was overwhelming. It had started late last night and grown until he could barely think of anything else. Thank the Mother, Anaea had told him to meet her at Nero's house later. He was certain he wouldn't have made it through breakfast. He probably wouldn't have made it from the kitchen down the hall to the foyer, and he needed to be in full control when he went with Anaea to face her lawyers today.

The compulsion twitched through him and he strode past his living room, packed with floor-to-ceiling shelves filled with movies: every format, every language he could speak, as many as he could get his hands on.

He marched down the hall to his bedroom, the compulsion driving him to his wardrobe. He pushed aside his suits and removed a small hidden panel, revealing the keypad to the locked door of the secret compartment along the back.

Realization flooded him. The only thing in the compartment was the Handmaiden's grimoire. The spell she'd cast on him, woven into his mind, must have activated. She needed her book back.

No. The word flashed through him. The Handmaiden didn't want her book back. He needed to give it to Anaea.

His throat tightened. Giving the book to Anaea had to mean the Handmaiden wasn't returning. She wouldn't just give something like her grimoire away—even if the grimoire wasn't necessary for the Handmaiden to cast spells. Sure, he'd never fully understood or felt he knew the Handmaiden, even though he'd been sworn to her service for almost seven hundred years. And there were moments when she'd seemed something more than just a dragon, but that was because of what she was, the only dragon sorcerer. She'd single-handedly built Court and rebirthed souls to keep their species alive —more or less. He didn't want her to disappear. He wanted to continue serving her, have her fend off his playful flirtations.

But the spell didn't confirm or deny that she was returning.

Except what else could giving the book to Anaea mean?

He typed in the code and opened the compartment, revealing the leather-bound book.

Her last words to him had been to reread one of her diaries and deliver the grimoire when the time came. She hadn't said she was leaving forever. Of course, she hadn't said she was coming back, either.

He grabbed the book. Electricity snapped through his hand and with a yelp, he dropped it. It fell open at his feet beside the wardrobe.

It had never done that whenever he'd touched it before, but maybe the activation of her spell in his head had triggered something in the book as well.

He reached again for the grimoire, a little more tentatively this time, but stopped before touching it. The book lay open to the rebirth spell. In a blink, the page was seared into his memory. Every detail, letter, and age stain was now there forever. The spell required great concentration and power. Interestingly, it didn't actually require a medallion. The medallions had been made to save a dragon's soul in the event the Handmaiden wasn't present at death. Any spell the Handmaiden had in her grimoire, she could also cast by strength of will alone.

He flipped the page, blinked, memorized between one heartbeat and the next, and blinked again. Half of this page he already knew. It was about vessels, bodies. The rebirth spell could put the spirit back into the same body—she'd done that to Payne, now Gig.

What Grey hadn't known was that the spell wasn't just restricted to dragons. It could be cast on any being, if that being had enough of a connection to the earth's magic. He also didn't know that the spell affected the rebirthed being's soul magic, making it stronger. If he begged the Handmaiden to rebirth him, he might become a faster healer. He'd lose all his memories, everything that made him *him*, but that horrible night would be forgotten and would never haunt him again.

He reached to turn the next page. The last sentence talked about the affects on the rebirthed being's memory, but before he could focus on the words, his bedroom shimmered, the reek of garbage flooded his senses, and water dripped around him.

Mother, not now.

"How fast can you heal?"

Not fast enough. Blood had poured from his neck through his fingers. He was helpless and they were going to finish what they'd started and remove his head.

"Not now," he growled. He shoved at the memory and grabbed the grimoire—the compulsion flooding him again, consuming his memories and making him snap the book closed and hug it to his chest. It didn't matter if he didn't understand all the ins and outs of the spell—and concentrating on what he'd unintentionally memorized would make his flashbacks worse. He had to get the book to Anaea. Dragonkind needed her to learn how to rebirth souls. And maybe she'd do what the Handmaiden had refused. Give him peace.

15

The youth center operated out of an old, reclaimed church on Well Street. The red brick was stained black with a century's worth of grime, and the front steps, while they had been cleared of snow and ice, were crumbling. Snow drifted in fat, lazy flakes, muffling the sounds of the city around Capri, as if the church sat outside of the earthly dimension, like the Dragon Court.

Capri rubbed her temples. Her headache, the one she'd gotten in Elmsville and which had taken her over a week to get rid of, was back. Or maybe it had never gone away. It certainly hadn't been drinks last night. She'd barely touched her margarita and had begged an early—or rather *earlier* than usual—night to do some digging around on Miller.

She popped two painkillers, choking them back without water. They probably wouldn't do much, they hadn't last time—and her soul magic had done nothing to ease the pain, either, for some reason —so there was nothing else she could do but grin and bear it and pray a miracle happened and the pills worked. She sighed and got out of her SUV to wait for Miller.

Hiro hadn't lied. Melissa Slater, a then up-and-coming reporter, had ripped Miller's career to shreds. Internal Affairs hadn't had proof he'd set that fire and killed that kid, but there were too many unanswered questions. The suspicion had been laid. From the look of it, no one had stood by Miller—except for maybe Hiro, but the

Medical Examiner's voice hadn't counted for much since she wasn't a cop. Capri knew all too well how dangerous it could be when your coworkers didn't have your back.

No, Miller's only option had been to agree to a transfer, and it seemed the only place willing to take him had been small-town Elmsville. Which didn't explain why Miller was back and digging into Andy Reynolds's decapitation.

Miller's navy Camaro pulled onto the street and parked behind Capri's SUV. He got out of the vehicle and ran a hand through his dark locks.

Capri's heart stuttered. He looked so much like Eric it hurt. Why the hell had she kissed him? It only made everything that much more difficult. She had no idea how she was going to concentrate now, knowing how his lips felt against hers. Just like Eric's... better than Eric's.

Heat swelled across her cheeks. She shouldn't have kissed him, and she certainly shouldn't have agreed to work with him. But while the first had been pure foolishness, a loss of her senses, the second was practical. He didn't strike her as someone who gave up, and if he was determined to pursue this case—even if it was an illegal pursuit —it was better to keep him close than be constantly tripping over him.

"Hey," he said, and jerked his chin toward the youth center's steps. "Shall we?"

"Yeah." But she couldn't help feeling he was asking something else, something more intimate.

She bit back a growl. Foolish drake. Focus on the job. She needed to know what was going on, or at the very least, have an idea of what was going on, before Hiro told Tobias. A drake caught off guard was often a dead one, and she hadn't survived this long by being caught flat-footed.

Miller tugged open the heavy front door and motioned for her to enter first. Eric used to do the same thing. Miller had more in common with Eric than just looks. And his lips—

No. Focus.

Hiro might think a fling with a human was a good idea, but Capri knew differently. The only thing to come from it was heartache. She couldn't let herself forget that.

The old church's small lobby appeared unchanged from its church days. The hardwood floor was worn in a track leading into the sanctuary. The aroma of dust and wood polish enveloped her. Beyond, the pews had been removed and replaced with folding chairs and tables. The place was quiet—which didn't surprise her since it was mid-morning in the middle of a school day—and cold, which did surprise her... although maybe not. Heating an old church probably cost a lot, and she doubted the center had a lot of money.

A narrow door at the back opened, and a man stepped out. With a wide chest, muscular arms, and short hair, he looked like a cop or an army vet. Certainly, the way he walked toward them and how he held his body said he had combat training of some kind, which was probably a good thing to have when dealing with potentially troubled youths.

"Can I help you?" he asked, his tone wary.

Capri pulled out her badge. "Special Agent Jones. This is Detective Miller. We're following up on Andy Reynolds's death."

The man narrowed his eyes. "I've already talked with Detective Cooper about Andy."

"We just have a few follow-up questions, Mr....?" She resisted the urge to use her earth magic. It would be better if Miller didn't notice anyone acting strange—and Capri had a feeling Miller was attentive enough to notice someone conveniently spilling whatever information she needed as strange.

"Hastings. Sam Hastings, counselor, janitor, whatever else needs to be done." He crossed his arms.

"But you're not the administrator?" Capri asked.

The muscle in Sam's jaw twitched. "No. That's Ms. Mitchelle. From the Steele and Westwood Corporation."

Interesting. Capri schooled her features. Steele and Westwood was owned by Nero, the doyen of the Major Black Coterie, and his Third in command was Raven Mitchelle. This was certainly a dragon connection to Andy Reynolds.

Ryan frowned. "So your youth center is run by a corporation?"

"And we're grateful for whatever money we can get. What do you want?" Sam asked.

"We just have a few questions," Capri said.

Sam glared at them for a moment then blew out a harsh breath.

"It's been a difficult few days." He snorted. "A difficult couple of months, actually."

"Months?" Miller asked.

"They say things happen in threes. I never believed it, but Andy makes three." Sam turned back to the narrow door. "Let's talk in the kitchen. It's warmer down there."

"Big corporation doesn't pay the heat and upkeep?" Miller asked.

"I'm sure we're just a tax write-off. They pay enough, just enough, and for the most part leave us alone."

They followed Sam down a narrow, rickety staircase to a tired kitchen that was only marginally warmer than the empty sanctuary. Six youths, an even mix of boys and girls, huddled around a table at the back. Beside them, on another table, sat a makeshift shrine with three pictures, each with a small lit candle beside it. Two of the pictures were of kids, while the third, on the end, was of Andy Reynolds.

All six teens glanced up at them, their expressions hard. But Sam shook his head ever so slightly, and they turned back to their conversation.

Light wavered around two of the kids: a girl with spiky green hair and half a dozen piercings in her face, and a heavy-set boy with gorgeous chocolate eyes and a bad case of acne.

"Can I get you anything? Coffee? Tea?" Sam asked.

Flickering halos enveloped the heads and torsos of the two teens. Capri blinked. It had to be a trick of the light. But the auras remained.

"Special Agent?"

"What?" She dragged her attention back to Sam. He didn't have an aura.

"Coffee? Tea?"

"No, thank you." The teens' auras flickered at the edge of her vision.

Damn it. Things just got complicated. She'd seen that aura twice now in as many weeks. These kids were mages, humans with the ability to cast an earth magic spell or with enhanced physical abilities. The very thing dragonkind feared. The very thing Diablo and the Asar Nergal were in the process of hunting down because of

Zenobia, former doyen of the Major Green Coterie, and her attempted coup.

"Like I told Detective Cooper, I don't think Andy's murder is connected with my kids' accidents," Sam said.

The girl with spiky green hair shifted. Her aura rippled, and Capri struggled not to stare. If there were mages in this youth center and the Asar Nergal knew about it, perhaps that explained what Diablo had been doing in Reynolds's house last night. Maybe this was the dragon connection to Reynolds.

Somehow, Reynolds had been connected to Zenobia and her coup. One of Zenobia's drakes had been body-sharing with these kids until they'd developed a connection to the earth's magic—since that was the only way they could have a mage's aura—and because the coup had failed, someone had killed Reynolds, tying him up as a loose end.

Of course, Zenobia using Nero's youth center was even more ballsy than Capri would have given the green drake credit for. There was no way Nero would have been involved in the coup. He was a Traditionalist and solidly aligned with Regis. If Zenobia had used Nero's center, it was as a fuck you to Nero, and there was no telling what he would get Regis to do to Zenobia once he learned the truth.

"Can you think of anyone who might have wanted to hurt him?" Miller asked.

Sam sighed as if he'd been asked the question over and over again. "No one wanted to hurt Andy. Everyone liked him. He was dependable. A great guy. We could always count on him."

Green Hair shifted again, the light from her aura flickering against her brow and lip rings. That girl knew something. But of course she did. She was a mage. Although using children was a new low, and from an army perspective, not particularly advantageous— and if Zenobia was anything, she was a drake who took full advantage of every possible situation.

Capri turned to the table of teens. "Can you think of anything?"

The heavy-set boy with the aura dropped his gaze and shook his head. A brunette girl, not much bigger than Capri, stood and glared. "Stop pretending like you care. Come on."

The others at the table stood, their chairs squealing on the linoleum floor, and they shoved past Capri. She grabbed Green

Hair's elbow, subvocalized her power word, and slid a thread of magic into the girl's mind.

"What do you think?" Capri had to be careful that Miller didn't notice anything.

Green Hair jerked her arm free of Capri's grasp. "You don't really care about what I think."

"Sure I do, and it's clear you have an opinion." Capri slid more magic, just a little bit more, into the girl. She was dying to share, to show up the cops who knew nothing, prove how smart she was.

"Do you know something, Vicky?" Sam asked.

"All I know is that Andy had a fight with Mr. Pimm last month at Tyler's funeral. Then last week, I saw Mr. Pimm and Andy arguing in the parking lot. Mr. Pimm was really upset."

"About?" Miller asked.

Vicky glanced at the memorial, and Capri drew on more magic, but didn't push it into the girl, hoping she wouldn't need it.

"Tyler Pimm died in a warehouse fire last month," Sam said. "Howard Pimm and his son hadn't gotten along in the last year or so. Every couple of months they'd have a fight. Last month, Andy found out Tyler had been squatting in a warehouse on Second Avenue, but hadn't been able to convince him to go back home."

"His dad was a freak. I wouldn't have gone home, either." Vicky flicked her lip ring with her tongue. "But I don't know why he was at the warehouse. He could have crashed with Kevin."

"Kevin?" Capri asked, forcing her attention away from Vicky's aura. She didn't want to believe there was something diabolical about this kid, and Capri couldn't ask with Miller and Sam there. She would have to track down this girl later. There were days when she really hated Court politics.

"Kevin's a graduate of our program," Sam said. "Sometimes he lets the younger kids stay at his apartment when things get rough at home."

"Which is where Tyler should have been," Vicky said.

"Which one is Tyler?" Capri nodded at the pictures on the shrine.

"The one on the right," Sam said.

The kid on the right looked about sixteen and didn't fit the stereotype of a troubled youth—at least as far as appearances went. He had clean-cut looks with short blond hair spiked at the front, a clean-shaven jaw, and soulful brown eyes. He looked more like a teenage heartthrob or the star quarterback or something.

"Thank you for your time." Capri held out her hand, subvocalized her power word, and slid a thread of magic into Sam's mind. She and Ryan were never there. Sam had never talked to them about Andy. "If you think of anything else, please tell Detective Cooper."

Ryan tensed beside her for a second then relaxed. "Yes, thank you."

Sam shook their hands and they climbed the stairs back to the sanctuary. Ryan held the door for her again, and she stepped into a brisk wind that stung her cheeks.

"What was that?" Miller asked, his voice dark.

"What was what?"

"If you think of anything tell Cooper?"

"Detective Cooper is the lead detective on the case." And she couldn't risk leaving her card with Sam and have Cooper discover she'd been investigating his case. "If Sam calls him, I'll know about it." The lie twisted her gut. Good grief. This was ridiculous. She lied to humans all the time. She'd spent years lying to Eric. Lying to Miller shouldn't bother her.

"Right." Miller ran a hand through his hair, mussing it, making him look even sexier.

Mother of All. She wasn't going to last another day with him, let alone another minute.

His gaze fell to her lips, and his pupils dilated. He wanted to kiss her again. The desire was clear in his eyes.

Her earth magic billowed to life without her summoning it and slipped toward him.

He leaned closer, and his hand brushed her arm, drawing sizzling fire from deep within her.

Her magic snaked into his mind. His breath fluttered across her cheek. Somehow they'd drawn even closer, nose to nose. Magic caressed between them, swirling in her head. She was weightless and heavy, dizzy and swollen, all at the same time.

A growl bubbled in her throat, and her lips curled back in invitation. A challenge to a potential lover. Who would be the first to present meat? Who would find the best shiny? How could she add to his hoard and—

Oh, God!

She jerked away, wrenching her magic back. What the hell was she thinking? She was losing her mind. He was human. He didn't have a hoard. He wouldn't understand the real her. She'd never even shown Eric the real her.

Miller cleared his throat, his brows furrowed. "So, ah... what now?"

"Now I—" Grab you and kiss you.

For the love of—

He was not her lover. She would lived forever, and he wouldn't. Humans and drakes just couldn't have relationships. Focus on work. Work—

"Oh, crap." She glanced at her watch. She'd forgotten she had to check in with Swipe and Gig about the mages. She had ten minutes to get across town. "I have something I have to do."

"Sure. Yeah." He pursed his lips. She couldn't read his expression. He'd closed himself off to her. Never a good sign. This was such a mess.

"Let's meet up later. I'll call when I'm done," she said.

"Sure." He shrugged. "I've got things I need to do, too."

"Okay." Now she felt awkward, like a hatchling first reborn.

"Okay."

"Okay." She forced herself down the youth center's steps to her SUV and got in. This was such a complete mess.

16

R yan got into his car and watched Capri drive away. He should have just grabbed her and kissed her. He had no idea why he hadn't. She'd radiated ferocious passion, a desire that threatened to drown him. He'd never met anyone like Capri before, and he wanted more. He wanted all of her.

It wasn't just infatuation, or the allure of danger—because an FBI agent with a disgraced cop was dangerous on so many levels. No, there was something more, something primal igniting within his very cells.

He'd never believed in love at first sight. Lust, maybe. But never love. And maybe it was just lust, and he'd convinced himself, because he really did want a lasting relationship, that his irrational attraction to Capri was more than just that.

God, he was back to using her first name, too. She obviously wanted him. Their kiss yesterday and their almost kiss just now was proof of that. But she had more sense than he did by stopping them. He was lying to her about everything. That didn't make a good foundation for a relationship. And what relationship could they really have? He couldn't come back to Newgate and she couldn't move to Elmsville.

Jones. Just keep thinking of her as Special Agent Jones. Not sexy, vivacious Capri.

Oh, man. He was in deep trouble. Sticking around and continuing to work with Ca— Jones was a disaster waiting to happen. Except, if he ran right now, he'd miss his meeting with Melissa this evening, and his ex would ruin Jones's career.

The air outside his windshield shimmered, and he gripped the wheel, focusing on the cold biting his fingers. But that only made him think of the cold last night and their kiss. The future flash rippled, gaining strength.

No, damn it. He had to stay in the here and now. He already knew what his curse was going to show him. Capri hurt. A gunshot. A scream.

The security door materialized in the middle of the hood of his car. It banged open. Capri rushed out.

He squeezed his eyes shut, but the vision didn't stop. The gunshot exploded around him, and the scream tore across his nerves.

He couldn't run away from this. If Capri was in danger, he had to do everything in his power to save her. There had to be a way to change the future. No matter how many times fate proved he couldn't do anything.

Silence pressed around him. He opened his eyes. A normal, snowy, gray street stretched ahead of him. The future flash was gone.

There were three things he had to do: save Capri, figure out how Pete could be murdered twice—if, in fact, the victim in Hiro's morgue was Pete—and come up with something to tell Melissa tonight.

The first, he had no idea when it might happen, so he had to wait. The second kept him close to Capri, which helped with that first problem. So two sort-of-birds with one stone. The third required some thought.

He had less than a day to come up with something, and he'd gotten next to nothing from the youth center. Well, he supposed almost next to nothing. It was awfully coincidental that the teen, Tyler Pimm, had died in a fire. Fires were becoming his other curse. The child he hadn't been able to save had died in a fire. So had Pete... maybe. And maybe if the body in the Medical Examiner's office was Pete's, it meant he'd faked his death all those years ago. It seemed crazy, but not impossible. They'd been best friends. The idea that Pete would just abandon their friendship didn't make any sense, and yet—

The wind gusted, blowing snow from the youth center's roof, sprinkling it on the Camaro's windshield.

And yet Pete had been different. At the time, Ryan hadn't fully understood what *different* meant. All he'd really known was that Pete had withdrawn from everyone and everything except Ryan. Pete's parents had become worried. They'd sent him to psychologists and therapists and special camps until everyone in school thought he was a freak.

Maybe he'd been a freak. Maybe he'd been cursed, just like Ryan.

Then the fire had come. Ryan had foreseen it. Flames night after night. But he hadn't understood what it meant. Not until fire engines had screamed down the street and Pete's house had been engulfed in flames.

Even if Ryan had known what the vision had meant, he couldn't have done anything.

Just like he couldn't have done anything for that child in the apartment fire, either.

The air outside his windshield shimmered again. Son of a—

He fought back the future flash. They were getting stronger and more frequent. With the exception of Pete's death, the flashes came maybe once or twice a year. They'd been short, fleeting moments, often over before he realized what was happening. But now, they were coming stronger and stronger, hard, shocking moments tearing him from reality. He didn't know what that meant, though. Maybe he really was going crazy.

This time he wouldn't fail.

Third time was the charm, right? But before that, he needed to figure out what to do about Melissa.

He started his car and turned the heater on. It blasted cold air even though it hadn't sat for long on the street outside the youth center. He pulled out his phone and stared at it. He needed information, about Pete, the youth center, maybe even about Mr. Pimm— their only small lead. But he hadn't had many friends on the force when he'd left, and even just the idea that he'd set that fire so he could save that kid and look like a hero made everyone distance themselves from him—regardless that Internal Affairs couldn't find any evidence.

Of course, they hadn't found anything that led them to anyone else, either, which was why he'd been strongly encouraged to take the transfer to Elmsville. The only person who'd stood remotely by him had been Dr. Hiro Yoshida, which was why he'd approached her yesterday about Pete's— Andy Reynolds's body.

He didn't want to bother her much more, but if he wanted to get on top of this case and keep Capri— *Jones* in the dark about why he was really interested in the murder, and then keep Melissa away from Jones, he was going to have to give Hiro another phone call. Here was hoping she had something he could work with.

CAPRI DROVE HER SUV HALF A DOZEN BLOCKS, JERKED THE VEHICLE into a coffee shop's parking lot, and pressed her forehead to the steering wheel. She couldn't do this. So much for being a predator. She wanted—irrationally, desperately—wanted Miller like she'd never wanted anyone else before. Eric had never made her feel this desperate, but then she'd never had to resist her feelings for him.

She had to get away from Miller. Run fast and far. The idea of running made her furious, but she couldn't continue with the way things were. Her magic had manifested without her power word. She was out of control. He *made* her out of control. The best situation was to finish the investigation as fast as dragonly possible, use what he knew about Reynolds, and then get the hell away from Ryan Miller.

Her lips tingled at the memory of last night's kiss.

Focus. Those kids at the center had mage auras. Zenobia had turned them into mages for her coup. But that didn't make sense.

Zenobia's attack force had been comprised mostly of homeless people from various Third World countries. People who wouldn't be missed. She'd also had them mind wiped—the less pleasant manifestation of the type of earth magic Capri possessed—to make them easy to control. The spell, while in effect, eliminated self-will and essentially overrode the effects of soul sickness that developed in humans when they shared a body with a dragon to connect to the earth's magic.

But the mind wipe also made it impossible for those humans to function in human society. If Zenobia had made these kids into mages, she must have had other things in mind for them since they were still out and around and functioning like real people.

Of course, that was all assuming they had been a part of Zenobia's plan. If they weren't, that meant there was another dragon breaking the law.

This was becoming more complicated and completely disgusting. It was dangerous to body-share. The human became soul sick, going crazy, and the odds weren't great that the drake doing the sharing wouldn't fall soul sick as well. Dragonkind had discovered that the hard way after the terrible spell, the Great Scourge, had destroyed dragonkind's physical forms.

The Mother of All, dragonkind's goddess, had sacrificed herself to power a counterspell to save her children, but she could only save their souls. When the Great Scourge was cast, dragons had to take whatever human vessel was closest, whether there was already a human soul in the body or not. Insane human mages had been created, as well as insane, soul-sick dragon spirits. From everything Capri had been told—since she'd been reborn in the late 12th century and couldn't remember the time of the Great Scourge— those early years had not been good.

Laws had been created and the Asar Nergal had been organized by King Constantine—now soul-sick himself. Dragons didn't body-share anymore. At least not until Zenobia and her coup, and the only reason her army had succeeded was because her chief of Coterie Security had the earth magic ability that turned many of those humans into puppets.

But not all. And those who weren't puppets were back in control of their bodies. They had to be destroyed to protect dragonkind. All mages did.

She growled and squeezed the steering wheel. It just wasn't right. Those kids in the youth center were just that, kids. But if they were mages, dragon law said the Asar Nergal had to kill them.

Maybe they were just on the brink and hadn't developed anything yet. If they weren't full mages, maybe she wouldn't have to mention anything to Tobias. And maybe the Asar Nergal wouldn't notice them.

She couldn't believe she was actually considering keeping this hidden from her boss, and hence Regis.

Okay, maybe she could believe she'd hide it from Regis. If the teens weren't body-sharing with a drake at that moment and they hadn't completed a connection to the earth's magic, they couldn't be a threat to dragonkind. There would be no need to senselessly kill them.

She wasn't going to be responsible for murdering children, and if she told anyone, Diablo would do it without a second thought. She had no doubt about that. He'd probably grin and laugh through the assassination.

Now she had to figure out what all this meant. Had Reynolds learned something he shouldn't have and been killed? Had Diablo done it? Which didn't explain why Diablo had a key to Reynolds's house—unless he'd taken it from Reynolds's body. If Reynolds was a part of the body-sharing plot, had he decided it was wrong and wanted to back out and was murdered? That was assuming he was human and not a drake. And what was the connection to Kardas, the first victim?

She needed time to figure this out, and time wasn't something she had a lot of. By the end of today, Hiro and Cooper would have to report the second decapitation to Tobias. Then the issue would become a part of the political turmoil at Court, and while she had no problem cleaning up another dragon's mess for the sake of all dragonkind, she wanted... no, needed to know the truth. Particularly if Regis was the problem. If he was becoming unstable, something needed to be done. Hell, something should have been done years ago, before Zenobia killed six dozen drakes in her coup, irrevocably losing their souls into the universal ether.

If Regis was responsible for the deaths, who knew what he'd do next. No one would be safe. With the Handmaiden gone, no drake could be reborn. That meant any death, sanctioned or otherwise, diminished their ranks.

Her phone rang. Jeez, she couldn't even get a moment. She wasn't late to meet with her team yet, but it seemed Swipe was begging for her to vent her frustration on him with a few more bullet holes in his designer coat. "What?"

"I need you," Grey said, panic filling his voice.

Her heart stuttered. "What's wrong? Where are you?"

"Downtown, at Anaea's ex's lawyers' office."

"You're what?" That didn't make sense… well, it did, but what was Grey doing at a lawyers' office with Anaea? Where was Hunter?

"Never mind. Are you alone?"

"Grey—?"

"Are you alone?" he growled.

"Yes."

Air buffeted the SUV's windshield and a black vortex burst from the concrete wall in front of her. Grey staggered through. His hands slapped against the SUV's hood, and he gasped for breath. Sweat slicked his brow and blood smeared across his forehead.

"Mother of All." Capri rushed from the SUV. "Are you crazy? Someone could have seen you."

"We don't have time." He grabbed her arm and yanked her back to the concrete wall. The black void opened as they hit it, and the world tilted. Darkness and nothingness pressed against her, then something solid hit her foot, and the world erupted into chaos.

apri's heart stuttered. Papers, glasses, pictures, briefcases, and jackets roared around a conference room caught in a vortex of telekinetic magic. Sparks of fire flashed around them, threatening to catch the papers, but the wind of the vortex extinguished them. Voices screamed and whimpered, but the fury of the wind drowned them out.

At the center of it all stood Anaea. She was gorgeous, powerful, and terrifying. Rage radiated from her— No, not just rage, fear and frustration and hurt. So much hurt. All of it focused on one man, squashed against the wall of floor-to-ceiling windows. Tears streamed down her cheeks, and her chest heaved with desperate, choked breaths.

A drinking glass slammed against the window beside the man's head. He screamed. Four other men, cowering under a heavy conference table, screamed as well.

Grey's grip on Capri's arm tightened. "Stop her."

Mother of All! "How?"

"Use your magic."

"She's a sorcerer."

"She's still human," Grey said.

Yeah, and when Capri focused her earth magic on Anaea, all that terrifying power would be directed at Capri.

"I promised Hunter," Grey said. "Capri, please."

Another glass slammed beside the man's head. Then a water pitcher. An office chair swept off the floor, flying toward Capri.

Grey jerked her back. "Please, try."

"If we survive this, you owe me." Capri yelled her power word. No need to be subtle, and the force of the summoning sometimes helped with how much magic she could draw.

Another office chair swept into the air. It ricocheted off the wall, breaking off an arm that shot across the room and embedded in the opposite wall.

"Anaea." Capri's magic crackled around her. No longer soft and sensual like when it had manifested with Miller, but powerful, forceful.

Anaea jerked around. Her eyes and face were red with tears. "Stop me," she gasped.

Capri's brain stuttered. Not the response Capri had been expecting. She'd anticipated a woman's rage, a sorcerer's rage, not complete desperation and fear.

"Please." Anaea's knees buckled, but her out-of-control magic swept her up, raising her a foot off the ground. Her head wrenched back, and with a howl, more magic exploded from her. The conference table trembled, and the rest of the chairs shot into the air, shattering against the walls into sharp, dangerous projectiles. Paper burst into flame, blazing through the air, billowing smoke. The sprinklers went off, dousing them in water, but the magical fire couldn't be extinguished.

"Stop. Me."

Capri's pulse raced. She blasted her earth magic at Anaea full force. There wasn't time for gentle. Anaea wanted to stop, but somehow couldn't. That should make it easier. Mother of All, the power within that one woman was terrifying.

Capri's magic slammed into Anaea's head, but didn't latch onto her thoughts.

A chair leg shot toward Capri. Fast, so damned fast. She twisted, but it sliced across her hip. Pain shot over her side.

She struggled to stay focused. Anaea wanted to stop. So just stop. Take a deep breath, Anaea. That will help.

Grey yanked Capri to the side again. Another piece of chair shot past. She hadn't even seen it coming. She'd never be able to control her magic and dodge chair pieces. She needed cover, but there wasn't any.

"Come on, Anaea. You can control this." Capri's magic slid across Anaea's mind, like fingernails on plate mail and completely useless.

"Help me out here, Anaea." Capri's magic skidded again. There was no way into Anaea's mind.

"I'm trying."

"This is your fault, you crazy bitch?" the man pressed against the window yelled.

The vortex swept stronger.

"Not helping," Capri growled. "Come on, Anaea. A deep breath. You're stronger than this." She locked her gaze on Anaea's. She could do this. They would do it together. Just take a breath. Let it go. Capri had her back. She didn't need to be afraid.

Anaea blinked, something snapped, and Capri's magic swept into her head. Thank the Mother.

Her calming chill swept in.

Take a deep breath. Control it. Anaea could control it.

Anaea drew in air and that something snapped again. Fire roared over Capri's mental thread. Terror and rage swept down it, erupting into an inferno in Capri's head.

Her knees buckled. She shot her hand out to grab the wall to keep standing, but it wasn't there, and she was falling.

Grey's arms wrapped around her, jerked her up, and held her close.

"Anaea, stop," he yelled over the roar of the vortex.

"I can't." Anaea's body shook. Her wind ripped the tears from her eyes and tore at her hair and clothing.

Capri's head burned. She could barely focus past the agony. "You have to."

Another chair shattered against the wall. The pieces flew toward the window. The man screamed. Capri struggled to focus her thoughts. Stop. Just stop.

The pieces hit the window, and it shattered. The man's eyes flashed wide. For a heartbeat, he hung suspended in the air, with shards of glass catching light around him and the Newgate skyline behind him.

Then time lurched up to speed, and he fell out the window.

Grey's arms around Capri tensed. Heat blasted through her head. Anaea screamed. The vortex whooshed out the window, seized the man, and tossed him back inside. He tumbled across the conference table and landed in a heap on the floor.

The telekinetic wind vanished. The chair bits and glasses clattered to the floor, and the flaming papers fluttered around them.

Anaea sagged to her knees, and Capri's earth magic snapped off.

"You all right?" Grey asked.

"All right enough. Go check on Anaea." Capri's head pounded. She didn't think she'd be able to move to check on the human herself.

Grey released Capri, and she staggered to the wall, but even with its help, she couldn't stay standing. She slid to the floor, praying her head would stop hurting. Sirens wailed in the distance. Someone had called 911. But then a window had blown out on a skyscraper and the sprinklers had gone off. Lots of people had probably called 911.

Anaea sobbed onto Grey's shoulder, and one of the men under the conference table peered out. This was one hell of a mess. Tobias was going to have a fit. The only good thing in all this was that Capri was already here to adjust everyone's memories.

She leaned her head back against the wall, closed her eyes, and said her power word. Her earth magic flared, and pain sliced through her temples.

Mother of All, she'd never experienced so much pain using her earth magic like this before.

Her magic stuttered and fizzled.

And she'd never had that happen, either.

But then, she'd never tried to control a sorcerer before.

Note to self, never do that again.

She said her power word again. Her magic flickered, and she seized it, focusing past the agony and putting all her concentration into it. There was nothing else in that moment except her earth magic.

It wavered then gained strength. Not nearly as strong as it usually was, but it would have to do.

She eased it through the room, sliding it into the minds of the men under the table and the man who'd almost plummeted to his death. The window had a flaw in it. A freak burst of wind shattered it, and the sprinklers had malfunctioned. That's all that happened. You're lucky and grateful to be alive. Who'd have thought a burst of wind could do that to a window and the sprinklers.

It wasn't a great fix to their memories, but it would have to do.

Their memories eased, taking on the new thought, mostly because that made more sense than what they'd actually experienced —thank the Mother of All for that. She didn't think she'd be able to fight with anyone at the moment.

She pressed her magic out of the conference room. The fire in her head threatened her concentration. Just a little more. She needed to catch anyone who might have gotten out of the room before she'd arrived. But there wasn't anyone else in the office.

She sent out a blanket thought about the flawed window and sprinkler system through the rest of the building. That sent another burst of agony pounding through her. Her hold on her magic faltered, and the thread snapped away. That was the best she was going to be able to do.

Firemen, cops, and paramedics rushed into the room. She wasn't sure if they arrived all at the same time or not. The world stuttered around her, caught in flashes of bright agony and blissful nothingness.

Someone helped her stand, wrapped her in a blanket—even though she still wore her winter coat—and escorted her out of the office to a chair—one half of a seating area—beside a bank of elevators. Cops started taking statements from the men who'd been under the table, and Grey and Anaea sagged into the couch across from Capri.

She couldn't believe that someone only five inches taller than her and completely human could be so powerful. But then, Anaea wasn't completely human anymore. She was a sorcerer, a full one, able to cast spells, not just in control of one or two earth magic abilities. She was the thing dragons had feared since the Great Scourge. The real thing. Regis might claim that there wasn't a difference between a mage and a sorcerer, but Anaea's power made the differences perfectly clear.

And she was Hunter's inamorata. Mother of All, Capri had to focus on that. Hunter trusted her. His soul had chosen Anaea in a bond between spirits that could never be broken.

Dragons didn't soul-bond often. Not even when they'd had their dragon bodies. It happened even less now that they were stuck in their parasitic spirit states, trapped in human corpses. The bond was unbreakable and lasted for life. If Anaea had refused Hunter as her mate, he would never love another. Sure, he could have other relationships, but he'd spend the rest of his eternity knowing he was incomplete.

It was a good thing that when Anaea's earth and soul magic had been awakened, so, too, had been the magic that made her immortal and made a soul bond possible. She was inamorated with Hunter as well and they could have an eternity together.

A curl of jealousy slid through Capri, but it was small, just a twinge. She was happy for Hunter. If anyone deserved an inamorata, he did. He was a good drake, who, regardless of his previous occupation as prince's assassin, did the right thing. It was just that Capri had found love. She hadn't been inamorated, but what she'd had with Eric had been the next best thing. She wanted that again, and yet didn't want to face the inevitable heartache it brought.

Grey murmured something to Anaea. She sniffed and wiped her eyes. Although right now things weren't great for Hunter and his inamorata, and this disaster wouldn't help. Prince Regis was furious that Hunter had left his employ to clearly break dragon law by letting a human sorcerer live and have a relationship with her.

It also didn't help that he held one of the last two medallions used to save dragon souls for the rebirth process. But better him than anyone else. He wasn't crazy like King Constantine or Prince Regis, and no one could get to the other medallion, since it was embedded in the heart of the arena. It would be best if Hunter stepped up and claimed leadership of his new coterie, but that wasn't really Hunter's style, no matter that dragons were flocking to his unofficial banner. Hunter had never wanted to play Court politics, and she doubted he'd ever want to be a doyen. Which left Grey holding it all together.

Anaea sniffed again.

And apparently helping to hold Anaea together, as well.

"Where's Hunter?" Capri asked.

Anaea drew in a ragged breath and squared her shoulders, visibly pulling herself together. She was as tough as a drake. Capri had known that the moment she'd watched Anaea take out Xanthic during the coup, but to see it again, to watch her battle all that emotion, proved why Hunter's soul had picked her.

"He's trying to find the Handmaiden," Grey said, keeping his tone low so the emergency responders wouldn't notice.

"He left—" The words slid out before Capri could stop them. In the early days of being inamorated, separation was actually painful. No wonder Anaea was struggling with her emotions, and if what had happened in that room was any indication, her magic was directly affected by her emotional state.

"Your people need her more than I need him right now," Anaea said.

"But—" Capri couldn't work her throbbing head around the idea that Hunter would just leave Anaea.

"This is a dangerous time for all of us," Grey said. Sweat glistened at his temples. It might have been water from the sprinklers but his pallor was gray again. His wet blond locks were plastered to his head, making him look even more bedraggled and sick.

"Are you all right?" Capri asked. He hadn't been looking well for at least a week now. No, not since the whole fiasco with Hunter and Anaea had started three weeks ago.

The muscles in Grey's jaw twitched. "I've been better."

Capri waited for more, but he didn't elaborate and she didn't have it in her to pry. Her head pounded. The fluorescent light in the ceiling panel was too bright. Even her teeth and soggy hair hurt.

A cop approached, notebook in hand, and she bit back a sigh. All she really wanted was to go home. And the best way to do that was to convince him it was a blown-out window and they didn't need to make any kind of substantial statement. She subvocalized her power word and slid it into his mind. He already knew what had happened. The other men who'd been in the room had given him more than enough information.

"Have the paramedics seen you?" the officer asked. He had a gentle smile that went with his boy-next-door looks.

"We're good," Capri said, pushing past the pounding in her head. They were fine. Just let them go.

The officer glanced at Grey and Anaea.

"Just a little shaken up," Grey said.

Anaea nodded her agreement. If Capri looked past the soaked

clothes, red-rimmed eyes, and too-pale complexion, she wouldn't have known Anaea had just had the scare of her life.

"All right." The officer motioned to another cop by the elevators. "Take them downstairs."

The other cop pressed the elevator call button. Capri pulled herself out of the chair, the hall twisting for a gut-wrenching moment then steadying. The elevator dinged and the door opened.

Capri eased in beside Grey, with Anaea and the officer on his other side, and they rode down to the lobby in silence, leaving a puddle of water on the elevator floor. There was a lot that needed to be said, but couldn't because of the human beside them, and Capri wasn't sure she wanted to have any kind of conversation at the moment. Her head pounded, and the pain just wasn't easing up, not like the pain in her hip. That cut had already healed.

Her phone rang, and all eyes glanced at her.

"Jones," she said.

"Where the hell are you?" Swipe growled.

Oh, crap. She might not have been late when she'd left the youth center, but she was more than late now. "I got tied up."

The cop's eyebrows rose.

Yeah, tied up was one way to describe the situation, and the cop didn't even know what had really happened.

"I'm on my way now."

"And by 'now' you mean?"

"Ten minutes." Except she had no idea where she was. "Twenty if traffic is bad."

"I can give you a lift," Grey said.

"Who's that?" Swipe asked, his voice darkening.

"I'll be there in ten." She hung up before he could argue. She was losing control of her team. She was losing control of her life, too, but pulling that together would just have to wait.

"You know I didn't mean for—" Grey shrugged, unable to say anything with the human beside him, but she knew what he meant. And really, she couldn't hold any of this against him, or even Anaea. There was no way they could have predicted what had happened. The only person who knew anything about being a sorcerer was the Handmaiden, and she wasn't around to give Anaea help at the moment—another possible reason Hunter might have gone looking for her.

"Swipe will get over himself." And if he didn't, Capri could just shoot him. That might even make her feel better. "But I will take you up on that lift."

"I'm parked out front."

The elevator dinged, and the doors slid open. Voices roared over them, and a crowd of reporters surged toward the open door. Cameras and lights and microphones surrounded them, and people started yelling questions. The lights were too bright, the noise too loud.

Capri fought to breathe past the agony in her head. The cop pushed forward, trying to create a path for them through the crowd. Grey draped a protective arm across Anaea's shoulders, and kept them close behind Capri.

They inched forward a few feet. The crowd jostled against them, and the noise billowed. Mother of All, her head hurt, and she had no idea how to make it stop hurting.

A man in the crowd said something, then turned away and a brunette with perfectly coiffed hair took his place. She shoved a microphone in front of Capri.

"Special Agent Jones, can you tell me why the FBI is here? There are law offices in this building. Are they connected to the recent murders?"

"The what?" Capri's attention jumped to her.

The cameraman at her shoulder shifted. A red light on his camera blinked. He was filming this.

"Can you tell me what the FBI has discovered on the recent decapitations?" It was the woman from the Medical Examiner's parking lot. The one who'd been talking to Miller.

"I can't discuss an ongoing investigation." The words spilled out on instinct.

"So the FBI is involved?"

Ah, shit. If that made it to the news, Tobias would discover she was investigating something she hadn't been assigned. This was bad.

"And how is ex-Newgate Detective Ryan Miller involved?"

And bad just went to worse. Now she had no way of keeping Miller off Tobias's radar. "I can't discuss this. Excuse me."

Capri shouldered the woman aside with a little more force than necessary. The woman bumped into her cameraman, knocking his camera and ruining his shot. Another group of officers broke through the crowd from the other end, and they opened the way up. Capri strode across the vast lobby to a wall of glass doors and rushed out onto the street, her head pounding and her thoughts whirling.

With two quick questions from some stupid woman, her life and Miller's were in jeopardy. She might be able to convince Tobias that Miller was just some human she was using, but there was no way she could convince Tobias her looking into the decapitations was anything other than what it was: her disobeying protocol. She needed to come up with an explanation and a backup plan for when the shit hit the fan. She had until the six o'clock news if her luck sucked, and the eleven o'clock news if her luck held. And that was all the luck she was going to get.

18

Capri strode into the Clean Team's conference room, her head still pounding. She'd contemplated changing first but her winter coat had protected her from the worst of the sprinkler's water and she really just wanted to get the impending fight over and done with—and Swipe was guaranteed to want a fight.

"Took you long enough," Swipe growled. He didn't even look up from whatever he was reading.

"What happened?" Gig asked, his eyes wide.

Maybe she should have at least glanced in a mirror. "Nothing. What have we got?"

"A fingerprint off the cell phone." Swipe glanced at her, and his scowl deepened.

Gig flicked a finger, summoning his earth magic, and turned on the big screen on the back wall. He pulled up the print and mug shot of a dark-haired, dark-eyed twenty-something man in desperate need of a shave and a haircut—in the very least, a comb.

"It belongs to Eddie Boyd. Real catch, this one. In and out of prison, mostly for small stuff. Obviously not bright enough to learn his lesson or to figure out how not to get caught." Swipe's tone darkened at the end, as if there was a double meaning to his words, but Capri's head hurt too much for her to even try to figure it out.

It seemed too much of an effort to engage in a fight, no matter how much she usually enjoyed them. What the hell was wrong with her? "Does he fit the profile for Zenobia's choice of mage stock?"

The screen changed and Gig sat forward. "Yep. It doesn't look as if there's anyone who'd miss him."

"Not even a parole officer?" Capri pressed her palms to her temples and fought to focus on the screen.

"Apparently he's between sentences," Swipe said. "It also doesn't look like the phone was Boyd's. His prints aren't on the buttons, only the outside, and there are other prints on top."

"So he handed the phone to someone." Capri was sure there was something important about that, and as soon as her head stopped hurting, she'd figure it out.

"I think this other number, saved in call history, belongs to Boyd." Gig flicked his finger again and a list of phone numbers—

No, not numbers, just one number, filled the screen.

"Regardless of whether this number belongs to Boyd, whoever had this phone called that number a lot," Capri said.

"Notice the most frequent days," Swipe said.

The call history stopped yesterday. But there'd been almost a dozen calls that day between 9 a.m. and 10 a.m.

A chill raced over Capri. That couldn't be right. "When did Diablo find that hideout?"

"Around 10 a.m. But I suspect he got the lead and informed the Dugga and who-knows-who-else around 9 a.m." This time Swipe's dark tone was clear.

"Someone in the Asar Nergal is warning the mages." She hated to say it, but she'd bet if she checked the other call clusters they'd coincide with whenever Diablo went hunting.

"It would explain why Diablo can't seem to do his job," Swipe said.

"But the Asar Nergal wouldn't— They've sworn—" Gig turned too-big eyes on her. "That would mean— I don't even know what that would mean."

"It means the Dugga is going to need to clean house." And Capri wanted to be as far away from that as possible. She had no idea who the Dugga was—that was a secret only Regis and Tobias knew—but warning the mages was as treasonous as making them. Someone, possibly many someones, would be spending time with Odyne.

Capri rubbed her temples again. Keep her distance and her head down—and pray Tobias didn't watch the news that night—and everything would be okay.

If there was a traitor in the Asar Nergal, her team needed to find the mages and call in Diablo at the last possible moment.

"All right." She straightened. "See if you can get a location on that other phone number. We need to take charge of this mess."

"Got it," Gig said.

Swipe leveled a hard look on him. "And go do that somewhere else."

Gig swallowed and glanced at Capri. She nodded and he fled.

"Are we really going to do this now?" Normally it was fun to argue with Swipe, but her head hurt so damned much.

"What's wrong with you? You should be glowing at the prospect of an argument with me."

"It's been a difficult morning."

"You're not yourself."

She met his gaze. "You just asked me if I was all right. You're not yourself, either."

"Actually, I asked what was wrong with you. Completely different than caring about your welfare."

She snorted, sending a spike of pain stabbing through her head. "Yeah, totally different."

Swipe flashed her a hint of teeth in challenge. "Just get it back together. Now is not the time to piss off anyone in Court."

"Particularly a mentally unstable prince."

"I wouldn't say that too loud in public," Swipe said. "Actually, I wouldn't say that in public at all."

"Only among my closest friends." And even in private, suggesting that Regis was unstable, like his father, was dangerous. You never knew who might be listening.

"We are not friends." Swipe scowled at her.

Yeah, right. And she was a baby gold drake in disguise. But she wasn't going to push it. They weren't friends like she and Hiro, they were co-workers, but she was pretty sure Swipe would have her back if push came to shove... although not if the person shoving was Tobias or Regis.

She sighed—even that made her head hurt—and stood. "Tell Tobias our suspicions about a leak in the Asar Nergal."

Swipe's eyes narrowed even more. "Isn't reporting to Tobias your job?"

It was, but she needed to get back to Miller and two decapitated bodies before Tobias locked her up for breaking just about every rule dragonkind had. "I need to follow up on... on that human. Make sure my earth magic is holding."

"Why don't I believe you?" He rolled his eyes at her and strode out of the conference room.

Capri pressed her palms to her temples again and squeezed her eyes shut. She just needed a moment. The urge to sit and put her head on the table teased her. But if she did, she wouldn't get up again, and she was running out of time. Who was decapitating people? And who was the leak in the Asar Nergal?

Someone cleared his throat behind her. For a heartbeat, she imagined it was Miller and heat swept through her.

"Got a minute?" Gig asked.

Not Miller—not that he could ever be in the Clean Team's base, but she was still disappointed. "Were you standing in the hall the whole time?"

Gig leaned in the doorway, but didn't look at ease. "Maybe."

Which meant, of course he had been. He'd heard whatever he'd heard and she'd deal with any fallout later. "What do you want?"

"I looked into that guy you wanted me to, and there's nothing unusual save that his place of employment is funded by one of Nero's corporations."

So nothing she hadn't already known.

"His life is pretty average for a human," Gig said.

"So why was he targeted with Kardas?" It just didn't make sense. There had to be a connection.

"Kardas? As in the drake who was killed?" Gig asked. "Isn't looking into that Cooper's job?"

"It is. I just don't want us caught off guard."

Gig straightened. "But if you're caught poking into Cooper's work, Regis could get pissed."

"That's why you have no idea why I asked you to look into this guy."

Confusion flooded his boyish features. "But I do know, sort of."

"No," she said, willing him to understand. "You don't."

"Oh? Ooooohhhh. Right." He winked. "I don't know. But my curiosity has gotten the better of me and I think I'll do more digging on this guy."

Capri offered him a smile. "Thanks."

"You bet." He grinned back at her and left.

Here was hoping if the shit hit the fan, Tobias would think Gig was too naive to really know what he was doing.

Here was hoping the shit *didn't* hit the fan. If she were smart, she'd stop poking her snout where it didn't belong. But being caught unaware and looking incompetent was just as bad. There were just so many messes and she had no idea how to control it all.

She blew out a quick breath. First things first. Miller.

Desire burned within her.

Jeez. Not Miller. Her investigation into the decapitations.

She pulled out her phone to call him.

An investigation that just so happened to require her to be close to Miller.

That was so very very good, and so terribly terribly bad.

19

Tobias stared at the stone dragons carved into the pillars in the rebirth chamber. The beasts, riddled with cracks and missing chunks, bared teeth as long as his forearm and spread massive wings.

He reached out his arms, willing, praying, for the earth magic of metamorphosis like Hunter, to turn into a dragon. Mother, please. From the moment he'd fallen from the sky and was shoved into this frail, minuscule body, he'd wanted his dragon form back.

Just for a moment. A second. A heartbeat.

He needed to feel the sun warming his scales and the wind caressing his snout. He needed to feel powerful, not helpless.

He roared and slammed his fists against the Handmaiden's altar. He was tired of being weak. He'd been tired of it since the 1500s when he'd taken to the sea to fight and steal and just be. Sailing had been the closest he could get back then to flying. But the sea had proven it wasn't the same and wouldn't reach that desperate, broken place in his soul.

He drew back to pound the altar again.

"You know she won't like it if you ruin the place," a sultry voice said.

Tobias searched the shadows for the owner. "I don't think she'll notice one more crack." The rebirth chamber was already in ruins from the attack on the Handmaiden two weeks ago.

"You really want to bet on that?" A dark form separated from the

shadows by one of the pillars, and Ophelia—head of Internal Inspec-
tion—eased into sight.

"No." But maybe if he broke something she'd come back and talk
to him. Except she hadn't even told him she was leaving. What made
him think she'd come back for him? He'd thought, after all the time
they'd spent together, she would have said something. He'd thought
she'd cared and thought—

Apparently thought things about them that weren't true. He was
just another drake, like her sworn servant, Grey. That was all.

"She's not back yet?" Ophelia crossed her arms. She wore her
usual black pantsuit. It blended with her dark skin, helping her to
hide in the shadows. Six hundred years ago, she'd been Constantine's
Spymaster. Now, she was still spymaster, just the title had changed.

"No. And you haven't *heard* anything about it?"

Ophelia raised an eyebrow. Only a select few knew about her
earth magic ability to hear thoughts—and only Tobias and Regis
knew she was the spymaster.

A thread of jealousy cut through Tobias. She had magic. She
wasn't completely helpless in her human form like he was. His
human hadn't given him anything but suffering. He had no earth
magic at all. He couldn't call wind, and didn't possess increased
strength. He couldn't use a gate even if the gate was anchored. Not
that he was going to let anyone know. Only Ophelia did, since she'd
read his thoughts years ago.

"You really have to learn to let that go." Her tone softened. "You
are the most powerful drake in Court."

"But if someone challenged me for my position—"

She barked a throaty laugh. "No one wants your paper, Tobias.
No one is going to challenge you to combat for the position of chamberlain."

"Unless Regis puts them up to it."

Ophelia's expression darkened. "I wouldn't put that past him. Last
time I was near him, his thoughts were practically salad."

Tobias went cold. "Are you sure?"

"Completely tossed, just like his father. The jumble didn't last
long, but—" She shrugged.

"We need a contingency plan." If Regis was becoming soul sick
like his father, Tobias needed to set the wheels in motion for new

dragon leadership. They couldn't be without a clear successor to the throne.

"You need to be careful of Regis. If he even suspects you of betraying him, he'll send you to Odyne."

If his prince didn't outright kill Tobias and send his soul into the ether. "How long have we got?" Maybe there'd be enough time for the Handmaiden to return—from wherever she was—and rebirth King Constantine. The king would lose all his memories, his soul would reset back to its primary state—that he was a gold drake—but the soul sickness would be gone.

"One problem with that plan," Ophelia said in response to his thoughts. "Constantine is missing."

"So Regis has already made his move." A reborn Constantine was the only drake who could rightfully claim the throne from Regis. So far the prince had kept the king confined to his quarters instead of having him reborn, claiming the situation helped stabilize dragon politics. And, for about five hundred years, it probably had. But after Zenobia's coup, and Hunter renouncing the Royal Coterie, everything teetered on the edge—including Regis's sanity, apparently.

"I'm not sure he's killed Constantine, though."

"What do you mean?"

Ophelia frowned. "There are moments when his thoughts suggest he has killed his father. But there are other moments when he's desperate to find him. Sometimes it's hard to tell the difference between wishful thinking and real thoughts."

"So Regis may or may not have murdered his father, but regardless, Constantine is missing?"

"Yes. I've confirmed that with a number of sources."

"Wonderful." Now there wasn't a clear line of succession. Hunter would likely be the majority of the dragons' next choice—even many of the doyens' choice—but Hunter would never step up. Which left the doyens fighting each other for the throne.

"It gets worse."

"How does it get worse than the possibility of civil war?"

"The Dugga is starting to suspect there's a leak in the Asar Nergal. He asked me to do a little nosing around for him."

Just great. "I was wondering why it was taking Diablo so long to catch a few mages. Do we think the leak is Diablo?"

"No. Not unless he knows I can read his thoughts, which I highly doubt. The drake is ready to blow a gasket at not being able to catch them."

Tobias blew out a long breath but it didn't make him feel any better. "Let me know if there's anything I can do."

Ophelia flashed him a hint of teeth, her gaze charged with sexuality. "Anything?"

"You know what I mean."

She dropped her invitation. "I do. She'll come back to you."

Tobias's throat tightened. "I'm not sure it's me the Handmaiden will be coming back for."

"I'm sure she will be."

Except Ophelia had never been able to read the Handmaiden's thoughts. And self-pity was just pathetic. He was a stronger drake than that.

"Yes, you are. Come on. We've got to figure out how to keep this place together so the Handmaiden has something to come back to."

THE ADDRESS WHERE MILLER HAD TOLD CAPRI TO MEET HIM WAS FOR A modest red-bricked century old house with two gables and a wide front porch. Sitting in an older neighborhood, the ice and snow-slick road was still cobblestones, and it was clearly a private residence. It seemed familiar, but that could be because it looked like all the other houses on the tree-lined street—and therefore many of the houses in Newgate.

She parked her SUV on the street and strode up the driveway, her footsteps crunching on hard-packed snow and salt. The idea of visiting his house simmered within her—even though it wasn't really his house since he lived in Elmsville. Still, he'd invited her someplace private, personal. Not that they could openly discuss the case in public, but he could have picked somewhere else.

She couldn't decide if the knot in her chest was the same strange feeling that had compelled her to kiss him or just plain discomfort.

It had to be discomfort. Her head still throbbed. Things were still complicated with Court politics, and—

The door opened. Ryan stood in the entrance in a T-shirt and jeans, his hair mussed as if he'd been running his hands through it or had just woken up.

Her breath vanished. Everything but him vanished. Just looking at him made her chest and gut ache, and it was no longer the ache of having left Eric. It was a want that threatened to consume her. It did consume her.

He drew in a sharp breath, as if he, too, could feel her desire for him.

Maybe he could. Maybe she was making him sense it with her earth magic.

But no magic curled from her. At least none she could sense. And yet, there was something there, an electricity, a spark.

"We should—" His pale eyes, the color of new leaves pierced by sunlight, held her captive. She would never be able to find a shiny that could match their intensity.

"We, ah…" He stepped aside to let her enter. "The, ah, case."

Right. The case. She was there to talk about the case and find out what he knew. That was all. Jeez, that was all. She wrenched her gaze from his and entered. "So, where do we stand… on the case."

He closed the door. It didn't catch. He shut it again, turning the lock to keep it closed. "Let me take your coat."

He stepped close, his hands brushing her arms. Heat enveloped her. More than just the normal heat of coming in from outside.

She slid out of her coat. He held it, poised behind her. His breath fluttered across the back of her neck. Tentative. Tempting.

"Reynolds is the second victim?" He reached around her, hanging her coat on the top of a banister.

She turned into him. "Yes."

They stood so close. If she took a deep breath, her breasts would brush his chest. Her stomach quivered in anticipation.

"Do we have a connection between the two?" he asked.

"So far, no." Since she couldn't tell him about the possible dragon connection. Mother of All, she needed to have her hands on him.

"So we have a youth counselor, no girlfriend or boyfriend, who maybe had an argument with the father of one of his kids." His gaze dipped to her lips.

Her heart stuttered. "And I'm not sure that's connected because of Kardas Grigas, the first victim."

"Unless that father is also a serial killer." He inched closer. So close, but not nearly close enough. Nothing but having him deep inside her would be close enough.

"What are the odds of that?" she murmured.

"Anything is possible." He dipped down and captured her lips with his. Sizzling desire swept through her. Her breath caught in her throat.

His tongue teased across her lips. The need within her grew. It flooded her senses, every nerve, every fiber of her dragon spirit.

With a growl, she twisted, pulling him around and shoving him against the banister. He groaned into her mouth and jerked her tight against him. Mother of All, he felt so good. She slid her palms down the muscular planes of his chest, following the ripple of chiseled abs to the waistband of his jeans and easing open the button on his fly.

He drew in a ragged breath, stealing hers from her lips. "Capri," he breathed.

Her name rippled over her, sensual, hot. It vibrated with something at the center of her being, something primal. It sparked a ferocious need that was so much more than what she'd ever experienced before. She hadn't thought it possible, hadn't thought she could contain such desire. And she couldn't. It seared through her, igniting her earth magic and burning across her senses.

She yanked his T-shirt from his jeans, needing to feel his flesh. In return, he flicked open the buttons on her shirt, his own fierce desire clear in his quick breath.

He slid her shirt off her shoulders, revealing her breasts and the black lacy bra containing them. His pupils dilated, the darkness leaving only a bright ring of green that shimmered as if with earth magic like a drake. Then he dipped forward, trailing his lips down her neck and across her collarbone.

Desire gripped her and she dug her nails into his flesh, unable to contain herself. A growl bubbled in her throat, soft, round. Not quite a growl. Something else, something—

Metal clicked on metal on the other side of the front door.

Capri froze, her heart still pounding, desire coursing through her. Ryan froze as well.

The click came again, then the telltale sound of a key sliding into a lock. A shadow moved on the other side of the door's frosted glass window, and that shadow had a key.

Ryan jerked away from Capri, reaching for his open fly. "Ah, shit."

Shit was an understatement. She wrenched her back to the door, tugging her shirt over her shoulders and fighting to do up her buttons. Why were they so hard to do up when she was in a hurry?

But it wasn't her buttons. It was her fingers and the trembling need still thrumming through her. Not to mention a roaring dose of frustration. Mother of All, if it was another drake behind that door, she'd shoot him. But the odds of that were next to nothing.

The door opened. "Oh!" a feminine voice said, her tone clear she knew something was up.

Heat raced over Capri's face. God, what was it with this man, this human? He made her lose all reason. She shouldn't have kissed him. She shouldn't want to kiss him.

She tugged her shirt straight and turned to the woman in the doorway. Two women, actually, although one was just a kid. The teen... maybe pre-teen, it was hard to tell... was a miniature copy of the woman, dark hair, dark eyes, and a heart-shaped face. Except the kid wasn't glaring.

Cold seeped from the still open door, freezing Capri's inflamed cheeks.

"So." Ryan cleared his throat. "I thought you weren't going to be home for another hour."

"Jess's class was canceled. Something about a bomb scare." The woman ushered the girl into the hall and closed the door. "It was just a blown-out window on a skyscraper, but still. I thought I could spend some time with my brother. But it seems you have other plans in mind."

Miller's gaze slid to Capri, and a renewed heat swept over her face.

This was ridiculous. She was a drake. A predator. One woman and a kid couldn't embarrass her, and yet, boy, was she embarrassed. Somehow, she'd lost control. All Ryan had to do was look at her and she lost all common sense. He was human, for goodness sake. No matter how much she wanted him—and man, did she want him—only heartache could come from being with him.

The woman hung her coat on a hook by the door that Capri

hadn't noticed before—probably because when she'd entered all she could focus on had been Ryan. "Jess, go start the kettle."

The kid, Jess, glanced from the woman, to Ryan, to Capri.

"The kettle," the woman said.

Jess blew out a heavy sigh, shrugged out of her coat, and rushed past Ryan to the kitchen at the back of the house.

The woman grabbed Jess's coat from the floor and leveled a dark glare on Ryan. "Care to introduce me to your... friend?"

"Right." Ryan cleared his throat again. "Capri Jones, my sister, Trisha."

Trisha raised an eyebrow, and Capri fought the urge to bare her teeth. "Capri? As in the pants?"

"No, the color."

Trisha's gaze dipped to Capri's cleavage, and her expression darkened even more.

Yeah, if Capri had had more time she would have managed two more buttons on her shirt, right up to the neck to avoid suspicion. As it was, the door had opened and Capri hadn't had time, and she was sure right now she looked like a sex kitten playing sultry executive.

Trisha's eyes narrowed. "Right. The color."

Well, this was awkward.

Capri ground her teeth. She could kiss whoever she wanted, and look like a sex-kitten, too—as much as there were a few dragons who'd find that immensely amusing. So why the hell did Trisha's interruption piss her off? Capri should be relieved. Trisha had saved her from making a fool of herself. Except now how did she introduce herself as one of Miller's co-workers? From Trisha's perspective, it was clear Capri wasn't.

"Will you stay for tea?" Trisha asked, her expression saying, 'I dare you to say no'.

"Ye—" Capri's phone rang. Thank the Mother. She'd never been so happy for the damned thing to go off. "Jones."

"We got another one," Hiro said.

All embarrassment, frustration, and desire snapped away—well, not all the desire, but she'd just have to ignore it.

Ryan tensed. He'd caught her change, as subtle as it was. "Is it...?"

And he was smart enough to figure out it was case related. "Yeah. I've got to go." Capri reached for her coat.

Ryan grabbed it before she could. "*We* have to go."

She opened her mouth to argue then snapped it shut. Her emotions were still strung so tight, arguing would just turn her on.

At the thought, a slick thread of attraction slid through her.

"Fine." She yanked her coat from his hand.

Trisha pursed her lips, her gaze sliding from Capri to Ryan and her expression clear. The *interview* over tea might have been avoided, but it wasn't canceled, merely postponed.

He grabbed his jacket. "And I'm driving."

"Are you cra—?"

He brushed his thumb across her lips. More attraction sizzled through her, and his pupils dilated again. He knew what his touch did to her. God damned traitorous body. It wasn't even hers, just the corpse of the daughter of a twelfth century laird. Stupid human form.

Ryan flashed her a grin, not knowing how much of an invitation showing that much teeth was.

Mother of All, she was in deep deep trouble.

20

Ryan marched down the hall of the Medical Examiner's building beside Capri. His sister had the worst timing ever…

And yet, maybe it was for the best. He needed to save Capri's life, not complicate it. And he was sure he was a complication. He was cursed. That wasn't something a person should bring into any kind of relationship.

But there was just something about Capri he couldn't resist. It didn't make any sense, and he had to ignore his attraction. Once he knew what was going on and Capri was safe, he'd have to go back to Elmsville. He certainly couldn't stay in Newgate, which meant there couldn't be anything between them.

Capri shoved open the exam room door and strode in. Hiro glanced up from a decapitated man on her table. Her gaze jumped from Capri to him.

"Well," Hiro said, "this is—"

"The body," Capri growled.

Hiro frowned, her surprise at Capri's abruptness clear. She slid a questioning look at Ryan. He'd left her a message that morning after he and Capri had finished at the youth center, but he doubted she'd expected to see him with Capri. Certainly, the look on Hiro's face said this was a development she hadn't expected at all.

Capri cleared her throat. "The body?"

"Absolutely, Special Agent Jones. We've identified the latest victim as Don MacCabe. A manager at a motorcycle parts store on Liberty. Same decapitation. I'd say a single stroke to the neck with an edged weapon like a machete or a sword."

Ryan leaned closer to the body. "Single stroke would suggest a certain level of strength." The victim was average on just about every level. Average build, average height, average looks—if that could be determined after death. He was a middle-aged man with a faded skull tattoo on his right forearm and another on his left shoulder.

"Kardas Grigas was an executive at a software company, Andy Reynolds a youth counselor," Capri said. "Now we have a motorcycle parts salesman. Two in their early 30s, now MacCabe here is probably in his 50s. Our unsub isn't picking them based on looks or occupation."

"So when we find out what the connection is between them, then we have our murderer," Ryan said. The catch was figuring out what that was.

"Yeah." Capri settled her gaze on him. A hint of ice slid across his sinuses. "Could I have a moment with Dr. Yoshida?"

"Sure." Was she trying to get rid of him? He supposed it was official FBI business, but he'd thought he'd convinced her to let him into the investigation. Except maybe with their kiss—

The chill shivered across his face and down his neck.

"It'll just be a moment," Capri said. Had her voice softened? He couldn't tell. "Detective?"

Of course. She needed a moment with her friend. It wouldn't take long, and really he wanted to give her everything she desired. "I'll be in the hall."

He stepped into the hall, unable to remember the five steps across the exam room to the door. A fluorescent light a few feet down the institutionally bland hall flickered. Capri just needed a moment...

No, Special Agent Jones. He was thinking about her in her first name again. This was bad. Of course, kissing her wasn't great for impartiality, either. And yet, he'd had no choice but to kiss her. He couldn't have refused. Just like he couldn't refuse her request now.

But the kiss hadn't been something she'd requested. It had been his own desire. His own foolish desire. And if his sister hadn't walked in on them, they would have done more than just kiss.

Why did his head feel too heavy all of a sudden, and why the hell had he left the exam room? He needed to know what was going on with the case. Now he'd have to ask Jones and there was no guarantee she'd tell him everything, or rather, tell him that little insignificant detail that might explain why Andy Reynolds was an identical twin to Pete Matthews.

He rubbed his face, letting the heat from his palms ease away the chill in his sinuses. He needed to get back in there. Why was it so difficult to stay focused?

He jerked away from the wall and turned back to the exam room door.

"Hello, child killer," a deep voice growled from the far end of the hall. Detective Cooper.

Ah, shit. Ryan unclenched his hands and forced them to relax. An encounter with Cooper was bound to happen sooner or later, since the decapitations were his case. Ryan had just really hoped they'd meet up later. Much later.

"Hello to you, too, Cooper."

Cooper snorted and strode toward him. He had the typical pretty-boy football star look. Clean-cut blond hair, square jaw, piercing blue eyes, and broad chest and shoulders. If he hadn't chosen law enforcement for his career, he could have been a model or an actor. Except, save for his face, he oozed a sense of dark violence, a predatory ferociousness. The same sense Capri gave off, although bigger, darker, and much more masculine.

Ryan blinked. He had to be imagining it. Cooper and Capri had next to nothing in common. They were both efficient, trained law enforcers. That was all.

And yet, he couldn't shake the sense that beneath their skin, they were something else, something inhuman.

Which was ridiculous. If Ryan didn't pull it together, Jones would ensure he never saw the inside of a police station again. Certainly not during her current case.

Cooper sneered, as if he were a bear flashing his teeth to intimidate a rival. "Didn't think you'd have the courage to show your face in town."

"Did you learn that line from a bad movie?" Ryan would be damned if Cooper forced him to leave the city again. He'd run the first time. He wouldn't do it again.

Cooper's expression darkened. "What are you doing here?"

"Hanging out with a friend. An FBI friend."

"And does this *friend* know you're a fire starter and a child killer?"

"She's FBI. I'm sure she's heard your gossip."

Cooper's eyes narrowed. "You can wait for her outside."

"It's freezing outside."

Cooper grabbed Ryan's arm and yanked him close. "Start a fire. I hear you're good at that." He shoved Ryan back, slamming him against the concrete wall. The air burst from Ryan's lungs. Cooper rammed his forearm against Ryan's neck. "Or do I need to charge you with trespassing?" His smile said he really wanted to arrest Ryan.

Ryan wrenched against Cooper's arm and rammed his fist into the other cop's gut. Cooper grunted and the pressure against Ryan's neck eased. Ryan shoved and reached for Cooper's wrist to lock his arm behind his back, just as Capri had done to him last night, but common sense kicked in, and Ryan staggered back instead.

He wasn't there on official duty. He could get charged for assault, and with most of the force thinking him responsible for that kid's death—even if Internal Affairs had cleared him—his fellow cops would take a long time processing him.

"Tell Jones I'm waiting by the car."

"Jones?" Cooper's eyes narrowed even more. "Now I know you're full of shit."

Ryan bit back a nasty retort and stormed to the back door. Cooper could think what he wanted. It didn't matter. So what if that asshole didn't think Capri would be interested in him.

Except why was she interested in him? She was FBI and he a disgraced cop. Maybe he only thought he saw an attraction to him.

No. She'd kissed him back. Her desire had been real, but was it real enough for anything more than a bit of fun? And God dammit, he wanted more than just fun.

21

The exam room door flew open and Cooper stormed in. "Miller? Really?"

"That's none of your business." Capri fought the urge to snarl at him and reveal how frustrated his disgust made her.

His gaze slid over the decapitated body on the table. "It is when it's my investigation. The man starts fires and kills children so he can pretend to be a hero."

Hiro did bare her teeth at him. "That was never proven."

"Let me guess, getting the human involved was your idea."

"No, it was mine," Capri said. Although *getting involved* with the human had definitely been Hiro's plan. Capri raised her chin and squared her shoulders. She might not be able to shoot Cooper in the M.E.'s office to get her point across, but that didn't mean she wasn't going to stand her ground. She was higher in status than him in Court, and she wasn't beyond using that to get what she wanted.

And Cooper knew that. "Fine," he growled. "What have you got?"

"A whole lot of nothing. I still don't know if the second victim was a drake," Capri said.

Cooper sighed. "Neither do I."

"But I'm pretty sure this third one is all human." Hiro handed him the file.

Cooper scanned the first two pages. "So that means Kardas was an accident?"

"Someone accidentally murdered one, maybe two drakes? That's a pretty lucky accident." But then Capri had no idea how any of that explained the other two murders. It looked liked drakes, specifically, weren't targets, but they could somehow be a part of the target group.

The memory of Vicky, the girl with the green hair at the youth center, flashed across Capri's mind's eye. Vicky had an earth magic aura. What were the odds that their latest victim had some connection to the youth center? Reynolds had worked there. Maybe that was the connection.

Kardas had been a member of the Minor Brown coterie. Or at least that's what everyone thought. But Zenobia had recruited across coteries for her coup. Maybe Kardas had switched allegiances. If so, the connection between victims could be human mages. Which would mean all these murders were sanctioned by the Asar Nergal. That would explain Diablo's presence at Reynolds's house.

But if these were Asar Nergal assassinations, why not be more subtle about it? And why not inform her, Hiro, or Cooper about them? With three so public and so close together, the humans were bound to notice. The Asar Nergal would have to call in the Clean Team to fix the mess at some point. But no one had called, which meant—

She had no idea what it meant.

Cooper growled. "There's nothing in the financials or phone records. The first two victims have nothing in common."

"The only connection to drakes that we have is that we know Kardas was a dragon and Mr. Reynolds worked for a dragon's company, but not necessarily directly with any drakes," Capri said.

"Trust me, that's a dead end, and if you go poking your nose into Nero's business, it could very well be a real dead end," Cooper said.

Hiro frowned. "Maybe this third body will help connect the dots somehow."

"All right." A hint of pain slid through Capri's head, and she rubbed her temples. "Well, Kardas's body was found on Fountain Street near his office. Reynolds's was by the youth center. Where was MacCabe found?"

"On 5th Avenue in the alley beside his bike shop," Hiro said.

"So they're being targeted at work." Cooper chewed on his

bottom lip, then his gaze jumped to Capri. "It doesn't look like there's a drake connection. Get that human away from my case. He can mess up the Clean Team's stuff."

"We haven't figured out anything, let alone whether there's a drake connection or not." More pain oozed through her.

"I know that I don't want Miller anywhere near this. Drop it or I'll tell Tobias you were nosing around where you shouldn't have been," Cooper said.

For the love of— "You invited me to nose around."

"And now I'm telling you to butt out. I see you or Miller anywhere near this, and Tobias will be the least of your worries."

"Is this really a game you want to play?"

"Keep that human away from my case." He bared his teeth and stormed from the room.

"Well," Hiro said, her voice a little too bright. "The CSU is done with MacCabe's scene... if you want to swing by and have a look."

"You're not supposed to be encouraging me." Even though checking out the latest crime scene was at the top of Capri's to-do list.

Hiro's expression turned serious. "I don't believe for a second that anyone knows what's going on here, particularly Cooper."

"Still, it is his investigation and for some reason he doesn't like Miller."

"I think he has a soft spot for human children."

"Who'd have thought?"

Hiro snorted in agreement. "I'll stall him. Tobias won't learn about Reynolds's murder until tonight. You have until then to learn everything you can."

"Let's hope I don't need it. Who knows? Maybe someone really did accidentally kill a drake."

"Who knows," Hiro said, but she didn't sound convinced.

Outside of the exam room, the hall was empty. Cooper must have threatened Ryan and told him to get lost. He was probably waiting by the car, so Capri marched to the back door. Her head was now pounding as much as it had been after helping Anaea. Cooper had that effect on people.

She rounded the final corner, and there, staring out the glass door, stood Ryan. Pale sunlight cut across his profile, lighting his eyes with that magical luminescence again.

A part of her needed him to be magical. As ferocious and immortal as she.

He glanced at her, the light now shining through his hair, giving him a halo.

Her breath caught in her throat. He wasn't a drake, he was an angel, a powerful warrior of divine beauty.

He shoved away from the door, taking a step toward her and out of the light. The halo vanished, revealing his human self. Even if she defied dragon law and pursued anything with him, he wouldn't live forever and she'd be heartbroken again. She couldn't do that to herself. She'd made a promise. Never again.

Except it had never before been such a hard promise to keep.

"So," he said. "Any connection with anything?"

"No. Which leaves us with the one lead we got yesterday. Mr. Pimm."

"Actually, we got two yesterday. Pimm and the administrator of the youth center," he said.

She'd been hoping he'd have forgotten about that. Her, with a human, interviewing a drake was a bad idea. "Do you think the other two victims are connected to the center?"

Miller shrugged. "I don't know. I just get the feeling there's more going on at the youth center."

Of that, she was pretty sure. But the real question was whether Nero knew about it. It was his center. Surely he knew youths there were being turned into mages. But that didn't make any sense. Nero was a Traditionalist. He was Regis's right hand. There wasn't a drake more devoted to dragon law than Nero. Unless that was all a disguise and he really had been helping Zenobia with her coup.

And none of those questions could be directly asked. If Nero wasn't involved, even a hint of the suggestion that he was connected with Zenobia's coup could be Capri's death—and with the Hand-maiden missing, it would be a real death, not just rebirth. Nero wasn't the kind of drake who took accusations to his honor lightly.

Although, maybe if Miller went asking around, asking human questions…

Now that was a terrible idea. Remember? Showing up with a

human was a bad plan. But it might be enough for Capri to get a read on Nero and know if she needed to be suspicious of him or not. She would have to ensure Miller's memories were more than taken care of, but she already knew she was going to have to deal with that.

Her stomach churned at the thought. That kind of magic could destroy his mind. And it would mean he'd forget her completely.

She cleared her throat and headed outside. "Why don't we swing by our third crime scene and start there."

Perhaps they could avoid Nero altogether. Well, perhaps Miller could. She, however, was going to have to find a delicate way to ask serious questions of Nero's Third, and pray it didn't get her killed.

22

Ryan drove to 5th Avenue, unable to stop glancing at Capri in the passenger seat. One moment she'd be looking at him with obvious lust, the next, a scowl. He was dying to ask what Cooper had said about him, but Ryan was pretty sure he already knew: Ryan was no good, he was an arsonist and a child killer. The real question was, did Capri believe Cooper?

5th Avenue was in an old section of downtown, five blocks from the latest revitalization project. The buildings were grimy from years of dirt and a few were abandoned and boarded up. Slush disguised potholes in the road and icicles hung from eaves, suggesting less than adequate insulation in the attics.

Ryan drove to MacCabe's motorcycle shop and parked two spots down. Capri got out and scanned the area, but didn't go anywhere. The crime scene would have already been processed by the CSU. All evidence would have been collected and taken back to the lab. All he and Capri could do was try to get a feel for the location.

Ryan got out of his car and joined Capri on the sidewalk. Salt crunched under his boots, fending off the ice in front of the door to MacCabe's shop. The front window was grime-free, and a slick new Harley sat on display.

Beside the shop was a shoe store with fluorescent platform shoes in the window. On the other side lay an alley. Given that Andy... or Pete... or whoever it was had been found in an alley, MacCabe had likely been discovered in one as well. Which meant while the murderer killed in public, he wasn't brazen enough to do it in plain sight.

Capri shifted near him. "Do you see that?"

Yeah, the move made her closer, but not close enough to imply the intimacy they'd had back at Trisha's house. Whatever Cooper had said must have changed her feelings for him.

She raised an eyebrow.

Right. She'd asked a question. What was wrong with him? They couldn't have a relationship anyway. Why was that so hard to remember?

He dragged his attention to where she'd pointed across the street. A square building with a sign reading Newgate Savings and Loans sat on 5th and a side street. And there, beside the front door, was an ATM.

"Do you think it has a camera?" he asked.

"Let's find out," she said.

They crossed the street. Sure enough, the ATM had a small camera. Capri pulled out her phone and dialed.

"If we're lucky," she said to him, "the camera will have caught something. Hey Gig, I need you to pull up some video for me. An ATM at 5th Avenue and—" She glanced at the street sign on the corner. "5th and Kress."

She turned to Ryan, a satisfied smile lighting her eyes. God, she was so beautiful. "It's a long shot—"

"But it could be something." This was the thrill of the chase, finding pieces and putting them together. "Let's see if we're on a roll and talk with Mr. Pimm."

Capri's smile deepened. It warmed him to his core. She loved the chase as well. He could fall in love with this woman. Hell, he already had.

This was bad, and impossible, and... and bad.

He got back into his car. He couldn't be in love with a woman he barely knew. It had to be lust. Plain and simple. Except there was nothing plain or simple about the situation.

Capri slid into the passenger seat. Just her presence turned him on. She didn't even have to touch him or look at him. She radiated strength and passion and it seared across his skin. It burned hot and sensual, invading his senses, invading him.

He forced his attention to the car. Drive to Pimm's and figure out who killed Pete. Really. That was his goal. Determine if the body in the morgue was Pete. It had nothing to do with who the murderer was or being with Capri.

The air above the car's hood rippled.

Not. Now.

A gunshot boomed and someone screamed. He clenched the steering wheel, praying the flash wouldn't fully materialize.

"Miller?" Capri brushed his arm.

He jumped and jerked to face her. The flash vanished. Pete or not, his real goal was to protect Capri, to prevent what had always before been inevitable.

She pursed her lips. Lips that had pressed against his, felt right against him, were—

He was not going to go there. "What?"

"Are we actually going to visit Pimm? Or are we just going to sit in your car?"

Ah, shit. He had yet to even turn the engine on. Wow, he didn't need Cooper to tell her he was crazy. He was doing a fine job at that himself.

"Right. Sorry." He started the car and drove down the street.

"What were you thinking about?"

You! "Just, ah… you know… how the pieces in this case fit together." *Oh, man. That was lame.*

"What pieces? There's next to nothing."

He turned right, stealing a glance at her. "That's what I mean."

"That you were thinking about nothing? You're a man. I'm sure you were thinking about *something*." She flashed him a wicked smile. It promised nights and days of incredible pleasure.

God, he loved that smile.

Down, boy. Remember, bad idea.

He clenched the wheel. Hard. "No, I mean that there's nothing. These aren't murders of opportunity. This murderer is taking forensic precautions. He's planned this. These men must have been killed for a specific reason."

"The question is, what reason?" she said. "If we knew the why, we might be able to figure out the who."

And how did that help him figure out if Pete was Andy or how to protect Capri from the future? "That would be the question."

He pulled onto Pimm's street and stopped at his address. His house sat on the corner of two narrow streets. It was a small structure with siding more gray than pale brown, peeling paint along the windowpanes, and a rust-stained storm door. A bushy pine crowded the living room window as well as the three steps to the door, throwing the front of the house into perpetual shadow. Snow, frozen in the shape of dozens of footprints, covered the steps and driveway, and a rusty silver van sat beside the house.

"Looks like he's home." Capri slid from the car. "Let's see what he has to say about his argument with Mr. Reynolds."

Ryan fell into step beside her as if they'd been partners for years. He rapped on the door as she reached for her identification.

Nothing.

He knocked again. If he was still Newgate P.D. he'd announce himself, but he wasn't, and this was Capri's show.

She glanced at him and he shrugged.

"All right." She cleared her throat. "Mr. Pimm. Special Agent Jones. Can we talk about your son?"

Heavy footsteps pounded, slow and steady and drawing closer, on the other side of the door. That had gotten his attention.

"What do you want?" The door jerked open and a tall, bulky middle-aged man with a shaved head stood on the other side. His expression twisted, as if he fought myriad emotions then settled on mildly pleasant. "What's this about?"

Capri showed him her badge. "Special Agent Jones. Detective Miller. Can we talk, Mr. Pimm?"

"Well, I—" Pimm glanced at Ryan then turned back to Capri.

"We'd like to talk to you about a youth counselor your son had contact with. Can we come in?" Capri asked.

"I was just on my way out." Pimm shrugged, his gaze jumped to the left of Capri, his eyes unfocused, then he snapped back to her. "I really have to go. But I do want to discuss this." He held out his hand. "Do you have a card?"

"This won't take long," Ryan said.

Pimm's gaze slid to the space between Ryan and Capri again. "I'm going to be late for work, and I can't afford to lose this job. I'm sorry." He grabbed his coat from a hook beside the door and stepped onto the tiny front porch with them. "Excuse me."

His gaze jumped again, then he shifted around Ryan and rushed to his van. With a roar and a belch of black exhaust, the van lurched out of the driveway and down the street.

"What was that about?" Capri asked.

"I have no idea."

23

Howard eased his van around the corner and parked at the end of the street, his heart racing. The demons had found him, and they were FBI. He'd suspected they'd infiltrated the highest levels of law and government, but he'd never before had proof.

All he'd known was that he'd needed to protect himself. His crusade was important, and he couldn't allow even his fellow humans, unaware of the hidden evil, to stop him. The demons were responsible for the death of his son. They were responsible for the death of his wife, too, although he hadn't been able to see the truth when Lizzie had died.

And really, he shouldn't be so surprised they'd found him. He knew every time he rid the earth of one of those monsters he was putting himself in danger. Lizzie had warned him. An angel sent from God to open his eyes that only he could hear and no one—not even he—could see. She'd whispered the truth over and over again. Demons were real. Demons were dangerous. Look and you shall see. And he did see. But he'd had to protect his child, so he'd done nothing, stayed hidden in his house ignoring the spirit of his wife.

His throat tightened. He'd done nothing. And now Tyler was dead. God had punished him for his uncertainty and Tyler was dead.

And now the demons had found him. He couldn't figure out how. He'd done everything right. Worn gloves. Made sure his scalp and beard were freshly shaved so he didn't leave behind any hairs. He only wore each set of overalls once and then burned them after the job was done. He was careful about fingerprints, DNA, everything.

He cut the engine and shifted to see past a tree branch and get a better view of his house. The demon—the short woman who claimed to be FBI—and her human slave peered through the window in the front door, then walked back to the driveway. But they didn't head to their car. Instead, they wandered around the side of the house toward the backyard.

Howard's pulse raced. He had to stop them. He couldn't let them discover all his plans. But he wasn't prepared to fight right now. He didn't have his weapons with him. Demons were hard to kill. Lizzie had warned him, he'd only get one swing to remove the beast's head.

Still, if they knew—

The wind swept through the trees. Wait. Wait. He wasn't caught yet. Even if they knew, he could change his plans. There was always another demon... just not one as powerful or with such a good opportunity to get close to it.

The demon emerged from around the house and marched down the driveway. They hadn't been in the back long enough to have entered the house.

Relief washed through him. They didn't know. Lizzie had protected him and they didn't know.

The man the demon was with said something. She glanced at him, one hand on the open door of the car sitting at the curb, and said something back. The man, a handsome guy with dark hair and a square face, nodded. The fool was beguiled by her. It was clear he was the demon's servant. And a demon's servant was almost as dangerous as the demon herself.

It didn't matter. They didn't know the truth about him. If they had, they would have killed him right there. And they hadn't gone into his house, so they didn't suspect him. One of the brats at the youth center likely had given them his name and that's why they'd knocked on his door. Not because they knew he'd killed their fellow demon posing as a counselor.

He was safe and tomorrow he'd be ready. The demons and their slaves would never see him coming.

CAPRI GOT INTO THE PASSENGER SIDE OF RYAN'S CAMARO. IF HE hadn't been with her, she would have broken into Howard Pimm's house and thoroughly searched it. Or maybe not. The man had acted strangely, but not in any way that suggested a dragon connection. And really, wasn't that the point of the investigation: to find any dragon connection to the murders?

And while there had been two kids in the youth center with mage auras, it didn't prove they were connected to the three decapitated victims.

Ryan got into the car, his presence sliding across her skin. "Not really enough evidence for a warrant."

"No." The urge to grab him and kiss him was overwhelming.

"One strange man, though, even if that doesn't make him a murderer."

"It doesn't discount him." Of course, it didn't discount anyone in the Dragon Court, either.

"Well, the only other lead we have is the coordinator of the youth center. What was her name?" Miller pulled out his notebook and flipped through the pages.

"Mitchelle." Raven Mitchelle and Nero's Third in command, who currently resided at his Newgate residence. "I'm not sure talking to Ms. Mitchelle will do any good." Aside from making this mess more complicated.

Her showing up at Regis's favorite Traditionalist's doorstep to ask questions about a murder she wasn't supposed to be investigating was beyond dangerous. Even if Nero wasn't there, Raven was certain to tell him the moment the door had been closed in Capri's face, and Nero would certainly report back to Regis.

"Perhaps she has some insight into what Andy was involved in."

Capri slid her gaze to Ryan. Just looking at him made her insides warm.

She jerked her attention back to the frozen road outside the windshield. "I doubt that. He worked closer with Sam Hastings, and Sam didn't have anything to offer."

"Well, then, perhaps Ms. Mitchelle knows what's going on with the deaths connected to the youth center."

"What has that got to do with anything?" But if Andy was

murdered because of the teens being turned into human mages, those deaths had everything to do with it.

Those kids had likely fallen to soul sickness, their spirits unable to withstand sharing a body with a more powerful dragon spirit. Their insanity would have been difficult to hide and detrimental to Zenobia's plans. She would have had to get rid of them and *accidental* death was efficient with few hanging questions. Better than just disappearing. With disappearing, there was still family searching for their missing child. With death, nothing more could be done.

If Raven was somehow involved with that, Capri had to know. The third in command of a coterie had a certain amount of autonomy, so it was foreseeable that Raven had changed allegiances and acted without Nero's knowledge. But the odds of that were slim, and that put even more doubt on Nero's true intentions. Who would be in a better position to take the throne when all was said and done than someone so close to it? For all Capri knew, Nero could have manipulated Zenobia into attempting the coup.

Miller sighed. "I know it's grasping at straws, but until we can talk to Pimm, or Hiro and the CSU come up with anything, we've got nothing."

"Maybe we just need to think about it. Take a step back," she said. Anything to give her time to interview Raven by herself.

"We have three decapitated bodies in less than two weeks. I'm not sure we have time to mull this over." He shoved his notepad into his inside coat pocket. "But you're right. We should probably take a moment and think about this. I've got some errands I need to run. Maybe doing something completely different will shake something loose. I'll drop you back off at your SUV at my sister's house."

She glanced at him again. He looked tired, and sexy, and just like Eric when he was lying. There was a hint of determination in his eyes, the glimmer of a plan. If she hadn't had years of seeing it already, she would have missed it. He was going to go talk to Raven without her. "So, errands, huh?"

He rubbed his chin and stared out the windshield.

Just like Eric used to.

"If we're going to work together, we need to trust each other." She subvocalized her power word and pushed a thread of magic into his mind. Her head pounded as if her headache from earlier had never gone away.

"Yeah, errands," he said.

She pushed harder. Mother, the pain! The muscle in his jaw clenched.

"I really think we need to talk to Ms. Mitchelle." His words spilled out in a rush.

Capri focused on her magic. No, they didn't want to talk to Raven. It wouldn't do any good. She wasn't going to know anything. It was just wasting their time.

"I know it's a waste of time." He pressed his palms against his cheeks. "But it's a mistake to ignore talking to her. Particularly since we've got nothing else to go on."

Pressure built in Capri's head. Her headache roared. "It would be better to take a break, a step back." Take a breath, look at the big picture.

"I don't think we have enough of the picture yet." He squeezed his eyes shut.

Pain snapped through her head. Sharp, agonizing.

"I'm talking with Ms. Mitchelle," Ryan said. "I don't care if it's not important. I need a better feel for the youth center, and she's the person to talk to."

Another crack of pain. Capri's magic burst from his mind. It seared over her, burning through her veins, blinding her.

"You can take my car. I'll call a cab." He opened the door to get out.

"No." She fought to clear her vision, catch her breath, anything to feel even the slightest bit normal and not reveal her agony. "No, we'll talk with her together."

Mother of All. She'd never experienced anyone resist her earth magic like that before.

24

Nero's estate sat on a large swath of property on the outskirts of Newgate. Capri struggled not to grind her teeth as Miller drove up the winding driveway to the massive house sitting on the hill. Her head still pounded with agonizing beats, and the sun, which had finally broken through the clouds, sat low on the horizon, eye level, burning into her brain. It was only 5 p.m., but this time of year, the sunset came early, making it feel much later in the day than it actually was. But perhaps that had more to do with her headache—the one neither painkillers nor her soul magic could touch—and her inability to figure out how Miller had broken her earth magic compulsion.

"Ms. Mitchelle lives here?" he asked.

"The estate is owned by Nero Tassinari."

"The man's name is Nero? As in the Roman emperor Nero? Wow, talk about a pretentious family."

Oh, he didn't know the half of it. "Mr. Tassinari has holdings all over the world. I suspect the youth center is an attempt at tax breaks."

"How do you know this?"

"Previous investigation," she said.

Ryan parked in the circular driveway before the massive front steps and equally impressive front doors. "And was Ms. Mitchelle a part of that investigation?"

"No." Capri eased from the Camaro. Pain snapped through her head, and the icy world twisted and darkened. She grabbed the door. She wouldn't faint. Mother of All, she couldn't faint.

"You all right?" Eric asked—

No. Ryan.

"Fine," she growled. "Let's see if Ms. Mitchelle is home." She shoved away from the car and, with force of will keeping her upright, marched up the stairs and rang the doorbell.

"You sure—?"

She bared her teeth at him. "Yes."

His eyes widened, and he inched back a step.

Oh, shit. She'd revealed a hint of her drake-self. His mind wouldn't know what he'd just seen, but his instincts would know she was a predator.

"Miller, I'm fine. Really. Just—"

The door opened, and Miller straightened. A pretty drake stood in the doorway. She looked about thirty, but Capri got the sense that she was old. Her aura was edged with brighter, multicolored light. The bigger and stronger the edging, the older the drake—or at least that's what Capri saw. Other drakes might see something else. This was a drake who could remember the Great Scourge, and a drake didn't live that long, or avoid rebirth, without being smart. Wonderful.

"Is Ms. Mitchelle home?" Ryan asked.

The drake slid her gaze from Capri to Ryan then back to Capri.

"This is Special Agent Jones. We have questions for Ms. Mitchelle about her employee, Mr. Reynolds."

The drake's eyes narrowed. "Of course. Please come in. I'll go get her." And then, of course, call Nero and tell him what was going on.

They stepped into a large foyer with a church pew sitting against the left wall and a pedestal table with a pot of flowering nightshade against the right. The drake motioned to the pew, indicating they should sit, and then she headed down the hall.

Ryan sat, the wood squeaking with his weight, and pulled out his notepad. She glanced at the spot beside him. Just the idea of sitting there made her twitch with the need to get the hell out of there— even though she'd already done whatever damage she was going to do just by showing up. But another part of her, the part that pounded in her skull and throbbed around her heart, wanted to sit and feel his warmth, just *be* beside him.

He glanced up, his pale gaze meeting hers. Fear flickered across his expression, along with desire and something else she couldn't quite discern. But there had still been fear and that desire could have been her magic influencing him. She shouldn't have let him see her drake. She shouldn't have made him kiss her. She needed to erase that, make him forget everything.

He shifted, his gaze jumping back to his notebook, and her heart contracted. She had to fix this.

But maybe it was for the best. If he was afraid of her, then she couldn't fall in love with him, or rather back in love with who he reminded her of. What she felt for him wasn't real. It wasn't him she loved.

She inched to the edge of the foyer and stared down the hall. Polished wood floors, paneling, doors, and furniture. Even in the soft light of the crystal chandeliers, everything gleamed.

A door at the far end of the hall opened and a teenage girl stepped out, her ponytail bouncing with her giggles. A bright green aura pulsed around her. Capri's exhaustion froze. Even the pounding in her head froze.

She was staring at a mage. Mother of All, she was so young. Fifteen at the most.

Maybe she was a drake. Her aura was bright. Nero would never have a human mage in his house, unless his claim that he was a Traditionalist was a lie, a way to get closer to the throne.

No, the girl had to be a drake. But the Handmaiden didn't rebirth drakes into immature bodies, because the bodies stopped aging and would never reach adulthood. Even Gig, while looking like a teenager, was in the body of a twenty year old.

Capri had to have seen wrong. That was it. Her head hurt. Miller awoke wonderful and terrible memories. She wasn't thinking straight, and she certainly wasn't seeing things straight.

The girl turned back to the doorway and giggled again at something said from within the room. Her aura flickered again.

Ah, shit. Without a doubt, she was human and a mage. A powerful one at that, from how bright her aura was. Which meant whoever had made her into a mage had to have resided in her long enough to ensure a strong connection to the earth's magic.

The girl turned toward Capri and froze, her eyes large. Her aura beat stronger, the radius expanding around her. Mother of All, whatever earth magic she possessed was incredibly strong.

Capri tensed, her hand inching to her sidearm. But the kid's eyes were so large, so scared.

Dragon law said the girl had to be killed. Their race needed to be protected, needed to be kept secret. But that didn't make sense anymore. Hunter's inamorata was human. She knew about them, and she wasn't going to betray them.

A boy, a few years older then the girl, stepped up behind her, placing his hands on her shoulders. He, too, had the wavering aura of a human mage. His eyes widened as well.

Capri subvocalized her power word. She didn't want trouble, but the kids hadn't moved. They kept staring at her while she kept staring at them. And now her head pounded even more.

The door opened again, and Anaea stepped into the hall.

What the—?

Anaea said something to the teens, and they rushed down a side hall a few feet away. She turned to Capri, her aura a brilliant, unwavering white.

"Capri?"

Miller's footsteps sounded behind her. "What's up?" he asked.

Damn it, now he knew she had a connection to someone here. There was going to be one hell of an argument once this interview was over. A part of her thrilled at the idea. But she was going to have to pull rank, tell him it was FBI business, say he didn't have security clearance, or something, or rip into his mind and erase everything.

"Ms. Salis."

Anaea's eyes narrowed, and Capri took the magic she'd activated when she'd subvocalized her power word and slid it into Anaea's head. It had sort of worked back at the lawyers' office. Maybe if Anaea wasn't freaked out, Capri would have more success.

"Capri—?" Anaea's aura flared in response to Capri's magic.

Capri struggled not to squint against its glare. If Ryan saw her, he wouldn't understand what was going on since he couldn't see auras.

She willed Anaea to listen to her, trying to use her magic to alert the woman to use caution.

"Detective Miller, this is Anaea Salis." Please don't ask too many questions. It's not safe.

"Ms. Salis." There was an edge to Miller's voice that Capri couldn't quite place. It probably had to do with the secrets he suspected Capri was keeping from him. Boy, if he only knew the truth...

He'd probably lose his mind like every other human.

A small voice within her reminded her that Anaea hadn't lost her mind. She wasn't soul sick and she, a human, knew about dragons.

But Anaea was a one-in-a-million kind of human.

"I didn't know you worked for Mr. Tassinari."

"Mr.—?" Anaea's gaze darted to Ryan. "Oh, no. My... fiancé has business with him."

Her fiancé. The love of her life. The pain in Capri's head radiated down her neck and across her chest. Not every drake was fortunate enough to find her inamorato. Most drakes didn't. And really, Capri was happy for Hunter. But why would Hunter have business with Nero? Hunter hadn't come out and said he was against the Traditionalists, but hell, he was eternally bound to a human sorcerer. That flew in the face of all dragon traditions.

Except there were human mages wandering around Nero's house. And what the hell did any of this mean? It couldn't possibly mean Nero and Hunter were involved with Zenobia's mages. That wasn't either drake's style. These kids were also younger than the mages Diablo and her team had been chasing, like the kids back at the youth center. Which meant...? She had no idea.

Movement at the end of the hall drew her attention. Grey headed toward her, his gaze jumping from her to Anaea.

"Capri?" he asked.

"Do you know everyone in this house?" Miller asked.

Grey opened his mouth.

"This is Detective Miller. We're investigating Andy Reynolds's death. We're here to talk with Raven Mitchelle," Capri said. Please, let this farce end so she could corner Grey and find out what the hell was going on.

"Of course," Anaea said. "Absolutely, Special Agent Jones. I'll go get Ms. Mitchelle for you."

"No need," a soft feminine voice said from the far end of the hall. A leggy brunette with a long ponytail, the tip brushing her waist, strode toward them. "Ms. Salis, I suggest you continue your research."

"Of course, Raven." Anaea nodded, grabbed Grey's arm, and dragged him down the hall.

"What can I do for you, Special Agent?" Raven asked, her tone dark.

"You're the coordinator for the Newgate Youth Center?" Miller asked.

"Yes." Raven's glare never left Capri. Once the human, Ryan, was gone, they were going to have a serious conversation.

Oh, yes, they were. Did Nero even know there were human mages running around his house? How could he not? He was the coterie's doyen.

25

The heavy front doors closed behind Ryan, and he fought the urge to pound on them and demand the truth. Raven Mitchelle had lied to them. Bold-faced, blatantly lied. That boy in the hall had been the same one whose picture stood enshrined at the youth center, Tyler. The one who'd died in the fire, just like Pete had. But the more Ryan thought about Pete's death, the more it felt fake.

Seeing that kid made it really feel fake. Except Ryan had no proof of anything. Just a gut feeling, and while a good detective didn't ignore his gut, he also looked for proof. And right now, he couldn't grab the teen and demand DNA to prove whether he was Tyler Pimm or not. Not without looking completely insane.

"Are you coming?" Jones stared at him. She stood halfway to the Camaro, bathed in twilight. Between entering the house and exiting, night had fallen and so too had the chance to learn anything. Even she looked exhausted and pained, but about what, Ryan didn't know. There were too many options. Top two being the fact that the case was going nowhere, and that she was keeping secrets from him—not that he could be too upset about that. He was keeping secrets as well. Regardless, there was no hint of the monster he'd seen earlier, and while she didn't look as if she was going to faint, she still didn't look good.

"When was the last time you slept?"

She cocked an eyebrow, sassiness overwhelming the exhaustion. "Excuse me?"

"You look tired. We should take a break."

"A break?" A hint of that monster edged her expression. No, not a monster, a primal, ferocious... creature. Like a panther or a hawk. Wild, free, and crazy sexy.

Jeez. He lost all common sense around this woman. She was so vivacious and confident. Maybe his mind turned her into a creature because his brain couldn't recognize such strength in such a small, sexy package.

Even more ridiculous, he wanted to be chivalrous and do things for her—and watch her resist his kindness, fighting it tooth and nail.

"What the hell are you smiling at, Miller?" she asked.

Oh, yes, let's play this game.

He strode off the steps, his boots crunching in the salt, and marched to her. "Let me take you home."

"My car is at your sister's house."

"I'm not sure it's safe for you to drive in your condition."

She leaned forward, her breath, a frosty mist, curling around her face. "My condition?" Heat flared in her eyes.

"You almost fainted when we arrived. I should drop you off at home for a power nap. Then we should do dinner. Get your blood sugar up." And that would give him a chance to return here and find out what was really going on with a kid who should be dead, but wasn't—if in fact that was Tyler Pimm. Not to mention figure out why everyone in that house seemed to know Capri on a first-name basis.

Capri rose on tiptoe, drawing her nose closer to his. "My blood sugar is fine, I didn't faint, and I don't need a power nap."

His heart pounded. An inch, less than an inch, and their noses would touch. "I said *almost* fainted."

"Dinner, however, sounds like a solid idea." But her eyes said she wanted more than just dinner.

The front door banged open and Jones's gaze jumped over his shoulder.

"Did you need anything else, Special Agent?" Raven asked.

Capri growled. She actually growled.

Something had really gotten under her skin.

"No, Ms. Mitchelle," Ryan said—it didn't look as if Capri was going to answer. He slid past Capri to the car, got in behind the wheel, and waited for her to bring all her ferocious energy into the confinement of the Camaro.

The passenger door jerked open, and Capri slid into the seat beside him. Her expression was dark, but it was an anger mixed with electrifying attraction. "We need to talk."

Talking wasn't exactly what he had in mind. "Yes, we do."

Her phone chirped, and she pulled it from her pocket. "Jones."

Someone said something, the voice a deep rumble. Her expression hardened. "Got it."

"What's up?"

"I have to go." She glanced at the mansion, her expression dark. The same sudden shift of expression she'd had when Hiro had called about the third victim.

"Where to?"

"You can't come."

"You're not taking my car and leaving me here. I'm not standing around Ms. Mitchelle's driveway while I wait for a cab." Certainly not after she'd lied to him. Of course, if Capri left him here, he could pound on the door and demand real answers.

"You can wait on the road."

"The cold back road thirty minutes out of town? I don't think so." No way in hell was he letting her go alone. His future flash could happen wherever it was she was going. "Besides, you're in no condition to drive."

"I'm perfectly fine." She growled again and ice slid across his sinuses. "Get out."

He ground his teeth against the sudden freeze. "No. Where are we going."

"I don't have time to argue with you."

"So tell me where to drive."

The cold billowed, rushing over his head. He wanted to get out. Let her do her job. He didn't want to get involved with FBI business.

But he didn't want to leave her alone. What if wherever she was going was where his future flash would take place? He needed to be there to save her, since she'd never believe him if he told her the truth. "Where. Am. I. Driving?"

"You're not." A chill edged her voice. It joined with the freeze in his face. So damned cold. He wanted to get out.

But it was colder outside than in the Camaro.

Get out.

He reached for the handle.

No. He couldn't leave her alone.

He turned the engine on. "Where. To?"

The ice in his face snapped, exploding in frozen agony behind his eyes.

Capri gasped. She pressed her thumb to her temple. "We're going to The Mansion, the club near Ingram and Orchard."

"See, that wasn't so hard." But God, that might have been the hardest thing he'd ever had to do, and he had no idea why. He forced a smile, but from Capri's dark look and growl, he must have bared his teeth instead.

CAPRI'S HEAD HURT. MOTHER OF ALL, DID IT HURT. SHE'D NEVER FELT anything like it, not in the hundreds of years she'd been able to manipulate humans. And now twice in as many days Miller had resisted her earth magic. It just wasn't possible.

And yet a part of her thrilled at the thought. Here was a man who could resist her manipulation. But it wasn't supposed to matter. She was supposed to have relationships with drakes. She couldn't manipulate her own kind. But she didn't want any of her fellow drakes. She wanted Ryan... No, Eric... No—

She didn't know anymore. And yet, she did. Eric had never flashed his teeth at her like Ryan had. It had taken everything she had not to grab him and kiss him right there.

He gunned the Camaro out of the driveway, and she clutched her seat belt, focusing on it digging into her hand. Ignore the headache. Ignore Ryan and the hot desire burning through her.

Swipe had said they had a line on one of the mages who'd escaped from the warehouse, possibly Eddie Boyd. That was what she needed to focus on. One thing at a time. She'd deal with all the questions about Nero and Grey once she had time to sit and really think about it.

Right now, she and Miller were only five minutes away from Boyd's location at The Mansion, a popular gentlemen's club in a massive old Victorian house that sat atop a hill on the edge of town— except there was nothing gentle about the place. It was a strip club, with gaudy lights, bad food, and overpriced beer that drew the dregs of male society and the curious young.

Given how this was just a cell phone ping and Gig wasn't certain if there was actually a mage on the other end, they weren't going to inform Diablo. That and the leak in the Asar Nergal made contacting him before the last possible minute a bad idea. But that didn't mean someone shouldn't get there as fast as dragonly possible.

With luck, the phone would be on one of the mages, Capri would be able to recognize him, and they'd be able to corner him. And corner him in private, since containing the memories of a large crowd was difficult at the best of times. Worst case, she'd search the club and not notice a mage aura, then Gig would show up and pinpoint the phone.

Here was hoping nothing magical happened. With her headache, trying to manipulate a crowd was going to be a nightmare. Without a doubt, she wouldn't be able to convince Miller to stay in the damned car, which meant she was going to have to deal with him and Swipe in the very least. This was going to be one head-aching mess.

The Camaro fishtailed around a corner. Miller turned into the spin, the wheels caught, and he evened out into his lane as if nothing had happened.

No, the mess— the *nightmare* was what she was going to have to do when all this was over. The more time Miller spent with her, the more likely he'd figure out something weird was up—if he hadn't already. He'd never be able to figure out the truth, never know she was a dragon, that was beyond human understanding.

But Ryan was starting to resist her earth magic. She didn't know if she'd be able to surgically erase the last few days. And doing a full memory wipe was out of the question. She wasn't going to do that to him. But not doing any of the options meant disobeying Dragon law.

Miller pulled into the parking lot at the club and cut the engine. "So."

No matter what she wanted, the odds of getting him to wait in the car were next to nothing. Even if she made him promise to stay, she was certain he'd sneak out after she'd gone inside. It would be what she'd do.

"So. I'm here to see if I can recognize a suspect. Eddie Boyd. 5'9", Caucasian, dark wild hair and beard. In desperate need of a shave and haircut."

"And if we see him?"

"We keep eyes on him until the rest of my team can get here." And Miller stayed out of the line of fire. The last time they'd run into these mages, Swipe had gotten shot. He could heal. Miller couldn't. "Listen, these guys are dangerous."

He cocked an eyebrow. "You did not just say that. I'm a cop, remember."

Yeah, but he wasn't used to this kind of danger. She still didn't know all of the earth magics these mages possessed, but regardless, any magic was dangerous for a human. Mother of All, she shouldn't have let him come along.

"Fine." She shoved open her door. "Stupid, stubborn..." God damned human.

"I heard that."

Oh, shit. Did she say that out loud?

"It's a Y chromosome thing. We men, we get ridiculous ideas in our heads that our friends may need backup, and then you just can't shake us."

Relief flooded her. Thank God. He thought she'd been talking about his gender.

She marched across the icy lot to the path leading to the front door.

Ryan fell into step beside her, as if they'd worked together for more than just two days. "Don't worry, we grow on you."

"Kind of like a fungus?"

"Gee, couldn't think of anything wittier to add?"

She shot him a heated look and flashed just a hint of teeth—she couldn't resist.

He grinned back. A stunning show of teeth that flamed the burn within her into an inferno. She didn't care he was human. And most of her no longer cared that he looked like Eric. Eric never smiled at her like that. He'd never thrilled at the prospect of a fight. Mother of All, she wanted to *know* Ryan Miller.

And that wouldn't happen if some stupid mage killed him.

"Tell me you're carrying your sidearm."

"Yes. I've got your back. It is just surveillance."

Yeah, and in her line of work surveillance could turn ugly. When Swipe showed up and saw Miller, it certainly would get ugly.

She'd cross that bridge when she got to it.

"Remember, I'm in charge."

"I wouldn't dream of it any other way."

Snow at the front of The Mansion had been cleared from the front walk and the three dozen narrow steps leading up to the porch, but that was as far as maintenance seemed to go with the place. The building sagged, and a heavy slick of filth coated the blacked-out front windows. Music blared through the door, rattling the windows in their frames. A heavy-set man wearing an open leather jacket—that likely couldn't close around his girth—greeted them with a scowl, but didn't give them trouble.

Inside, throbbing music and a cloud of machine-made smoke enveloped them. The smell of the place hit Capri before her night vision kicked in: stale beer, vomit, and unwashed bodies. Yeah, gentlemen's club indeed.

She and Miller stood at the mouth of what would have been a vast, sunken living and dining room. Tables and chairs filled the area between them and the stage at the back. The entire left side was the bar, and on the right were booths for more private seating.

The place was packed with mostly men but there were a few women among them. The music changed and the crowd by the stage cheered as a woman in a gold bra and thong and a gauzy something over top strode out to perform.

Ryan leaned close. "Do you see him?"

His breath slid across her neck and cheek, drawing a delicious shiver that she struggled to ignore. She searched the crowd, but even with her night sight, there were too many people for her to find anyone at just a glance. "Not yet. We need to get to a more suitable vantage point."

"I agree."

He slid an arm around the back of her waist and drew her close. Another shiver raced over her. The heat from his body enveloped her. She could be this way forever, wrapped in his arms and pressed against him, but with less clothes—definitely less clothes.

She bit back a groan. Focus on the damned job. She could undress him later.

No, never later. He was a human.

She eased away, putting space between them—horrible, desperately needed space.

"Let's try over here." She slipped through the crowd toward the bar, knowing he'd follow. She could feel him at her back, his aura brushing hers. Which was impossible. She couldn't sense auras that way—only see them—and besides, he didn't have one.

She forced her gaze to slide over the crowd, searching for a real aura, any telltale flicker that could indicate a mage. The music pounded around her, bodies pressed close.

Ryan pressed close...

Focus.

There. A flicker of something at the edge of the stage, near the back. Wild dark hair, bushy beard. It was Boyd.

"Hey, isn't that the guy from the warehouse?" Miller asked.

"Yep." She checked her watch. Ten more minutes until Swipe and Gig showed up. She pulled out her phone and dialed Swipe.

"Yeah?" he growled over the phone.

"I've got eyes on Boyd. What's your ETA?"

"Five minutes. Keep your head. The others might be there as well."

Ryan stepped close again.

Keeping her head would be easier said than done.

Boyd's gaze jumped over the room. Capri pulled Ryan around, putting him between her and Boyd. She leaned into Ryan's chest, letting his warmth and strength envelope her again.

"He's searching the room, isn't he?" Ryan asked.

Why did he have to be sexy and smart, too? It made everything so much more complicated. She fought to concentrate past that thought and the feel of Ryan's rock-hard chest under her fingers. But, boy, was it difficult.

She peered around his biceps to watch Boyd. The mage shifted on his stool, his gaze still jumping over the crowd. She couldn't tell if he was waiting for someone or just keeping a nervous watch for trouble.

Then his gaze landed on her and his eyes widened. He couldn't have possibly recognized her, hiding behind Ryan. But the recognition was clear. He had to be able to see auras and knew she was a dragon.

He scrambled off his stool, jerked to the back, and dashed through the *employees only* door.

"Shit." Capri pushed around Ryan and shoved through the men between her and Boyd. She shouldered open the employee door and drew her firearm. Boyd raced to the end of the hall. He shoved aside a girl in fluttery red feathers and stumbled to the back exit.

He was getting away and they needed him alive to identify the rest of the mages.

She subvocalized her power word and shoved her magic into his head. "Stop."

Pain exploded across her temples. Her knees buckled, and she grabbed the wall to keep her balance.

Miller drew his sidearm.

Boyd staggered. He wrenched around to face her, his expression going blank for a heartbeat. With a growl, he drew a gun, but his hands shook, ruining whatever aim he had. "Get out of my head, snake!"

"Put the weapon down." Agony burned through her. Her earth magic wavered, the thread in his mind thinning and growing weak.

The muscle in Miller's jaw twitched.

"I said, get out!" Boyd fired. The bullet zinged into the wall beside her head.

Miller yanked her behind him and fired, hitting Boyd in the shoulder.

Boyd scrambled out the back door.

Son of a—

"We need him alive." She grabbed Miller and jerked him to face her. "And if you pull me behind you again, I'll shoot you myself."

She shoved past him and rushed to the door. Boyd was getting away and all she wanted was to stay in the hall and kiss Ryan.

26

Ryan rushed after Capri, out the back door and into the parking lot. He had no idea what the hell had just happened. Capri hadn't shot at Boyd even after he'd fired at her. She'd just stood there, staring at him. Instinct had kicked in—protect Capri—and he'd fired.

If he'd been thinking, he should have known Capri would have been pissed at that. And yet, she hadn't fired back. Even a rookie on his first day knew that when shot at by a cornered suspect, you fired back.

Now Eddie Boyd had probably gotten into a car, and they'd lost him. But Capri ran across the lot to the snow bank on the far side. She crouched, her gun in one hand, her other pressed against the frozen asphalt. She squeezed her eyes shut, her pain clear. Something was wrong, but he hadn't seen any blood on her in the hall, so she couldn't have been shot.

"You got him good." She pointed to the dark blood in the snow.

"I should have aimed for his leg."

"Center of mass is always the safer bet when they're firing at you." She pulled out her phone. "Boyd recognized me and ran. He's injured and in the industrial park behind the club. Have Gig zone in on my phone."

She pocketed her phone and straightened. More pain flashed across her expression. With a growl, she climbed over the snowbank.

Beyond lay twenty feet of unfenced yard with towering evergreens and maples. Three paths had been trampled into the snow, each going to adjoining streets or parking lots. Capri scanned the ground for a second, no more than two, then followed the one to the right. There, a few feet down, were more drops of blood.

Ryan had no idea how she'd managed to spot that in the dark so fast. There was so much more to this woman than met the eye. "What's the ETA on backup?"

"Three minutes." She picked up the pace.

Ryan followed, scanning the area for signs of Boyd.

The uneven path led around a clump of pines and down a steep incline to an auto wrecker's lot. Skeletons of dead vehicles crowded the partially plowed lot, creating dark nooks and towering walls of rusted metal.

Ryan held his breath, straining to hear Boyd's steps on the icy ground. The man had to be running. It was the only way for him to get so much distance between them, but the wrecker's yard was silent. The wind hissed and the dead vehicles groaned, but still no sound of Boyd. Where the hell was he?

Capri knelt and pressed her fingers to something dark on the trail again. More blood. They were still on his path.

"This way," she said, her voice low.

She skirted around a row of school bus shells into a wider area with a squat metal structure on the far side. A large garage door took up most of the one side, big enough for a big rig to drive in. Beside it stood a small human-sized door. A light above the small door cast an orange semi-circle on the ground, catching in the ice, and revealing streaks of sand that had been haphazardly strewn on the ground.

Capri stopped at the edge of the buses. "The trail leads to the door."

"How—?"

"The door handle. It's smeared with blood."

He squinted. There might be a dark smudge on the door, but from this distance, it was barely visible and might not be blood. "I'd say that's just a guess."

She flashed him a quick smile. "Or maybe I'm just that good." Her tone suggested she was good at other, more intimate things as well.

"I'm sure you are."

A hint of pain edged her eyes, and she blew out a quick breath, the mist curling around her face. "He's bleeding and needs medical attention. I'm guessing he's hoping there's a first aid kit in the garage. At the very least, we have to check the doors and clear it, unless we can find a blood trail going around the building."

"I'll—" He was going to say take point, but doubted she'd let him. Even if she was feeling bad enough that she needed him to take point, she couldn't risk letting a detective from a different town with a questionable record ruin this, whatever this was. "I'll cover you."

"No. You need to go around back and cut off any possible exits."

"You can't go in alone."

"I'm not. My team will be here in a minute. We're just checking the door and getting eyes on Boyd again."

Yeah, how much did he believe that?

"Unless you think you can't follow that order?" she asked. "It's going to be difficult enough explaining why I have an Elmsville detective assisting on a federal case." That sense of feralness glowed from her pale eyes. Even with the pain, she was determined to follow through. She was more than just a petite strawberry blond in a pantsuit. She was stronger than her diminutive package suggested, and he'd be a fool to stand in the way.

The air around her rippled, and a security door flew open behind her. Gunfire exploded. He ground his teeth. *Pull it together.*

Her eyes narrowed. "Can you follow orders?"

He nodded. Another explosion rattled through him. Capri didn't react. It wasn't real. It. Wasn't. Real. "Let's do this."

She slipped around the front of the buses, her gun held ready, and rushed across the parking lot toward the door.

Ryan sucked in a quick breath and followed, running through the imaginary security door. He angled to the side of the real building, slowing as Capri reached the small entrance. She met his gaze and tried the door. It opened a fraction, and she froze. With a jerk of her chin, she told him to secure the back. She'd probably only give him a few seconds before sneaking in.

He forced himself to turn away and creep along the side of the garage to the back. Yep, covering the back was important, but so was covering your partner. She'd already been distracted in The Mansion's back hall. Whatever was wrong hadn't been fixed.

Sure enough, there was a back door. Ryan eased up beside it. A cloud scuttled over the moon, enveloping him in darkness. Something glimmered from under the edge of the door. There was definitely a light on inside, but that didn't mean there was someone there.

"We've got to get moving," a harsh voice said on the other side of the door.

Ryan froze, holding his breath and listening. Maybe Capri *had* seen blood on the door.

"Eddie needs a doctor," another voice said. This one sounded young, maybe a teen.

"I'm fine," a third voice growled. That had to be Boyd.

There were at least three men in there. Cold seeped into Ryan's coat, biting his cheeks and neck. He resisted the urge to call Capri's cell and warn her. If he did, the guys in the garage might hear it, and he'd heard no indication that backup had arrived.

Besides, as much as Capri didn't look like she was at the top of her game right now, he had to trust she knew how to do her job. She wasn't some rookie he'd been assigned to train. She was an FBI agent. Except that was all he really knew about her. He had no idea how long she'd been on the job, or even what her team did.

"We have to get moving. The snakes are on my trail," Boyd said.

"You brought the snakes here?" Young Guy's voice jumped an octave.

"What the hell made you think to bring the snakes here?" Harsh Voice asked.

"They shot me. I wasn't thinking," Boyd said.

"Fucking moron," Harsh growled.

Something whooshed on the other side of the door.

"What the hell?" Harsh yelled. "Snakes."

"Not just any snake. Death," a slick new tenor said.

Someone screamed. Something clattered to the floor, and two shots exploded. Something else boomed. It sounded like it was on the far side of the garage.

"Son of a—" That was Capri.

Another burst of gunfire.

Ryan yanked on the back door. It wouldn't open.

More gunfire.

Shit shit shit. He had to get in there. Had to know what was going on. This could be his future flash coming true.

He kicked at the door. It still didn't budge.

Another scream. High pitched. He couldn't tell if it was a man or a woman.

He kicked the door again. Come on. Come on. He wrenched back to kick again, and the door flew open. Boyd stood in the opening, one hand pressing a rag to his shoulder, his eyes wide.

Ryan yanked his gun up. "Freeze."

Faster than Ryan thought possible, Boyd leapt forward, knocked Ryan's gun aside, and shoved past him.

Ryan staggered back. His foot hit ice and swept out, slamming him to one knee. Someone inside the garage screamed again. Inside, the man he and Capri had hid from, back at Andy's house, pounded his fists into a large man's gut. A small man on the ground scrambled away, while four more men rushed toward Ryan and the door.

Capri raced after them from the other side of the room, her eyes narrowed with pain. "Stop," she yelled. One man stopped, his expression stunned. The other three stormed toward Ryan.

He fired, hitting one man in the leg, dropping him to his knees. The other two barreled past, the first man seizing the front of Ryan's jacket and tossing him against the side of the garage.

He slammed into it with so much force the air burst from his lungs, and his head snapped back. Pain raced across his chest and skull, and his knees buckled. He struggled to catch his breath, breathe past the agony.

The man from Andy's house zip-tied his unconscious suspect to a pipe then raced to the back door. He was on the far side of the garage one second and then beside Ryan the next, glaring at him. Ryan tensed, gun raised.

"He's with us," Capri said, but Ryan couldn't tell if it was directed at him or the man.

She grabbed the man Ryan had shot, yanked him over to the back door, and zip-tied him to the handle. "Funny seeing you here, Diablo."

The man, Diablo, snorted. "Didn't think you'd need help." His gaze jumped to where the other men had fled. "When were you going to tell me you had a line on their den?"

"When I had them in custody. Now do you mind? They're getting away."

"Give it a moment." Diablo's eyes grew unfocused and he rolled his shoulders as if trying to relax. "Two went to the left, one to the right."

Headlights flashed across the garage from the front door.

"Looks like your backup is here. I'll start with the single then go after the double."

"Not if I catch them first. Miller, stay here." She bolted to the left, along a path between the shattered carcasses of cars.

"Hell, no." He raced after her.

"I said, stay with the perps."

"They're secure, your team has them, and I'm not leaving you without backup." There were two of them, one of her, and she still looked like she was in pain.

"I said, stay with the perps," she growled, still running along the path.

"And I said, no."

She wrenched toward him, radiating that feral monster again, making her seem bigger, more powerful than her tiny frame implied.

He squared his shoulders.

She hissed and flashed him a hard smile—he wasn't even sure it was a smile.

"They're getting away, Special Agent."

Her expression darkened and turned sensual. Standing his ground against her turned her on. "What am I going to do with you, Detective?"

"I can think of a few things." It turned him on, too.

She jerked to the path, gun ready, back on the hunt.

He followed. He had no idea what had just happened, but a part of him really liked it.

They chased the men out of the trees onto the street of a new development. The road twisted down into a valley where half of the lots were empty and the other half had houses in various stages of construction. Capri picked up her speed and Ryan pushed to match her, worry and excitement pounding through him. His breath puffed around him in white clouds that sparkled in the street-lights, but he stayed focused on the men.

The smaller of the two, a man with a torn jean jacket and a wild blond beard, stumbled. The other, a broad-shouldered black man with a jagged scar running down the side of his face, didn't hesitate. He careened to the right, into the shadows between two partially sided houses. The first man, Blond Beard, shoved up to his feet and headed left.

Ryan glanced at Capri. With a nod, she headed after Scar. That was all the communication they'd needed. No words. Again, he was struck with the sense that they'd been partners for years.

Blond Beard ducked up the driveway of a finished house and rushed into the shadows beside it. If he managed to get back into the woods behind the development, Ryan might not be able to find him.

Ryan put on a burst of speed. His chest burned from the cold air and effort. He raced into the fenced-in yard.

Blond Beard staggered to a stop before hitting the fence at the back.

Ryan trained his gun on him. "Hands where I can see them."

The man spun around, hands up. He glared at Ryan.

"On your knees."

The man pursed his lips, his gaze sliding over Ryan. Then his lips curled back in a sneer. "You're not a snake."

Ryan widened his stance. "On your knees."

"No." The man leapt at him.

Ryan pulled the trigger. The shot shattered the quiet of the subdivision. Blond Beard gasped and pressed a hand to his chest, but continued to barrel forward. With his free hand, he slammed his palm against Ryan's gun.

The weapon ripped from Ryan's hand and smashed into the wall beside him. Flecks of brick shot into the air, stinging his face. The force was stronger than anything he'd ever experienced. How the hell was the man still moving? He'd shot him square in the chest.

Blond Beard grabbed for the front of Ryan's jacket. He twisted out of the way, but the man snagged his shoulder and yanked, tossing him into the backyard.

He crashed into the packed snow. Cold bit his face and neck. His chest burned. So did his cheek. He couldn't tell if the ice had sliced it open or not. He shoved up to his feet, but Blond Beard pounced, hammering a fist into Ryan's chest.

More pain exploded within him. Something cracked. He'd never encountered someone so strong before, and would have never guessed the man would have that kind of strength, given his slight stature and the gunshot wound. He should be hurting more than Ryan.

Blond Beard swung at Ryan's head. He ducked, sending spikes of pain shooting through his chest, and rammed his fist into the man's kidney. It felt like hitting a brick wall. Blond Beard grunted, twisted, and wrenched Ryan's arm up.

Pain sliced through his shoulder, and Ryan ground his teeth against the agony, fighting the darkness swarming the edge of his vision. He clawed at Blond Beard's hands, but couldn't break his grip.

Cold air swept over him with a whoosh. The man growled, wrapped an arm across Ryan's neck, and spun around.

The dark-haired man from Andy's house, Diablo, stood on the edge of the patio, his sidearm in his hand, hanging at his side. Ryan couldn't figure out how Diablo had gotten into the yard so fast. He'd gone in the opposite direction at the wrecker's yard.

"I'll kill him, snake."

Diablo shrugged. "Go ahead."

"Gee, thanks," Ryan gasped.

The man tightened his arm around Ryan's neck.

Ryan tensed to ram his elbow into the man's gut. Diablo jerked his gun up and fired.

The man's head snapped back and his grip on Ryan loosened. Ryan leapt away. The man staggered, but didn't drop. Instead, he straightened and ran his thumb over a red welt on his forehead.

"Want to try again, snake?" he said. "Your bullets don't bother me."

Ryan's brain stuttered. What the hell?

Diablo snorted. "I can think of other things that will hurt."

The air around Ryan gusted, blowing up snow from the ground, and Diablo vanished. With a whoosh, he reappeared in front of the man. Diablo seized the man's coat, and with another whoosh, they both disappeared.

Ryan pressed a hand to his side and stared at the spot where they'd just been. Every breath was agony, but every thought hurt more. He couldn't figure out what had just happened. He must have blacked out or something... twice. People didn't just disappear. That wasn't possible.

ONE OF THE CLEAN TEAM'S MANY SUVS PULLED TO THE CURB BESIDE Capri, and Swipe stormed out. "I thought I said to get rid of the human."

Capri yanked the big black mage with the jagged scar running down the side of his face to his feet and pushed him toward the vehicle. "I took your suggestion into consideration."

"So why is he still around?"

She shoved the mage into the back seat and wrenched around to face Swipe. There wasn't time for this. She had to back up Miller before the only remaining mage hurt him. "Because I have uses for the human, and I'm still the team leader. You want the job, take it from me."

Swipe hissed and leapt at her. She shot him in the gut. He staggered, and she grabbed the front of his coat and slammed him beside the SUV's open back door. The mage yelped but stayed in his seat.

"Still the leader." She pressed her gun to Swipe's heart. The shot wouldn't kill him, but it would hurt a lot more than a gut-shot.

"What's wrong with you?" Swipe growled, his eyes hard.

"I've got the human under control."

"It doesn't look like it to me."

He was right. She didn't have anything under control. But there was no way she was going to admit that. "Look closer."

The air whooshed around them and Diablo gated in beside her. He raised a sculpted eyebrow in question.

Capri turned from Swipe to face Diablo. He was alone.

"Where is your mage?" And why was Diablo gating around like humans couldn't notice him?

"I've got the mages contained."

Swipe growled, stormed back to the driver's side of the SUV, and got in. Diablo grabbed her arm and tugged her a few feet away, out of casual earshot. "You need to take care of your human."

"Excuse me?" Just great. Everyone had seen Miller and everyone thought it was their business to tell her how to handle hers.

"He's seen too much. Do your thing." And by *thing* he meant wipe Miller's mind.

"What did you do?" Damned cavalier drake, not caring who his lack of discretion hurt.

"The mage was bulletproof with enhanced strength. The most expedient solution was to gate him into confinement."

"You gated in front of Mil— a human? I should report you."

Diablo leaned close, but there was nothing sensual about the action. It was all menace. "I figured you'd rather wipe the human's mind than go to his funeral." Who was this drake? Diablo didn't care if a human died. At least he never had before. "If you don't want to take care of things, I'll be forced to make his family pick out his coffin."

Mother, no. She grabbed his jacket, and pressed her gun to his shoulder. "You wouldn't dare."

"The law is the law." He leaned into her firearm, as if daring her to shoot. The shot would hurt, but again, the damned thing wouldn't kill him—although she wasn't sure how fast he healed. If she was lucky, the wound, and the accompanying agony, would last minutes instead of seconds.

"Do your job, or I'll do mine," he said.

Damned fucking Asar Nergal. She shoved him back and holstered her gun. "So you screw up, the humans pay, and I have to clean up the mess. Just great. It's always the way."

"I'm pretty sure it wasn't me who screwed up first. You have until dawn to deal with him." He grabbed her arm and the disorienting twist of his rare, rapid, free-gating ability swept around her.

Blackness swallowed the street where she'd grabbed her mage. Her stomach heaved and the sense of the world tilting flooded her. Then the darkness receded. Her foot hit asphalt, her knees buckled, but she managed to keep standing. She now stood on a brightly lit suburban road. The streetlights shimmered in the snow and ice lying across postage-stamp sized lawns. Houses in various stages of construction lined the road.

Diablo pointed down the walk of a fully finished house. "Your human is back there."

"He's not *my* human."

Diablo flashed a hint of teeth. "Of course he isn't."

With a whoosh, he gated away.

Capri followed the path to the back of the house, keeping her footsteps quiet, uncertain of what she was going to walk in on.

Ryan sat on a crate beside a pile of unlaid patio stones. He pressed his arm to his side as if it hurt to breathe and his expression kept sliding from confusion to disbelief to blank then stunned.

She wanted to roar, go back to Diablo, and rip his thoughtless head off. He didn't care about anyone but himself. Humans were nothing to him, toys he discarded once they no longer suited him. If she could gate without an anchor, she'd return to the SUV and shoot him.

Except he wouldn't be there anymore. He would have taken the mage and returned to the Dragon Court. The only drake left at the SUV would be Swipe. And while she could shoot him to vent her frustration, that wouldn't help the situation. Swipe had told her to lose Miller—whether his reasons were to protect Ryan or not was beside the point. If she'd just listened to Swipe, she wouldn't be in this mess. Ryan wouldn't be in this mess.

She stepped into the yard, purposefully crunching ice so he'd hear her.

His head shot up, his gaze searching the darkness. All confusion was gone. In its place was determination, wariness, surety. This was the man she admired. So much like Eric and yet so different. She could almost believe she'd mistaken the confusion for something else, something innocent. But that was fooling herself. Even if his mind didn't break at the impossible, dragon law demanded she wipe his memories or kill him. The kindness was the memory wipe.

She subvocalized her power word. Lightning snapped through her head. She swallowed back a gasp. A thread of magic flickered to life then slipped away.

If she was going to do this right, she'd need time. Ryan had already resisted her compulsion. If she didn't want to completely wipe his mind and turn him into a blathering idiot, she needed a place to relax and concentrate.

His gaze found hers in the darkness. "Hey."

"Hey." More pain lanced through her head. What she really needed was a few days, but Diablo wasn't a drake to forget his words, particularly when it came to humans. He'd said she had until dawn. "You okay?"

"I'll live." He sucked in an uneven breath, wincing. A hint of light flickered from his eyes. Mother, how she wished it was real and that he was a drake and possessed magic.

In a way, he did. She no longer saw him as Eric's doppelgänger, and she still felt something for him. Whatever that something was, it was more than what she'd felt for Eric... maybe not more, just different?

Her heart contracted. And maybe she was fooling herself. What she felt for Ryan *was* more, strange and uncontrolled.

"Any idea how far from the car we are?" The light flickered again, sliding across his cheeks and forehead.

"I'll call a cab. I think that'll be easier." God, her head hurt. Now it felt as if everything about him radiated light.

"Are you okay?" Ryan asked. "Do I need to get you to a hospital?"

She snorted, sending a spike of pain through her head. "I should ask the same of you." But if they went, she'd have to wait to wipe his memories.

"I've got bruised ribs. Nothing I haven't had before, and nothing a doctor will be able to do much about." His gaze grew unfocused and a hint of his earlier confusion slid across his expression. "What I could use is a drink."

"I know just the place." God damn it, she was going to take him home. Not to have her way with him like she wanted, but to erase every last bit of herself from his memory. This hurt so much more than just leaving Eric.

28

Capri slid her key into her front door. She couldn't get her heart to stop pounding. Mother of All, she didn't want to wipe his mind. She wanted the complete opposite. She wanted him to know everything, know what she really was and accept her. But that was impossible. He was already struggling with what Diablo had let him see, and knowing the truth would drive him insane.

Ryan shifted behind her, easing closer. His heat, his presence, permeated her senses, as if his aura brushed against hers—an aura he couldn't have because he wasn't a dragon. God, she was going crazy with want. The drive here, in his too-small Camaro, had been too much to bear. She'd convinced herself it was the guilt of what she had to do that made her flash from hot to cold and back again. Except it wasn't what she *had* to do, but what she *wanted*.

She'd been through this before. With Eric.

She couldn't do it again.

"Having trouble with the lock?" he asked.

How long had she been standing on her front step? "No."

She turned the key and opened the door. A rush of emotions, guilt, fear, and desire, flooded her. Since Eric, she hadn't brought anyone home, human or drake. This was her sanctuary. The only place safe and untouched by dragon politics and fleeting human relationships.

And here she was, inviting Ryan in to deal with both in one foul, mind-destroying moment.

He followed her inside, staying close, as if he, too, was magnetically pulled to her. Her pulse stuttered. Which way should she go? Follow her duty or follow her heart?

She turned to him, pulled, drawn, controlled by a force she couldn't explain, and met his gaze. Pale green irises ringed pupils full and filled with a matching desire. The world fell away and all that remained was Ryan. Her want burned hotter, darker, more than her want had ever been for Eric. She'd thought she'd loved Eric, and while she had, what she'd felt had been light and fleeting. What flooded her now was deep, threatening, consuming. She could lose herself in Ryan and not care. Dragon law be damned. She would defy them all for this man. She would die for him.

"Capri." He breathed her name.

It shivered over her, fluttering to the center of her being, and a purr trembled deep within her in response.

She froze, an ice sweeping over her.

The purr threatened again. A dragon only purred for her—

No. This was wrong. So wrong. She jerked away from him, heading to the kitchen.

"You wanted a drink?" she forced out as she glanced back at him.

"Yeah." His gaze said he wanted something else.

God! The purr rumbled again. Except it couldn't be a purr. She was mistaken. She *had* to be mistaken. Dragons only purred for an inamorato. And she was not, could not, be inamorated.

She pulled out her bottle of Glengoyne and two glasses. The lip of the Scotch bottle rattled against the tumblers as she poured. She fought to make her hands stop shaking but couldn't.

She had to wipe his memory. It was for the best. Diablo would kill him otherwise. But Mother, she didn't want him to forget her. She wanted—

Another purr bubbled low in her throat.

God damn it! It was not a purr! She was not that drake, the one destined for a love that could never happen.

"This is one heck of a house. You should have told me the FBI makes way more than a local cop," he said. "I would have changed jobs."

She grabbed the glasses and forced herself to look at him. He stood in the doorway to her greenhouse, one hand on the door frame by his head, the other pressed to his side as if that would help ease the pain of his bruised ribs. He looked completely at home, framed by the greenery and orchids as if he belonged right there. As if he'd always been there.

She crossed to him, an agonizing push-pull within her, drawing her inexorably to him no matter how much logic told her she had to keep her distance.

"It's a family home." She offered him the Scotch.

He reached for the glass, his fingers brushing hers. Electricity zinged up her arm. Her breath caught in her throat and the zing turned to a scorching, liquid heat that rushed straight to her core.

The purr rumbled in her throat, soft, sensual, and all too real. No, no, no.

She shoved past him, heading into her hoard, not caring where, only knowing she needed balance in a world that wouldn't stop twisting.

This was a disaster. She wasn't supposed to be inamorated with him.

Just the thought sent more need searing through her.

Mother, please no.

But her spirit had chosen. Against all common sense, crossing species lines and defying dragon law, her spirit had picked Ryan. All her desire had never been because he reminded her of Eric. It was because she was inamorated with him. A human.

Her throat tightened, tears burning her eyes. She emptied her glass, but the alcohol didn't burn away the hurt and desperation and soul-deep craving. It didn't help put the world back into place. Nothing could be in place anymore. Ryan was human, and unlike Anaea with her magic, Ryan would live a too-short human life.

The thought was overwhelming and agonizing. Her soul had destined her for a few years of bliss and then an eternity of heartache.

"Capri." He drew close, his impossible aura tingling across her senses.

Her pulse pounded. Perhaps a few years of bliss would be enough. If she was lucky, it would be sixty or seventy years. The joy and pleasure of that time could fill the rest of her lonely eternity. It would be enough. It would have to be enough.

But that didn't solve the problem that he'd age and she wouldn't. She'd have to leave early, like she had with Eric, or tell him the truth.

Mother, she *wanted* to tell him the truth.

Except her love couldn't save him from going crazy.

Her breath hitched in her throat again.

The only way to salvage this situation was to wipe his mind of every thought and feeling and memory of her. She had to remove everything, erase herself from his mind. It was the only way to keep him sane.

"Where are you?" he asked, his breath sliding warm over the back of her neck.

She wanted his hands and mouth there, not just his breath. "I'm... I'm thinking about the case."

"No, you're not." He drew closer, his hard chest brushing her back.

The electric attraction snapped around her. She could just lean back, give her body to him, and let the world, dragon politics, her duty, everything vanish in his embrace.

But if leaving Eric had been hard, leaving Ryan would shatter her. It would be easier not to give in and not take that final step to a true merging of souls.

She stepped away from him. The agony of even that single step was excruciating.

"The case," she forced out.

"God damn it, Capri." He grabbed her arm and yanked her back to him, softly grunting in pain with the sudden movement.

"You should watch your ribs."

"We're not talking about my ribs. We're talking about us." He tipped her head up to look her in the eye. The world fell away again, and she was drowning in his essence. If she could just stay there with him.

No. She had to stop it before it started. End it before his death could destroy her... or her very presence hurt him.

That was the only thing she could give him. She couldn't present him with shinies and meat and pieces for his hoard. She couldn't spend his too-short life lying to him. And she couldn't spend her life knowing the heartache that awaited her.

This way was better. Fast. Rip off the bandage. Erase his memories and save him. She subvocalized her power word, but he captured her lips with his and all concentration vanished. All that remained was the feel of him and the heat he fueled within her. Every nerve burned with need and desire and rightness.

He wrapped an arm around her back, drawing her closer as if he couldn't get close enough. And it wasn't. She needed him in her, filling her, searing his soul to hers.

Warmth rushed over her, pooling between her legs. She slid her hand under his shirt, trembling with the effort not to release her dragon and rip the cloth from his body.

A purr bubbled. He devoured it, kissing and nipping, teasing her dragon-nature.

She growled and tugged at his shirt. He eased it off, then pulled her tight against him again, as if unable to withstand even a second of separation. The pain of his bruised ribs was still there, clear in his eyes, but there was a stronger, consuming passion there, too. His erection pressed against her, hard, more proof that he wanted her as much as she wanted him.

Her purr trembled through her.

He moaned. "God, Capri. I want you so much."

The purr broke out in full. She couldn't hold it back and didn't want to anymore.

He drew back, the separation aching, but his fingers slid down her neck to the buttons on her shirt. Her breath hitched. He flicked open one button, then the next. Slowly. So damned slowly. Heat built within her, growing with every button he reverently released. His fingers traced her flesh, his touch so light, so sensual.

She closed her eyes, giving in. Her soul had chosen and if she was only going to get one night with her inamorato, she was going to enjoy it.

His breath burned across her neck. She tilted her head back, offering him more, offering him all of herself.

He took the invitation, his lips brushing against her throat, his hands trailing to the button on her pants.

Her heart pounded faster. He slid his lips down her neck to her breasts while he slipped her pants over her hips, letting the fabric ease down her legs.

She dug her fingers into his hair. His restraint was driving her crazy. She wanted him, all of him, now. She'd never felt so hot, so needy in the hundreds of years she'd been alive. She was so sensitive even the thought of him touching her made her burn.

He leaned back, a wicked, sensual gleam in his eyes. "Feel good?"

She growled. "What do you think?"

"I think I'm going too fast."

"You're not going fast enough." She grabbed the front of his pants, tugged him close, and undid the button.

He matched her growl and shoved her back against a worktable scrubbed clean and ready for work… she just never thought it would be ready for this.

He unhooked her bra and caressed one of her breasts, teasing the nipple into a fierce, straining point. Pleasure built, quivering, undulating, growing. His gaze burned into her, searing him completely on her soul. His other hand skimmed the edge of her panties. Lightning zapped at his touch.

Oh, God. She was melting. His fingers skimmed closer to her core. More heat rushed in response, so hard she ached. Then his fingers brushed her, darted away, then brushed again.

She was breathless, heady, desperate. She pulled at his pants and underwear, palming his thick, full erection.

He moaned and slid a finger into her. Yes, oh, yes. She shuddered, the sensation rushing through her. She arched back. More, please more. Electricity built within her as he stroked, consuming every part of her. But it wasn't enough. She had to have him, all of him. The need to give herself to him, bond her soul to his completely, was overwhelming. Male or female, when a dragon's soul had chosen, that was it. There was no one else. They wouldn't love another, wouldn't bond with another. She was his and he was hers.

She caressed his erection, struggling to be gentle, and drew a moan from him. She stroked harder, matching him touch for touch. His breath came fast and hard. Like hers. She wrapped her legs around his waist and drew him closer, pressing him against her, drawing his tip to her center.

A purr released in full. He pressed a little harder, teasing again, with the slow, agonizing pleasure of what she wanted, needed. Him in her. Them joined. He had to feel it, too. The energy swirling around them. The crackling of their auras against each other.

She'd never experienced anything like it in her life. It stole all breath and thought. All that remained with the truth of them.

Then he thrust into her. That truth erupted between them on breath and motion. His lips captured hers and he thrust again. Pumping harder, faster, filling her, filling the soul-bond. Her dragon roared, its passion white-hot, building into a ferocious climax. Climbing. Swelling.

It crashed over her, sweeping her up, filling every cell, every fiber of her being. Ryan cried out, he pulsed within her, sending more glorious ripples shuddering through her.

This was right. This was the way it was supposed to be. He had claimed her in the most personal way a human could and her soul had claimed him. He was her inamorato. Whether he accepted her or not, he was her soul's completion.

29

R yan brushed a strand of hair from Capri's face and she sighed, a fully satiated feminine sound. They'd curled up on a wide, cushioned bench in the middle of her greenery and flowers and had cuddled that way, half dozing, for... Ryan had no idea for how long. It could have been an eternity, and he wouldn't have cared.

This was a perfect moment. One he didn't want to end. They'd found meaning, understanding. It was a connection he couldn't put into words. There was something about Capri that reached to the center of his being, and he liked it.

He couldn't explain it. It certainly didn't make any sense. He barely knew this woman, and yet he knew, soul-deep, she was the one.

Which was ridiculous. Love at first sight didn't exist. His need to be with Capri, to protect her—not that she needed protecting—to have her permanently in his life was...

He didn't know what it was. But he knew, without a doubt, this was more than just lust. Sure, there was lust involved. Just the thought of her—and the feel of her skin pressed against him—made him hard.

But it was more than that. And so long as they stayed where they were, nothing could change and take whatever this was from him. Except neither of them could stay in this greenhouse, suspended in the glow of their connection, forever. They'd have to face the world and he couldn't let his ruined career destroy Capri's.

His heart jerked.

"What?" Capri asked, her voice soft and sensual like her body.

"What time is it?" He'd forgotten about Melissa.

"Got somewhere important to be?" she asked, her blue eyes bright with playfulness. She was stunning. Her skin was luminescent with satisfaction. That ferocious creature within her glimmered in her gaze, promising more passion and a fierce dedication to him if he accepted her.

And if he didn't get to Melissa, his ex would destroy this amazing woman's life. Just being associated with him could jeopardize it. If he cared for Capri, he couldn't accept what was promised in her gaze.

"I forgot, I have a meeting with someone." He eased off the bench, his bruised ribs complaining with the motion, and grabbed his pants. He felt for his phone, but it wasn't in his pocket. It must have slipped out.

"I didn't think you were that kind of guy. The love 'em and leave 'em type." She bit her bottom lip, her gaze traveling down his body, filled with heat and passion.

God! He could lose himself in her, take her again right now. But he couldn't let Melissa hurt her. When whatever this was with Pete or Andy or whoever was over, Capri would come to her senses.

"I'm sorry. This is important. I won't get another chance to deal with it if I don't make this meeting."

A phone rang, the tone bright and cheery. It wasn't his.

Capri sighed. "Looks like the world has returned." She fished through their clothing and pulled out her phone, but met Ryan's gaze before answering. "What we started here is not finished."

His pulse pounded, his desire swelling. No, it was definitely not finished.

"Jones." She pulled on her panties and bra, a black lacy set that accentuated her pale skin. "You sure?"

She eased around a table half-filled with plants and opened a laptop hidden among the pots. With a few clicks, she pulled up her email. "I'm opening it now. Thanks."

"What have you got?" he asked.

"Gig, ah— Special Agent Valverdis came through with the ATM footage." She opened the file.

A grainy recording filled the screen.

"Hiro put MacCabe's time of death at around ten last night." He needed to get to Melissa, but he couldn't pull himself away from a possible lead to a murder suspect.

"And Gig says there's only one person on the footage at that time."

A man walked into the picture, his back to the screen. Capri hit pause. The picture wasn't great. The man was bald or had a shaved head and he was Caucasian, but that was it.

Capri hit the play button, inching the footage along. "Come on. Look at the camera."

The man shifted. Over his shoulder, the light in MacCabe's bike shop went out.

"Does look like he's waiting for someone." Ryan leaned closer, savoring the heat radiating from Capri's skin. All they needed was a clear profile, then they could try facial recognition programs and get an ID.

The man shifted again. The door to the bike shop opened and MacCabe stepped out. He turned his back to the man, likely locking the shop's door.

The man stepped forward, away from the ATM. They were going to lose him without even getting a hint of his identity.

Then the man glanced over his shoulder. Capri hit the pause button, capturing a perfect, grainy profile of Howard Pimm.

Movement flickered in the dark computer screen. Ryan leaned closer to get a better look. What was in the video? What tiny detail could there be?

"What do you see?" she asked. Her breath caressed his cheek, drawing shivers of need and desire.

It was so damned distracting. He needed to focus on whatever was moving in the video.

Wait. She'd pressed the pause button. There shouldn't be any movement on it—

Which meant it was a reflection of the greenhouse window behind them. Capri's house sat on a large old lot. He'd barely seen the neighbors' houses when he'd parked in the driveway, and only darkness had lain beyond the greenhouse windows when he'd first entered—although he had been rather distracted at the time.

Maybe he hadn't seen anything at all. Tree branches in the wind or something.

The movement flickered again, something looming, drawing closer?

Cold dread filled him. He turned and time suddenly moved too slowly. A man, outside, straightened in the bushes, a gun in his large hands.

Ryan's heart jerked. "Gun."

Capri wrenched around. The shot exploded, roaring through the glass and slamming into Capri's chest. She lurched back and her hands flew to the entry wound as if that could somehow staunch the bleeding. Blood poured over her bra and across her pale skin.

Oh, God!

He reached for his sidearm, but it wasn't there. It lay on the floor on the other side of the table with his shirt and her clothes.

The man fired again.

Ryan yanked Capri down and dragged her beyond the table into the cover of the plant-filled shelves, adrenaline consuming away any hint of pain from his ribs. "We have to get you to a hospital."

"I'm fine."

Another shot exploded around them, but from the other side of the greenhouse. Glass shattered.

He pressed his hands against hers, adding pressure to her wound. "Your phone is on the table."

"It just grazed me."

The hell it did.

"I'm fine." Light radiated from her eyes. The ferocious monster she'd revealed on Raven's steps earlier that day slid across her expression. "I'll take care of this."

She pushed him aside, leapt up, and rushed around the shelf.

Ryan scrambled after her. The man from the window fired again. Another man, a stocky guy with a flattened nose, fired from the doorway to the kitchen.

Blood flared along her arm, but she didn't even stumble. She raced at the man in the doorway, Flat Nose, and batted his gun aside.

The man in the window, a bald guy with a spiderweb tattooed over his scalp, fired at Ryan.

He dove back for the table. Another gunshot slammed into the wood inches above his head.

He leapt up to grab Capri's phone, but Tattoo fired three quick shots. Ryan jerked back and bolted for his clothes. Tattoo fired again, forcing Ryan away from his weapon and phone. His gun was so close. He could see it peeking out from Capri's shirt.

Someone yelled. Capri broke Flat Nose's elbow and seized his gun. He relinquished the weapon but wrenched around fast, so damned fast, and rammed his fist into her face.

She fired—she still had to be stunned from the punch—and hit him in the chest.

Ryan yanked his attention from her. She could handle herself. But that was when she wasn't bleeding. She'd been shot in the chest. Except she wasn't moving as if she were in any pain.

Tattoo fired again. Ryan dove for his gun again, spiking pain through his ribs. He drew it from its holster and fired at the window. But Tattoo twisted to the side.

How the hell—? The man had literally dodged a bullet.

Tattoo sneered and fired again. *Bang. Bang.*

Ryan scrambled around the table for cover, abandoning the chance of getting a phone. Capri raced toward him. Behind her, two more men crowded the doorway to the kitchen, holding MAC10s.

Shit.

Blood smeared Capri's face and chest. She looked ferocious, terrifying, and wild. "Run."

He didn't need to be told twice. He fired at the men behind her and bolted with her between the shelves and around a corner.

Machine gun fire exploded around them. Bullets tore through plants and shelves. Glass shattered.

The gunfire paused. "Come out, little drake," someone called.

Capri glanced around the shelf. "Shit, shit, shit."

"What?" Ryan peered around her. Two more men with MAC10s had joined the first guys. "You have got to be kidding me. We have to get out of here."

Something rattled, metal against the tiled floor. *Click, click, click.* And a grenade bounced into sight.

"Holy Mother!" Capri leapt up, hauling Ryan with her, and they dove through the window. An explosion roared behind them. Ryan hit snow and rolled, leaving blood smeared across the pristine white. The cold stung his bare skin and it hurt to breathe. He leapt up, gun ready. Capri crouched beside him. The men in the greenhouse rushed toward them and more movement in the surrounding trees caught his attention.

Another explosion ripped through Capri's house. Someone yelled and a woman materialized out of thin air beside Capri. The woman screamed and slashed at her with a machete.

Capri jerked back and fired, but the woman vanished and reappeared behind her.

Ryan's mind stuttered, but someone rushed from the shadows beside him and he didn't have time to think, only react.

The man punched. Ryan wrenched back, pointed his gun, but the man was too fast. He batted the gun down and rammed a fist into Ryan's gut. Pain roared through Ryan's chest. He yanked his gun back up and fired, hitting the man in the side. The man howled and staggered back but another took his place. Dark, shadowy-figured men and women dressed all in black surged around him.

A MAC10 spat bullets into the ground beside him, and he twisted out of the way into an assailant's grip. That man's hand seared Ryan's flesh, sending agony up his arm.

The man slammed his free hand against Ryan's bare chest. More agony. Burning, core deep. Ryan wrenched back, but the man held tight. The air shimmered around them and the world twisted with the promise of a future flash.

Not. Now.

Agony roared through his chest. The future flash continued to build. Behind him, a woman screamed. Ryan's heart froze. He didn't know if it was Capri or not.

His vision shot out of him and whirled above him. Men and women swarmed around them. Three bodies lay at Capri's feet. Flames engulfed her house.

A man trained a gun on Ryan's back and fired. Ryan jerked to the side and the bullet slammed into the man holding him.

The future flash rippled, the agony from the man's touch vanished as he dropped to the ground.

Ryan staggered, his senses half in his body, half whirling above his head. He leapt at the man who'd fired at him. The man staggered back, but his foot caught in the snow and Ryan snagged his hand, seizing the gun.

The future flash yanked Ryan's senses up. A man with a MAC10 aimed at him. He grabbed the man in front of him and forced him around. Machine gunfire slammed into the assailant's body.

Capri screamed, her eyes wide. She shot the MAC10 guy and rushed to Ryan.

"Run," she roared at him.

A woman swept around behind Capri.

The future flash wrenched Ryan from his body again. The woman leveled her gun and fired, hitting Capri in the back, in the heart.

Pain lanced Ryan's side. Capri gasped. Her knees buckled, and he grabbed her. She clung to him as if that would keep her from falling. But the shot was fatal. Blood poured from her, staining the snow.

"Run," she growled.

But he couldn't leave her. He shot the woman who'd shot Capri.

The future flash shot up. There were too many. He had less than half a clip left—if he was lucky.

Another MAC10 guy raised his weapon.

Capri shoved back from him. Somehow she'd found the strength to stand. "I. Said. Run."

30

"Run," Capri growled.

Not without her. Ryan wrapped an arm around her waist, took most of her weight, and shot the man beside him. The man staggered back and Ryan shoved past him. Machine gun fire spat through the snow beside him.

He hauled Capri deeper into her yard, away from the street and possibly more dangers. She needed a hospital, but he couldn't help her if she was dead.

She shoved against his grip. "What are you doing?"

"Getting us the hell out of here." But his vision swept out of his body again. The assailants followed.

One of them, a scruffy middle-aged man in a torn suit, raised his gun. He pointed it at Ryan's back.

Ryan wrenched to the side. The bullet slammed into a tree by his head.

"We're not going to get out of here." She twisted out of his grip, grabbed his hand, and pulled him into the pine grove a few feet away.

How the hell—? She shouldn't even be standing. Maybe he hadn't seen what he'd seen. But she'd been shot—twice… maybe more?

"There are six coming up fast," she said.

His vision trembled. He leaned against the tree beside him to keep his balance and trained his gun on the closest assailant. *Bang.* The woman dropped.

"Now there are five. And I'm out of bullets."

"Get that woman's gun and take out one more."

"What are you going to do?"

She flashed him a fierce smile filled with heat and wildness. "Take the rest."

She leapt at the next guy, seizing his arm and slamming him into the tree behind her.

The next man was on her a second later. He stabbed a sword at her, but she sidestepped the strike and kicked out his knee. He fell and she cracked her elbow against his face.

Holy shit!

His vision shot to a man standing back, raising his MAC10.

Right. The gun. Ryan had to take out at least one more.

He scrambled for the woman's body, only half seeing. His vision twisted from bird's eye to within him to just above his shoulder. This strange non-future flash was growing stronger. His adrenaline was fading and so was his control.

The flash flickered to Capri. A new man punched her, knocking her to her knees. Blood poured from her nose and mouth.

The man grabbed a sword on the ground. "I know how to kill a drake," he said.

Ryan blindly grabbed the gun.

The man raised the sword as if to chop off Capri's head.

Ryan's vision twisted. He fired, but his vision had jumped to the MAC10 guy before he could tell if his shot had hit. Ryan jerked the gun to him and fired again. MAC10 guy's head snapped back and he dropped.

The world wrenched around Ryan, twisting, rippling, out of control. Pain flooded him and he fought to breathe.

"Are you hit?" A hand grabbed his shoulder. Capri's hand, hot and radiating a sizzling electricity.

"What?" He couldn't think past the electricity and the churning world.

"Are you hit?" Her hand trembled. "We can't stay. You need a hospital."

He snorted. Somehow that jerked him out of the future flash or whatever the hell was happening to him. "You need a hospital. You were shot. Twice. I saw it."

He raised his head, his gaze hitting hers. He was falling into a blue sea, a Capri-blue sea. The fierceness was still there, but so too was a softness. Affection, directed at him.

His mind stuttered. She'd been shot. His gaze dropped to her chest. She still only wore her black bra and panties. She was covered in blood, but there weren't any entry or exit wounds in her chest.

"How—?" His mind stuttered again. It didn't make sense. It was impossible.

He yanked his attention back to her face. Her nose and mouth no longer bled. But the injuries had only been seconds...? Minutes...? He didn't know anymore. Nothing felt right. Nothing *was* right.

"You're not— You should be dead. You should—"

"I'll explain later." She grabbed one of the dead assailants beside her and shoved him at Ryan. "Take his coat and boots. We don't know if there are others still in the house."

He glanced toward the house. Flames engulfed it. It sat on a rise in bright roaring contrast to the night and snow and quiet surrounding them. But it hadn't been quiet moments ago. Blood and bodies littered the ground.

"Ryan."

He wrenched his attention back to her. She should be dead. He saw her get shot. Saw it before the weird future flash thing had happened.

"Coat and boots. We need to get out of here. Now. Then we need to figure out who set this up."

She eased to the woman and pulled off her boots.

Right. Immediate danger first. He could fall apart later.

CAPRI PUT ON THE DEAD WOMAN'S BOOTS AND SHRUGGED INTO HER coat. Her chest hurt. Mother of All, did it hurt! She was a pretty fast healer—the bleeding had stopped shortly after the shots—but it still hurt. She hadn't taken a beating like this in hundreds of years.

Ryan pulled off the man's boots. He looked like he was on automatic pilot. At least he was moving.

"Do you think the attack had anything to do with the decapitations?" Uncertainty filled his expression, but it wasn't uncertainty of who'd attacked them. He'd seen her shot. His mind was on the verge of shattering, unable to accept what he thought was impossible.

"I don't know. If it is, does this eliminate anyone in our suspect pool or move anyone to the top of the list?" Keep him focused on a mundane problem, something he was familiar with. Just long enough for her to get them someplace safe.

She checked the woman's coat for a phone, found one, and ensured she could call for help. Now they needed to get moving. They'd spent too much time there as it was.

Ryan shrugged into the man's coat. He shoved his hands into the pockets and pulled out a wad of bills.

"That should come in handy." Money for a taxi would be useful. "Let's go."

He nodded, checked his gun, and she led them deeper into the grove. There was a gate in the fence at the back of her property. It led through a gully to the semi-major street beyond. Never before had she wanted to be able to gate without an anchor. Diablo's rapid gating ability would have been really handy right at the moment. There wouldn't be any footprints for their assailants to follow and she could get them away in a hurry.

Ryan slipped and grunted. He pressed his arm against his side and panted. He was losing his mind and losing blood. The question was, which was going to kill him first?

His impossible aura, the one she wasn't supposed to be able to feel, flickered around him, now fully visible. Except he didn't have an aura. He couldn't. He was human and not a mage.

It was the stress of the situation, the agony still searing through her, and the panic of her inamorato's life being threatened. That was it. But man! He glowed like all the assailants had.

Her aura sight must be messed up. Getting a beating could do that to a girl. Her headache was back in full force. She'd tried using her earth magic on the first guy in her greenhouse and an agony she'd never experienced before had torn through her. After that, she'd been unable to summon her earth magic at all.

And all of that just meant her aura sight was unreliable. She needed a place to hole up, take care of Ryan, and then figure out what the hell she was going to do. The question was, where to hide? The magic used in the fight proved the assailants had been mages.

She didn't recognize any of them as drakes, so they had to be humans. Which meant—

Mother, why did her head have to hurt so much?

It meant Ryan's question still stood. Was the attack related to the decapitations or not? Not a lot of people knew where she lived, so it could have been the leak in the Asar Nergal. Or it could have been someone else.

No. The attack had been big. At least a dozen mages, maybe more. That required resources. But whose? And God dammit, whoever that was owed her an entire hoard. All her beautiful flowers, burning.

She pushed that thought away. Focus on the immediate danger. Losing her hoard was heartbreaking, but losing Ryan would destroy her. Find who did this. And end them.

That was the goal.

And because of all the mages involved, it had to have something to do with catching Boyd and the others earlier that night. Retaliation or something. She and her team had to be getting close to something big and someone powerful behind the mages. It was the only logical explanation. But who?

"The only person I can think of, who would have had the funds and the balls for an attack of that scale on an FBI agent, is Raven Mitchelle," Ryan said, as if reading her mind. "But that still doesn't make any sense. Her business is too legit for something this stupid."

Unless it wasn't legit. But she couldn't say that and put Ryan onto Raven's trail. She needed to keep him away from drakes, not get him more involved. But all those mage kids, not to mention Anaea—a human sorcerer—and Grey in Raven's house implied the black drake was somehow involved in something more. Except Anaea wouldn't be part of an attack on Capri. That didn't seem her style and it certainly wasn't Grey's or Hunter's. Not to mention that none of the mages who'd just attacked her had been kids. "So who else could it be?"

They cleared the gully and cut between two squat office buildings. To the left and up the hill was a strip mall with a twenty-four-hour coffee shop. The cold didn't bother her much—her healing took care of that—but Ryan needed warmth.

Mother, he could have died. He had almost died. Panic raced through her. She needed to figure this out.

They reached the coffee shop, rage and panic thrumming through Capri. She needed to deal with this. Make Ryan safe. But once they stopped moving, she'd have to deal with his shattering mind—except he hadn't broken apart yet. Maybe there was hope. Please, let there be hope.

Bright, warm light lit the coffee shop's front window, giving her a clear view of the entire seating area. At this hour, it was empty.

Thank God, and the Mother, and any other deity who might be listening.

Inside, a chime rang as the door opened and heat flooded over her. Ryan sagged onto a plastic chair at a table that gave him a clear view of all the windows and the front door. His skin was pale and sweat slicked his brow. She couldn't tell how much blood he was losing beneath the baggy stolen coat. Without a doubt, they'd left a trail to the shop.

Which meant she needed to call for help now, before more mages showed up.

A middle-aged woman shuffled out from the back. Her eyes grew wide and froze on the table. Ryan had set the gun in front of him.

"Sorry," he mumbled and pulled the weapon under the table.

"The minute we leave, I want you to call the police," Capri told her.

"Why don't I call them now?" the woman asked.

"That would do, too." It wouldn't give them a lot of time, but if more mages arrived, Capri didn't want the woman alone and helpless. The catch was, were the police involved in this whole mess? Cooper or Ptolemy could have had enough of her. They could be connected to the mages. Anyone could—

Except Grey. Grey would never try to kill her. He was too good a friend.

She pulled the phone from her pocket.

"Can we trust whoever you're calling?" Ryan asked. "You can't rule out that whoever was responsible knows you and has connections."

"This guy is safe." She hoped. No, Grey was safe. He'd help her. She just had no idea how she was going to pay him back.

She dialed Grey's number. It rang once, twice, three times. It started a fourth and clicked. It was going to his messages. But instead of the answering machine response, a gruff voice said, "Hello?"

"Grey?"

"Capri?" Grey cleared his throat. "This isn't your number. And it's almost one. What's wrong?"

That's what she loved about him. Smart. Always knew when someone was in trouble. He was going to make some lucky drake very happy.

"Capri?" he asked, panic edging his voice. "Where are you?"

"At the coffee shop on Meyer." Shit. The words had jumped out before she realized what she was saying. She really needed a break, time to ground herself—and get rid of this damned headache.

"I'm coming over."

"No, don't—" He couldn't see Ryan. If Grey knew he was her inamorato he'd… she had no idea what he'd do.

Grey strode around the outside of the building. In a blink of an eye, he'd gated in.

Damn. "Wait here," she said to Ryan and went outside to meet Grey. All she'd wanted was a safe place to stay. He could have given her that without showing up, but he hadn't given her a chance to ask. This face-to-face was dangerous for both Ryan and Grey. If whoever attacked her knew Grey was as good a friend as this, he could be in danger, too.

"You were supposed to just talk to me, set me up with a safe house," she growled, "not show up."

"You sounded like you needed help." His gaze traveled up her body, over the ratty blood-stained coat. "And it looks like you need it."

"Yes, but if they see us together—"

His eyes narrowed and the muscles in his jaw tightened. "Who's the drake?"

"The drake—?"

"Yeah, the guy sitting in the coffee shop glaring at me from the corner of his eye."

"There's no—" The only person in the shop was Ryan.

"I don't recognize him. But he's dressed as badly as you."

Grey was seeing a drake, or rather a drake's aura. Which meant Ryan's aura wasn't a figment of her headache or stress. It was real.

Mother, somehow Ryan was now a mage. But no dragon had body-shared with him... unless being her inamorato changed things within him, awakened his magic. Except that wasn't possible. Only a dragon's spirit could connect with the earth's magic and that took time. At the minimum a day and the maximum was years.

"He's a friend. He was visiting when... when trouble came calling."

"That's pretty vague." Grey squinted. "He looks like the human you were with at Nero's."

Shit. Capri yanked Grey around so he couldn't see into the coffee shop. "He's not." Her stomach roiled, and she bit the inside of her cheek. She hated lying to Grey, but it was best for him. He was already in Regis's black book for keeping Hunter's inamorata a secret and joining Hunter's unofficial coterie. If it came out that he knew of another human mage, she doubted even Hunter could protect him. "So can you set us up for the night or what?"

The vein in Grey's temple pulsed, and he turned his gaze back to the coffee shop. "What did you say his name was?"

For the love of—! "I didn't." Now was not the time for him to suddenly become jealous. He'd quietly waited for her for centuries, and she supposed she'd quietly waited for centuries for him to give up.

"I really don't remember his aura."

Her stomach flip-flopped again. Would he refuse to help her if he realized Ryan was a mage... or worse, her lover? She hadn't thought Grey was a vindictive kind of guy, but did she really know him? Did any drake let another get close enough to truly know him or her?

"You can't remember everything."

Grey raised an eyebrow. Even in the frigid air, sweat slicked his temples. "Wanna try that again?"

"I—" She had no idea what to say. In that moment, she'd do whatever it took to keep Ryan safe from dragonkind. Mother of All, she'd lost her mind.

She jerked away and ran a hand through her hair. It was loose. Ryan had pulled the chignon free in the greenhouse. Heat swept through her at the memory of his hands and lips caressing her human flesh. Of him sliding thick and hot inside her.

He glanced up from his coffee and met her gaze through the glass. A hint of a smile softened his expression and her heart thumped in response. Hers. Her heart belonged to him and no other. She had to keep him safe. No matter the cost.

"Ah, shit," Grey said.

She whirled back to him. He stood so still. All sense that he was fighting to hold himself together had stopped. If she hadn't known he was alive, she might have mistaken him for a statue.

"He *is* that human, isn't he?"

She held his gaze, trying to figure out what to say. Did she need to protect Ryan from Grey or not?

"How did I become the go-to man for saving the asses of human mages?"

A growl bubbled within her. "I can save his ass just fine. What I need is a place to hole up until I figure out who's trying to kill me."

"You didn't want me involved because he's a mage, you stupid drake?" Grey met her growl and bared his teeth.

"I think you knowing about him will put you in danger." She grabbed the front of his coat and yanked him close. Rage shook her, but she didn't know why. Grey was going to help. She didn't doubt he would. But why did he have to figure out what Ryan was? Why did Ryan have to be anything other than what she'd thought he was? She hadn't wanted things to be more complicated, for either of them.

Grey jerked from her grasp. "Your little mage is the least of my worries."

"He's not so little."

He flashed his teeth. "You don't say."

Something within her broke. She didn't know what. Ice swept over her, and her rage turned to fear. Grey's smile turned fierce, as if her fear were painted on her face. He'd come to a realization about her, one she was sure she hadn't figured out for herself yet. In that moment, she knew he wasn't just a good friend to Hunter, he was one to her as well. And she had no idea how the hell she was going to be able to repay him.

His gaze dropped to her feet. "Those boots are way too big for you." He frowned. "And where are your pants?"

That was all he had to say? "It's complicated."

"Complicated?"

"Yeah, someone blew up my house."

"Holy shit. Any idea who?"

"If I knew that I wouldn't be coming to you for help. It could be anyone in Court."

Warm air swept over her and the chime above the coffee shop door rang. "What's going on, Capri?" Ryan asked.

"Just arranging a safe place to stay." If she didn't wipe his mind, they were going to have to have a long conversation—part of which involved whatever his earth magic might be. Hopefully it was something subtle, like enhanced strength or speed.

She bit back a growl. What the hell was she thinking? They couldn't have a conversation. She had to wipe his mind, and if she could wipe hers, she would. Except now he had an earth magic ability, which meant dragon law demanded he be killed.

The apartment Grey sent them to was a loft in a renovated warehouse in a seedier part of town. Ryan had remained quiet for the taxi drive, the climb up the stairs to the third floor, and the march down the dimly lit hall. He looked strained, as if the events of the evening had finally sunk in: they'd had sex. Her house had been blown up. He'd seen things he shouldn't have seen. Impossible things.

And there was nothing she could do to fix that.

His aura flickered, brighter now than before. Whatever earth magic he'd developed, it was growing stronger. She just couldn't figure out how that was possible. He hadn't shared his body with a drake—sex didn't count—so there was no way the magic asleep within him had been woken. Only the magical strength of a dragon's spirit could activate a human body's connection to the earth's magic.

Unless being her inamorato had something to do with it. Maybe his soul magic had also been strengthened. Maybe he wouldn't live a normal human life and she wouldn't be faced with an eternity of loneliness after he died. That still didn't solve the problem of him losing his mind once he realized the truth.

This was such a mess.

She slid the key Grey had given her into the lock and opened the door. Weak illumination from a streetlight outside the bank of windows on the far wall created a sense of foreboding. She found the light switch and flicked it on. The place was basic and it didn't look as if Grey had been in the loft for years. Most of the right side of the space was a gym and boxing ring. Dust sheets had been pulled from a kitchen table with three mismatched chairs, and from a bed by the bank of windows, mostly hidden by a series of paper screens. At her feet were two shopping bags, one with clothes and the other with food. Grey was a better friend than she deserved.

"Wow, you take me to all the best places," Ryan said.

"I'm not sure we're in any position to complain." She dug through the bags, looking for bandages for Ryan.

"I'm still trying to figure out what that position is, exactly." He closed the door and leaned against it, arms crossed, waiting for an explanation.

What could she tell him? "It's complicated. Now let's look at your injuries. I know your ribs were grazed."

Now was the moment when she had to do her duty. Except she couldn't kill him. She'd never be able to kill him. It would be easier to kill herself—and that wasn't an easy proposition since the only real way to kill her was decapitation or maybe fire.

In the very least, she needed to erase his memories, save his sanity. But she didn't want to rip into his mind and make him forget about her. She wanted him to know her, the real her, and accept her for who she was. But that was completely dangerous.

He didn't move from the door. "Well, use small words so I can understand it."

"I didn't mean you wouldn't understand." Except that was exactly what she'd meant. "I just—" She thought about her power word. Just thinking about it made her head hurt.

Damn it, just say it and be done with it. But she couldn't. She couldn't make herself do it.

It wasn't fair. It God damned wasn't fair.

"There are things you don't understand. Take off your coat."

"Then help me." He meant help him understand, not help take the coat off, but her gaze lingered at the sliver of bare chest peeking from beneath his collar.

Mother, she wanted him so badly. "You're bleeding. Let's deal with that."

"You're bleeding, too." He grabbed her arm, pulled her to him, and opened her coat, revealing the dried blood around what should have been a gunshot. "I know you were shot. I saw it. And I saw that man disappear and reappear. I know what I saw. I'm not crazy."

"No," she said between gritted teeth. "You're not crazy." She was in so much trouble. There was no good way out of this. But she had to tell him the truth. Her soul demanded it. She couldn't lie to her inamorato, no matter how much it was for his own good. "There are things you need to know."

"Then tell me."

She pulled away before she melted into his embrace and forgot herself in his lips and body. This needed to be done. If he went completely crazy, she could wipe his mind. If he didn't accept her, at least she'd told the truth. It was all she could do now. Where was Diablo when she needed to shoot something?

"Take off your coat and let's see if Grey left us something to drink." She grabbed the shopping bags and took them to the kitchen table. Grey had sent them a change of clothes—including boots—a couple of microwave dinners, a new cell phone, and a first aid kit. She pocketed the phone and pulled out the kit. "No liquor, but at least we have bandages."

"You're stalling."

Yes, she was.

The muscle in his jaw worked, as if he were considering his options. Then he blew out a long breath and slid off the coat.

He was gorgeous, all ripped muscle promising strength and protection. And only hours ago, she'd run her hands over his flesh, felt him move within her, shared his breath, bonded her soul to his in a way she couldn't explain to him.

Heat swept up her neck. She didn't want to leave him, didn't want to hurt him, and had no idea what she was going to do.

She struggled past that thought and the memory of his skin under her fingers and focused on his wounds. Red bruises and small lacerations covered his chest, arms, and face—he was going to look terrible in about a day—but blood only really wept from the graze along his ribs.

Thank goodness it wasn't bad. It was actually a miracle he'd gotten through that with only scrapes and bruises.

"Are you going to say anything?" He meant her unfinished

complicated explanation, but there was a heat in his gaze that said he wanted to talk about something else.

She opened a package of gauze and pressed it to his side. "Hold this. I just need to cut some tape."

"And when we're done with me, you're taking off your coat."

Her heart stuttered, the memory of his body against hers drawing shivers. "I'm not injured."

She cut the tape and pressed the first two pieces to his body.

He captured her hand as she applied the third piece. "I don't believe you."

"You've seen it. I'm not hurt."

He drew even closer, capturing her between his arms and the counter. The warmth of his body seeped through the thin coat. He brushed his lips across her cheek and down her neck. His hot breath caressed her too-sensitive flesh and threatened to bring on another purr.

"Stop stalling. You're going to bleed to death."

God, he felt so good, so right, pressed against her. So right. "I'm not going to bleed to death."

Why couldn't they just be like this forever?

"But I saw you get shot. Twice."

"I know." She sucked in a quick breath but it didn't steady her. "You can't turn back from this. Once you know, you know."

"For the love of—" He jerked away.

She grabbed him and yanked him back, capturing his gaze with hers. "Knowing is dangerous."

"As dangerous as someone blowing up your house?"

"Possibly more dangerous."

His eyes narrowed. He didn't believe her. "If you don't start talking, I'm leaving. I can look after myself."

"Can you look after your sister? Your niece?" Except it could already be too late for them. No. The destruction of her house had nothing to do with Ryan. His family was still safe. He could still be safe if she could convince Diablo she'd wiped his mind.

He tensed, his body trembling under her hands. "Are you threatening me?"

"No, God, no. But you need to understand. Once you know, your life will change. Everything will change."

"So what?" He rolled his eyes. "You'd tell me but then you'd have to kill me?"

"Something like that."

He slammed his hand on the counter beside her. "Cut the secret agent crap," he roared.

Yes, there was a spirit strong enough to stand against her inner drake. Hot anticipation swept through her. She bared her teeth, unable to resist sending him a challenge. His eyes flashed wide.

"It's not secret agent crap," she growled, revealing more of her dragon.

He shifted, but stood his ground, even raised his chin in defiance.

If he flashed a hint of teeth, she'd rip the rest of his clothes off. "This is the truth. There is magic in this world, and I am not human."

He blinked, as if he didn't understand her words, then barked a harsh laugh. "Bullshit."

She grabbed his hand and pressed it to her chest where she'd been shot. "You said I was shot. All this blood came from somewhere."

The muscle in his jaw twitched.

"I'm not human. I look human. I'm in a human's body, but I'm different, I'm—" Oh, crap. Do it. Just do it. Rip off the bandage. "I'm a dragon."

"This is ridiculous. If you don't want to explain what's really going on, just say so."

"Yeah, we tried that two minutes ago. This is the truth. You have to know I'm different, have to sense that there's something else, something you can't explain about me."

"There is something." He pulled away, running his hands through his hair. "Now I think it's that you're crazy."

This wasn't working. How the hell had Hunter explained it to Anaea? Of course, Hunter had been stuck in Anaea's body. She could have just seen in her head what Hunter was, no explanation necessary.

A cold, foul weight roiled in her gut. That was the answer. It was the fastest, most certain solution. She had to transfer into Ryan's body and show him the truth. It was the only way to make him understand. It broke even more dragon laws and risked his sanity and hers. She'd never body-hopped before, but it was the only way.

Before she could change her mind, she captured his face between her palms and kissed him. He wrapped an arm around her, drawing her close, and she deepened the kiss, teasing his mouth open. Her desire swelled. This was her inamorato, she'd do anything for him, sacrifice her life for him, defy all laws, dragon and human, for him. And right now, she needed him to understand.

She seized at her essence and imagined it pouring into Ryan through their connected lips. Heat seared through her, and Ryan's aura flared bright.

He gasped and grabbed her shoulders, trying to push her away, but she held tightly to his head, keeping their lips locked. Her essence burned up. Light flooded her senses. She was weightless, energy, too bright, too hot, too much. She screamed, but couldn't tell if the cry was just her soul or her body. It wasn't working and she was somehow losing herself.

She dropped to her knees, clutching Ryan's limp body in her arms... except Ryan was too small, too fragile. Or she was too big, or—

"Capri?" Ryan's voice rattled through her head... his head... their head.

It's all right. I'm all right.

He froze. "What the hell? How are you—?"

We don't have a lot of time. The longer my spirit shares your body, the greater the risk to both of us.

"This is not happening. It's a dream. I'm crazy. I'm unconscious. We didn't get out of the house before the bomb exploded. We—"

Ryan. Focus. His panic pressed against her, squeezing her tight. There were so many things she wanted to know. It would be so easy just to dip into his memories and find out. Like, what his earth magic was—of course, he might not even know that yet. But more importantly, if he felt the same way about her as she did about him.

Her thoughts slipped into his mind, reaching for his memories. She jerked her attention back to herself. No. Focus. Relay information and get out before she made things worse.

This is the truth. She sucked in a breath... or Ryan did—she wasn't going to pay too close attention to the feel of his body—and concentrated on her knowledge of her reality: the truth about dragons. How she was just under a thousand years old, that she was a blue drake in the service of her prince. She let the truth about earth magic and soul magic rush out of her and into him, and the truth about the Dragon Court and politics and everything else. Everything, unable to choose what she imparted, including the truth about how she felt about him, how her spirit had picked him, forever.

His pulse raced and his breath drew sharp gasps—and her soul magic started to heal his injuries. She felt his chest heave, felt the whirl of information threaten his sanity and his consciousness. She held on to his essence as tightly as she could. She would not lose him in this mess, and he would not lose himself.

With one last blast, the last of everything she knew poured into him, and she forced him to kiss her unconscious body—she was not going to think of it as dead, even though it was.

More heat and pain seared through her, and she gasped. Her head pounded. Mother of All, it hurt so damned much. But she was back in her own body. Ryan's strong arms held her and his too-wide green eyes searched her face.

"I don't— I can't—" He shoved her from his lap, scrambled to his feet, and pressed his palms to his temples. "What did you do?"

"It was the only way."

He staggered to the kitchen table, clutching it to keep upright. "It's not possible."

"It is, Ryan." She stood and reached for him.

He jerked back. "Stay away. Whatever you are."

"I'm a dragon. An ancient spirit surviving in this human body."

"You're a monster. A beast."

"Ryan, please. You have to understand. This was the only way you'd understand."

"Understand? I don't understand. It's impossible. There's no such thing as magic. Not the kind of magic you're talking about. Dragons aren't real. You aren't real."

"I am real." If she could just hold him, let him feel her, kiss him and show him with her lips and body how real she was, he'd believe what had happened. He would root back into his mind and he wouldn't go crazy. She took another step closer.

"No." He wrenched away. "This isn't real. It's not real."

She reached for him, but he batted her hands aside and shoved her with more force than he ever had before. She stumbled into the table, toppling it over, and crashed to the floor.

He grabbed his coat and ran out the door.

She rushed after him, but the hall was empty. The phone in her pocket rang. She ignored it. Ryan was more important. She had to make sure he was all right, that he processed everything she'd shoved into his mind. He could handle this. She knew he could. He *had* to handle this.

But the phone didn't stop ringing. Whoever it was, wasn't leaving a voice message, just kept calling back.

"What?" she growled into the phone.

"You've got trouble," Grey said. "Tobias is on a rampage. Something about working a case you're not supposed to be working and with a human, and a news report about it. Swipe has tried to cover for you, but you need to get to the chamberlain's office and deal with this now before Regis proclaims you're a traitor and sends an assassin after you and your mage."

Everything within her froze. "Does he know about Ryan?"

"As a normal human, yes. As a mage, no. You're safe there, for now. But you need to deal with this before anyone finds out."

"I can't leave him."

"Not you, too? What is it with dragons falling for humans? You're starting to become a cliché. Your inamorato will be fine for a couple of hours. Trust me."

"No, I— I tried to explain things to him and—" Her throat tightened. She'd made such a mistake. Body sharing with Ryan had only sped up his insanity. "Let's just say he didn't take it well."

Air whooshed around her. The black vortex of a gate burst into life at the end of the hall, and Grey leapt through. "Where is he?"

She could have cried with relief, or collapsed, or both. She felt she'd been torn in two and she couldn't explain it. She was a stronger drake than this, and yet Ryan had left and was going crazy and—

"Capri." Grey grabbed her shoulders. "Where is he?"

"I don't know." A sob threatened to break through and her eyes welled with tears. She growled and wiped at them. "What's wrong with me?"

"It's an inamorated thing. Makes drakes do crazy things."

"We have to find him." She moved to shove Grey aside, but Grey held her tightly.

"You're putting on clothes and I'm gating you to Court. You're going to deal with Tobias."

"But Ryan—"

"I will find your human." He yanked her back into the apartment, grabbed the bag of clothes, and shoved it against her chest, making her take it. "This is starting to become my thing."

More air swept around her. A black void burst into life beside them, and Grey yanked her into another gate. The world twisted, then her foot hit hard floor, and a dimly lit hall of gray granite surrounded her. They were in Court. Grey had gated her to Court.

She shoved him against the wall, dropping the clothes and reaching for a gun she no longer had. "I have to find him."

"No. I will find him. You stay alive."

32

Ryan staggered down an alley, tripped over something hidden in the shadows, and stumbled into the wall. The uneven brick dug into his palms, but he barely felt it. His head was too full. There was too much information. Information that wasn't possible.

He pressed his forehead to the brick and clutched the wall as if that would make the world stop whirling. But it wasn't the world that whirled, it was him, his mind, his very essence.

Magic was real. The thought that there were two kinds of magic, earth magic and soul magic, flashed through him. They were Capri's thoughts or memories or whatever they were.

He wasn't supposed to know any of that. It was dangerous for him to know the truth. He could go crazy.

Also Capri's thoughts.

He was pretty sure he already was crazy.

There was no way she could just give him her thoughts.

But she *had*. She'd also given him her essence, her spirit. It was just for a second, just long enough for her to reveal… everything.

His heart pounded and even with his eyes squeezed shut, he could feel the world wrenching around him.

She'd even revealed her core-deep affection for him. A love that confused and terrified her, but one that—no matter how hard she fought it—couldn't be denied. That emotion spoke to him. It resonated with something buried within him, something he hadn't known existed. And yet he didn't want to examine it. That would mean what now churned through him was real.

It couldn't be real.

It just couldn't.

He shoved away from the wall and staggered toward the mouth of the alley and—

And what? Safety? Surety?

He couldn't get back the sense that he knew how the world worked. He hadn't even known he'd been so sure of things until Capri had broken that misconception.

Sure, he knew that something was different, at least with him. He saw flashes of the future. Real flashes. Horrible flashes. But for some reason that seemed sane, normal. The idea that dragons lived in human bodies, possessed magic—

No, only a handful of dragons... drakes, possessed significant magic. It had something to do with their now human bodies. Something to do with that body's connection to the earth's magic.

And then there were gates and interdimensional spheres and enhanced strength and speed and night sight—

Oh, God, stop. Just stop.

He rushed onto the street. Deserted. But at this time of night, in this neighborhood, that didn't surprise him. He picked a direction— it didn't matter which—and ran. His feet pounding, his breath burning, as if he could outrun what was in his head. He had to outrun it. He didn't want to know any of it. He could feel it burning him up from the inside out, devouring his mind, his thoughts, everything that was him.

It was too much. She shouldn't have done whatever she'd done—

Transferred her spirit into him—

She hadn't had the right. But she'd had no choice. He wouldn't have believed her otherwise.

He ran for blocks—he had no idea how many—until he found a wider street. Here most of the streetlights were actually working, and two blocks down, red neon lights flashed, promising "Cold Be—" "Mechanical Bull" and "Op-n." A taxi, its 'In service' light on, sat in front of the dive bar.

Ryan pulled out the wad of bills in his pocket that he'd found when he'd put the coat on. It looked like tens and twenties. Enough to cover cab fare. He rushed to the vehicle, opened the back door—managing to control himself long enough not to wrench at it—and slid inside.

"Where to?" The driver glanced into the rearview mirror, caught Ryan's gaze, then glanced back to the meter.

Where to? He had no idea. He needed to get free from the knowledge whirling in his head. But he couldn't escape himself. "25 Montgomery Street." It was the first address that popped to mind. The address of his childhood home, now Trisha's home.

"Sure thing." The driver hit the meter and pulled away from the curb.

Ryan squeezed his eyes shut. Words, thoughts, images pounded through him. He fought to ignore them, to think about anything else, to think of nothing. Nothing would be wonderful right now. A dark, empty abyss, where there wasn't him or Capri or anything else. Magic wasn't real. He wasn't crazy. Capri didn't love him.

Jesus, she loved him.

He shoved that thought back. For all he knew, none of it was real. The explosion had rattled his mind, broken him somehow. His curse had taken a new horrible twist, and now he was stuck in some unreality. Was he even in a cab going home?

The cab pulled into a driveway, the wheels crunching on ice and salt. Ryan opened his eyes. The familiar red brick Victorian, with its wide front porch and twin gables, sat before him. Home. Safety. In the very least, a place where he could regain his bearings and figure out how crazy he was.

Dragons were dangerous. They had laws—

Just stop.

He paid the driver the entire wad—it was too much but whatever. He rushed into the dark house and pressed his back against the front door.

Only a few human bodies could make a connection to the earth's magic. Humans and dragons could share bodies, but the human spirit wasn't strong enough to withstand the connection. The human spirit would become soul sick and go crazy.

The thoughts pounded against his mind. He already was crazy. This couldn't be real. He couldn't have seen the things he'd seen.

He staggered into the kitchen and filled the kettle to make tea.

Tea made everything right for Trisha. He didn't know how it could make things right for him, but it was the only thing he could think of... which wasn't true.

There were dragons in his head. Great, monstrous spirits crammed into fragile human forms.

He pressed his palms to his eyes.

There. Were. No. Dragons.

It wasn't real. Somehow, Capri had lied to him. Maybe she'd drugged him. Maybe that was why he felt the way he did. Something in the water, or her kiss, or...

The kettle squealed. He took it off the element and opened the cupboard for the tea box. It wasn't there. He couldn't remember anymore if Trisha kept the tea in the cupboard or not. He scanned the counter—not there, either—then he glanced at the kitchen table. Trisha's white ceramic tea jar sat on the table, surrounded by photos. Jess's school project.

He reached for the tin, his gaze sliding over the photos of him, his sister, his whole family, during happier times. Aunts and uncles, cousins, grandparents, and great grandparents all smiled back at him, laid out in chronological order. At the top, by the tea jar, was the black and white photo he'd seen earlier, of the two couples in stuffy 1900s clothing. Trisha had said he looked a lot like Great-great-great-uncle Eric.

Ryan picked up the photo and shifted it so the light over the stove illuminated the picture. Yeah, he looked a lot like Eric. And the woman beside him...

He drew the photo close. It looked like Capri. He'd thought that the first time he'd seen the photo. Then, he'd believed it was his imagination playing tricks on him because she compelled him, drew him to her. Now... now he wasn't so sure.

No. Drakes were old. Capri had received her current human form in the twelfth century.

The knowledge was just there, just like everything else. She'd known Eric. Loved Eric, and had been forced to leave him because of dragon law.

Her ache for his long-dead great-uncle flooded him. He gasped against the weight of it. She'd mourned that man's loss for a century.

She'd lived for centuries before then. She was spectacular, and fero-cious, and impossible.

It was all just so impossible. He couldn't contain it, couldn't begin to fully understand it. The burn, the tornado of thoughts, exploded within him again. He gasped and clutched the counter, struggling to keep standing. But he couldn't find his balance. He couldn't tell reality from fantasy, couldn't sense up from down. He was drowning in thoughts and knowledge and the impossible.

33

Capri rushed along the Lesser Promenade, every nerve thrumming. She'd changed into the shirt, jeans, coat, and boots Grey had given her before heading to Tobias's office, but what she really wanted was to find Ryan and make sure he was safe and sane.

Please. Let him be sane. The flurry of emotions overwhelmed her. She had to get back to him, except he didn't love her. He didn't believe her.

That hurt seared, flooded, consumed her.

He didn't love her. He'd rejected her. There was nothing left for her. Her damned soul had picked him and human souls didn't work the way drake souls did.

Her throat tightened. This was worse than losing Eric again. Her chest was too tight. Her eyes too hot. All she wanted was to curl into a ball and cry. She was losing her mind. All she could think of was Ryan and that horrible moment when he'd shoved her away and run out the door.

He'd looked so wild, so hurt. Humans couldn't accept the truth. Every drake knew that. She should have just accepted her heartache and wiped his mind. Then only one of them would be hurting. But no, she was selfish. She'd wanted him to understand, and she'd only made it worse. Sharing his body, infusing him with all her knowledge of dragonkind, had broken him and shattered his mind. She'd made him soul sick and then let him run away.

She couldn't be in Court. She had to find Ryan. Maybe if she used her earth magic she could make it right, make him love her.

Her stomach churned at the thought. He didn't love her. Accept it. Just accept it and move on. She would deal with Tobias and Court politics. Then she'd wipe Ryan's memory to save him, and hide from everything until it stopped hurting.

And to do that, she needed to trust Grey to find him and keep him safe while she dealt with Tobias. It wouldn't help either of them if she was executed for treason.

Except there was no guarantee Tobias would allow her to leave Court once she'd talked to him. There was also no guarantee that Tobias wasn't involved in the attack at her house.

But if that was true, then Tobias was somehow involved with the mages. Which was impossible. Tobias was loyal to Regis. He wouldn't be involved with Zenobia and her coup.

Of course, she'd never believed that there would be mages in Nero's house, either, and without a doubt those kids had been mages. Grey and Anaea had been there as well, which meant...

She had no idea what it meant. She didn't think they were involved with Boyd and his group of mages, but did that mean there was more than one group of mages out there? And what the hell was Grey doing, involved with that and at Nero's house?

None of this made sense. Nero was a Traditionalist and Regis's favorite doyen. An association with Hunter, even if it was through Grey, was unheard of. Hunter was Regis's least favorite drake. If Hunter didn't possess the last free medallion and have a sorcerer at his side, Regis would have sent every wannabe assassin after him. But Nero didn't just have a casual association with Hunter. If Anaea had been in his house, free to wander around, he had a direct link.

The Lesser Promenade widened. She passed a pair of patrolling guards, and while they glanced at her, they didn't stop her, which meant there wasn't a warrant for her arrest—or they'd yet to check in and learn about her. She was getting closer to the stairs up to the Greater Promenade and the Chamberlain's Office. Grey had said Tobias was furious that she'd been investigating something she hadn't been assigned. She'd known that might happen when Hiro had called her to her office. At least she had a solid lead with Howard Pimm—thanks to Gig finding that video. But she couldn't explain Ryan. And if Tobias was angry about him, that meant that reporter had aired Capri's slip-up at that lawyers' office.

She could fix this. Mother of All, she would fix this. Tobias would understand. She just needed to spin this as done in the best interest of the Royal Coterie. She'd suspected Ryan had known something and needed to keep him close until she'd discovered the truth. Yes, she should have informed Tobias right away, but she hadn't wanted to jump to conclusions.

Oh, yeah, Tobias wasn't going to believe any of that. He'd call her headstrong and stupid.

All of which right now was completely true.

She reached the massive staircase curling up to the Greater Promenade and took the stairs two at a time. There was no good way out of this and maybe she deserved it for what she'd done to Ryan.

Tears filled her eyes, and she blinked them back. She'd hurt her inamorato, broken his mind. She deserved whatever punishment Tobias gave her.

She hit the second to last step and almost rammed into Katar, Barna's Second.

"Going somewhere?" he asked.

"Yes, I have a meeting with the chamberlain."

"No, you have a meeting with me," Regis said from the top of the staircase. He flashed a hint of teeth, challenging her to argue with him… or was that sexual invitation? With Regis it was hard to tell since this kind of situation turned the bastard on. His gaggle of sycophants drew a step closer and nodded their agreement.

But Capri couldn't muster even a hint of teeth in response. She didn't want to fight. She wanted to cry. No, she wanted to fix the situation with Ryan. "Of course, my prince." She dropped her gaze to his feet in submission. "What would you like to discuss?"

"I think it has something to do with a particular human," Katar said, his voice low. Satisfaction gleamed in his dark eyes.

"A human?" Rage and fear exploded through the grief. She fought to keep her gaze down. Regis hadn't told the guard yet because he wanted to torment her himself first. If they hurt Ryan—

"Don't play coy," Regis growled. "You've been digging your nose into dragon matters with a human and without permission."

If anything happened to Ryan, she'd rip out Regis's throat. But threatening Regis would just draw attention to Ryan. "It's just a human who potentially has some good information. I intend to wipe his mind the moment he's no longer useful."

Katar eased down to her step and leaned close. "You still don't have permission. You're still breaking the law, little drake."

"I might be small, but I still bite like a drake." She met his gaze in direct challenge. Mother of All, she wanted to grab the slimy drake and beat him senseless.

Katar sneered. "Too many drakes have taken liberty of your generous graces, Your Highness. They think you're weak."

"I don't think you're weak," she forced out. She thought he was crazy and far too powerful, but definitely not weak.

"Her actions say otherwise. Obviously Zenobia's public lesson wasn't enough for some drakes." Katar shot her an evil grin. "She's supposedly sworn allegiance to your coterie, but disobeys your laws. She lives in the human realm and has relations with humans."

"My lord prince—" She didn't have time for this. She needed to deal with Tobias then get back to Ryan.

"She's disgraced you," Katar said. "Other drakes will think it's all right to disobey you because members of your coterie already are."

"I have not disobeyed you." Her hands burned with the need to shoot the asshole. But he was with Regis, which meant he was somehow in the prince's favor, and shooting a favored drake was never a good idea—even if she'd had a gun handy, which she didn't.

"Tobias has summoned her. Obviously she's disobeyed you."

Regis narrowed his eyes, his anger burning red across his cheeks. His sycophants inched back. They stood too still, as if hoping Regis— a stronger predator—wouldn't turn his attention on them.

"Will you stand for that?" Katar asked. "Will you let her make you look weak among your own coterie?"

Capri's frustration froze to fear. She had to calm Regis down, make him see reason before Katar goaded him into doing something terrible. "My prince—"

Movement behind the half-dozen courtiers caught her attention. A shaggy head of black hair peered around the shoulder of the farthest drake. Gig. His wide eyes were locked on her.

"Disobeying the chamberlain means disobeying me," Regis hissed, his fury sweeping across his forehead and down his neck.

"I haven't disobeyed the chamberlain." Please just let it go.

"Doesn't look like that to me," Katar said, showing all his teeth in dark satisfaction. "She must think she can get away with it. She thinks you don't deserve her respect. That you're weak."

"I'm not weak," Regis screamed. "Seize her."

No. She couldn't be taken. She had to get to Ryan. Had to—

Katar grabbed Capri's arm. She wrenched free, but he shoved her against the railing, then grabbed the front of her coat and tossed her up the remaining stairs to the Greater Promenade at Regis's feet. Two of his guards leapt on her, pinning her to the floor.

Gig tensed. She captured his gaze, willing him to stay still. She couldn't stand it if she put him in danger, too. He trembled but didn't move.

Regis bent over her. "Tobias would complain too much if I killed you, but I will not tolerate insolence." He kicked her in the face.

Her head snapped back and pain sliced through her, making her headache pound anew.

"I'm loyal," she gasped. Black specks danced across her vision. The pain from the blow should have faded by now. She was a faster healer than this.

"You will be when Odyne is done with you."

She jerked against the guards' grip. Not Odyne. She couldn't get locked up, not when Ryan needed her… but he didn't need her. He didn't want her. "Please. I haven't broken the law. I'm still yours to command." Her words sounded weak even to her.

"You'll not make me look weak or a fool. Tell Odyne I need her whole, but contrite." A wicked gleam darkened Regis's eyes. "Very contrite." He strode away, a guard and the half-dozen sycophants following him, while Gig was nowhere to be seen.

Her throat tightened again. Ryan didn't want her.

The two guards holding Capri hauled her to her feet. Katar slammed his fist into her face. Pain exploded through her head again and her knees buckled.

"It's a shame I have business elsewhere," Katar said. "I love watching Odyne work. The things that drake can do with a touch."

Ryan woke in the guest bed in Trisha's house, clutching the photo of Capri and his great-uncle, still in the filthy winter coat and the jeans he'd worn when he'd run from Capri's burning house. He had no idea how he'd gotten to his room. He couldn't remember anything past recognizing Capri in the photo.

Capri, the dragon. Blue drake, actually.

He jerked up, his heart pounding. Dragons were real. Magic was real. The guest room shimmered around him. A gunshot exploded behind him, the security door opened, and Capri rushed out, blood staining her side. He could see it now, the ferocious glint in her eye, that vivaciousness he couldn't explain. It was because she wasn't human.

Now he knew it didn't matter if she'd been shot. Her soul magic could heal her body. It made her eternal. She really had been the woman in the photograph. And all that eternal, ferocious passion was his. She'd chosen. He knew from the knowledge she'd flooded into his mind that a dragon only mated once and for life. If he rejected her, she'd never love another. When he died, she'd spend the rest of her eternity alone.

Just the thought made him hurt. Core deep. She didn't deserve that, but he couldn't protect her from it, and staying away wouldn't solve the problem. Her spirit had made its choice.

And so had his.

He could deny it all he wanted, but whatever had compelled her dragon soul to bond with his also compelled him. If he'd known what being inamorated was all about, he would have recognized his irresistible attraction to her for what it really was. True love.

It was crazy. He barely knew her, and he certainly didn't believe in true love. Of course, he hadn't believed in magic, either, even though he could see the future. Yeah, he was willing to agree that not believing, even with what he could do, was ridiculous, but sometimes people didn't make sense.

The future flash Capri growled and raced down the hall into darkness. More gunfire and a scream.

He fought back his panic. The vision was almost over and now he knew the bullets couldn't kill her. She was a blue drake. Her element was water. Only fire could hurt her. That and decapitation. The only sure way to kill a dragon was decapitation... which explained why Capri was so interested in the murders. If one of the victims had been a dragon, dragonkind was likely very nervous about these murders.

The future flash trembled around him, pulling at him, but he yanked against it. He was sick and tired of it controlling him. He would be in control for once, damn it. Capri wasn't in danger. He didn't need to rescue her. When the flash came to pass she'd be fine, he'd be fine, and they could figure out how they were going to defy dragon law and be together.

The rightness of that thought swelled through him.

The future flash jerked at him, the world twisting around him.

He fought back. He and Capri were meant to be.

And he'd run out on her when she'd revealed the truth.

The rightness churned, suddenly foul. He had to get back to her. Explain he'd been surprised, but that he understood everything now.

He shrugged out of the coat, dragged on a clean T-shirt, and opened the bedroom door. He had no idea where she'd taken them last night. It had been in an old warehouse, in a terrible part of town, but there was more than one terrible part of town in Newgate. This wasn't Elmsville with only one wrong side of the tracks.

"Shit."

"What did you forget now?" Trisha asked. She stood in her bedroom, holding a full basket of crumpled laundry. Bright sunlight streamed through the door behind her. That was important, but he couldn't remember why.

Trisha narrowed her eyes. "What's wrong with you? You don't usually sleep so late. And what happened to your face? Were you in a fight?"

The light. Her room faced west. Which meant it was past noon. Capri had been waiting for him all morning. No, Capri wouldn't wait. She'd assumed he didn't care for her the way she cared for him. Or she thought he'd lost his mind and was soul sick or both, and—

"Crap. Melissa." He was supposed to have met her at midnight. She'd probably run her damning story about him and Capri that morning.

"What about Melissa?"

"I have to go." He rushed to the stairs. They twisted and wavered, and he shoved back at the future flash.

"What's going on?"

"I'll explain later. Just—" A new horrible thought flooded him. He had no idea who'd blown up Capri's house. If Melissa had run her story connecting him to Capri, whoever had targeted her could target Trisha and Jess. "Take Jess and go to—"

He had no idea where to send her. Mom wasn't in town, but a connection to him and Trisha was also a connection to their mother. The only person he could trust was Capri... and Hiro.

"Take Jess, go to the Medical Examiner's office, and ask for Doctor Hiro Yoshida."

"You're scaring me."

"It's all right. Just a precaution." The flash tugged, stronger. The security door banged open.

"A precaution against what?"

He squeezed his attention to Trisha. "I don't have time. Just do it. Now. Please."

Trisha held his gaze for a too-long heartbeat. Then she dropped the laundry and shoved past him to the top of the stairs. "Jess, get your coat. We need to visit a friend of Uncle Ryan's."

He squeezed her shoulder. "Thank you."

"You've got a lot of explaining to do."

"And I will. I promise." He rushed down the stairs, and grabbed a coat and his extra car keys.

Except his Camaro wasn't in the driveway and Capri's SUV still sat at the curb. Right. His car was at her place—or what was left of her place.

Oh, man, she was going to hate him.

He wrapped his coat around his arm, smashed the back passenger-side window on the SUV, and unlocked the doors. If there'd been time, he would have been more subtle. But there wasn't time. He needed to find her. The compulsion to find her was overwhelming.

He slid into the driver's seat, yanked out the wires under the driveshaft, and hot-wired the vehicle. With only a vague idea of where that apartment had been, his best bet wasn't to drive aimlessly around town. He needed to find someone who knew how to get in touch with her. There'd been at least two people who'd recognized her at Raven Mitchelle's residence, and one of them had been the friend who'd set them up with the apartment.

Trisha and Jess rushed out of the house and got into Trisha's car. Thank goodness his sister was actually listening to him for once. He didn't know if she was in danger, but he wasn't going to risk it.

He paused at the stop sign at the end of the street, found Hiro's number in the SUV's call directory—thank you, technology—and dialed.

"Hello?"

"I have a strange favor to ask." Please say yes.

"Ryan? Is everything all right?"

"I don't know. Someone blew up Capri's house—" The security door banged open again.

"That was *her* house on the news? Oh, my God. And you were there? Are you guys all right? Do you know who's responsible? Wait, what were you doing at Capri's house?"

"It's a long story." He squinted past the future flash and turned a corner too fast. The SUV's rear started to slide out. He corrected, the wheels caught, but he didn't slow. "My sister and niece are going to come visit your office. Could you keep an eye on them until I've cleared this up?"

"Absolutely," she said without hesitation.

"Thank you."

"And Ryan, things with Capri could be dangerous."

He snorted. "You don't know the half of it."

"Just keep your head."

"I intend to." He hung up. Keeping one's head had a terrible and literal meaning in the dragon world. Hiro couldn't possibly know how accurate that statement really was.

Ten minutes later, Ryan pounded on the door to Raven Mitchelle's residence.

Please let Raven know how to find Capri. At the very least, she had to know how to contact Capri's friend, the one who looked like a Viking.

The future flash whipped around him, the security door banging open again and again. The impossible information Capri had shoved in his head still whirled, threatening his already shaky grasp on reality.

He clenched his teeth. He was not crazy. He would not be crazy.

A gunshot exploded.

Why wouldn't the damned flash just disappear?

Capri would be fine. He just needed—

No, he *had* to tell her he hadn't meant to run out on her, that he was drawn to her the way she was drawn to him. It didn't make any sense, but he knew, soul-deep, it was true.

Raven's heavy door wavered. More gunfire. The vision twisted, wrenched back to the beginning, and the security door banged open again. Capri raced through him. His stomach lurched. An inamorated drake whose love wasn't reciprocated had nothing to live for.

Focus. Find her. All he needed was a conversation and he could make this right.

He pounded on Raven's door again, unable to see it through the vision. Come on. Open up.

The door flew open, and Raven Mitchelle stood in the entrance. Her eyes flashed wide. "Oh, my God."

"I need to find Capri."

Raven squinted at him. No, not at him, at something just beside him. "I'm not sure that's the best idea."

It was the only possible idea.

"Holy shit," a masculine voice said from behind Raven. It was the man from last night, the one who'd disappeared and reappeared in the blink of an eye, Diablo. He strode down the long hall toward them, radiating fury and feralness. He had to be a dragon.

A gunshot boomed around Ryan, but Raven and Diablo didn't react. "I need to find Capri."

"I'm sure you do. Of all the stupid things she could have done." Diablo grabbed Ryan's arm, yanked him inside, and slammed him against the wall.

The air burst from Ryan's lungs. The foyer twisted, darkened, and the hall flooded in around him.

Diablo's face materialized out of the darkness, close, sneering. Without a doubt he was a dragon. "What have you got on her? She's not this dumb."

"I haven't got anything," Ryan gasped.

A sharp wind snapped between Ryan and Diablo and the dragon jerked back.

"Let's not overreact," Raven said.

"Overreact? Men his age just don't develop earth magic," Diablo growled.

"It's not common, but not impossible."

"Listen. I don't want any trouble. I just need to find Capri." The future flash eased, the gunshots faint, like a TV turned down low.

"If she didn't make you, then you really don't want to find her." Diablo paced to the far side of the foyer with ferocious steps. He turned his dark glare on Raven. "You can tell the difference. Did she — You know, or not?"

Raven squinted at Ryan. "I can't tell."

"It usually takes a lot longer than a few minutes of body-sharing for a human body to connect to the earth's magic," Ryan said. He drew in a steadying breath and pushed the future flash back even farther. "Listen, I just need to get in touch with Capri."

"Damned stupid drake." Diablo growled and leapt at Ryan. "You could only know that if she body-shared."

The wind whipped around them again and yanked Diablo back. He roared and twisted toward Raven.

"He's an unnatural," Diablo said.

"He deserves a chance to explain. The dragon taint on his aura isn't very strong." She set her hands on her hips and turned to Ryan. "Start talking."

"Listen, I'm not here to cause trouble. Capri did what she had to do to make me understand." He snorted. "I'm still not sure of everything she shoved into my head."

Raven pursed her lips. "So she shared your body and gave you her knowledge?"

"Yes. Now, can we move on to finding her? If you can't, put me in touch with her Viking friend." He didn't want to go into details. He'd already said too much. Sharing a body with a human defied dragon law, and revealing what he had to Diablo now put her in danger. But it didn't seem as if Raven would let him go if he didn't share something.

"So you know everything?" Raven asked.

"I think so. I'm trying hard not to really think about it. Right now, I need to apologize to Capri and then we need to go after Pete's— Andy's murderer."

"What do you know about Andy's murder?" Diablo asked.

"We got a solid suspect on video just before the third victim was killed."

Tyler Pimm stepped into the end of the hall and stared at them. He'd supposedly died in a fire just like Pete had. There was something about that, something about them being here.

Diablo yanked against the invisible bonds holding him back. "Raven, let me go. I'm not going to do anything."

Raven rolled her eyes at him, but the wind slipped away. She turned back to Ryan. "Who killed Andy?"

She seemed to know about this magic thing, and she was awfully close to Diablo. Pete had had an uncanny ability to know what other people were feeling.

Capri's knowledge pulsed through him. Pete had empathy. He had magic. But only a human who'd shared a body with a dragon's spirit could connect to the earth's magic.

"Who killed Andy?" Raven asked again.

Except that wasn't true. He was pretty sure Pete had never shared a body with a dragon, and before Capri had shoved her essence into Ryan's head, he'd already had his ability to see flashes of the future.

"It's all wrong." He met Raven's gaze, as if somehow she'd confirm the truth. "Humans *can* connect to the earth's magic without a dragon's spirit."

She nodded.

"Then why don't dragons know this? Why does their law assume all mages are made by body-sharing? Why does the law assume all are soul sick?"

"Other dragons don't know because they don't deal with them," Diablo said. He glanced at Tyler, then jerked his chin, a clear command to leave. "Other drakes don't have to kill children."

Tyler's gaze jumped from Diablo to Ryan, then he hurried away.

Realization flooded Ryan. "You don't kill them, do you? You're supposed to, but you don't."

"Not the natural ones. They don't deserve it," Diablo said, his voice dark, the threat clear: don't jeopardize his kids.

"That's what Pete— I mean Andy, was doing here. He was helping you save these kids. They can't be accepted in the human world, and to keep dragons safe, the idea that magic exists needs to be kept a secret. He faked his death all those years ago and now he helps— helped others like him do the same."

Diablo grabbed the front of Ryan's shirt. "And if you tell Capri, I'll rip your head off."

Ryan grabbed Diablo's hand but couldn't pry the man's grip free.

The invisible wind whipped around them, but didn't seize Diablo.

Raven's gaze flickered to the space just beside him. "I'm not sure Capri is a drake we have to worry about. She has to know Detective Miller is a mage. Even if she can't see the difference between mage and drake, you didn't have an aura yesterday and now you have one. She's smart enough to figure out the truth, and she didn't kill him."

She couldn't have killed him even if she'd wanted to, because she'd become inamorated. All of which brought him back to the need to find her. "Capri isn't a danger. Even if she can see…" There was something about auras.

He tugged at Capri's knowledge. Not all drakes could see the difference between a dragon's aura and that of a human mage. "Is that what you're looking at? When you glance just beside me?"

Raven frowned. "Yes, why?"

"Howard Pimm looked at Capri the same way."

"Tyler's dad? What has Howard got to do with any of this?" Diablo growled.

"Pimm was the man on the video before MacCabe was murdered. Did you know MacCabe? Was he a drake or a mage?"

"A mage," Raven said.

That was the motivation. "Pimm is killing mages."

"His first victim was a drake," Diablo said.

"All right. So he's killing anyone with an aura. He can't see the difference or doesn't care." Ryan's heart stuttered. "He's seen Capri. He knows she's a drake."

"I think Howard Pimm and I need to have a conversation," Diablo said, his tone dark, implying that a conversation wasn't what he had in mind.

"You can't just kill him."

Diablo flashed his teeth, looking even more feral than before. "Why not? He's killed two of us and a drake."

"Everyone deserves a fair trial."

"Consider me the jury of his peers." Diablo shoved away from Ryan. The muscle in his jaw tensed, and Ryan knew he was going to pop away like he had during the fight last night.

Gate. That was what it was called. He was going to gate to Pimm's.

"No." Ryan lunged at Diablo and seized his arm. The world lurched. Gut-wrenching blackness flooded Ryan's senses, then his foot hit something hard. He staggered and Diablo slammed his fist into Ryan's face.

P ain exploded across Ryan's cheek and specks flashed across his vision. Dingy white siding swam into focus and the bite of freezing air stung his face.

"No hitchhikers," Diablo growled.

"You can't just kill someone in cold blood."

"I've been doing it for a long time. This one at least deserves it." Diablo swung at Ryan again.

Ryan wrenched back, sending agony shooting through his bruised ribs and body. "But it isn't what you do anymore."

"Oh, it is. I just don't kill innocent kids. What do you think is going to happen to him? You arrest him? Dragonkind still needs to figure out if he's a danger. If he isn't, Capri and her team has their way with him and he's left a shell of a man. If he's a danger, the prince's assassin will finish him and Capri will help hide the evidence."

"That's what she does?" He couldn't believe it, but it made horrible sense, and if he thought about it, the truth was there, in the memories she'd given him. Ryan just had never imagined that she used her FBI credentials to cover up crimes.

"What else did you think she did?" Diablo barked a harsh laugh. "Did you actually think she worked for human law enforcement? It's all about keeping our secret. The only way we care about you is whether or not you're going to go crazy and try to kill us. If you're just crazy, we might arrange for you to spend the rest of your life locked up in an insane asylum, because, hey, who's going to believe you? But more likely, we'll just end you. It's better that way."

"You don't really believe that. You wouldn't be saving those kids if you did. Do you really want to murder the father of one of those kids? What would he think of you?"

Diablo glared at him, then growled and jerked away. "Fine. Let's get Howard into custody. Then we'll figure out how to deal with him."

"Fine."

They marched from the back of the driveway to the front steps. Diablo pounded on the door. No answer. Pimm's van was gone, as well.

"He's not home. I have to get to Capri and warn her." Pimm could be halfway to where she was right now. Except if Ryan had no idea where she was, how could Pimm?

Diablo slid his dark gaze at Ryan as if he could see into his soul, weighing him.

Ryan shuddered. Maybe Diablo had empathy, like Pete, and could see how Ryan felt about Capri. What would this dragon do, knowing that a human had fallen in love with a drake? Or that Capri's soul had picked Ryan? Without a doubt, there were laws about that.

The knowledge flashed through him. Yep. Big laws.

"I think we should see what Howard is up to." Diablo grabbed Ryan's arm, the world wrenched into blackness, then materialized into a musty hall.

Ryan staggered and grabbed the wall beside him to catch his balance. One minute they had been on the front step, the next two feet inside the door.

"Do you have night sight, mage?" Diablo asked, glancing through the arch beside him into the living room.

"Do I have what?"

"Can you see in the dark?"

"You can see in the dark?" More of Capri's knowledge rushed through him. Capri could see in the dark. Night sight was a pretty common earth magic. He squinted but couldn't discern anything through the gloom. "I don't think I can."

"You might get it later." Diablo strode down the hall, his footsteps silent even with his heavy boots. He radiated a predator more than ever.

Ryan followed, his steps quiet, but not Diablo-silent. At the end of the hall sat a kitchen, shrouded in even more gloom. A heavy curtain, shot with half a dozen holes, covered the window over the sink, and a blanket had been nailed over the back door—likely an attempt to keep out winter drafts.

Beside them sat the door to the basement. Diablo reached for it then glanced at Ryan. Dark gold light radiated from his eyes, like the blue light Ryan had thought he'd imagined glowing from Capri's eyes the other night.

"Before we break all of Grey's horror movie rules and go into the creepy basement, what is your magic?"

"It's not useful."

Diablo's lips curled back in a wicked smile. "Not telling me won't ensure your safety."

"I haven't told anyone. And if you wanted me dead, you would have killed me by now."

"Maybe I respect Capri too much for that."

Ryan raised an eyebrow, trying to match Diablo, predator to predator. "I'm not sure you respect anyone. I'm certain you don't respect Capri enough to spare me."

Diablo shrugged. "Keep your secret for now. I'll find out soon enough."

"You're so sure of that?"

"If you don't want to lose your mind, you'll find your way to Raven and get training. What Raven knows, I know."

"Ah, the power of pillow talk. You know you can't always trust what a woman says in bed."

Diablo grabbed the front of Ryan's shirt and jerked him close. "Say that again about my sister and I really will kill you."

Holy shit. "Fine. You want to know my curse? I see things." Ryan met Diablo's gaze, facing the predator and offering a direct challenge even if he scared the crap out of Ryan.

Diablo's grip eased. "What kind of things?"

"Deaths." The word rushed out, and the moment Ryan said it, he knew it was true. He didn't just see flashes of the future. He only saw flashes where people died. "I see when someone dies."

"You're a death augur? Well, that's grim."

Which meant if his future flash was showing him Capri in danger, it was life threatening. Except that might not be entirely true. Pete hadn't died in that fire... well, he had. Pete had died and Andy had been reborn.

God damn it. He bit back a growl. Wow, he was becoming more and more like a drake. Capri might not be in physical danger, but the life she knew had to be. He knew in his soul he saw permanent ends. In a world where dragons could be reborn, a process that stripped away everything they were was as much a death as a physical one.

Real or spiritual, he couldn't let her die. He had to get to her, warn her, stop it somehow. Except they were at Pimm's house. They might be able to confirm if he'd murdered Pete or not. From Diablo's reaction, the dragon wasn't going to rush to help Capri, and Ryan still wasn't sure he could trust him. "Can we finish with Pimm, now?"

"Got somewhere you have to be?"

Ryan glared at Diablo. Just finish this, for goodness sake.

Realization flooded the dragon's face. "You keep saying you have to find Capri. You've seen something, haven't you?"

"Yes. Now, let's find Pimm." Ryan jerked his chin to the basement door.

Diablo opened it, revealing a rickety set of stairs descending into darkness. He crept down, glanced around, then pulled the string of an overhead light. The naked bulb flared to life, exposing a small room filled with photos and papers and scribblings. The mess covered every wall as well as a homemade worktable sitting in the back left corner.

A thick book sat open on the worktable. A picture of Capri had been glued to the page, with notes: *demons can be spotted on television, works for FBI, has human servant.*

Ryan flipped the page. A picture of a middle-aged man with a strong jaw and hard eyes stared back at him. The man looked familiar, but Ryan couldn't place him.

"What's he doing with a picture of Barna?" Diablo asked, nudging Ryan aside so he could get a better look at the book.

That was it. The man was Gregory Barna, the businessman who owned half of Newgate. The notes beside his picture were a flurry of scribbles, something about the biggest of the demons, and dinner. Beside the book were more notes and pictures.

Ryan shifted through them, using the tip of his pen. He couldn't make out a lot of the writing, stuff about demons and duty.

"Here it is. Proof he killed Kardas, Andy, and Don." Diablo tapped the book under a picture of Pete with the note: *trial complete*.

Diablo flipped the page, revealing a picture of MacCabe with the same note.

Now the question was, where was Howard Pimm? From all the notes and pictures of people scattered across the desk, his work wasn't done. It looked like it was just beginning.

Ryan shifted to another pile of pictures at the end of the table. They were of men and women in white shirts and black pants, and half a dozen different angles of a white van with a catering logo. None of the previous victims involved catering. Was this a murder no one had discovered, or was this one that hadn't happened yet?

Diablo had flipped back to Gregory Barna's picture. No completed note at the bottom.

There was something about the caterers. Something about Gregory Barna. Well, he was rich, he probably used catering all the time. In fact, he always hosted a charity ball every year.

"When is Barna's ball this year?" Ryan asked.

Diablo glanced up from the book, light seeping from his eyes. "Tonight."

That was it.

"Barna is his next target. Howard is dressing as a caterer to get in." Ryan flipped over another note. In bright red ink were the words: *They unnaturally heal and the world must know. I will prove it and the world will take up the fight.* "And Howard is going to reveal dragons to the world."

"Just yelling it out won't do anything, no one will believe him," Diablo said.

"I have a feeling he's going to do more than just madly scream it. He knows about dragon healing. There will be news cameras at that gala. He's going to prove dragons exist."

Diablo's eyes flashed wide, more light seeping from his whites. "That can't happen. I have to get Capri and deal with this before it gets bigger than she can handle."

Footsteps crunched outside, toward the front door.

"I have to stop him before he starts." Diablo vanished with a whoosh of air.

The footsteps crunched up the front steps. Diablo whooshed back beside Ryan and grabbed his arm.

"Not Pimm?" Ryan asked. If it had been Pimm, Ryan doubted Diablo would have returned without attacking first.

"No, Cooper."

"Detective Cooper?"

"And he can't see you. I don't know if he can tell the difference between a mage or a drake, but Raven says you're a natural mage and not an unnatural one, so I'm not risking it."

"Cooper is a dragon?"

The world wrenched around Ryan. Darkness swarmed over his senses, then his foot hit floor and he stumbled into Raven's foyer.

"Detective Cooper is a dragon?" Ryan grabbed the large table in the center of the foyer to steady himself. "I suppose the name should have been a giveaway."

"What's wrong with his name?" Diablo asked.

"Gee, Capri, Raven, Diablo, Cooper? Are there any dragons named Bob or Eddie?"

"Well, no."

Raven rushed down the hall toward them. "What happened?"

"Cooper showed up. Makes sense. It is his case."

"Did he see you?"

"Of course not." Diablo pulled out his phone. "But we've got a bigger problem. It looks like Tyler's dad did kill Andy and is now planning to kill Barna and reveal dragons to the world."

"Capri needs to be in on this."

"Already dialed." He flashed Raven a fierce smile.

"If you dialed her cell, that number won't work. It was blown up with her house last night. Why do you think I'm here asking for a way to get in touch with her?" Ryan still couldn't believe Cooper was a dragon. Although if he really thought about it, Cooper gave off the same predatory vibe that Capri, Diablo, and—now that he was paying attention—Raven did.

"Fine." Diablo dialed a different number and someone growled into the phone after the first ring. "Hello to you, too. I got a line on a big mess that's going to need your attention."

The voice growled something and Diablo frowned. "What do you mean, you can't find Jones? ...Yes, I'd heard her house blew up, but I know she's fine... How do I know?"

"Grey," Ryan hissed.

"Her silver drake friend, Grey. You better grab Gig and get to Barna's. There's going to be trouble... Fine, don't believe me, but you and I both know Capri's magic can't influence a whole city. If there's even a chance that dragonkind will be revealed, you need to be there. This needs to be contained... I'll find Capri... Yeah, I know. Consider this my one and only caring moment this century."

Diablo hung up and dialed again.

"What's going on?" Ryan asked.

Diablo held up a finger to silence him. "Hey, Grey... no, actually. I need to find Capri... She what—? God damn it. Well, that will make it difficult for her human to find her."

That didn't sound good. "What's going on?"

"What do I know about her human?" Diablo asked, ignoring Ryan. "That it's a mess that's at least found its way to Raven's doorstep."

Air whooshed through the hall, the front door turned into a black vortex, and Capri's friend Grey stepped through. His gaze jumped from Diablo to Ryan and narrowed.

Yeah, this was a mess. Ryan wasn't going to deny it. But it could be fixed. All he had to do was talk to Capri.

"The human doesn't need both of us. Someone needs to help Capri." Diablo pocketed his phone.

"Tobias is more likely to listen to you. I promised Capri I'd find her human."

"For the love of God! I'm standing right here and I have a name," Ryan said. "And what's going on with Capri?"

"Who says I'm going to bother the Big Man?" Diablo flashed a wicked grin. "Don't go anywhere and don't do anything," he said to Ryan.

"What are you going to do and where the hell is Capri?"

Grey growled. "Don't make this worse for her. Tobias will understand."

"It doesn't matter if he understands or not," Diablo said. "I need to get her to Barna's gala before Pimm puts all of us in jeopardy."

"I'm going with you," Ryan said. They were not leaving him out of this.

"No, you're not." Diablo's gaze jumped to Raven then Grey. "Keep him here." Then Diablo vanished.

"What the hell is going on?" Ryan asked.

"I don't know. But Diablo is right. You need to stay here," Raven said.

"Capri is in a little hot water with her boss," Grey said.

"Would that be the chamberlain or the prince?" Ryan could prove he wasn't an idiot. Capri had given him the gift of knowledge and he would use all of it to ensure her safety—even if it put his sanity in jeopardy.

"How do you—?" Grey asked.

Ryan tapped his temple. "Got the fast track of drake knowledge."

"Which couldn't be good," Raven said.

"I'm fine enough to help Capri. So who is it? Chamberlain or prince?" If it was the chamberlain, Capri's knowledge said he was fair and would listen to reason. Prince Regis, however, was another story.

Grey sighed. His gaze darted up to the right—he was about to lie. "The chamberlain."

"So, it's really the prince. You'd think with all your extra life, you'd be better liars."

"Diablo will take care of it." Raven gestured to the hall, an invitation to further enter her house. And an invitation to sit on his hands and let someone else deal with it.

Yeah, not his style. He was a cop. He was capable of taking action. At the very least, he could help bring Pimm to justice—even if that might just be human justice. That, and his future flash hadn't gone away. He was a death augur, damn it. Which meant Capri was still in danger.

As if thinking about it gave it strength, the foyer rippled around him. Grey and Raven gasped, their gazes jerking to the space just beside him. His aura must have flared.

"I need to get to Capri. If Diablo is going to get her to the gala, then that's where I need to be." He fought to control the vision and not let it overwhelm him.

Raven crossed her arms. "You can't go. The place will be crawling with drakes. If they figure out what you are, they'll kill you."

"They won't figure out I'm a mage," Ryan said.

The air in the foyer rippled again. Ryan shoved at the vision. He'd seen it before. He didn't need to see it again. But it surged, flooding over him. The fire door banged open, and Raven's foyer vanished with the noise.

Blood stained Capri's side and was smeared across her cheek.

Ryan fought to return to the foyer. He couldn't help her while caught in a vision.

The future flash spun, wrenching him around. Capri ran down the dark hall. Gunfire exploded and someone screamed.

Ryan's pulse raced. It felt so real. But it wasn't. Not yet.

More gunfire from the darkness. He tensed and reached for his sidearm, but he didn't have it. Panic swept through him.

He fought to calm down. Focus. It was just a flash. Capri couldn't be killed.

She was all right. She—

Bang. Another gunshot. Details of the hall flooded around him, incomplete construction, naked girders above him, an unfinished concrete floor. Where the hell was he? This wasn't the hall he'd seen before, was it?

The vision lurched, wrenching him with dizzying swiftness.

The security door flew open again, and a man raced into the hall, holding a bloody sword. It wasn't Howard Pimm. Ryan had never seen this man before. Tall, Caucasian, short-cropped dark hair. He radiated the feral ferocity Capri and Diablo did. Light flickered from the man's eyes. He was a dragon and he knew how to kill one of his kind.

The man glanced toward Ryan, but his gaze slid through him, then turned toward the hall.

The future flash burst apart, throwing Ryan back into the foyer. He fought to catch his breath. "Capri is in real danger."

"Diablo will take care of it," Grey said.

"No. He won't. I—" God, he was going to tell two more people about his curse. This was becoming a bad habit. "I see things. Diablo said I was a death augur. I know who's going to kill Capri."

"You have to stay here," Raven said. "If a drake sees you—"

"He'll think I'm just another drake. There are only a few who can tell the difference between a mage and a drake."

"You're not supposed to be using Capri's memories to justify putting yourself in danger," she said.

"Describe the guy and I'll stop him," Grey said.

Ryan raised an eyebrow. "Tall, white, dark hair. Definitely a dragon."

Grey frowned. "That could be a lot of people."

"Yeah, why do you think I didn't suggest that in the first place?" That and Ryan wasn't going to sit around while he knew Capri was in danger. He might not have saved anyone before, but he wasn't going to give up now when it really mattered. "Yes, it's dangerous. Yes, I need to avoid Cooper. And no, I'm not going to sit here while Capri is in trouble. You're either going to help me or not, but I'm going."

Grey growled. "Fine. Mother damned, stubborn humans."

Diablo gated to the Greater Promenade outside the Chamberlain's Office. There wasn't a drake in sight, not even inside the maze of cubicles and filing cabinets. For a second, he feared Tobias wouldn't be in his office and he'd be forced to choose between searching for the chamberlain or heading straight to the dungeon and Capri. But a man-sized shadow passed behind the closed blinds. Tobias was pacing.

That wasn't good.

Diablo gated to Tobias's door and knocked.

"What?" Tobias barked from the other side.

Diablo opened the door and leaned on the frame, feigning a casualness he didn't feel. He was on the verge of catching Andy's killer and dragon politics was getting in the way. "Hi."

"What do you want?" The chamberlain jerked to his desk and sat, sliding his hands over the open folders before him.

If Diablo hadn't known the folders were part of the chamberlain's hoard, he wouldn't have noticed the action. But he did know and the movement revealed just how stressed Tobias was. Diablo hadn't seen him this upset since Regis took the throne from his father in 1521.

"I need Jones." Maybe if Diablo kept the conversation to business it would remain civil.

Tobias rolled his eyes and growled.

Okay, so Jones was probably part of the stress and this particular business wasn't going to avoid the problem.

"Listen," Diablo said." I know there are issues."

Tobias snorted. "Jones is indisposed."

"Jones was arrested. Let's not mince words."

"She broke the law."

Diablo jerked away from the frame. "Did she?"

Admittedly, Diablo knew she'd broken the law, but he doubted anyone else—even her team—knew that.

"She was working a case she hadn't been assigned with a human."

"We both know there isn't a law against that."

"It was all over the news. Her relationship with the human—a disgraced cop—and their investigation into the decapitations."

"You've dealt with this kind of thing before." Diablo bit back the urge to grab Tobias and shake him.

Tobias sighed and stroked the folders again. "I can't go against my prince."

Diablo cocked an eyebrow. Tobias went against Regis all the time. It was mostly little things to keep the peace between the doyens or to ensure dragon safety when Regis did something thoughtless—kind of like locking up the leader of the North American Clean Team.

Tobias met Diablo's gaze. The drake looked exhausted. Something else was going on. It was a dangerous time to be a drake in the Royal Coterie. Probably even more dangerous to be employed in such a visible position.

"Release her for this. Special circumstances and all that. We've got a human who plans to reveal drakes to the world."

"Talk to the Dugga. This is business for the Asar Nergal."

"Actually, it isn't. The man hasn't made the Dugga's awareness, so he isn't a mage." Truth. The Dugga of the Asar Nergal had magic that made him aware of mages. But if a mage wasn't strong enough to endanger dragonkind, the Dugga's magic didn't acknowledge the mage. It was a shame, since Howard Pimm—while only having aura sight—didn't register as a threat and clearly was.

"I can't release Capri," Tobias said, his tone saying he wished he could.

Footsteps clattered behind Diablo and he stepped into the office, clearing the doorway. Swipe and Gig rushed up.

"For the love of—" Tobias crumpled a paper under his hand.

"We need Jones," Swipe said. "There's a situation."

"Let me guess. A mage who isn't a mage is threatening to expose dragonkind," Tobias said.

"No. What?" Swipe glanced at Diablo.

"My problem," Diablo said.

"Really?" Swipe asked.

Diablo shrugged. "Yep."

"Well, I need her first. We've recovered a text message from the damaged cell phone. Someone has hired Zenobia's mages to assassinate Barna at the gala tonight."

Tobias threw his hands up. "You're certain of this?"

Swipe stiffened. "This is not some ploy to get Jones out of prison. This is big. Gig has already associated half a dozen phones with the mages and they're already at the gala. It's happening right now."

"Fine." Tobias yanked out a notepad and scribbled on it. He stamped it with his signet ring and held it out for Swipe. "Don't fuck up."

Swipe flashed his teeth in aggression. "Have I ever?"

Tobias glared at him, and he—with Gig at his heels—rushed out of the office.

"There's more going on, isn't there?" Diablo asked. It was a dangerous question. Tobias wasn't likely to open up, and suggesting any kind of trouble could put Diablo in a cell beside Capri if Regis got wind of it.

"Do your damned job, drake."

Oh, yeah. There was a lot of trouble going on. He and Raven were going to need to keep their heads down if they were going to protect their kids. He could only pray whatever was going on would blow over soon.

CAPRI FOUGHT TO BREATHE PAST THE AGONY SEARING THROUGH HER. She sat in the corner of her tiny cell, pressing as much of her aching body to the cool stone wall as she could, but it did little to ease the pain. Nothing could. Mother of All, it burned from the inside out. She'd never imagined Odyne's earth magic, searing touch, was so powerful. Sure, she'd heard stories and watched Zenobia's sentencing, but Mother!

A wave of agony skittered along every nerve. She had to find a way past it and get out of here. Ryan was likely soul sick, lost in insanity, and it was all her fault. She shouldn't have shown him the truth. She should have wiped herself from his memory, prayed whatever earth magic he'd developed wasn't too noticeable, and let him live his normal human life.

Except she hadn't wanted to let him go. Her soul had picked him, for the rest of her life, and she was selfish. She wanted to give in to that, be with him.

Another wave of agony seared through her, stealing her breath. How long was this going to go on? Odyne wasn't even in the cell anymore. The guards had held her while Odyne had gathered her magic, growling her power word over and over again. Capri had felt the energy building, snapping through the air, then the guards had released her, Odyne had grabbed her face, and agony had consumed her.

That had been... She couldn't remember when that had been. It could have been minutes or hours ago, bookended by blackness and agony. The only thing still clear had been Odyne's eyes. Hard, black. She would never forget those eyes.

The memory of Odyne's eyes bled into Ryan's pale green ones. They radiated light, as if he were a dragon. No, not a dragon, a mage. She hadn't been mistaken when she'd seen his power that night while they'd been hiding from Diablo in the snow. She'd seen a glimpse of his earth magic. She didn't understand how he could possibly have magic. Human souls weren't strong enough to ignite the connection. Only a dragon's soul could. But his flickering aura was real. She hadn't imagined it. And after being in his head, even if it was only for a brief moment, she knew he hadn't shared his body with another drake.

A shiver, not of pain but desire, slid through her at the thought of sharing his body. But sorrow quickly followed. She wanted to share bodies again, like they had in her greenhouse, wanted the intimacy of lovers, of being with her inamorato. But that wasn't what was best for him. Her world was dangerous for humans. Mother of All, her world was dangerous for drakes.

She was done with her service to Regis. She didn't know what her people would do about keeping dragonkind's secret if she quit. A part of her didn't want to care anymore if humans found out about dragons, but that kind of revelation could have disastrous effects. How many humans would become soul sick, unable to accept that magic was real? No, she couldn't abandon her team, but then she couldn't ask Swipe or Gig to renounce their service to the Royal Coterie.

She shifted so her other cheek pressed against the cool wall. This was a mess, and she was sure if the pain just stopped she'd be able to think it through.

Footsteps rushed down the hall. Odyne and the soldiers were returning. Guess it had been closer to hours than minutes since their last visit.

Capri drew breath to will herself to stand and face what was coming like a drake. Pain screamed through her. She clung to the wall and struggled to her feet.

Hot and cold swept over her in waves. Sweat slicked her hands and face, and down her back. Her breath cut out of her lungs and through her throat as if the air was laced with razorblades.

The door opened and framed Swipe, his broad shoulders inches from either side of the doorway, his expression hard.

Capri's brain stuttered. "What are you doing here?"

Movement behind Swipe drew her attention: Gig peering from behind the bigger, older drake.

What the hell?

A wave of agony snapped through her. She sucked in a breath, determined not to let her team—particularly Swipe—see her this weak. "Not that I'm not happy you're here, but you shouldn't have risked Regis's ire by coming here."

Swipe rolled his eyes. "We're not doing this for you."

"Speak for yourself," Gig mumbled.

Swipe shot him a dark look, then turned that glare back to Capri. "Regis is a fool for not recognizing the value of our team. The European and Asian Clean Teams won't be able to pick up our work-load, and save for the two drakes on those teams, you're the only other one able to manipulate the minds of humans."

"So you're doing this for the sake of all dragonkind?" Yeah, no love between them, that was for sure.

"In part. I'm also doing it because Regis is a dick and I know he just sent you to Odyne for his own sick amusement. I'd also be a really shitty Second if I didn't make an effort."

"Gee, I never knew you cared." Another wave of agony shot through her. She bit back a gasp, but Swipe's eyes flashed wide. He'd noticed.

"That, and you think I'd trust anyone else to watch my back while I'm tranced out, cleaning up some stupid drake's mess?" He snorted and stepped back, giving her room to ease out into the hall. "Besides, Gig managed to get that stupid cell phone to talk, and boy, did it talk."

"Oh, yeah?" Right now, she couldn't care less about human mages and her job to protect dragonkind's secret. She needed to get to Ryan and protect him. More agony swept through her. Her knees started to buckle, and she ground her teeth, willing herself to stay upright.

Swipe's hands twitched, as if he wanted to reach for her. "Seems like a drake has been in contact with those mages."

"We already know drakes had been in contact with them. They were a part of Zenobia's coup."

"No," Gig said. "This is after the coup. Like recently. And he—or she—wants Barna dead."

There were so many possibilities for who and why, Capri couldn't wrap her aching head around them. Any one of the doyens could want to kill Barna for any number of reasons. Barna's coterie, the Major Brown, was the wealthiest—aside from the Royal Coterie—and Barna controlled large chunks of real estate in Newgate, the city with the largest number of dragons living there and with the largest number of dragon visitors. Barna had been laughing all the way to the bank after his investments in the little town of Newgate started paying off.

"We need to get to the gateroom," Swipe said. "And we need to get to Barna's gala. Even Diablo said something big was going down, which means it must be big for that drake to call us for backup."

That did have to be big. Diablo never called anyone for anything.

She forced herself to stride down the hall toward freedom, fighting the agony pounding through her—although how free she really was could be debated. The moment this mess was over, Tobias would be obligated to toss her back into the dungeon. That was, if she returned to her service with the Chamberlain's Office. After she wiped Ryan's memory and saved him from going insane, she would need the distraction of work. But returning wasn't an option. Regis would want her head and she doubted he'd care if he permanently destroyed her soul and lost a valuable member of the Clean Team.

She rounded a corner. The dungeon's main arch towered before her, marking the exit and the edge of the magical ward preventing dragons with the ability to gate without an anchor from leaving.

"All right." She tried to pick up speed, but another burst of pain swept over her, threatening her balance. "Our best bet is to find Barna and discreetly protect him, use him as bait." And then she could call Grey and see if he'd found Ryan. Please let him have found Ryan.

"That still doesn't help us figure out who the drake is that hired them," Swipe said.

"Once we've got a mage in custody, I can make him talk." She'd rip her earth magic into whomever they caught and learn the truth. But she didn't want to waste time fighting mages and protecting Barna. She wanted to find Ryan. To hell with her duty. Dragonkind didn't give a damn about her—

Which wasn't true. It was only Regis who didn't care. Hiro and Grey and Gig and even Swipe, they cared about her. They wouldn't understand how she could be inamorated to a human mage—well, maybe Grey could since he and Hunter were like brothers—but that didn't matter. They were still her friends and their secret needed to be protected. And really, humanity needed to be protected from the truth, too. How many humans would fall to the soul sickness, unable to fully comprehend the truth of their universe? How many would fear dragons and want to destroy them, like those humans who'd cast the Great Scourge all those years ago? And how many would want to control the dragons and use them for their own evil purposes?

No, for the sake of Ryan and her friends, she needed to protect their world with the magic she'd been given. No matter how much she despised Regis.

They reached the arch, and Swipe pulled an *asru* bead stone from his pocket, a mini portable gate anchor. "Use this and gate to the base. We'll meet you there."

Before she could take it, air whooshed around them, and Diablo materialized beside her.

"How about we just skip that part. She'll meet you at the gala." Diablo grabbed her arm and the world vanished.

Air whipped at her face then her feet hit the floor, sending an agony roaring through her body. She staggered, but Diablo's grip kept her from falling.

They stood in a dark hall. Only a hint of light bled around the cracks of half a dozen doors evenly spaced on either side of her. Her night sight kicked in, showing the unfinished cinder block walls, open ceiling, and wires snaking around her.

"We need to talk," Diablo said, his voice dark, his grip on her arm tightening.

Fear froze her gut, but hot rage quickly followed. Had he found out she hadn't wiped Ryan's mind like he'd told her? But if he didn't know, she wasn't going to tell him. "We never need to talk."

"There's always an exception to the rule."

"No, there isn't." She wrenched at his grip, but he held tight. Agony roared through her, like the very first time Odyne had touched her, stealing her breath. Mother of All, when would the pain stop?

"Jesus, Jones." Diablo's expression hardened. "Did you give in? Did you tell Odyne about the human?"

"What about the human?" she growled.

"That you didn't wipe his mind? That he's a mage? Did you tell Odyne?"

Fury consumed the agony, tainting everything she saw red. Ryan was dead. He had to be. Diablo had killed him. That's what Diablo did, he was the self-proclaimed death to all human mages.

She couldn't breathe past the overwhelming pain and fury. He was dead. Her inamorato was dead. She grabbed Diablo's throat, wrenched him around, and pounded him into the cinder block wall.

Air buffeted her. He slipped from her grip, no, vanished. He gated out of her grasp. She whipped around as he materialized behind her on the other side of the hall, not within striking distance.

She leapt at him. The only thing left for her was to avenge Ryan's murder. He hadn't deserved to die. Dragon law and Regis and anyone else who thought differently could rot in hell.

"Jones." Diablo raised his hands.

She swung at his head. He jerked out of the way but didn't punch back.

"Would you just listen." He blocked another punch and scrambled to the side.

Why wouldn't the murderer just fight back? It wasn't fair if they didn't fight back. Just like killing someone because they might have a magic that could hurt you. "Why couldn't you have just trusted me to deal with it?"

Diablo snorted. "This is how you deal with it?"

She swung again. He gated away and reappeared behind her, wrapping a thick arm around her neck.

"I dealt with it the right way. The fair way." She wrenched against his hold.

He tightened his grip. She fought to draw air past his arm, past the knot in her throat, and past Odyne's agony burning every nerve.

"You body-shared so he'd understand you. Do you know how dangerous that is? You could have turned him into everything Regis fears."

"I did what I had to. He was going to leave. I couldn't let him leave. I couldn't—" Mother of All, this was worse than Eric. He was dead and it was all her fault and—

Wait a minute. "How did you know I body-shared with him? When did you start having conversations with your prey?"

"If you would just calm down."

A burst of agony swept through her. The world darkened, and she gasped.

"Just breathe through it." Diablo eased her to the wall so she could lean against it. "Just breathe."

"Yeah, how would you know?"

He cocked a dark eyebrow and somehow she knew he did.

She drew in a ragged breath. The pain ebbed then billowed again, stealing her air. "How do you know I body-shared?" she asked between clenched teeth.

"First tell me. Is he your one?"

"What do you care?" What the hell was Diablo getting at? None of this made sense and she wasn't sure it would make sense even when Odyne's magic had finally stopped.

"I need to know if you know."

"What do you mean?"

"Well, it's kind of obvious you've lost it for this mage. In the hundreds of years we've worked together—"

She snorted. "Oh, yeah, we've spent so much time working together." He always growled something, then gated away, leaving her to do the clean up.

"Fine. We're not besties. But this isn't like you. You follow the rules, keep your head down. There are only a few things that could change that."

"And if I find out you've killed him—"

"Relax. Your inamorato is not dead. Confused and barely holding it together, but not dead."

Capri breathed out a sigh. Thank God. "I have to get to him, wipe his mind so he doesn't go crazy."

"I'm not sure that's the best idea."

"For the love of— Just tell me what the hell is going on. I've had a rough twelve or so hours."

"Yeah, who blew up your house?"

"Don't know, and not the question I asked."

"Fine." Diablo blew out his own breath and ran a hand over his perfect ponytail. "The short of it is that Raven runs a school for natural human mages."

"She what?" Capri couldn't have heard that right. "But how does she find those mages? What does she teach them? In Nero's house?" Diablo had to be messing with her. Raven taking mages into Nero's house was not possible. "And why are you telling me this?"

"Your human is going to need Raven's help if he isn't going to go crazy."

"But—"

Diablo raised a finger, silencing her. "Just let me finish answering your first questions before we move on. I send her the mages, children, really. Those humans who've naturally connected to the earth's magic."

"A human's soul isn't strong enough to make the connection."

"So you've been told. But the humans who cast the Great Scourge hadn't body-shared to get their magic. Natural mages are just very rare."

Pain swept over Capri and she struggled to stay focused on Diablo. "There's no way Raven has a house full of mages without Nero knowing." But if that were true, it would explain the kids Capri had seen there, as well as Grey and Anaea.

"Nero doesn't believe in murdering children, either."

"But the law?"

"Nero is the Dugga. He assigns me the mages to hunt, and I determine who dies. Innocents don't die."

"And here I thought you were a heartless asshole."

Diablo flashed her a lopsided smile. "I still am. But even assholes can have standards. I don't drown kittens, and I don't murder children. Everything else is fair game."

He was not the drake she'd thought he was. Although apparently neither was Nero. And keeping her secret—that she was inamorated to a human mage—also meant keeping their secret.

"So what now?" she asked.

"Howard Pimm is responsible for the decapitations, and he's coming here to kill Barna."

"And so are Zenobia's mages. Wow, which god did Barna piss off to make him such a target?"

"Some drakes are just lucky, I guess. I say we deal with the mages and Pimm and then worry about what's next after that." Diablo shrugged. "Who knows, maybe saving dragonkind twice in one evening will put you back in Regis's good graces."

"Nothing can do that. Regis doesn't have anything good about him." But Diablo was right. If Ryan was holding it together for now, she needed to deal with the immediate threats, and then figure out the rest of her life.

H oward approached the loading docks of the king demon's office complex, his heart pounding. This was it. The demons were drawing in on him, and he needed to make the world see them, know they existed.

He just hadn't expected so many of them to be working the king demon's gala. Howard would have thought they'd be guests, not servants, but he'd seen a dozen coming and going along with all the other humans. The lesser demons were security guards and caterers and florists and who-knew-what else, and Howard had to pass by them to get inside.

Sweat slicked his palms, and he gripped the strap of his duffel bag tighter. The FBI demon and her servant hadn't known he'd been ridding the world of their evil. She would have killed him on his doorstep if she'd known. Which meant none of these demons knew, either. He just had to stay calm and stick with the plan.

"I'll protect you," Lizzie said, a whisper caressing his soul. "This is too important. It must be done."

The world had to know.

"Then we'll be together again."

Yes. With Tyler.

Light flickered at the edge of Howard's vision. Lizzie was walking with him. He wouldn't be able to see her if he looked directly at her

—guardian angels couldn't be seen like demons and no one else could hear her—but he could sense her with him.

"Not with Tyler," she said.

Sickness squeezed Howard's chest. The demons had possessed him before Howard had realized the truth. But Lizzie had been looking out for him. She'd burned the demon and saved Tyler's soul. But Tyler wouldn't be a guardian like Lizzie. His soul hadn't been strong enough to resist corruption.

"But yours is," Lizzie said. "That's why you were picked for this."

And that was why he couldn't fail.

He rolled his shoulders, trying to ease the tension clawing across them. He was less than twenty feet from the first demon.

The woman, directing humans unloading a florist's van, glanced at him, but her gaze didn't linger. One of her humans pulled out a large vase and her attention turned fully to him.

Howard strode past her. His confidence grew with every step. They didn't know who he was. He moved through the chaos of people and demons swarming the loading docks and slipped past security behind a group of waiters.

He was doing it. Lizzie protected him. The demons had no idea he was coming and soon the world would know the truth.

———

RYAN GOT OUT OF THE BEAT-UP TRUCK GREY HAD BORROWED FROM Raven, as Grey grabbed the sword—also borrowed from Raven—and hid it inside his calf-length winter coat.

"A sword?" Ryan asked, still fighting the future flash as it tugged at him. The security door banged open... again and again. "Really?"

"More effective than a gun against a drake."

Right. Ryan knew that... from Capri's knowledge.

Grey shrugged. "Just think of it like *Highlander*."

"Like what?" Now, that was something he didn't have in his new memories.

"You know, the movie, with Sean Connery and Christopher Lambert. It's a classic. Don't you know anything?"

"Apparently not."

They headed across the parking garage to one of the many

lobbies in Barna's business complex. They were on the opposite side to the gala, but Grey's plan was to slip in a back entrance and avoid as many drakes as possible.

The future flash tugged harder at Ryan, and he fought to keep it at the edge of his senses and not let it envelop him. Get to Capri, stop that man... or rather drake—hopefully not with Grey's sword—and the flash would end.

It had to end.

Then Ryan would get his chance to talk to her and make things right.

Grey opened the door and glanced in. "All clear."

Good. The fewer drakes they ran into, the better.

Inside lay a hall with a pair of elevators, a couple of maintenance doors, and the opening to the lobby. The complex took up an entire city block, a combination of new office towers and restored original buildings. The gala was in the newly renovated section of the old buildings, but that didn't guarantee the best bet for finding Capri.

They headed down the hall. Grey stopped at the entrance to a massive lobby. It was filled with people. Business people, people dressed for the gala, and everyone in between moved from outside to inside, to shops and offices at the perimeter, or to the vast staircase leading to the upper levels.

Even on this far side of the complex, there were signs of the gala. The theme was a celebration of fire and ice, and giant spiky sculptures of metal and glass dotted the landscape. Fake fires were made of colored silk over a fan, and flashing red and orange lights "flickered" within the art. Glitter, glass, and metal shimmered, catching the light, in myriad decorations—all of them types of modern art sculptures. They hung from walls, pillars, decorative trees, and even from the glass and steel walkways stretching two-, five-, and ten-stories up, connecting one side of the complex to the other.

A bank of glass elevators sat on the far side of the rotunda. To the left, a massive stretch of windows looked out onto an outside courtyard created by two sections of the complex. Red bled across the sky. The sun was setting already. It was close to 5 p.m., which meant the pre-gala events would start soon. How was he going to find Capri in this, or the man he'd seen in the flash?

"How many of these people are dragons?" Maybe Grey could help narrow down the options.

"A lot. You really shouldn't be here."

"The odds of anyone noticing I'm a mage and not a dragon are slim."

"Still, not odds I like."

"Well, deal with it. I'm the only one who can point out the drake who's going to kill Capri."

Grey growled. "Fine. I'd say our best bet is to find Barna. That's where Capri will be."

"Agreed." Pimm was after Barna and Diablo had gone to get Capri to stop him. If Ryan was running the operation, he'd stake out Barna and wait for Pimm to show up.

"If Barna hasn't headed to the gala, he's probably in his office. In the very least, someone there might be able to track him down," Grey said. "East wing, top floor."

"Which is why you parked in the east garage."

"I do have a little experience with this kind of thing." Grey flashed a hint of teeth—a sign of dragon excitement, among other things. "Come on."

They stepped into the crowd and headed to the elevators. Ryan searched the people, his mind whirling and the future flash tugging at him. A familiar coif of brown hair caught his attention. Melissa. She turned and caught his gaze before he could hide. Shit.

Her expression darkened, and she stormed through the crowd toward him.

"Bringing a big friend to confront me isn't going to stop me from running my follow-up story," she said.

"Bringing a what—?" He had no idea what she was talking about.

Her gaze jumped to Grey then back to Ryan. Her eyes were even harder than before.

Swell. She thought Grey was hired muscle, an attempt to scare her into not running the story… wait a minute—

Her words rushed through him: *stop me from running the follow-up*.

Shit. Shit. Shit. She ran it. The bitch ran the story connecting Capri to Ryan.

"You almost got lucky," she said. "Someone's house blew up and I almost got bumped, but they squeezed me in. You should have met me at the boat house."

Movement over her shoulder caught his attention. A tall man with short-cropped dark hair, wearing a tailored suit, strode toward the elevators.

The future flash billowed, jerking his vision closer to the man. It was the guy Ryan had seen going after Capri.

Someone grabbed his arm, wrenching him back to his body. Melissa. "Didn't you hear what I said?

"And I've got more important things to worry about." Like saving Capri's life. He yanked out of her grip. He'd deal with the fallout of her story later. It was the only thing he could do. He nudged Grey.

"What?" Grey asked.

"Over there. It's him."

"You can't just brush me off." Melissa stepped in front of Ryan.

He grabbed her shoulders and moved her aside. "Honey, you've done your worst. You've proven you're still a selfish bitch. I hope you're happy. Now, get out of my way. I have lives to save."

Her mouth dropped open. "You what? You're not working. You're—"

He shoved past her. He was done with her and had more important things to deal with right now, like not losing this guy.

The man entered the elevator, and Ryan pushed past a couple dressed for the gala.

"Hold the door," he called.

The man met Ryan's gaze, then glanced up and over—likely at Grey. He pursed his lips, and the doors slid shut.

Ryan hit the call button, the doors to the next elevator opened, and they rushed in.

"Are you sure that's the guy?" Grey asked.

"Yes."

"Shit."

"Let me guess. You know him?" Ryan kept his gaze locked on the other elevator. He needed to know what floor the guy got off on.

"Yeah. That's Katar. He's Barna's second in command and a rising star with Regis." Grey pulled out his phone. "Oh, and I'm guessing that was an ex back there."

"Uh huh." Ryan didn't want to talk about it.

"You're with Capri now. She's family, or as family as it gets with us. That means your problems are my problems. Just say the word…"

He shifted and the tip of the sword poked out from the bottom of his coat.

"Thanks, but not the way I usually solve my problems."

Grey jerked the sword back up and dialed his phone. "I didn't mean *that*. Financial ruin is more my thing."

"I'll think about it." Not that he wanted to destroy Melissa, but a part of him didn't want her to get away with ruining Capri's career.

The man, Katar, got off on the ninth floor.

"That's weird," Grey said, pulling Ryan's attention back to the chase. "I wonder why he didn't go up to Barna's office."

"Maybe he has an office on nine." Ryan hit the button for that floor.

"I doubt that. Hey," Grey said into the phone. "Give Capri a heads-up to watch out for Katar… Yeah, from her human."

He hung up as the elevator door slid open. The hall beyond was empty, filled with painting equipment and tarps, but it wasn't in the stage of construction as the future flash.

Regardless, Katar couldn't have gotten too far. Ryan stepped out and Grey followed.

A voice rumbled somewhere down the hall. Ryan glanced at Grey, whose expression hardened—and not just as a ferocious creature trapped in a human's body, but as a warrior who'd seen years of battle. Sweat glistened at his temples. He was a warrior who'd seen too much. Ryan had noticed that look before on cops who'd been in bad situations.

The voice rumbled again. Another one, higher pitched, answered.

There wasn't time to ask if Grey was going to keep it together or not. Ryan was just going to have to pray he would. The man was a dragon, after all. That had to count for something.

Ryan headed down the hall. His future flash rippled at the edge of his senses. Grey was silent behind him.

"The mages are going to start in five," the rumbling voice said. He sounded down a bit and around the corner. "Barna is set in the arboretum, where he usually is before the gala."

Ryan slowed, edging to the corner, and glanced down the hall.

Four men and one woman were in a sitting area covered with painting tarps. A door to an unfinished office stood open. Two of the men had pulled aside one of the coverings and were sitting on a black leather couch. The others leaned against the walls. All looked at Katar, who stood with his back to Ryan.

Ryan jerked behind the corner, his future flash vision whirling his sight back down the hall.

Katar checked the time on his phone. "Remember, none can be left alive."

"And I've got the boss man," the woman said. She flipped a lock of platinum blond hair from her eyes and slid her hand to a long knife —or was that a short sword?—hidden in the folds of her long coat, just like Grey's.

It sounded like they were plotting Barna's murder, and those mages who were starting in five were somehow part of the plot but were going to be betrayed.

"So where's Fletcher?" the middle-aged man on the couch asked. He was squat with sandy blond hair and while he didn't look imposing, he still gave off the predator vibe that everyone else in the group did.

Behind Ryan, the elevator dinged.

"Crap," Grey hissed. "If I'm recognized, this could be bad And there are too many to stand our ground."

Except there was nowhere to go. Behind them was whoever was in the about-to-open elevator, and they needed to walk past the hall in clear view to escape.

No time.

Forward, past the hall, was the only option. Maybe no one would notice.

Ryan rushed forward, and Grey followed.

"Hey," a voice said.

Damn. They'd been spotted. Ryan's vision twisted back to the seating area. The old guy had spotted them. Katar swung around, scowling.

"Was that the Handmaiden's bitch?" the woman asked.

"Grey," Katar growled.

Grey grabbed Ryan's shoulder and his vision shot back into his body. A vortex whirled in front of them. Behind, the man from the elevator rushed toward them and Katar and the others raced around the corner, guns and swords in hands.

The woman lurched through the vortex, her blade drawn.

"Whatcha doing, silver drake?" she asked. "And who's your friend? He's cute."

"Back off, Ginger," Katar said, his voice low and threatening. But the menace—and his gun—wasn't directed at her. It was fully on Grey. "Seems we have a problem."

"Yeah. We're lost and you're ugly," Grey said.

"Not the problem I was thinking of." Katar flashed his teeth, looking even more feral. "You've stumbled across major brown business."

"And it's none of mine. Whatever happens with the Major Brown Coterie stays in the Major Brown Coterie," Grey said.

"Why is it that I don't believe you?" Katar asked.

Grey frowned. "I really don't know. I'm quite a trustworthy guy."

"Oh, yeah, now I remember." Katar tapped his gun to his temple. "Trustworthy to your friends. And your blue drake friend can't keep her nose out of my business. She and her team just keep going after my mages, my hired and groomed assassins."

"Don't forget fall guys, too," Grey said.

Katar snorted. "Yeah. It would be bad if they died too soon. Which is why Capri is such a pain. See how I did that? Full circle."

"Well, you know, when anything involves mages, it's kind of Capri's job to stick her nose in," Grey said.

Ryan's sight tugged at him, jumping from the woman back to the men. He struggled to stay focused. "I do like the plan." The only way out of this was to talk. There were too many of them and they were too well armed for a fight—at least Grey still hid the sword. That could be a useful surprise at the right moment. "So you hired the mages—"

"Repurposed them from a fellow, but overly ambitious, green drake," Katar said.

"Okay, repurposed them." As if they were tools that could be taken and not people. "You hire them to attack your boss and then you swoop in to save him so you'll look like a hero."

"He'll look like the new doyen," the woman, Ginger, said.

The older guy glared at Ryan. "Who the hell are you?"

"No one. Just visiting from out of town." Ryan shrugged. "You know, if your mages are showing up in five minutes, you should probably get moving."

"We'll stay here," Grey said.

"Yeah, you will," Katar said. "Fletcher, you were late. You watch them. A security detail will be up in two minutes."

"Why can't I kill them?" Ginger whined.

"Because I say so. They might end up being useful." Katar jerked his chin. "Search them, Cestus."

Shit.

The older guy, Cestus, patted them down and confiscated Grey's sword and phone—so much for that—while another man, a guy in his mid-twenties with shaggy blond hair, called security.

"When this is done, maybe I'll think of letting you go. Or maybe I'll ask Regis to throw you in with your blue drake girlfriend for a time with Odyne, until the Handmaiden comes back and Regis has you reborn."

"Really not necessary," Grey said.

"Just remember. Start to summon a gate and Fletcher will shoot you. You're not Diablo. You can't gate like he can." Katar glanced at Ryan. "No one can gate like he can, and I doubt he can gate faster than a bullet."

Katar snorted and strode down the hall to the elevator with the others following, taking Grey's sword and phone with them.

"So." Grey rocked back on his heels. He slid his gaze from Fletcher to Ryan and raised an eyebrow.

This was their only chance to escape. The security team would be here any minute, and right now it was two against one. Only there were still the terrible odds that one of them would get shot.

"So." Ryan's vision shot up, swirled around him, then flew down the hall. It swept around a corner to a plain security door. The door banged open and four security guards rushed out of the stairwell.

It was now or never.

He lunged at Fletcher. The drake leapt back. He yanked his aim from Grey to Ryan, but Ryan had leapt too close and slammed his hand up and the shot hit the ceiling. Fletcher twisted, trying to point the weapon at Ryan. Grey grabbed Fletcher's shoulders and tossed him back. He slammed him against the wall. Ryan grabbed for the gun.

Fletcher bucked against Grey's grip, yanking the gun out of Ryan's reach. Someone yelled at the end of the hall. The leader of the security team. He pointed his gun at Ryan, while another man pointed his at Grey.

"Shoot them!" Fletcher smashed his elbow back, skimming Grey's cheek.

Grey jerked away and Fletcher spun around. Ryan grabbed at his gun but Fletcher rammed the butt against Ryan's hand. The security team leader fired. The bullet slammed into the wall by Ryan's shoulder.

Grey grabbed Ryan and tugged him back. "Let's go."

They scrambled away from the security team. Bullets blasted into the wall beside them. They raced down the hall toward the sitting area. Ryan could only pray there was a way to hide or get to the stairwell unseen—since waiting for an elevator right now wasn't an option.

They bolted around another corner. Ryan's vision swam around him, jumping from the security team and back to him. The team chased after them, guns ready. They'd seen which hall Ryan and Grey had rushed down. They had to lose them. The question was, how? And Ryan needed to find Katar again. It was the only way to save Capri.

"We need to get out of here. Can you make a gate?"

The security team stormed into sight.

"I need a bit more breathing room than what we've got."

Ryan's vision shot down the hall, away from the security team. Two more men were coming the other way. They were going to be trapped if they didn't take the element of surprise.

"Come on." He rushed down the hall, hit the corner, and surprised the two extra men.

The first guy yelped. Ryan punched him in the face. He staggered back and Ryan snagged his gun, while Grey rammed his elbow into the second guy's throat. The man went down, coughing.

Ryan and Grey bolted around another corner, and Ryan grabbed at the first door in the hall. Locked.

Grey tried the second door. Unlocked. They scrambled in, and Grey flicked the lock on the door but it wouldn't catch. Swell.

C apri reached for the door to the arboretum as Odyne's pain washed through her again. The hall darkened and she gripped the door handle to keep standing.

"Breathe," Diablo said, his voice low, close.

She sucked in air and the door to the arboretum swam out of the darkness. Her reflection in the glass panel stared back at her—too pale, too drawn. Diablo stood at her shoulder, close but not touching her. A touch could set off more pain. Behind her, Gig watched with big eyes, while Swipe scowled. He was probably going through the odds of how useful she'd be in a fight and realizing she wasn't going to be much help.

Yeah, well. She wasn't here for a brawl. None of her team really were magically set for a fight. She was here to contain whatever any humans remembered.

She yanked open the door, sending a shock of pain searing through her and drawing a growl she tried to swallow.

"Hey," Swipe said.

"What?" she asked through clenched teeth.

He held out his backup gun. "I hope you won't need this."

"You mean stand back and let the big boys handle things?" She couldn't look weak, not even in front of her Second—maybe particularly not in front of her Second. Swipe could use it as an opportunity to take control of the team. But did she really want control? With Ryan in her life, being a member of the Royal Coterie became complicated. And so far, Swipe hadn't made any move to oust her—which he could have done back in Regis's dungeon.

"That wasn't what I meant," Swipe said.

"Sure it was." Diablo flashed his teeth. "Capri, you're next to incapacitated and we need you ready to use your earth magic. Containing situations is your team's goal."

Capri took the offered gun. "Way to charm a girl, Death-to-all-mages."

Diablo's smile deepened. "The truth is the truth. I thought girls liked guys who didn't lie."

"Okay, this is great and everything," Gig said. "But those mages' cell phones are getting closer and we've yet to find Barna."

"How close?" Swipe asked.

The elevator at the end of the hall dinged and the doors slid open, revealing four men and two women. Their auras flared around them with the promise of power and danger.

The woman in front—a tall blond—raised a sword and yelled. Lightning shot from the blade and arced down the hall.

Diablo shouldered Swipe and Gig deeper into the arboretum and slammed the door shut. The lightning shattered the glass and crackled over the metal frame.

Swipe fired through the now-glassless door, hitting the lanky black man beside the woman. The bullet ricocheted off him, drawing a chuckle. Swell. She had lightning and he was impervious. It was likely the rest of the group had just as powerful earth magics, too.

"Capri, you and the kid find Barna. Swipe and I will hold them off," Diablo said.

Swipe fired again, but the impervious guy jumped in the way, protecting the others.

"That's a terrible idea," Swipe growled.

"Oh, yeah? What have you got that's better?" Diablo asked.

Capri sucked in another breath. The mages were human and her magic could deal with them. "Gig. Find Barna. I'll take care of the mages."

Diablo's eyes flashed wide, as if he'd figured out what she planned and didn't like it. "That's a worse idea. Capri—"

She subvocalized her power word. Pain exploded across her head, the agony as fresh as if Odyne had just touched her.

Diablo yanked her behind a large raised flowerbed.

Her connection to the earth's magic vanished, but the pain still coursed through her.

Lightning snapped past them. Swipe and Gig scrambled in beside them.

"What the hell?" Swipe fired another two shots.

Capri fought past the pain. More lightning snapped. She drew breath to summon her magic again.

"Don't," Diablo said. "Swipe and I can handle a couple of mages."

"Sure we can," Swipe said, sarcasm dripping from his words. "Just six is more than a couple."

Wind whipped around them, snapping branches from the trees.

"And now they have wind as well as lightning." Swipe fired again. "I really hate wind."

"Don't be such a scaredy-drake, earth dragon. So a little wind limits your healing. Just don't get hurt." Diablo flashed his teeth. It was clear this was what he lived for. "Save your magic for when you really need it," he said to Capri. Then he vanished with the whoosh of one of his sudden gates.

"Just don't get hurt. I'm going to kill him," Swipe said.

Wind swept around them, and Swipe shuddered.

"Okay, the plan." Capri ground her teeth. "We get to Barna and we get him to his security team."

Someone yelled, and the impervious man barreled around the planter. Gig squeaked and shot him in the face. Impervious man roared and grabbed the younger drake.

"Great. Can we trust his security?" Swipe asked. He lunged at Impervious, and Gig squirmed away.

"When you think of something better, we'll do that." She glanced down the hall. Three of the mages were gone. All that remained was Lightning Woman with her sword, Impervious, and a heavyset man moving his fingers like a puppet master—likely Mr. Wind. He twitched and a tree limb snapped free and hurtled toward her.

"Get moving." Swipe wrenched in Impervious's grip. "The others must have gone after Barna."

"But—" Gig said.

"I'll be fine," Swipe said.

A black vortex formed behind Puppet Master. Diablo leapt out and grabbed the drake. Another vortex swept around them and they vanished.

"See? Better already. No more wind," Swipe said.

Lightning Woman shot a blast at them. Capri shoved Swipe and Impervious out of the way.

Gig fired at Lightning Woman. She dove to the side, shooting another bolt of lightning at them. It exploded into the planter, showering them with dirt and cement and foliage.

Another vortex formed behind her. She scrambled out of the way with a wild swing as Diablo appeared.

"Go!" Swipe said.

Diablo dodged the woman's swing, lunged past her guard, and grabbed the front of her coat. She shoved a palm against his chest and lightning exploded from her hand, slamming Diablo back over two raised planters and into a massive pillar.

Gig grabbed Capri's arm, sending a shock of pain searing through her.

"We don't know what any of the others can do or how many more there are," he said. "We have to get to Barna."

Yes. She staggered away from Swipe and Impervious and raced deeper into the arboretum. This was her job... sort of. Keeping dragonkind safe was her job and this had the potential to put everyone at risk. Including Ryan, who now had magic and was neck-deep in her world.

R yan scrambled around an office partition and crouched beside Grey. He checked the clip in his gun. Out of ammo. The security team had followed them into the office and now it was a game of cat and mouse through the maze of office furniture. All the while, Katar was getting closer to Capri and fulfilling Ryan's future flash. Grey had already tried to make a gate, but they'd been shot at before it could fully form and they'd had to abandon it.

"We need a better plan," Grey hissed.

"I'm all ears." But even if they got past the security team, how was Ryan going to find Katar again?

The desk beside him wavered and darkened.

Not now.

Footsteps sounded nearby, soft thuds on the carpet signaling a careful approach.

Ryan's vision wavered again and a hall formed where the desk was.

The footsteps drew closer.

Grey tensed.

The muzzle of a gun eased into sight by the partition.

Ryan fought to stay in the present but his vision tugged at him.

The hands holding the gun slid into sight. Grey leapt. He grabbed the man, jerked him forward, and rammed his knee into the man's face.

"Come on." Grey shot the man in the back, grabbed a second firearm from the guard's boot, and held it out to Ryan.

Ryan stood, but the world tilted, no longer the office, but a hall.

"Come on." Worry darkened Grey's tone. He pressed the gun into Ryan's hand.

The office jerked back into place. The shot security guard was already climbing to his hands and knees—he had to be a dragon. Grey shot the man again, and he and Ryan raced around a bank of filing cabinets.

Gunfire slammed into the partition where their heads had been. Ahead lay an exit. They rushed through the door, returning to the hall under construction, but Ryan's vision wrenched back into the office, then back to the hall. His future flash seized him. Katar jumped into sight, except behind him wasn't the cinder block hall from the original future flash.

Grey slapped Ryan's shoulder and he sliced a mental gap in the flash to see reality. They raced around a corner and another.

Footsteps rushed down the other hall past them.

The future flash flooded Ryan's senses again, yanking him back to the other hall. It was brightly lit, shiny, new. Katar rushed along it with the five others he'd left with.

Ryan was seeing reality. The present.

He knew it soul-deep, just like he knew, when his vision shot out of him in the middle of a fight, it wasn't the future but imminent danger.

Katar chambered a bullet in his gun. Ahead of him stood a pair of glass doors. No, not glass. The glass had been shattered. It lay in chunks on the floor, catching the light.

"What the hell?" Ginger asked.

Cestus reached for the door handle. "Looks like the party started here."

"It wasn't supposed to," Katar said, his voice dark.

"Hey." That was Grey's voice.

The flash rippled. Ryan struggled to hold on to the flash—the irony not lost that every time before, he'd been trying to get rid of it —but he had to figure out where Katar was.

"Ryan." Grey again.

The flash paled. Ryan clenched his teeth. Hold on. Just a little longer.

Then Cestus opened the door and the room beyond flooded into sight. It was a magnificent indoor garden, flowers and bushes and even trees.

Magic crackled against Ryan's skin. The flash vanished and his jaw ached. A black vortex swirled around the wall.

Grey grabbed Ryan's shoulder. "Come on."

"Will that take me to Katar or Capri?"

"No. We don't know where they are and we need more weapons."

Ryan pulled from Grey's grip. "Katar is in some indoor garden or greenhouse."

"The arboretum? There's an arboretum in the building."

Someone yelled down the hall.

"We don't have a lot of time," Grey said.

"I need to get to the arboretum. Can you gate us there?"

Grey ran a hand through his hair. Sweat glistened on his face and his complexion was pale. Whatever stress Ryan had seen before when this had all started was pushing through, threatening to take over. "I wouldn't trust me to get us there right now."

Ryan met Grey's pale gaze. That confession had hurt.

"New plan," Ryan said. "Can you get yourself to safety?"

"That I can do, I just may end up in New Mexico or Canada."

"Can you distract them first?"

Grey flashed a fierce grin. "And give you a chance to get away. I can do that, too."

"Don't get killed."

"I'm a drake. We're hard to kill or haven't you heard?" A shadow flashed across Grey's expression, belying his words. He might be a drake, but something had made him all too aware of his mortality. Then the shadow vanished. "I'll join you when I can."

"You better."

Grey snorted. "Capri has no idea how good she's got it." He bolted from the hall and yelled to catch the security team's attention.

Ryan fought the urge to back Grey up. That wasn't the plan. Grey was a solid friend, a warrior who knew his limitations and didn't let his pride get in the way of doing what was right. Ryan couldn't help but wonder what had happened to Grey.

More yells and gunfire filled the hall.

Ryan tried to focus, see if Grey's death was imminent, but his vision wouldn't jump down the hall. With luck, that meant Grey might be in danger, but it wasn't mortal.

Please, don't let it be mortal.

Ryan wrenched his attention from the sounds of violence and raced in the other direction, toward what he knew for certain was mortal danger for Capri.

41

Capri and Gig rushed from Swipe and Diablo to the far end of the arboretum and found Barna faced with three mages from the elevator. Another mage with lightning shot a bolt at Gig, pinning him down, while a female mage with enhanced strength and speed swooped down on Capri. She slammed Capri with punches and kicks, and knocked her gun into the foliage.

Capri blocked another punch for her head by Strong'n'Fast, and Lightning shot more bolts at Barna and Gig. She couldn't believe there were two mages with lightning in the group of six. The odds of that were small, but then Zenobia had had the luxury to keep only the strongest mages for her coup.

More lightning exploded beside Capri. Strong'n'Fast punched again, forcing Capri to jerk out of the way, but Strong'n'Fast's knuckles skimmed her cheek, drawing an inferno of Odyne's pain.

Gig fired at the lightning mage—a stocky Chinese man—and the man leapt behind a pillar. Barna grunted and dodged a sword swing from his assailant—a man who'd probably been a body builder in his previous life. Telekinetic winds whipped around them, summoned by both Barna and his assailant, essentially negating each other.

A tree branch whizzed past Capri's head and Strong'n'Fast slammed her fist into Capri's gut, stealing her breath. Pain exploded through her, her knees buckled, and Strong'n'Fast grabbed her throat. More pain seared where Strong'n'Fast squeezed, and Capri dropped to her knees. Suffocation wouldn't kill her, but it could subdue her long enough for Strong'n'Fast to decapitate her.

She hissed her power word. Odyne's pain snapped, sudden and sharp. "Sleep."

Strong'n'Fast squeezed harder.

"Sleep." Capri struggled to concentrate on the thread of earth magic in Strong'n'Fast's mind. The woman was tired. She should just close her eyes. "God damn it. Sleep."

Strong'n'Fast's grip loosened.

Capri sucked in a ragged breath. Odyne's agony burned through her. "That's it. Just relax and sleep."

Strong'n'Fast squinted, fighting the compulsion. "No." She shook her head as if that would free her from Capri's magic.

Capri pushed harder. "I. Said. Sleep."

The woman wrenched her hand back to punch. An explosion sounded and blood misted Capri's face. Strong'n'Fast's eyes flashed wide. Blood seeped across the front of her shirt and she collapsed forward. Behind her, Gig stood ready to fire again.

"Thanks," Capri said.

"No prob—"

Lightning slammed into him, the force throwing him over a thigh-high planter. He disappeared behind the concrete box with a scream. Capri scrambled after him, shoving a thread of earth magic at Lightning Guy.

"Sleep!" Pain threatened her consciousness.

Lightning Guy shot off another bolt, blasting the top off the planter.

Gig sucked in quick shallow breaths, his chest a charred, bleeding mess. Capri reached for him, but Barna howled, wrenching her attention to the possible danger.

Barna's assailant—the body builder—yanked his sword from Barna's torso. Barna slammed his palms against the wound as if that would stop the bleeding—and given that he was a dragon, it might hold back enough blood. Body Builder lunged again. Barna jerked to the side, the blade skimming his ribs, drawing another yell.

"I'm good," Gig said.

"No, you're not."

"The mission is to stop the mages. So stop them already."

Capri sucked in a quick breath. The best way to stop them was to use her earth magic, even if that was going to be agonizing. She said her power word. Her earth magic flared to life again, and so, too, did the aftereffects of Odyne's magic. Capri's power stuttered, and she fought to stay focused and maintain the connection.

Lightning crashed beside her, and Body Builder tossed Barna, tumbling him down an aisle between planters.

"Sleep."

Body Builder raised his sword.

"I said, go to sleep." Pain roared through Capri.

Body Builder spun to face her. "Get out of my head, bitch."

"Go to sleep."

"No." He lunged toward her as a black vortex whooshed beside him.

Diablo appeared, grabbed Body Builder's sword arm, wrenched him around, and hauled him into another gate.

Capri's mind stuttered.

Gunfire and lightning boomed on the other side of the planter. Swipe had pushed Lightning Guy back to another pillar farther away.

Behind them, Katar and a security team with a dozen drakes rushed down the aisle.

Barna blew out a relieved breath and sagged against a tree, a hand still pressed to where Body Builder had stabbed him.

Katar's gaze jumped from Swipe to Capri and his eyes narrowed. Ice slid through her. Diablo had warned her about Katar, and even if he hadn't—or if the asshole hadn't convinced Regis to send her to Odyne—she would have disliked him.

"The Clean Team is in league with the mages," Katar said.

Four of the security team members growled and rushed into the fray, two going after Swipe, the other two rushing toward Capri. The others looked stunned, as if they hadn't fully registered what Katar had said.

"Our doyen is under attack, and the Clean Team needs to be stopped." Katar glared at the hesitating security team members. "Do your job."

The men and women split, rushing at Swipe and Capri.

"Stop," Barna gasped. "They've been helping."

"No, you're under Capri's spell," Katar said.

"My magic doesn't work on drakes." Capri glanced at Gig.

"I'll be good in a few minutes," he hissed, and he crawled—under cover of the planters—out of sight.

"Your magic can manipulate anyone."

Wind slammed into her, tossing her back.

"No," Barna said.

The closest member of the security team rushed toward him, a sword held low, almost as if she was keeping it out of sight.

"Watch out," Capri yelled.

The woman with the sword turned, last minute, toward Capri. More wind whipped around her. Gunfire sounded from Swipe's position. Barna gasped, calling for his team to stop, but Katar kept countering the commands and the team listened to the Major Brown Coterie's second in command instead of the doyen.

More of the security team rushed at Capri. A vortex formed beside her and Diablo appeared.

"Holy shit!" he said.

Wind tossed him back. He gated away and reappeared a few feet over.

A security guard punched at Capri and she twisted to the side. But another guard jabbed at her with his knife. The blade skimmed her arm, drawing a fierce sting enhanced by Odyne's magic.

Diablo shoved the man aside and punched another one in the face.

The woman with the sword turned back to Barna and swung at him. He stumbled, still injured from being impaled in the chest—seemed he wasn't a fast healer.

"What the hell?" Diablo's eyes narrowed.

Realization flashed through Capri—spiking with Odyne's magic. "Katar is the traitor. He hired the mages."

"Lies," Katar yelled. "She's using her magic on you."

Diablo snorted. "Her magic doesn't work that way."

A gunshot exploded. Blood sprayed from the back of Diablo's shoulder. He screamed and staggered.

Another security guard lunged at Capri. Behind him, Ryan rushed down the aisle, his pale gaze locked on hers.

She punched the closest guard in the face and turned to Diablo. "Gate Barna to safety. We'll regroup... somewhere."

"Yeah, I don't recommend staying here." Diablo seized Barna and dragged him through a gate.

"You bitch!" Katar pointed his gun at her and fired. *Bang, bang, bang.*

She dove out of the way, rolling to the feet of one of the security guards. No, not a security guard. It was the female drake with the sword. She was with Katar, but wasn't dressed like a guard.

Sword Woman bared her teeth and swung at Capri. She wrenched out of the way. Ryan tackled Sword Woman and slammed his elbow into her face. "There are too many. We have to get out of here."

"Swipe!" Capri yelled, grabbing Sword Woman's weapon from the ground.

No answer. The drake had either escaped, was hiding, or dead.

Her stomach clenched. He was not dead. Swipe was a hard drake to kill. Just like Gig.

Ryan grabbed Capri's hand, his gaze unfocused and his aura pulsing around him. "Swipe and Gig are fine. But—" He shot Sword Woman in the chest. "We're not. This way."

42

Grey's heart pounded. He bolted around a corner as gunfire peppered the wall behind him, and dashed down the hall. There, at the end, a freight elevator. The doors slid open, revealing two more security guards. Even if they hadn't been armed to the teeth, Grey would have thought the situation ridiculous. It was now seven to one—and he wasn't that dangerous a drake.

But maybe he could have the element of surprise and a means of escape if he timed it right.

He barreled for the men. The first guy saw him, but Grey didn't give him time to raise his gun. He leapt and rammed his fist into his face, knocking him to the ground.

The second guy froze. Just for a heartbeat. But a heartbeat was all Grey needed. The elevator doors hit his foot and jerked open. Grey seized him and tossed him into the hall.

Grey hit the close door button. The first guy groaned. The second guy rolled to his knees. Grey hit the close door button in a rapid tattoo. *Close, damn it. Close.*

Second guy fired.

Grey wrenched into the corner. A bullet slammed into the back of the elevator and the doors slid shut.

Thank the Mother.

It started to move, and Grey hit the stop button. He needed to get back to his den, grab some useful weapons, and then find Ryan and Capri.

He drew breath to concentrate and summon a gate. Tremors slid through his body.

They'd almost killed him.

The tremors increased. His knees buckled, and he pressed his palms to the back of the elevator to keep standing. There, at chest level, was the bullet hole. It could as easily have hit him as it had the wall and he wasn't a fast healer.

The world darkened and the smell of wet garbage flooded his senses. Water dripped and someone chuckled, an ugly grating noise.

"How fast can you heal, drake?"

"Not fast enough," someone else snickered.

Pain seared his throat. He clamped his hands against his neck, but remembered blood welled behind his fingers. He couldn't breathe, couldn't see into the darkness. Memory twisted his assailants' faces into hideous masks, then they jerked into crystal clear detail, every hair, every wrinkle, every freckle seared into a memory that just wouldn't fade.

He was going to die. He didn't have enough strength to fight back and he wouldn't heal in time to fight off that final blow. He couldn't concentrate enough to call a gate, and he didn't have any other magic.

The agony of his slit throat billowed. His pulse roared.

Except he hadn't died. Hunter had found him. It was just a memory.

He fought to concentrate past it and summon a gate. The darkness thinned in the center, revealing the elevator wall and bullet hole. He shoved through the gloom and planted his hand over the hole.

Magic snapped over his fingers, darkness whirled around his palm, growing, growing. A gate. To home. To safety. He'd been out in the human world more times in the last two weeks than he had been in the last seventy years, and dragons kept trying to kill him. But he'd also lived more in the last two weeks than he had in the last hundred years.

Someone yelled above and behind him and something pounded around the elevator. The security team was trying to get in.

The magic of his gate locked within him, attaching to the other side, and he leapt through. The world wrenched around him, and his foot hit the floor.

"How fast can you heal, dragon?" The memory's gloom swarmed him.

No. He would not let it take hold.

He shoved at it. Through the dark alley he saw rough-hewn walls. He was not in his suite in the Dragon Court. His gate had locked onto the main anchor at Court, and he was in the public gateroom.

The memory of his attack flooded around him again.

"Hell, no," he growled.

The memory snapped. A woman screamed, and water danced on sunlight.

Not that one, either.

Gunfire spat around him and air, heavy with heat and moisture, pressed against him. The Korean jungle swept in to replace the medieval courtyard.

Mother of All. No.

A sharp inhalation cut through the gunfire and screaming. The jungle faded and an angel stood before him. No, not before him, on the other side of the gateroom in the archway to the hall. She was mesmerizing, straight dark hair, large dark eyes, and pale skin. Her small mouth was open in a shocked "oh" and she stood tensed, as if ready to run. But what drew him the most was a sense of the present. No achingly long history like he felt with most drakes, like he knew most drakes had. Unlike almost everyone else, he couldn't remember her. Years of chance encounters didn't flash into his mind. There were no conversations, no thoughts, no concerns about her. She was fresh, new, and something about her stilled the memories raging through him.

"Who—?" He reached for her and staggered forward a step.

Her eyes widened even more and with a squeak, she fled down the hall.

The urge to run after her shot through him, but he stopped himself. Capri and Ryan were still in trouble. He needed to get to his den, arm himself, and get back to Barna's gala.

No. If Ryan's vision was true, there was a chance they could lose Capri's soul forever. Grey had to get Anaea and get her to Capri.

The woman from the hall, whoever she was, was now seared into his memory, and unlike every other memory, he was grateful he'd never forget their too-brief encounter. When this was done, he would find her and demand that she tell him how she could ease the storm of memories within him with just a look.

43

Capri and Ryan raced around a corner. They'd put distance between them and Katar's dragon security force, so she tugged his arm, stopping him, and pressed him against the wall.

"I thought—" Mother, she'd thought so many things: that he didn't love her, that she'd made him crazy, that she'd—

It didn't matter that they still had mages and Katar's security team chasing them. She'd deal with that. But right now she needed a second with Ryan to prove he was real and not some delusion.

He cupped her face in his hands and brushed his lips against hers. Electricity crackled over her skin, drawing an inferno of Odyne's magic. Capri gasped and gripped the front of Ryan's jacket to keep standing.

"Hey?" he asked, his voice filled with worry.

"I'm fine," she said, struggling to breathe through the pain.

"You don't look fine." He hooked a finger under her chin and urged her to look up.

"But you do," she said.

"You're not supposed to change the subject."

A shiver of agony slid through her. "Nothing can be done about it right now. So I'm trying not to think about it. How's your head?"

"I'm trying not to think about that, either."

"I'm sorry. It was the only way I could think of to make you believe." It had been selfish. She'd wanted him to know the truth about her, about everything. "If I'd been thinking, I wouldn't have—"

"Broken a major dragon law?" A wry smile pulled at his lips.

"Hell, no. I'd break every law there is for you."

"And I wouldn't ask you to."

"I know." But she'd do it to keep her inamorato safe. Except she hadn't being keeping him safe when she'd slid her soul into him. She'd wanted him to understand and love her. "Still, I wouldn't have been so selfish and risked your sanity."

"You needed me to know. I get that. I'm glad you did, because now a lot of things make sense." He pressed close, his lips a breath from hers. "I'm also pretty sure my sanity was already in danger."

"And yet here you are. Perfectly sane." God, she wanted him closer, wrapped around her, diving inside her.

"I don't think I was ever perfectly sane."

Someone yelled at the end of the hall.

"And speaking of insane, I still have a problem," she said.

"Yeah, and Pimm is still somewhere around here."

Right. She'd forgotten about Pimm. "Jeez. The day just keeps getting better."

"Oh, and Katar is going to try to kill you." Something dark flashed over his eyes as if he wasn't telling her the whole truth.

"How do you know? Aside from the obvious. Diablo said you'd called to warn me."

"Kind of my thing now." He frowned. "Although actually it's been my thing for a while. Diablo and Raven say I'm a natural mage."

"Still have trouble accepting that." Everything she'd been told said human naturally connect to the earth's magic. Their souls weren't strong enough.

"Me, too. But we've got more pressing matters like Pimm."

"And the security team Katar sent after us." Capri leaned her head against the wall and met Ryan's pale gaze. She could look into that gaze for the rest of her life—or rather Ryan's, since he was still human.

She shoved that heartache aside. They'd deal with that when they had to deal with it.

"Okay," she said. "Barna is safe, so we can forget about Katar and deal with him later." It would be a messy political situation, but given that Katar had ignored Barna's commands, it would be safe to assume the doyen of the Major Brown Coterie would deal with his Second.

"Pimm, however, is still here to reveal dragonkind to the world. What do you think he'll do if he can't find Barna?" Ryan asked, but the answer was clear in his gaze. He was a cop, he'd seen men desperate to get their message to the world. Pimm would do anything. If he couldn't find Barna, he'd kill another dragon. And the building was filled with dragons.

"How the heck are we going to find him?"

"We—" Ryan straightened. His aura flared and his gaze grew unfocused. He grabbed her shoulders and wrenched to the side.

Pain snapped through her at the sudden movement, and gunfire exploded into the wall where they'd been.

A dragon—an average-sized guy with short-cropped red hair—adjusted his aim and fired again.

Ryan yelled.

Capri yanked him behind her and shoved him back. The bullets tore through her shoulder and arm—thank God the drake was a terrible shot. Pain roared through her, more painful than just a bullet wound. She gasped, her brain screaming. She couldn't just stand there. She had to attack—hell, she'd take running if that kept Ryan safe. But the agony stole her movement, everything but the determination not to let her knees buckle. It lasted a heartbeat, no more, then she pulled her palm away from the healing hole in her shoulder.

Ryan grabbed her bloody hand and they scrambled down the hall. Gunfire slammed into the wall ahead of them. They hit an intersection and raced right.

Ahead stood two more security guards. One held a gun, while the other was empty-handed—although that didn't mean he was weaponless if he had earth magic—with a healed slash across his chest visible through his ripped T-shirt. Shock flashed across their expression.

"We've got eyes," the slashed-chest drake said into his radio.

"Kill them!" a harsh voice screamed back. "She tried to kill our doyen."

Ryan squeezed Capri's hand, and they raced in the other direction.

"But the laws—" Slashed Drake said.

"Are you questioning your Second?"

Gunfire exploded past them again.

Capri glanced back. The first dragon, the one who'd been shooting at them—Gun Guy—had joined the other two, who were now bolting down the hall after them. Capri's heart pounded. She'd never wanted to be able to gate without an anchor so much before.

They reached a set of wide glass doors and shoved them open, reaching one of the bridges cutting through the center of the complex and connecting two of Barna's towers. A glass half-wall and semi-opaque floor gave the bridge the illusion that it was invisible and those crossing it the sense that they were walking on clouds.

A whip of wind caught the door and tore it from Capri's hands, slamming it shut in her face. The glass shattered and she wrenched aside, stumbling through Ryan's open door.

More wind snared that door and slammed it shut. Gunfire roared around them.

Ryan's aura burned, almost blindingly bright. He shoved her aside and a bullet whizzed between them. Whatever his earth magic was, it had something to do with foresight, since there was no way he could have known in time where that bullet was going.

The magically summoned wind howled, growing in strength. It seized shards of glass and whipped them around her and Ryan. Pain sliced across her face, arm, legs, and across her back, pinpricks that healed in a second, but awoke Odyne's painful magic, curled within the center of Capri's being.

A black vortex formed at the far end of the hall and the dragon whose side had been bleeding—a wiry man with a flat nose that had been broken too many times before a dragon had take over his body —stepped through the gate. He held a thin longsword in his hands, but his expression said he wasn't convinced of his actions even though he'd now blocked their escape.

"What are you waiting for?" Slashed Drake said from behind them. The wind billowed. More pinpricks sliced at her.

Ryan growled. Blood from a cut on his cheek oozed over the clenched muscle in his jaw. His aura flared so brightly it was difficult to keep looking at him.

"Do it." Gun Guy fired, but nothing happened. He swore, ejected his clip, and shoved in another one.

The drake with the sword growled and raised his weapon, but screamed instead of rushing forward. The tip of a blade protruded through his chest. He sagged to the ground, revealing Howard Pimm behind him. The human's eyes were wild. He pulled his blade from Sword Guy and kicked him forward.

"Where is your king?" Pimm said.

"What?" Sword Guy gasped. Blood poured from the wound, pooling on the cloudy glass floor. He obviously wasn't a fast healer.

"I must know where your king is. Where's Barna?" Pimm asked.

"Not here," Slashed Drake said.

Pimm's gaze leapt up, landed on Capri and Ryan, and narrowed. "So the human slave has taken the final step and embraced a demon. I won't be able to save you."

"What are you talking about?" Slashed Drake asked.

"The world must know." Pimm gestured beside him, drawing Capri's gaze. "And I'm showing them, right now."

Her heart skipped a beat. They were two stories up, in the middle of the main lobby, and the place was packed. At the far end, a stage had been set up for Barna's big gala presentation, along with rows and rows of tables and chairs for the dinner. Set throughout the lobby all the way to the walkway, colored silk, lit with red and orange lights, billowed within spikes of glass and metal. People dressed in their black-tie finest pointed and gaped, and only a quarter of them had a dragon's aura. The rest were human. How long had they been watching? Had they seen Sword Guy's gate?

Glass shards clattered to the ground and the wind vanished.

Everyone had certainly seen that.

Pimm kicked Sword Guy forward. He scrambled to his feet, clearly less hurt than before. "Look and behold," Pimm yelled, drawing more eyes to the walkway. He slashed Sword Guy's arm, which bled but noticeably started to heal. People screamed and yelled and pointed.

God dammit. She had to do something. She really wanted to stop Pimm, but that would leave her vulnerable to Katar's men. Except if she didn't activate her earth magic now it would be harder—maybe even impossible—to contain this.

The stocky Chinese human mage with lightning rushed around the corner to the shattered door. How the hell was he still alive and not in custody?

He sneered, jerked his hand out, and yelled. Lightning exploded from his palm and slammed into Gun Guy. His firearm flew over the glass railing, and he collapsed to the floor, howling.

More screams roared from below and people started running in all directions.

Sword Guy leapt at Pimm, but he screamed and swung his machete. The blade slammed into Sword Guy's neck, severing muscle and bone.

Time jerked to a halt. Everything froze: the people on the bridge, the chaos below. Then Pimm's machete wrenched through Sword Guy's neck, his head toppled from his shoulders, and his body crumpled to the floor.

Slashed Drake yelled. Wind slammed into Pimm, crashing him through the glass doors on the far side of the walkway.

Lightning exploded beside Slashed Drake, knocking him to his knees. Gun Guy jumped at the lightning mage, who bolted back down the hall, while Pimm yanked a gun from under his coat, and fired. *Bang, bang, bang.*

Ryan jerked Capri to the side. Two panels in the glass partition shattered, and Slashed Drake dropped to his knees. More bangs. More shattering glass. Slashed Drake collapsed to his side, unconscious.

More screams rose from below.

Click. Click. Pimm was out of ammunition.

"Deal with that," Ryan said, pointing to the chaos in the lobby. "You're the only one who can." He bolted down the walkway toward Pimm as the man grabbed a fresh clip from his pocket. He slid it into the gun, but Ryan was on top of him. He kicked the gun from Pimm's hand. Pimm scrambled out of the way of the next kick, and punched at Ryan's head.

Capri wrenched her gaze from the two and yelled her power word. Magic flashed over her with a lightning agony. It stole her breath and threatened to steal her consciousness. Blackness washed over her with the promise of peace from the pain, but it wouldn't keep dragonkind's secret and it wouldn't keep Ryan safe. How many of the humans below, if they realized the truth, would become like Pimm? How many would see dollar signs when they looked at dragons? There would be a day when the world would know the truth, but today was not that day. Not if she could do anything about it.

She shoved back the darkness and drew a ragged breath past Odyne's pain. Her magic whirled through her, wild and unfocused. She said her power word again, concentrating on turning her magic into a thread, a brilliant, glowing thread.

It crackled and writhed, fighting her will.

Come on, damn it. Just become a thread.

Her head burned. Her whole body burned. The magic had never done this before. But then, it had been different from the moment she'd met Ryan. Even back in Elmsville, it had been different. Her magic had never been so unsure and painful before, as if Ryan weakened her.

No. Ryan didn't weaken her. He was her inamorato. He gave her strength.

Her magic billowed, and she saw that she wasn't out of control. It was stronger, bigger, more powerful than it had ever been before. She hadn't been losing her mind. She hadn't known she needed to compensate for the greater force she now summoned. It burned through her because she wasn't used to it. Her mental and magical muscles were being stretched and overworked.

And none of that helped her right now.

Odyne's magic still seared her every nerve, and the people below still panicked. Even the dragons were panicking. The emotion was palpable, crackling through the air, grating against her tenuous control.

She squeezed her eyes shut. A thread. That was all she needed, something she could weave into a net. Thin, electric, controllable.

Her magic snapped.

She ground her teeth, focusing on the look and feel of a magical thread. Just a hint of magic. That was all it was. She didn't need all the power she'd summoned, not this moment. Mother, it felt like she was a hatchling again and had just realized she could summon earth magic.

The magic writhed and seethed.

She'd controlled it then. She could control it now. The situation didn't call for a delicate touch. At this point, she'd take a couple of hours' memory wipe.

Please.

The magic jerked in her grasp.

God damn it! She seized a small part of it with her mind and wrenched it into a thread. It jerked again, then lengthened, maintaining its shape. More magic rushed to it, as if magnetically drawn.

She seized another small piece and set it across the first, and another. The flood burned but she wouldn't let go. Just keep breathing and focus. Just make a net.

44

Ryan wrenched back, dodging another strike to his head. Pimm was stronger than he looked—it explained how he could decapitate that security guard with one blow... how he'd decapitated Pete.

Pimm growled and rushed forward, his shoulder low. Ryan twisted out of the way—farther from the weapons—and shoved Pimm. The man crashed into the wall, but spun around as if the impact hadn't hurt him.

Swell.

The gun lay behind Pimm and the machete a few feet from that. Ryan had no idea how he was going to detain the man. Twisting his arm back into a joint lock wasn't going to hold him. Ryan might not even be able to lock the man's joint in the first place. But killing the man wasn't an ideal option, only a last resort. Whether the members of Newgate P.D. believed it or not, he was still a cop, and cops didn't just kill people, no matter what they'd done. If dragonkind felt differently, that was their business. They could deal with Pimm without Ryan. But right now it was Ryan against Pimm and he was going to do what was right.

Except he had no idea how.

Ryan's vision flashed from his body to the decapitated security guard. He lay a few feet from his sword with his firearm still holstered, and there on his belt were his handcuffs.

Pimm launched at Ryan again. He sidestepped the lunge, but Pimm's hand whipped out and seized Ryan's forearm before he could get to the fallen security guard.

Pimm yanked Ryan around, slamming him against the glass partition. The stainless steel railing topper dug into his back. His vision writhed around him, to above him, to the dead security guard, back into his head.

"You shouldn't have embraced the demon," Pimm said. "You could have still been saved."

Ryan grabbed Pimm's wrist and wrenched, but couldn't break his hold. "I can still denounce it. You've shown me the truth."

Pimm glanced beside him. "But—" he said to empty air. His expression hardened, and he swallowed hard. He turned back to Ryan and leaned in. "It's too late for you. I'm sorry."

Pimm tossed Ryan to the floor. The man jerked his foot back to kick. Ryan rolled out of the way but wasn't fast enough. Pimm's steel-toed boot skimmed Ryan's already bruised ribs. Pain exploded in his side. Something had snapped—maybe many somethings. He couldn't breathe. The agony burned across his chest.

Pimm jerked his foot back again for another strike.

Ryan scrambled away. He had to get to the security guard's body and those handcuffs. Only a few feet remained.

Pimm's foot slammed to the floor and his other foot rose to kick.

Ryan's vision shot from the security guard to Pimm. Ryan wasn't going to get to the cuffs or even the gun fast enough. Pimm's foot rushed toward him. Another blow could kill him. It could slam an already broken rib into his lungs or heart, and he wasn't a dragon. He couldn't heal from that.

His vision lurched to Capri. Sweat slicked her brow, and her complexion was pale. Her breath came in quick gasps. Whatever she was doing took all of her concentration.

Ryan's vision spun back to Pimm, who kicked at him. Pain roared through his chest and his vision darkened. He sucked in a breath and seized Pimm's foot.

Pimm tried to wrench free. Ryan scrambled to his knees. He shoved Pimm's foot up and toppled the man, then dove back to the security guard's body. He'd never be able to win a fistfight with Pimm—even without broken ribs.

He reached for the gun—it was closer—but Pimm grabbed his ankle and yanked him away. He seized Ryan's jacket, hauled him up, and slammed him back into the floor.

More pain seared across Ryan's chest and face. His breath vanished, and so did his sight. Only a black, airless vacuum surrounded him. He clawed at it, fighting to stay conscious. His magical vision lurched above him. He lay, gasping, blood oozing from his nose. His arms and legs twitched as if he tried to move, to stand, but couldn't. He was trying to stand.

Come on. Get up. But the vacuum clung to him.

Pimm lunged past him to the security guard's body and grabbed the man's sword. Behind him, Capri panted and trembled, and the dozens of people still below looked dazed.

Pimm stalked back to Ryan and raised the sword.

He had to get up.

His vision writhed and spun. Death was imminent.

Get up!

The blade hurtled toward him. His muscles spasmed with agony, and he wrenched to the side. The blade slammed into the semi-opaque floor with a squeal. More pain. More flickering darkness. He fought to ignore it and kicked Pimm in the knee. The man staggered, and Ryan shoved up and grabbed Pimm's sword arm.

Pimm yanked with his incredible strength against Ryan's grip. Ryan clung to him. He couldn't let Pimm get in a solid strike. Pimm slammed Ryan against the railing. Gasping, Ryan switched his grip, tightened it on Pimm's wrist, and rammed his palm against Pimm's elbow, snapping his elbow in the wrong direction.

Pimm howled and dropped the sword. It skittered to the far side of the walkway into a pile of broken, beaded glass. He turned to grab Ryan with his good hand. Ryan twisted and kicked Pimm in the knee. The man dropped to the floor.

Ryan scrambled for the sword. Pimm dove after him. Ryan's fingers brushed the hilt of the weapon, but Pimm scrambled past him and grabbed it. Ryan lurched for Pimm's hand. Pimm shoved him and rose to his knees, the sword raised above his head.

Ryan jerked to his back and slammed both feet into Pimm's chest, shoving him. His head hit the steel railing and his eyes flashed wide. Time froze for a heartbeat, suspended in the horrible image of

Pimm, his head bowed from the blow, the sword still gripped in his hand, and nothing below him.

With a scream, he fell. Ryan scrambled forward. Pimm slammed into a sculpture and a glistening spike jutted from his chest.

Someone wailed. People rushed toward Pimm's corpse, and away from it, while others just looked stunned.

Ryan dragged his attention to Capri. She pressed her forehead to the cool semi-opaque floor, her pale gaze locked on him. She was all right. Thank God. They were both all right—with a few broken ribs, but still alive.

Relief and love filled her expression, and that magnetic attraction that he hadn't been able to explain or deny filled him. Now he knew it was a soul bond, a connection between paired souls that couldn't be broken. It didn't matter that she had the spirit of a dragon and he a human. They were a match, a perfect pairing, bonded for life—and given that magic existed, beyond life.

Her gaze jumped past him and her eyes widened. His vision shot out of him. Katar, Ginger, and Cestus rushed to the shattered doors.

"Take care of them," Katar growled.

Ginger sneered and rushed onto the bridge with Cestus. Capri lurched to her feet, but she was too far away. Ryan scrambled to the security guard's body, his chest screaming in pain. He seized the guard's gun and fired, hitting Ginger in the heart. She staggered.

Capri leapt past him and rammed her shoulder into Ginger, knocking her over the railing.

Katar's eyes flashed wide. He grabbed Pimm's machete and bolted away down the hall.

"You take this guy. I've got Katar." Capri raced through the doors after him.

"No!" Ryan fired at Cestus. He had to help her. She was running straight into his future flash.

45

Capri rushed after Katar, her head pounding and Odyne's magic still burning through her. She couldn't let him get away. He had to answer for the laws he'd broken, if not to his new-found friend, Regis, then certainly to his doyen, who he'd plotted to murder.

That, and he pissed her off. He'd put everyone in danger, dragonkind, her team's lives, and Ryan's life.

He ran around a corner. She raced after him. He stood in the center of the hall, a gun pointed at her. *Bang.*

She jerked back around the corner, but wasn't fast enough. Pain sliced her side, making Odyne's magic billow. She pressed her hand to the wound and her back to the wall. Mother, did it hurt.

"Did I hurt you, blue drake?" Katar asked. "Don't you heal fast? Or is Odyne's touch still slowing you down? All that pain from just one little touch. It burns for a long time." Katar chuckled. "We did studies, Regis and I. You know, the effects can last for years."

Wonderful. "So I guess you know what's waiting for you when you return to Court."

"Regis won't send me to Odyne. I'm his favorite now."

She glanced around the corner. Katar was creeping closer, the gun shoved down the front of his pants and the machete raised.

"Who said anything about Regis? Barna knows you tried to kill him."

"Barna knows no such thing. All he knows is that I claimed you and your team were in league with the mages. For all he knows, it's true."

"Yeah. That's why we saved him."

"Minor detail that I can deal with. Starting with you." He leapt around the corner, swinging the machete for her neck.

She ducked and rammed her shoulder into his chest. He staggered, and she grabbed the gun from his waistband.

He slammed the machete's hilt into the mostly-healed gunshot wound against her ribs, drawing an agony augmented by Odyne's magic.

She gasped, the pain weakening her knees. He jerked back to strike again. She shoved forward, catching his arm with hers.

"You're not strong enough to stop me, little girl."

"I don't have to be." She flicked the safety from the gun and fired into his gut.

With a scream, he wrenched back. She fired again, skimming his ribs. He twisted and kicked her in the chest. The force slammed her against the wall. Agony and blackness swarmed over her. He raised his machete to strike. She raised her gun, and he bolted around the corner.

She scrambled forward on her hands and knees, trying to get her feet under her. He threw open a security door and rushed inside. Pain threatened her consciousness. She shoved up to her feet, fighting the agony, and raced after him.

Inside was a concrete stairwell. Katar's footsteps clattered above her and another security door banged open.

There, one flight above her. Light from the hall beyond the open door filled the stairwell. She raced up the stairs, opened the door, and rushed into the pool of illumination from a security light. Beyond, the hall lay in darkness. Ghostly plastic sheets and strings of wires hung from the unfinished ceiling. Doorframes stood empty, like hungry mouths, some dark, some with the promise of pale light, maybe from another security light or a window.

Katar didn't make a sound. His footsteps didn't pound in the hall in either direction. Wherever he was, he was lying in wait for her.

Ryan ran down the hall and around the corner. Empty. Panic pumped through him. Capri was in the middle of his future flash and he had to be there to stop it. He'd shot Cestus with his last two bullets—he'd wish it had been three—kicked him in the head, and knocked him over the railing. Then he dropped the gun, grabbed the sword at his feet, and chased after Capri. But he hadn't been fast enough. She was gone.

This was not happening. He might have told himself he was investigating Pete's murder, but really he'd spent these last few days trying to keep Capri safe.

Which way to go? Down the hall? One of the doors?

He strained to hear something, anything, but there was nothing but the mumble of voices from the lobby behind him.

Everything within him screamed to find her. Now!

But where? How?

The hall rippled and darkened. That damned security door banged open, and Capri rushed out.

He fought against the flash. He needed to stay in the present—and he was not going to think about whether the flash was now in the present or not. Knowing what was going to happen wouldn't help. He needed to find her.

The flash wrenched back and the security door banged open again.

Ryan's heart skipped a beat, and he squinted his mental eyes. There was something behind her, through the door. A dark line that cut on an angle behind her... like a railing.

She'd come from the stairwell. But to what floor?

The vision wrenched back again. *Bang.* The door swung open. He squinted harder, focusing all his concentration on the spot over her shoulder inside the stairwell.

There, behind the railing, was a thick black line painted on the cinder block wall. Part of a four. She was on the fourth floor.

He yanked free from the flash and rushed to the stairwell door, but the flash swarmed back around him. It poured over him, stealing his breath. He clutched the doorframe to keep standing. The world twisted and the security door banged open.

Yes. He knew. She was on the fourth floor.

Blood stained her side and smeared across her cheek. She didn't look in trouble anymore. Now that he knew what she was, she looked ferocious, a predator on the hunt.

He fought to see past the flash.

Someone screamed.

It sounded so real.

His flash jerked. Now he was in an unfinished office. Street and building lights shimmered out a bank of windows. A security light shone a patch of harsh light by a pillar and wires hung from the ceiling.

Capri fired but the gun clicked. She was out of ammunition. A man—Ryan didn't recognize him—with wild dark hair and dressed like a security guard, laughed and rushed toward her. Another security guard, with a square jaw and brush cut, stepped into the light, and beyond him, a shadow among the shadows, stood Katar, watching it all.

Ryan wrenched against his vision. Get up the damned stairs.

Someone yelled. The sound was strong, close. It didn't ripple or echo in the darkness. It was real. His future flash was happening now.

He bolted to the stairs, but they weren't there. He hovered above Capri's shoulder as the men rushed at her.

He fought to return to his body. He couldn't just watch. He had to help her.

46

Capri sidestepped a punch from a security guard with wild dark hair. She slammed a fist into his face and another in his gut, but he lunged around to grab her arm. She leapt back as the other guard, a handsome man with a square jaw, jumped at her.

She twisted away and kicked him in the knee, making him stumble.

"I said, grab her," Katar growled from somewhere in the shadows.

"Why don't you come out here and do it yourself?" she said.

Wild Hair punched at her head again. She ducked and scrambled away, pain burning through her. She needed to finish this fast. Except both of the drakes she faced were bigger than her, and without a weapon it meant they had the advantage.

The one with the square jaw grunted and pulled out an expandable steel baton. Neither man had a gun—half good, half bad. It meant they couldn't shoot her, but it also meant she couldn't take their guns and shoot them. Square Jaw rushed at her.

She ducked under his swing and rammed her fist into his kidneys. He jerked his arm back. She ducked under the swing again, shoved her hand against his neck, and hooked her foot behind his heel. With a jerk that sent agony searing through her, she shoved him down to the floor, slamming her knee into his groin as they hit.

His breath burst from him, showering her face with a spray of saliva. He tried to hit her with the baton but couldn't get the leverage for any force. She seized it, wrenched it from his hand, and slammed the tip into his neck.

The weapon hit. Flesh resisted then popped. She yanked the baton free. Blood flew from the weapon and splattered the pillar beside her. Square Jaw grabbed his neck. Blood oozed between his fingers. He gasped and gurgled. The wound wouldn't kill him, but hopefully it would incapacitate him for a long time.

Movement flashed at the corner of Capri's eyes. She dove off Square Jaw, rolling on her shoulder and twisting up into a crouch. Wild Hair leapt over Square Jaw's body, rushing toward her.

Capri rolled out of the way and slammed the baton against Wild Hair's leg. He screamed and staggered. She leapt up, whipping the baton against his ribs, arm, ribs again. He lurched back. She pressed her attack. Snap. Snap. Jab.

Wild Hair backed into the wall. There was nowhere to go. She jabbed again. The baton hit his chest. He grabbed it and twisted, wrenching her forward.

Her shoulder slammed into the wall. Pain roared through her. She released the baton and Wild Hair swung at her. She ducked under and rammed her foot into his knee. The joint shattered, dropping him.

She leapt up and smashed her elbow into the back of his skull. Bone crunched. His neck snapped, his face cracked into the wall, and he collapsed.

"Well done," Katar said, his voice too close.

Capri jerked down, and Katar's machete whooshed over her head. She seized the baton and wrenched around, bringing it up to block another swing. Metal squealed against metal as the machete skidded off the baton.

Katar swiped the blade up and around. Capri leapt toward him, snapping the baton against Katar's forearm. He roared and rammed his shoulder into her chest.

Agony shot through her. She staggered, and Katar slashed at her. She jerked back but wasn't fast enough. The machete sliced through the front of her coat, drawing a thread of fiery pain across her gut.

Katar slashed again. She wrenched back, off balance. Another slash. He was backing her up like she had Wild Hair. A lunge.

She sidestepped, snapping the baton down on the blade. The

machete's tip hit the floor, and Katar stumbled. Capri whipped the baton around and snapped it across the hand holding the machete. It clattered to the floor. Snap across his face. Snap—

He seized the baton. She twisted in, kicking him in the chest. Air burst from his lungs but he didn't let go of the baton and used it to wrench her toward him. She kicked again. He captured her leg and barreled forward, slamming her back to the wall.

Pain exploded through her. He twisted her wrist. Her fingers went numb, and she dropped the baton. He spun her around and slammed her to the floor, bringing his weight down on her.

Ribs cracked. Agony consumed her.

He grabbed the front of her coat, yanked her up, and drove her back down to the floor.

More pain. She couldn't catch her breath.

She clawed at his hands, twisted in his grip, anything to break free. But he was bigger and stronger than she.

He yanked her up and down again. Her head snapped back, cracking against the concrete.

Flashes of light and dark swarmed across her vision. She fought to focus past the pain. Katar's weight vanished. He lunged toward the machete. She scrambled for the baton only a few feet away, and wrapped her fingers around the rubber handle.

She wrenched around to block the strike she knew was coming, but the strength of the machete's blow knocked the baton from her still numb fingers. He kicked her in the gut, knocking her over, and raised the machete to decapitate her.

But a shadow dove out of the darkness and caught the machete's strike with his own blade. Ryan. Her heart stuttered with relief and fear.

Katar growled and slashed at Ryan, who parried and lunged in. Katar sidestepped and jabbed the machete into Ryan's side.

It happened so fast. Katar was the more experienced swordsman. Hell, Ryan probably had never used a sword before. One parry, a lunge, and a counterstrike. That was it.

The sword slipped from Ryan's fingers. His knees sagged, and he seized the machete, trapping it in his body. His gaze locked on hers with a fierce determination, his message clear: kill the bastard.

She seized Ryan's sword. Dragon laws be damned. Katar had to be stopped, and without a medallion or the Handmaiden nearby, death was the only option.

With a scream, she leapt forward. Katar's eyes flashed wide, and she swung the sword with all her dragon-enhanced might. The blade hit flesh and bone and then air. Blood sprayed the wall. Her yell boomed through the empty office space, echoing off the unfinished concrete walls.

Katar dropped, his head bouncing a few feet away. Ryan sagged to his side, and the square-jawed security guard staggered to his feet.

Capri jerked the sword in his direction and growled. He raised his hands and backed away.

"Oh, Mother," a soft masculine voice said.

Capri jerked her attention to the new threat. The need to help Ryan screamed within her, but she wouldn't be able to save him if they were still under attack.

Grey and Anaea rushed toward her.

A sob bubbled in Capri's throat, and her knees gave out, dropping her beside Ryan. The machete protruded from his side. He still clung to it, his breath shallow desperate gasps.

"This will be all right. I will make it all right," she said. She wanted to touch him, to kiss him, to hold him but feared any contact would make everything real. If she didn't touch him he couldn't be injured, couldn't be dying.

"Call 911," Grey said.

"They won't get here in time," Ryan gasped.

"I won't let him die." She would die with him. Her heart was already shattering. Odyne's agony was nothing compared to this.

Anaea knelt beside them. "Grey will gate you to the hospital."

"Done," he said. Just like that. No questions asked. No comment about how dangerous it was to gate into—or even near—a busy emergency room. Nothing about the laws they were about to break or the mess revealing a magical gate to humans might cause.

Grey pressed his hand to the wall stained with Katar's blood. A black vortex of a gate formed, slowly. The muscle in his jaw twitched, as if summoning this gate was painful.

Ryan brushed his bloody fingers against Capri's cheek. "It'll be all right."

But he didn't look all right. He was pale. Blood pooled around her knees. Even with the blade still in the wound, stopping the gush of blood, his life still wept from his body.

She captured his fingers, pressed them against her skin, and leaned into his touch. "You're going to be all right."

"That's what I just said." A hint of a smile pulled at his lips.

"Yes." Her throat tightened.

"Got it," Grey said. He nudged Capri aside, knelt, and slid his hands under Ryan's back and knees.

Ryan's eyes hardened. He gave a quick nod, and Grey lifted, drawing a sharp gasp that became quick pants, Ryan's agony clear. "Let's go," he said.

Grey turned to the gate as a man-sized shadow dove toward them. Wild Hair leapt into the pool of light, seized the machete handle, and wrenched it from Ryan's body.

Blood sprayed across Capri's face. Ryan's blood. He went limp.

Wild Hair raised the weapon to slash at Grey. With a growl, Capri lunged at him, but a sudden wind tossed her back. She fell to the floor as the wind seized Wild Hair and crashed him through the bank of windows on the far side of the unfinished office space.

Anaea growled. Her telekinetic wind whipped around her, pulling at her hair and clothes. Then the wind vanished and she sagged, her hands pressed to her knees as if to catch her breath.

Capri scrambled to Ryan. He wasn't moving, wasn't breathing. His head and arm hung limp, and blood stained the front of Grey's clothes and the floor at his feet.

Grey staggered to the gate, but it wasn't there. The shock of the attack must have broken his concentration.

"Call another," Capri said. Ryan needed help. He couldn't die. He couldn't. Mother, please.

"He's not breathing." Anaea pressed her fingers to Ryan's neck. "There's no…"

"He can't be dead." Capri wouldn't allow it. She was supposed to get at least fifty more years with him. A violent tremor seized her and dropped her to her knees. She'd just found her inamorato. He wasn't supposed to die. Mother, this was not happening.

This was not happening.

47

A sob clawed out of Capri. She couldn't drag her gaze from Ryan's face. He was hers. And he was dead.

"I'm so sorry, Capri," Anaea said. She reached for Capri, but light shimmered from the inside of Anaea's shirt and her eyes flashed wide. She yanked the medallion from around her neck and the light intensified, blindingly bright, burning away the shadows in the room.

"What's happening?" Grey asked.

Anaea's wind burst to life. It whipped around her again, rattling the wires in the ceiling, gusting dust and snapping the plastic sheeting.

"The medallion is absorbing his soul," Anaea said.

"What does that mean?" Capri fought to get to her feet, but the wind knocked her back. If the medallion had Ryan's soul, Anaea could put it back into his body—no, his body was too injured. Without the soul magic of a drake, he'd just die again. But Anaea could put Ryan's soul into another body and save him. He wouldn't remember anything. He probably wouldn't remember he was her inamorato. The bond might not survive rebirth. But at least he'd be alive.

Grey staggered, and the wind jerked him to his knees. Ryan's hand hit the floor, into the pool of his blood.

Anaea's wind pulled her up. The light from the medallion burned the color from her, turning her into a shimmering white entity. The humans would call her an angel. A dragon would say—

"Mother," Grey gasped, his eyes wide with recognition.

"No." Anaea shook her head, and the wind eased her to the floor, on her knees before Ryan. Her eyes were hard, her breath quick gasps, and her body trembled. Her magical power was incredible.

Her telekinetic wind snapped, swirling up miniature dust devils. She squeezed her eyes shut and it subsided, then she eased the medallion's chain over her head and clutched it with both hands.

Capri jerked forward. "Use me. I'll hold his soul until we can find a vessel."

Anaea glanced at her. The sorcerer's eyes burned white. No pupils, no irises, only shimmering, searing white. She blinked and Capri's heart stuttered with the movement, released for a split second from the ferocity of all the power, then captured again in its vortex.

"Please. I can't lose him."

Anaea's expression softened. Capri couldn't tell how. Her eyes remained burning suns, her face a hard sculpture, but there was kindness there, love, affection, understanding.

She turned back to Ryan, her movement slow, and pressed the medallion to his chest. Light exploded around them, blinding for a heartbeat and an eternity all at the same time. Capri was suspended with it, body, breath, and soul.

Then the light swept into a contraction, rushing out of the medallion and into Ryan. His skin started to glow. White light cut from beneath his eyelashes and between his lips. Darkness flooded behind Capri, as if Ryan and the medallion were consuming more than just the light it had created, but also the light from the emergency light and the glow from the office windows across the street.

It pressed against Capri's senses, pulled at her, called and cajoled. With a roaring whoosh, it jerked her forward. Her forehead banged against the floor. Pain screamed through her skull and someone gasped.

She wrenched up. Ryan gasped again, then screamed. He pressed his hands to the gaping hole in his side, clawing at his ruined shirt.

Capri rushed to him. "It's all right. It'll be all right."

He stared at her with no recognition and no understanding.

Her throat tightened. Of course he didn't recognize her. He was newly reborn, reset to whatever was in his human soul's base knowledge. And he was still injured. He still needed a hospital.

"Make a gate," she growled.

"No." Anaea pressed her hands against Capri's and Ryan's and eased them away from the wound. Or what should have been the wound.

"My side," Ryan said.

"His side." Capri glanced at Anaea. "How?"

"I don't know."

"What does it mean?" Capri needed answers. Had Anaea healed Ryan or did he now have soul magic strong enough to sustain his body? Was he now a sorcerer like Anaea or... or she had no idea what?

Ryan groaned.

"It'll be all right. We're your friends. I'm—" She swallowed hard, unable to tell him she was just a friend. She was more than a friend, she was his and he hers. But the rebirth spell had taken that away. Mother, he didn't remember her. "I'm a friend, too."

He grabbed her fingers, pressed her palm against his newly healed side. "Why are you talking like I don't know who you are?"

"Because— What? You shouldn't know who I am."

He flashed his teeth in pure invitation. "Soul to soul, blue drake. I'd never forget you."

"But how?" Her mind whirled. He wasn't supposed to remember. That wasn't how the rebirth spell worked.

"The Handmaiden has been keeping secrets," Anaea said. "Just like how there are natural human mages, the rebirth spell doesn't have to wipe a dragon's memories."

"And apparently it also works on humans," Grey said.

"I would guess only those who already have a magical connection," Anaea said.

"It doesn't matter." Capri met Ryan's gaze. He was alive, and he remembered her. Everything else didn't matter.

TOBIAS RAN HIS FINGER THROUGH THE ASH AND DIRT ON THE ALTAR IN the Handmaiden's rebirth chamber.

"We're beginning to make a habit of this," a sultry feminine voice said. Ophelia.

"Yeah, well. This is the only place I know of in Court that's warded against prying eyes."

"And ears." She flashed her teeth and leaned against a pillar.

Tobias sighed and fought the desire to run a hand through his hair. It was a habit he'd kicked two hundred years ago that was coming back. Being the royal chamberlain was not an easy job these days. "What do your ears tell you?"

Ophelia's expression darkened. "That we're in trouble."

"Us, personally? Or dragonkind in general?"

"Dragonkind, but given your position in Court, it might end up falling on you."

"Swell." Maybe it was time to take that vacation he'd been thinking about. Except he hadn't been thinking of taking a vacation, and there was nowhere he could go where Regis's drakes wouldn't find him. What he really wanted was to find the Handmaiden. But whether that was for the sake of dragonkind or his hurt feelings, he didn't know.

"Your plan worked. With your North American Clean Team and Capri containing most of the mess at Barna's gala, it was easy to set up the news story that this was a joint FBI-Newgate P.D. special investigation with Detective Miller as a deep-cover officer. Cooper's even marginally happy because you gave him all the credit and even Ptolemy joined in the ruse by awarding him a medal. The story from that reporter with KDKA—excuse me, formerly with KDKA—got discredited, so believe it or not, we're safe. I'd say this was one of your best cleanups yet."

"Try and convince Regis of that." The prince had locked Court up tight. Only those with the ability to gate without an anchor—since Regis couldn't control them—and those with special permission were allowed to leave Court. No matter how tidy Tobias and the Clean Team had made the situation, the events of the gala had sent him on a rampage. A dozen drakes had been sent to Odyne and a dozen more had been locked up, whether they'd had anything to do with the mess or not.

"That's my concern," Ophelia said. "Dragons are starting to talk. They're no longer just thinking of uprising, they're talking about it."

A coup would destabilize Regis completely. "Do you know who?"

Ophelia pursed her lips. She knew. The drake knew almost everything that happened at Court. But if she wasn't going to say who was involved so Tobias could arrest them that meant—

"You want a coup," he said.

"I don't know. But Regis brought Odyne back into service. That's not right. Not for the dragons she touches, and not for her."

If the rumors were true, Odyne didn't just give pain, she also received it when she used her magic. Regis had to have something against her to compel her back into service, but Tobias had no idea what that could be.

"I'll keep my eye on the situation, but..." Ophelia shrugged.

"But something needs to change." Tobias couldn't agree more. The question was, what? And would he be able to break his oath of allegiance and defy his prince when that time came? He might have been a pirate in a past life, but he'd never been an oath-breaker before.

Everything would be fine once the Handmaiden came back. Except he had no idea when that would be. And if she didn't return soon, there might not be a Dragon Court to return to.

DIABLO PACED HIS LIVING ROOM, BATTLING THE RAGE ROARING through him. It had only been a few days since the fight at Barna's gala, but all that gating, fighting—and getting shot—had weakened his control on the beast within and it was going to take time to quiet. Except Andy's murderer was dead, and Capri and her inamorato were fine. Even Grey was doing all right—although the silver drake still didn't look well. Things should be back to normal. He had to get things back to normal.

He'd tried everything: meditating all day, working out until he was exhausted, sleeping in, taking a day off work to spend it all with the kids he'd saved.

But the beast clawed at him, digging painful rents into his psyche that ignited at every noise, every flash of light, every thought of Andy's death.

Mother, Andy wasn't supposed to be dead.

But he was. Diablo couldn't turn back time. He had to move on and figure out how to calm the beast again.

He needed to kill someone, break something, destroy, maim. God, he'd never needed one of the humans' ridiculous wars so badly before. He drew back to punch the window and jerked to face the room before he shattered the glass. Andy's spindly table and fragile vase stood opposite him, taunting him. No. Reminding him. He wasn't the beast. The beast didn't control him. He controlled it.

The urge to destroy something crawled over him. He needed a drink. But drinking alone right now was a terrible idea.

He pulled out his phone and dialed.

"Hello?" Grey said after two rings. He sounded tired.

"Wanna get a drink?"

"Excuse me?"

"A drink. I could use a drink, but I... well, I could use some company more." The beast roared. He didn't want company. Company would stop him from starting a bar brawl.

Yeah, that was the plan.

"Are we friends now?" Grey asked.

Diablo snorted. "I have no idea."

"Fair enough. I'll be at your place in a flash."

"Sure."

"Where is your place?"

Diablo chuckled. "Third floor, 16 Eighth Street at Eighth and Lafayette." He pocketed the phone and grabbed his coat. Might as well meet Grey by the lobby doors and save the drake from climbing the three stories to his apartment.

He opened the door and a streak of black rushed out. Andy's kitten. Damn little escape artist.

He raced after it, caught a flash of something pale a few feet ahead of him, and stumbled to a halt. A woman crouched at the end of the hall, scratching Darkness under the chin.

She glanced up and gold light flickered from her hazel eyes. Perfect eyes. Warm and mysterious, in a heart-shaped face, framed by a cascade of honey-blond hair.

Diablo froze. Even the beast froze.

"Is she yours?" the woman asked.

His mind stuttered. She'd asked him a question, but the words muddled in his head. "What?"

"Is she yours?" Her gaze dropped to Darkness.

Right. The cat. Not the woman. "Yeah. Well... a friend's, but he's..." Mother, he was going to tell her Andy was dead. Way to impress a girl. "The cat is mine," he growled.

The woman picked Darkness up and the kitten's purrs grew louder. More light flickered from the woman's eyes. He hadn't imagined it. She was a mage.

"Mine likes to escape, too." She held Darkness out to him. "You'll get used to it and notice the signs soon enough."

He took the cat, who rubbed her face against his chest and curled into the crook of his arm. "Thanks. Are you visiting someone?"

Man, why had he asked that?

"I moved in last week. 306." She smiled, a delicate flashing of teeth that zinged through him.

"306," he said. Even the beast was stunned by her.

"Yeah." Her smile deepened, and she strode past him. Her door clicked open and closed and he still stood there, still stunned.

"Hey, who was that drake?" a new voice asked.

Grey stood in front of Diablo. He hadn't even seen the silver drake approach.

"I have no idea. But I intend to find out." And the beast within rumbled with agreement.

CAPRI EASED INTO THE DOORWAY TO THE SOLARIUM IN RAVEN'S AND Nero's house for human mages. Ryan sat among the flowers and ferns and bushes at one of the wrought iron café tables, bathing in early morning sunlight. It shimmered off the crystalline snow powdering the grounds beyond the large glass windows.

Only a few days had passed since her soul had chosen him and Katar had killed him and Anaea had brought him back to life. Capri's heart still stuttered at the sight of him, partly in fear because he broke so many dragon laws, but mostly in awe that their love survived. He should be dead. Her soul shouldn't have bonded with a human. And he shouldn't be a mage.

Yet he was, she did, and he lived on.

They both lived on and even the small things had worked out. Most of Katar's human mages had been killed at Barna's gala and the few who remained had been taken into custody by the Asar Nergal. Anyone involved in blowing up her house was either dead or arrested and she and Ryan were working on plans to rebuild. His ex's exposé had been discredited with some surprising manipulation by Tobias which made Ryan look like a hero. Even Cooper had been mollified by being given credit for ending a new-to-the-city gang's attempt to assassinate Barna.

And while Capri had yet to leave the Royal Coterie, she knew where her loyalties really lay. Her job with the Clean Team was still important—perhaps even more important—now that Ryan was a part of dragonkind's secret, but if a drake... say Hunter, decided to take the throne, she'd throw all her support behind him. Heck, if Nero wanted the throne she'd support that, too. There was a reckoning coming for Regis. She didn't know when or how, but it was coming.

Ryan reached for something on the table, but didn't pick up his mug of morning coffee. Instead, he grabbed his pocketknife and ran the blade across his palm. He hissed as blood welled from the cut, but it didn't ooze over his hand like it should have. He wiped what little blood there was with a tissue and frowned at his uninjured flesh.

He now healed like a dragon. He hadn't manifested a true sorcerer's ability like Anaea had, but whatever the rebirth spell had done to him, he was more than just a human mage.

"It's not changing," he said without glancing up. "Are you going to stand in the doorway and stare at me all morning, Capri?"

"And here I'd thought I'd been quiet." She stepped into the solarium and followed the narrow path to his table to stand behind him. "It's soul magic. Once it's activated, you can't make it go away."

His gaze leapt to hers, strong, filled with passion. It slid a shiver through her, fueling the desire she knew belonged only to him and no one else. She'd thought Eric had been the one, and she had loved him, just not the way she loved Ryan. They looked so much alike— which wasn't surprising since Eric was Ryan's great, multiple times, uncle. Perhaps those humans who believed in reincarnation were right, and Eric and Ryan shared a soul. Right family, wrong time period.

Ryan's frown deepened and his gaze slid to the knife on the table. "I just don't want any surprises. Anaea doesn't know what she did, but she claims my soul is like yours now. Not a dragon, but eternal. She says the notes in the Handmaiden's grimoire talk about how the rebirth spell can work on any being if his earth magic is strong enough, and that the rebirth process enhances that magic."

"And you don't believe her?" Capri hadn't believed Anaea at first, either. But every morning Ryan sliced his palm and healed. It was true. She knew it soul-deep—and she wasn't going to accept that it was just wishful thinking on her part. "Have you foreseen something?"

"No. Just… it's a little hard to believe."

"I thought we'd dealt with disbelief when I imparted everything I knew into your head in one fell swoop."

He flashed his teeth, part in challenge and part in sexual invitation—he was getting so good at that. Mother, it made her hot. "I'm a slow learner."

She snorted. "No, you're not. You've already figured out how to push my buttons."

"What buttons would those be?" he asked, his smile deepening, his fingers trailing a searing line up the inside of her arm.

She gasped, desire coursing through her. "Stop. Please. I have trouble saying no in greenhouses, and there are children around."

"There aren't any right here." He tugged her into his lap, his hands sliding under her shirt, skin on skin.

"Raven will kill us if we traumatize any of her children." Capri dipped her head close, brushing her lips against his. Two could play this game.

"I'd foresee it if she was going to. And—" He closed his eyes for a second then opened them, freezing her in place. "Nope. Nothing. No death for anyone on the immediate horizon."

His hand slid up her back, found the clasp on her bra, and unhooked it.

"You know you'll live forever. You can afford a little patience," she said.

"Later. Right now, let's pretend I'm still mortal."

He captured her lips with his, hungry and claiming, searing his essence again and again on her soul. A purr bubbled in her throat and she let it rumble through her. Hot, needy, safe. This was the true bonding of souls. Drake. Human. It didn't matter. They would fight for each other—they might even fight with each other—and they would face the world together. They didn't make each other whole. They were complete souls already. But their love made them stronger.

Don't miss the next book in the series!

HOARDING SECRETS
A Dragon Spirit Novel: Book Three

She can't remember. He can't forget

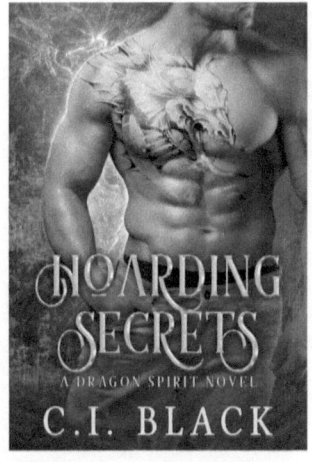

Once a powerful warrior, Grey's greatest battle now is with his out-of-control magic. What empowers him to remember everything also threatens to imprison him in his most horrific moments. He yearns for peace, but with the dragon sorcerer, the Handmaiden, missing, he has nowhere to turn. So when someone ransacks the sorcerer's chambers, he agrees to investigate, hoping he'll find her. What he didn't count on was having to work with an agent of the Dragon Court, who instantly captivates and soothes his writhing memories but endangers everyone he holds dear.

Tortured with a lack of memory, Ivy wakes each day not knowing who she is and having to learn again and again that she's the servant of an insane prince. All she wants is freedom. When she's assigned to the case of the Handmaiden's chambers and encounters Grey, she realizes she can use his secrets to force him to help her escape… if she can just ignore how he makes her feel.

But they soon discover the Handmaiden has hidden a dangerous, powerful magic and the first key to finding it has been stolen. Now they must put their desires aside and race against time, risking everything, to save dragonkind and each other.

OTHER BOOKS BY C.I. BLACK

ABOUT C.I. BLACK

C.I. Black has always lived in a world of imagination. When she's not daydreaming, she puts her flights of fancy down on paper writing urban fantasy, paranormal romance, and romantic suspense books.

She's the author of The Dragon Spirit series and The Medusa Files series. You can find a complete list of C.I.'s books at www.ciblack.com.